BULL & DUKE

Kati Wilde

BULL & DUKE

When one of the Hellfire Riders' deals suddenly goes sour, and Sara Abu-Hamdi sees something she shouldn't, Bull will do whatever it takes to keep her quiet. Even if that means keeping her in lockdown and forcing her to share his bed…

Duke is less than thrilled to discover he'll be playing bodyguard to a spoiled actress. But the woman he's watching isn't who she seems—and protecting her won't be as easy as he thinks.

LOOKING FOR CONTENT WARNINGS?
FLIP TO THE END!

To avoid putting spoilers up front where readers might accidentally see them, I've listed the content warnings on the very last page. If you are browsing through a "Look Inside" feature and can't flip to the end, please feel free to visit my website and look for the content warnings link in the menu.
www.katiwilde.com

BULL & DUKE

THE HELLFIRE RIDERS

KATI WILDE

BULL & DUKE

Also by Kati Wilde

*The Hellfire Riders
(Discreet Cover Editions)*

SAXON

BLOWBACK

GUNNER

BULL & DUKE

STONE

**The Hellfire Riders MC Series
(Original Covers & Ebooks)**

THE HELLFIRE RIDERS: SAXON & JENNY

THE HELLFIRE RIDERS: JACK & LILY

BREAKING IT ALL

GIVING IT ALL

CRAVING IT ALL

FAKING IT ALL

LOSING IT ALL

(Turn the page for more...)

The Dead Lands
Fantasy Romance

THE MIDWINTER MAIL-ORDER BRIDE

THE MIDNIGHT BRIDE

PRETTY BRIDE

THE MIDSUMMER BRIDE
(COMING SOON)

Wolfkin & Berserkers
Shapeshifter Romance

BEAUTY IN SPRING

HIGH MOON

TEACHER'S PET WOLF

SHERIFF'S BAD BEAR
(COMING SOON)

Other Romances by Kati

GOING NOWHERE FAST[1]

SECRET SANTA

THE KING'S HORRIBLE BRIDE

ALL HE WANTS FOR CHRISTMAS

THE WEDDING NIGHT

EVIL TWIN[2]

---

[1] Includes cameos by the Hellfire Riders
[2] Set in the same world as the Dead Lands

CONTENTS

FOREWORD

"Kati," you might be asking me, "why is this not Stone's book? Especially after what you pulled at the end of Gunner's story?"

It's a good question, because I had *intended* to write Stone's story after Gunner's...but a few things got in the way.

One was a very simple contractual issue. I'd signed with Berkley Romance for ***Going Nowhere Fast***, which features Aspen, a cousin of Stone and Anna's. But that contract had a clause which restricted me from publishing anything that might compete with their release. I couldn't publish a full-length novel for a certain period before and after it released. So instead I published two shorter works.

But the other reason was simply that Stone's book was long and hard and emotional, and these stories were easier to write and provided a bit of stress relief while I was fighting with Stone's book. And this was especially true when I was writing Bull! He was a character that was on the periphery of my original plans for the series (which centered on the core members of Saxon, Jack and

Lily, Gunner, and Stone) but from Bull's very first appearance, he was so much fun. He always had a joke or a way of easing the tension, and I wanted to discover what kind of life made him become that man: one who was a big cuddly bear (but who would also kill without hesitation.)

As for Duke, he was one of the Steel Titans who had originally been a Hellfire Rider, but who'd left the club when Lily was patched in. There was some simmering conflict there that I didn't get a chance to fully explore when the two clubs merged early in the series, because Val was such a jerk and took up all the page time being a villain. But since I was telling a side story anyway, I wanted to delve into that a little bit more. Duke isn't a misogynist, so why did he make that choice? And how can a man viewed as disloyal to a club ever win a place again in a brotherhood where loyalty is everything?

So although my original plan for the series didn't include these two stories, I ended up really liking how they filled out the period when Stone was gone, especially since the Hellfire Riders were missing their enforcer and needed someone to fulfill that role. And they both provide something a little lighter before we dive into the rough ride of Stone's book.

And I hope you love Bull & Duke as much as I loved writing them!

—Kati

A NOTE ABOUT READING ORDER

You have a difficult choice to make! You can read Bull's & Duke's stories...or you can skip to Stone's and read these two romances after you finish his.

From the foreword and series numbering, obviously my preferred order is to read these two stories first. While I was writing them, I was deliberately teasing and building anticipation for Stone's book, which serves as an epic conclusion to the series. However, the events from Gunner's book lead directly into Stone's! And it's so hard to wait to find out what happened!

If it helps to decide: although these were published before Stone's book, all three books overlap the same time period (much of the action of Stone's book occurs away from Pine Valley and the Hellfire Riders, while Bull & Duke's stories stay closer to home.) Stone's book spans a year's time—it begins before Bull's book and ends after Duke's book—whereas Bull & Duke's romances take place over the course of the same summer and autumn.

And if your taste doesn't run to epic conclusions, these books would provide a sweeter, less dramatic ending to the series. It's all up to you (and there's no wrong decision!)

Happy reading!

BULL

ONE

BULL

Used to be, I hated early mornings. Hated dragging my ass out of bed before dawn to spend an hour pumping iron at the gym. Hated grabbing a shitty breakfast and washing it down with shittier coffee before riding out to the job. Hated showing up at the site while the fucking bright-eyed birds were still catching their dickless worms.

Loved the work. I've been a foreman with T&E Construction now for a handful of years. It suits me. But the goddamn early hours that the job requires never did.

Not until Reggie's opened up across from the Hellfire Riders' old clubhouse in town. Not until Sara Abu-Hamdi started working there.

Now early hours and I get along real easy.

The light is shining bright through Reggie's front window when I come out of the gym, but it's still ten minutes before five, when Sara will unlock the door. The first hour is usually pretty damn slow, so she works the place alone, making customers' espressos and breakfast sandwiches in between filling the display case with baked goods and prepping for lunch. Another girl comes in at six, the pace starts picking up, and that's usually when I haul off to the job.

The old clubhouse where I work out sits back from the street, with an asphalt parking lot surrounded by a chain link fence. I leave my bike in the lot and head through the open gates. My hair and beard are still damp from my shower, and I'm wearing the jeans, boots, and T-shirt that'll get me through a day on a construction site. For now I'm wearing my kutte, since I'll be riding out to the job, but even though the Riders' VP is my boss and owns the company, rules state that the vest comes off when I get there.

Probably for the best. Midsummer, it'll end up being a jackass scorcher of a day, but right now the air's still carrying the deep chill that falls overnight in this arid part of central Oregon. And I love wearing the Hellfire Riders' colors, but breaking ground on a site in heavy leather under a blazing sun that wants to beat me into submission?

Not my idea of a good time.

When I hit the sidewalk across the street from Reggie's, I can't see anyone at the counter, which means Sara's still finishing up in the kitchen. Sometimes she's a few minutes late opening, and I start to worry, the back of my neck tightening and my gut uneasily churning, imagining her hurt back there, maybe she accidentally cut herself with a knife or some pervert was lying in wait for her when she went in at three-thirty, and just when I'm on the verge of busting through the door, she'll show up wiping flour from her hands and laughing at herself as she apologizes for losing track of time.

And I look at her dark eyes and her dark hair and that laughing smile and as long as she's all right, I'll forgive anything.

So I've got it bad. I have for a few months now. And it just keeps getting worse.

But it's all right. I'm a patient man.

I lean back against the chain link fence and pull out my phone. No surprise, no one's sending me messages at four-fucking-fifty in the morning. Got an email about penis enlargement, though.

Don't need that. My dick gets any bigger and it'll need its own kutte and a bike to get around.

Thinking about Sara does the job better than any herbal supplement, anyway. Thinking about her husky laugh becoming a husky moan and maybe one day seeing her thick hair out of its braid. Thinking about sliding my cock deep, feeling her hot and wet and writhing beneath me.

Hell, I'm half hard just standing here waiting for the moment I see her. And the moment I *do* see her?

There's a reason I always sit at her counter so fucking quick. I don't want to scare her with my cock trying to bust through my zipper like something out of *Aliens*.

That is, I don't want her scared more than she already is.

The familiar rumble of a Harley engine approaches. The headlight shines into my eyes as it heads for the old clubhouse, but I don't need to see to know who it is. Duke's one of the few other Hellfire Riders who comes in to the gym this damn early.

A good number of the brothers put in time on the weight benches and up in the ring during the afternoon and evening, but I hate that "change your clothes in the middle of the day and shower and get ready again" shit even more than I hate — *used* to hate — rolling out of bed early. I like getting ready just once, then wearing the same goddamn thing until I head for bed.

Though if Sara was a reason to be taking off clothes in the middle of the day, I probably wouldn't hate it so much. She already changed my mind about early mornings. I bet I'd take real well to getting dressed twice, as long as the naked time in between was with her.

Or better yet, I'd just get us naked midday and keep her curvy little ass in bed until the early morning. No getting ready again.

Win-win.

Duke turns toward the gates but stops his bike before heading through to the lot. We get along well, Duke and me. If there's one brother I had to go out with—*going out* as in a blaze of fucking fire, not *going out* as in holding hands—it'd be him. Now he takes a long look at me, then turns to look across the street at Reggie's.

And the genius says, "You could just ask her out," like I've never thought of that. Like I don't think of it every damn second of every damn day. Like either he's real fucking dense or he thinks *I* am.

So I give the only appropriate answer—a middle finger raised in his general direction. Considering the size of my hands, it's a damn powerful statement.

His laugh joins the rumble of his engine as he revs up and rides into the lot.

Because, yeah. I could ask her out. But I've been sitting at her counter for a few months now and I've seen what happens to every man who does—and because she's sexy and sweet, there's been more than a few who've asked. She shoots them all down.

But that's not all I've seen. I've seen the way she eyes them more warily the next time they come in. This early in the morning, it's mostly regulars. So it's not like they're strangers coming in.

She was comfortable until they asked her out. Then she wasn't so comfortable anymore.

And a few months ago, when she just moved into town, she was all-around more skittish—her gaze jumping to the door every time someone came in and only relaxing into a smile after she saw they weren't whoever the hell it was she was afraid might be coming through.

The first few days, I thought it was me. I'm a big motherfucker, built like a mountain and tattooed all to shit. The sight of me has frightened men who weighed in at twice what Sara does. Throw in the kutte and I make some people real nervous. And thinking she was afraid of me, thinking I was the reason she was so jumpy—it got me right in the gut.

Then I realized it wasn't me. Because she was always so damn friendly when I showed up, and she eased up around me real quick—but she still had that jumpy look when others came in.

Over time, even that nervousness has eased up some. I like to think she's feeling safer, knowing I'm sitting there.

But I figure that as the months pass, she's probably just not so afraid that whoever she believes is coming for her is ever going to come.

The way she shoots everyone down, though—then doesn't look at them the same way after? Makes me think that once upon a time, she said yes to someone. Or maybe she said no. And either way, it didn't turn out real well.

So I'll continue being patient. I'll continue holding

off until more of her fear bleeds away. Because that woman is worth waiting for.

In the meantime, maybe I'll find out who it was that hurt her. Maybe make sure he *never* comes through that door.

And it's about time for her to open. She's not out front yet, but I push away from the chain link fence, then wait for a long boat of a car sailing down the street to go past.

Instead the fucker swerves across the road and pulls over in front of me, right up across the clubhouse's driveway like he's cutting off the entrance. But I know the driver. Vern Woodridge isn't cutting anything off. He's just too fucking stupid to know better.

And he should know better than to stop and talk to me in front of the fucking clubhouse. Especially with what's supposed to go down tonight.

His wheels are a joke, a giant pink Cadillac that his grandma probably drove until she croaked. His weaselly little head jerks from side to side as he hastily cranks the window down. Inside, the floorboards and seats are covered with all kinds of shit—dirty clothes and Monster Energy cans and Jesus knows what else mixed in. Probably a few talking rats and magical portals to Dipshitland.

Genuinely fucking pissed and letting every bit of it show, I grip the top of the door and lean down. "Don't you *ever* stop to talk to me. You've got to the count of fucking three to move on before I start shoving you ass first through this Caddy from tailpipe to engine."

"Okay, okay! But listen to me, man"—his hands are flailing and he's high as fuck, eyes bright and glassy—"tonight's no good! Tonight's no fucking good! Osprey called it off."

"What the fuck do you mean, called it off?"

"He got spooked! He wants to change the meetup."

Fucking hell. "What time?"

"I don't know yet! I'm waiting to hear—" Abruptly his head jerks back, courtesy of my fingers fisted in his greasy hair, his scraggly goatee suddenly pointing toward the Caddy's ceiling. "I'm not bullshitting you, man! Ow! Ow!"

"What *time?*"

"I'll find out! But if you're in a rush, man, I can get the product from another— Ow! Shit, fuck!"

"Osprey." Because I want that fucker in my hands. "Only from Osprey. You understand?"

He tries to nod but I've got his head bent too far back. Instead he wheezes, "Yes!"

"The Riders gave you a nice chunk of cash to get this shit done for us. But it's not done yet and I'm not a patient man. You hear what I'm saying? You make us wait too long and when I take our cash back, maybe I'll also be taking a few fucking fingers. Maybe I'll bust a few fucking knees. You want that, Vern?"

"No, no, no." He's crying a little now, his Adam's apple bobbing in his skinny throat.

"Then you best not fuck me over, and you'd best get me what the hell I want. I want a new fucking meet up time, I want to know the fucking location where you're meeting him, and I want that fucking meth in my hands by tomorrow night—and you better fucking deliver all those things to me, or maybe next time you go for a ride in this Cadillac you'll be in that nice big coffin of a trunk. You understand?"

Another attempt to nod is followed by a wheezing, "Yes, man."

I ease off. "Now you don't ever fucking stop here again."

"Sorry, man," he babbles, still holding up his hands. "I just knew you'd be here and wasn't sure you'd get my message on that other number."

The back of my neck stiffens. "You knew I'd be here?"

"You're sitting at that counter every day, man. Every day." He's rubbing his neck. "I don't blame you because she's smoking hot even though she's a—"

"Don't you ever finish that," I say quietly.

With bulging eyes, Vern nods—not finishing it now because my hand's wrapped around his throat and squeezing, and his fingers are desperately trying to pull mine away.

I give him another few seconds, until it becomes real damn clear that my grip isn't ever going to loosen unless I want it to.

He gasps and wheezes some more when I let him go and say, "Now get your fool ass out of here," while stepping back from the Caddy. And he's not all stupid. Not a second passes before his tires are screeching and he's fish-tailing onto the street.

Then I turn and see Sara standing at the front door to Reggie's, watching me with her dark eyes looking big and round and her full lips parted, as if in shock.

And suddenly I wish I'd killed the fucker.

TWO

SARA

What do you say when you've just seen a giant biker choking the driver of a pink Cadillac?

Good morning doesn't seem to cut it. That's what I usually say to Bull. *Good morning, just your usual? And will you kiss me, please?*

Not that I ever really say the last. I think it, though. I've got a bit of a crush on the big guy—okay, more than a *bit* of one—but my instincts when it comes to men are obviously shit. I can't trust them.

Except now. Because Bull's only ever been polite and sweet and sometimes hilariously funny, but my instincts always said there was a darker side to him, something he wasn't letting me see. But then I told myself I was being a judgmental asshole, because he's huge—just freaking huge—and covered with tattoos and he wears that leather vest. And I know what it's like to have someone look at you and assume some crazy shit. Like, hey—*she's Muslim, so she's either a terrorist or she at least sympathizes with those extremist fuckers.* Or, hey—*she's a virgin, so she's going to fall in love with me the moment I stick my dick in her and our passion will be glorious to behold, until that passion turns insane and she has to flee across the country to get away from me.* So it didn't seem fair to paint Bull with a "maybe he's also into some illegal shit" brush just because he rides with a motorcycle club.

But it looks like my instincts were right. And it's kind of a relief, actually. Nothing sucks worse than not trusting your own judgement.

Actually, a *lot* of things suck worse. Much worse. Heartbreakingly worse. Some of those things happened because my instincts were so off when I met Raphael Wainwright four years ago. But right now, for the moment, I'm just basking in the relief of being right about someone.

And Bull looks as if he's about to chase after the pink Caddy and rip it apart with his big bare hands, but I'd rather have him at my counter. So I swing open the door and call to him, "Friend of yours?"

Instantly all the darkness lightens. He starts across the street, his long stride eating up the distance.

"Not a friend." With a shrug of his heavy shoulders, he shows me his phone before sliding it into his pocket. "I thought he was a Pokémon."

Laughter shakes through me so hard that I can't even move out of the doorway before he's right there. Wiping my teary eyes, I ask, "Gotta catch 'em all?"

"Trying to."

His gaze is searching my face as he says it, and I realize on a sudden shuddering breath that he's never been this close before. He's been within arm's reach—almost the same distance—and with a counter between us. But he's always sitting and although I can't mistake what a big guy he is, it's a completely different feeling when we're both standing together.

Maybe because the name on his vest fits him. Bull. Because he's so solid—and there's nothing lean about all the meat he's packing. He's barrel-chested and thick-thighed, yet none of it's soft. And although he works out every morning, the bulge of his biceps and definition in his forearms isn't the overdeveloped muscle of a body-builder, either.

He's just…strong. It's such a crazy turn-on.

And there's something about this closeness that's unbearably intimate. Maybe it's because I have to tilt my head back to meet his eyes, and that's what I'd do before kissing him. I'd tilt my head back, and his gaze would drop to my lips like it is now, and then his mouth would lower to mine.

But although Bull's looking, he's not lowering his head. Instead he's gripping the edge of the door that I was holding for him — now he's holding it for me.

"You ready to open?" His voice is as big and as deep as his chest.

"Yes," I say and can hear the husky note in my reply. If my apron didn't cover my breasts, my nipples would be poking right through my thin *Jem and the Holograms* T-shirt. "Just your usual?"

And will you kiss me, please?

"Whatever you've got for me," he says.

"Oooh, well then you're in luck." Suddenly full of anticipation, I head inside, pointing to his seat at the counter. "You sit. I've got something new."

This is the best part of working at Reggie's — the best part aside from having Bull's company every morning. My friend Minerva Vey owns the café, but she's given me a free hand with the menu and management. It's a long way from sous chef at the Michelin-starred restaurant where I used to work in Manhattan, but everything I loved about that job, I still have here. The head chef had been brilliant and exacting and always pushing us to send out food that will not only satisfy the customer but excite them with every bite — and that hasn't changed.

It just costs my customers a lot less.

Add in the challenge of tailoring it to the café setting,

where customers order at the counter and most of them are taking it to go? Not as easy as it sounds. We've got a limited menu as it is, with the old standards of bagels and croissants and assorted bakery items—pastries and desserts made here every morning, the breads from a local bakery. Sandwiches and soups rule the menu, and most of the time, customers want something familiar and substantial and comforting. They'll order the same thing every single day, at breakfast and lunch. And the weekly chef's special? The more similar to their usual that it is, the more likely they'll try it.

But not Bull. His 'usual' is whatever I put in front of him. Typically he doesn't even hesitate before digging in.

This time he does, looking down at the bowl I set on the counter, his spoon poking at the caramelized fried onions, cilantro, and cashews garnishing the top. "Is that oatmeal?"

"Kind of." At least, on the blackboard menu I'll be describing it as 'savory Hyderabadi oatmeal.' I catch my bottom lip between my teeth but I can't really stop my grin. "It's a variation of haleem—which is not traditionally a breakfast dish but I thought it'd translate best to one here."

"It's got meat in it," he says flatly. "You put meat in oatmeal."

"Bits of beef so tender they'll melt in your mouth. Nice and hearty for a growing boy who's got a long day of work ahead," I tell him. For customers who might not be as adventurous, I also made a vegetarian version, but Bull's as carnivorous and as courageous as they come. "Squeeze that lime wedge over the top and try it."

And I love this moment. When he takes that first bite. When the wariness in his blue eyes turns to something surprised. Then deeper, hotter, hungrier.

"Fuck me running," he says gruffly, already shoveling up another spoonful. "The way it looks, it shouldn't taste like that. What's in there?"

"Magic," I tell him, backing away from the counter with my hands up and my spirit fingers on high.

His grunt in reply is as good as any five-star Yelp review, because it means his mouth is too full to talk and he has no intention of letting it stay empty.

I head for the espresso machine and start making his americano. He orders just coffee, black—but one morning when I'd forgotten to start the coffee brewing before opening, I pulled one of these for him, instead, and discovered his taste runs a little deeper, a little less bitter than the drip coffee we serve. So it's been americanos for a while now.

I'm not sure he's noticed that I no longer pour his coffee from the carafe on the back counter. But he's probably disappointed with the coffee he gets anywhere else.

Just fine with me. I don't want him going anywhere else.

I set the mug beside his bowl—already half empty, so I'll probably be serving up another before he leaves—and head for the bakery display case.

And if I put a little swing in my hips, because from his seat at the counter he's got an unobstructed view of the way my ass looks in these jeans and how the ties of my apron accentuate every curve? All the better.

Because like I said—I don't want him going anywhere else.

I don't want any other customers going anywhere else, either, but I wouldn't work quite so hard to keep them in that chair.

"Did you do anything fun this weekend?" I ask him as I start arranging the chocolate croissants. A lot of weekend mornings he comes in like usual, but this past weekend he didn't. Now that it's summer, his motorcycle club seems to go on rides all the time. I see them pass through town sometimes, dozens of men—about half with women riding behind them.

I've never seen a woman riding behind Bull.

I don't know how I'd feel if I did. I don't have a right to feel anything, I suppose. Still, when I think of it, a huge ache opens up in my chest.

Just like it does when I wonder if the reason he doesn't come in sometimes is because another woman made him breakfast.

"Not fun," he says quietly. "A funeral."

Oh no. Feeling like a total ass for not remembering, I abandon the croissants and head back, my throat tight. His face is hard but I know there's hot and rough emotion swirling beneath. "That little boy?"

The son of one of the other bikers. I heard all about it last Sunday even before Bull mentioned it the next morning—how they'd been in the wrong place at the wrong time. A convenience store. The security footage caught it all. They'd been standing in line to pay for a slushie when someone came in with a gun. Not targeting the biker, just looking to rob the place. But the robber had started firing, the biker had tried to shield his boy. They'd both been hit. The boy didn't survive, but the biker did. Maybe. On Friday morning, Bull said his friend was still in a coma in a hospital up in Bend.

His nod is short. He's not eating now. Or drinking his coffee. Just sitting with his jaw clenched and his hands fisted on the counter.

"Has there been any improvement in his father's condition?"

"Not yet."

"They haven't caught the guy who did it?" Even though his picture is plastered over the front of the local paper and has been shown on the news every night.

And there's the look in his eyes that tells me every single one of my instincts was right. Because he's sweet and polite and funny. But I don't have one single doubt that if the shooter were standing here now, Bull would kill him in cold blood and accept whatever consequences befell him.

That part of him doesn't scare me. Maybe it should.

But instead my heart just aches for him. Sliding my hand across the counter, I fold my fingers over his fist and squeeze.

"I'm sorry," I tell him.

His throat works. He turns his hand palm up and for a long second, his strong fingers hold mine in his warm grip. Then he nods, lets me go, and begins eating again.

It's quiet between us after that, because light conversation seems inappropriate. Until a customer comes in, I make her no-foam latte, and she goes.

"Are you taking lunch today?" I ask him, because often he does. Sometimes he and the other guys at the site head out to the Wolf Den during their lunch hour, but usually he brown-bags it with a lunch from Reggie's.

So what if I make his sandwiches and portions a little bigger than we usually serve? He's a big guy. One of our best customers.

And I love feeding him.

"Yeah, I need one," he says, then looks up from his haleem with a hopeful gleam in his eyes. "You still have those barbecue wrap things?"

Last week's special. Seeing that look in his eyes, I wish I had more. But I shake my head. "This week it's a kafta plate. And there's hummus, falafel, pita." Going back to my roots, even though it hurts to make the kind of food I grew up cooking with my mother and grandmother. But Raphael took my family from me—and I'm not going to let him take everything. I'm not going to let him take even *one* more thing. "You'll like it, I promise. And if not, I'll make it up to you tomorrow."

Then I'll have two days off, and I won't see him again until Friday morning. Although, technically…I have *every* day off. Because I don't really work here. Not officially.

Something that will end up biting both me and Minerva in the ass, someday. Right now we're saying I'm part-owner so that the usual wage rules don't apply. But my name's not on any paperwork, and one day she'll get in trouble for paying me under the table and I'll get in trouble with the IRS and everything's going to be a huge freaking disaster.

But I haven't known who could help me get out of that mess. There's been a couple of people I've met who probably could, but there isn't anyone who I trust.

Until now. Maybe.

I glance at Bull. He's looking down at his phone, tapping the screen. Nerves churn in my stomach.

But putting it off won't help anything. So I take a deep breath and plant myself in front of him.

He looks up, blue eyes locking on my face. Immediately he must recognize that I'm nervous and that this isn't my usual 'plant myself in front of him' and chat mode.

His voice is low and deep. "You all right?"

"Yes." I sound breathless. "But I was wondering…if I could ask a favor."

"Name it. I'll do it."

"I…" That was fast. "I didn't even say what it was."

"Doesn't matter," he says. "You name it. I'll do it."

My heart's pounding. "Okay. It's just that— I don't want to make assumptions about anything you do or the people you know. So if I'm off-base, just tell me."

"Sara."

It's all he says but in that instant, the way he looks at me, I think I could ask for the moon and he'd say he could bring it to me, and that he'd get a little pissed if I doubt whether he can.

"I need new identification," I tell him in a rush. "And I'm wondering if you know someone who might be able to help me."

His gaze never leaves my face. "I thought you said you were born in Queens?"

"I was. I'm a U.S. citizen. It's not…" I don't know how much to say. "I've got a good driver's license, passport, birth certificate. But I need to be someone else. Because right now I'm not putting my name on anything and it's been really…hard."

No bank accounts. No utilities in my name. Minerva leased the house where I live and pays the rent for me out of my wages. I use cash for everything and don't feel secure about anything. And even though I should have switched over to an Oregon ID and vehicle plates, I've been afraid to update my license and my car's registration.

His slow nod eases the knot of anxiety twisting inside me. "I know someone. I'll make sure you get what you need."

Relief shoots out of me in a high-pitched laugh. "Thank you. And I'm happy to pay you— Or not," I quickly say when his face darkens.

"Yeah. You just hold the rest of that back." He looks at me for another long minute. "There's another option."

There is? I raise my brows and look at him expectantly.

"You tell me who scared you so bad that you're looking to change your name, and I make sure the body's never found."

I stare at him, waiting for the punchline. He doesn't give one and his gaze doesn't waver.

He's serious.

As if he'd offered to mow my lawn instead of kill a man, he evenly asks, "Too much?"

No. Well, yes. What he's offering would be too much. But *he's* not too much.

And I'm just so glad my instincts were exactly right.

"I have another favor to ask," I tell him.

"Sara." His voice deepens in warning. "Just name it."

"Okay." Pulse racing, I brace my hands against the counter. "Will you kiss me, please?"

And I never knew a man so big could move *so* fast.

THREE

SARA

One second Bull's sitting in front of me. The next second he braces his hand on the counter and launches his big body over it—and I don't remember stepping back, though I must have, because otherwise he'd have barreled right into me.

It's as if he's already thought about how to come for me, he does it so fast. As if the move was already all planned out in his head. Yet despite his speed, it seems to take forever before he actually kisses me. His big hand slides beneath the tail of my braid and cups the back of my neck, his broad thumb circling around to nestle in the hollow of my jaw. His gaze searches mine all the way down, as if he's waiting for me to change my mind, to pull away—then I close my eyes and his mouth captures my lips.

And he came for me fast, but now he takes his time, and I'm aware of everything. The soft brush of his beard against my chin. The firm warmth of his lips. The roughness of his callused fingers, the strength in his hands. The way he's not breathing, as if he's listening for my response and carefully waiting.

He doesn't need to be careful.

Rising up on my toes, I shove my hands into his thick hair and open my mouth beneath his in sensual invitation.

And he's a patient man, but he must be a hungry man, too. His left arm suddenly wraps tight around my waist and with a deep groan he hauls me up against the giant expanse of his chest. His tongue sweeps past my lips, not hesitant now, but devouring my mouth, sinking in for a long and ravenous taste.

With every stroke of his tongue, my heart pounds and fire sings through my blood. This kiss is everything I hoped it would be, hot and sweet.

And it's more than I hoped. Not just hot and sweet but absolutely consuming me.

A desperate moan rolls up my throat and I try to press closer. But Bull is already holding me so tight there's no closer, except for naked skin and him inside me.

Oh, but I'd love to have him naked and inside me now. Right on the counter. He could set me down and push between my legs and—

We'd probably scare off the customer who just came in. Which would be worth it. But Bull is already lifting his head and setting my feet back on the floor.

His big body blocks me from the customer's sight for a moment, so I have a second to find my composure again, and the move is so sweet and protective that if I wasn't already crazy about him, I would be now.

But I don't really find my composure. Not when Bull casually walks back out from behind the counter as if he was supposed to be there and takes his seat again. Not when the customer comes up to the register—a regular, one of the nurses who works at the urgent care center up the street, and who has been coming in every morning for as long as Bull has been sitting there. I greet her politely, as if she didn't just see me plastered against his big chest and my fingers buried in his hair. She responds just as politely, but her eyes are sparkling and she's repressing a grin.

I'm not even trying to repress mine. Each glance I steal in Bull's direction says he's just as pleased by what happened, and his eyes are hot as they follow my every movement.

When the nurse leaves, I wonder if he'll come for me again. He doesn't. Maybe because there's something else here with us in Reggie's now—a new tension, a feeling of anticipation that's hot and slick and oh, so good.

Maybe because the next time he kisses me, we better not be interrupted.

I head back to his end of the counter, my hands tucked into my back pockets because otherwise I'm going to grab him again. "So," I say. "That was all right."

His brows shoot up and his entire body seems to bristle. *"All right?"*

I just grin.

It's a challenge he doesn't back down from. *"All right,"* he echoes again with mock irritation lacing his deep voice. "I guess I'll have to do better than that. You busy tonight?"

My elated heart almost thuds through my ribs. I shake my head.

"Then I'll come for you at seven. I'll be on my bike so you'll want to wear jeans."

"Like these?" I turn and let him get another good look at my ass.

If his eyes were a fire I'd be immolated right now.

"Like those," he says gruffly. "You got a phone number?"

Some of the playfulness leaves me. "I don't use a cell phone. But I've got a landline at the house."

His expression darkens. "Give me his name."

Raphael Wainwright. A name Bull might recognize, even though Raphael is thousands of miles away. "He's no one."

Bull doesn't like that answer. "He's someone who needs getting rid of if you're afraid of him."

As I should be. Because even though he's thousands of miles away, Raphael has a hell of a reach. But as soon as I have a new identity, he'll never touch me again.

No need for Bull to risk his life when the solution is for me to get a new one.

"I'm not afraid," I tell him now, which is a huge lie, but I follow it up with the truth. "I'm just tired of hiding."

And Bull doesn't like that, either. But he doesn't push for more. Just comes up off his seat, leans over the counter and slides his hand around the back of my neck again, pulling me close for a fierce, hard kiss.

A possessive kiss. As if everything has already changed between us. As if the date tonight is just going through the motions of laying a foundation for a building that's already constructed.

As if I'm already his.

I don't know if I am. But I think I'd like to be.

My breathing is unsteady when he lets me go. Everything's unsteady. And wonderful. But still the world is shifting under my feet and I need to find my balance again.

I can always find that equilibrium in the kitchen. Backing up a step, I tell him, "I'm going to go…uh, make your lunch."

Something in his expression freezes and all at once he's looking at me in that careful way again.

"Am I pushing too hard?" His voice deepens and his body is utterly still. "I'll go slower, easier."

I *really* don't want that. "You couldn't push too hard."

"All right," he says and now his gaze holding mine isn't wary, but hot and hungry. "Then you make my lunch. I'll feed you dinner. But my dessert afterward is going to be your sweet pussy."

I stop breathing, stop backing away from the counter. Just stare at him with that sweet pussy already aching for his touch, already hot and liquid and I've got the feeling it's just going to get hotter all day, because I won't do anything but think of it.

I can't think of anything else *now*.

As if he didn't suggest anything more than a kiss on my front porch, he casually raises his coffee to his mouth, drains the mug before saying, "Too much?"

"No," I whisper hoarsely. "I think that's just right."

Satisfaction gleams in his eyes. "Good," he says and rises to his feet. Trembling all over with tension and anticipation and desire, I head into the back and pull together the box for his lunch, then toss in a chocolate chunk cookie for his dessert.

Tonight that dessert will be me, spread out beneath him.

At the register he pays cash, like he always does. His callused fingers slide over mine when I hand over his lunch, as they always do.

But nothing's the same. And as I watch him head for the door, it occurs to me that there's something I've never asked him before.

"Bull," I call out and he turns smoothly, walking backward. "What's *your* name?"

He grins. "David. But since my pop is the only one who uses it, you might as well keep calling me Bull."

I probably will, though I like his real name as much. But he's been Bull to me for so long I can't think of him as anyone else.

"Just David?"

"Masters," he adds, then his gaze darkens and turns speculative. "And come to think of it, maybe you shouldn't bother getting new identification. If you're going to be changing your name, Sara Masters sounds like a damn good one to me."

With that, he heads out and I'm left staring after him with my jaw dropped.

Because he *really* moves fast.

I GET OFF WORK AS soon as lunch rush ends. I've been floating all day, thinking of Bull and everything I need to do before I see him again at seven.

The first thing will be to go home and nap. Every morning, I'm up at three a.m., so I'm not used to late hours and I don't want to fall asleep halfway through our date — or halfway through dessert.

Just the thought of Bull's tongue on me sends a delicious shiver racing over my skin. All day, I've been wet with anticipation and aching from the memory of our kiss. His mouth on mine made me hotter and needier than I've ever been. So imagining his mouth anywhere else?

Nuclear meltdown.

And on second thought—maybe the first thing I should do is take a bath and shave *everything*.

But it doesn't really matter what I do, because the best part of it all is that I'm actually looking forward to spending time with a man. Take *that*, Raphael Wainwright. That bastard could have so easily ruined me. Instead he only hurt me.

He hurt me deeply. So deeply. But he didn't break me. Maybe because I was never in love with him, and he didn't have that power over me.

Instead he took everything I *did* love.

But I'm not letting him take anything more. And I won't let thoughts of Raphael dim my happiness now.

Still, I can't get away from him. When I leave Reggie's through the back entrance, I don't breathe easily until my gaze scans the parking lot and finds it empty. No Raphael waiting by my car, a smile on his lips but his eyes telling me that I'm a bad, bad girl as he asks whether I've been deliberately avoiding his calls.

At the drugstore, I can't shake the feeling of being watched and followed. I force myself not to look over my shoulder. He's not there, asking why I'm buying condoms and new razors and don't I know that I'm his? That I'll *always* be his?

And a part of me *wants* to use my old credit card, hoping that he'll see the purchases listed there. That he'll see the condoms and razors I bought, and know that I'm tidying up my pussy so that another man can lick it.

But I defied him before and he destroyed everything. I'm not going to let him touch Bull.

Because that's what Raphael would do. He wouldn't hurt me. Not physically. At least, he never has before. I wouldn't take bets on what he might do now. I disappeared six months ago and in that time, maybe his love has transformed into something else. It was a pretty sick version of love to begin with.

So I don't know if he would hurt me. But I know he *would* destroy anyone who stood between us. Anyone who tried to protect me from him. He'd burn down their house while they're sleeping in it.

He's done it before.

And as much as I'd love to throw a 'fuck you' into his face, I can't risk him finding me.

So I'll change my name. And one day, I'll stop feeling as if someone is always watching me. One day when I get home from work, I won't sit in my driveway, scanning all the cars parked on the street, looking extra hard at any I don't recognize as belonging to my neighbors. I won't stare at my living room window, watching for any hint of movement and desperately wondering if I'll find him waiting inside, as he waited for me before. More than once.

But that day isn't today. When I pull into my driveway and hit the garage door opener, I watch the window. The curtains are just as I left them—open wide. I care less about my privacy than not being surprised.

Everything looks okay.

I pull into the garage, grabbing my purse and the bag from the pharmacy before opening the car door.

And I fucked up. I fucked up so bad. Because I should have closed the overhead garage door right away. But I didn't. So my hands are full and I'm half in and half out of my seat when, out of the corner of my eye, I see the figure slip around the back of my car.

My heart leaps in terror, ready to run.

But it's too damn late.

FOUR

BULL

A WORKDAY NEVER SEEMED SO LONG. AND IT'S NOT OVER yet, because the work doesn't stop at the job. There's Hellfire Riders' business to take care of.

This morning I left a message for the prez, letting him know tonight's plans had changed. I didn't send details, nothing that can be traced back to us later. So I'm not surprised when he says he'll stop by my place around six. He'll want a face to face for a more thorough update.

Which ought to give me just enough time to fill him

in, then shower and stroke one out to take the edge off before changing into something clean and heading to Sara's.

And I was right—it is just like rolling out of bed early. I hate changing and getting ready twice in a day. But knowing that I'll be with her, I don't hate the thought of it so much.

Shit. I'm not hating *anything* today.

I moved in hard on her. Maybe too hard. But she seemed to take it all right.

And, hell. I wouldn't have moved at all—at least not yet—if she hadn't moved first.

Just flat out asked me to kiss her.

No way I could have held back. I'm a patient man. I'm a *damn* patient man. When I want something, I can wait forever for it.

Until I've actually got what I want right in my hands. Then holding back isn't exactly the strongest part of my personality.

But I'll try to go easy on Sara. Eat her pussy tonight, show her a real good time. Maybe wait until tomorrow before getting her sexy little body under me and my thick cock deep inside her.

And if our date runs past midnight tonight, hell—that's technically tomorrow.

It's blistering hot when I leave the job site at four, but on the bike the rush of wind makes for a sweet and cool ride. My place is a few miles out of town, up a long driveway shrouded with dried pine needles. The house is a big log cabin that my dad built for my mom, though she only lived there about a year before taking off. The house wasn't the problem—it's a beaut, set in an isolated clearing with a back porch overlooking a sparkling creek. It was my dad who sent her running.

I might have run, too, if I hadn't grown up with him and gotten real comfortable with his idiosyncrasies.

Pop's a bit paranoid—and a bit of a survivalist. Half the time he lives in a little shack deeper up in the mountains, so the government won't find him. The past few years, though, he's been spending more and more time at home. Those creature comforts calling to him, I suppose—though he says it's to keep an eye on me. To make sure I don't get into any trouble.

He's not real good at it, because I get into plenty of trouble while running with the Hellfire Riders. The trick is, just don't get caught.

Anyway, I figure some of his tendencies rubbed off on me. I'm not holing up in a shack or stockpiling MREs anytime soon, but sometimes being a Hellfire Rider means walking outside the line of the law, and that don't bother me none. The government's got its uses, like helping and protecting those who need help and protection. And, shit—we pay taxes, because we sure as hell love riding those government roads.

But the Hellfire Riders, we help and protect our own. And the law can stay the fuck out of our business.

So, yeah. Pop's rubbed off on me some.

Though some days I wish he'd take it easy on the stockpiling shit. I roll up closer to the house and see he's been at it again. A huge fucking pile of wood is sitting beside the house, as if a dump truck backed up into the clearing and just shat out a few cut-up trees.

He's already at the chopping block, cutting the logs into wedges with a maul. His dark hair started running to gray a few years back, and his body's a string of lean, wiry muscle. He's got his shirt off and sweat running down the back of the tan Carhartts that hang off his skinny ass.

Don't know where I got my size, but it wasn't from him. Maybe from my mom, though he says she was a little thing. Since I was about three months old when she took off, I don't remember her — and he doesn't keep any pictures around. For all I know, he went truly crazy for a while and fucked a she-bear.

"David, my boy!" Wiping his brow on his forearm, Pop tosses a split log onto the pile forming beside him. "You got time?"

"A little."

"Split or stack?"

I hate stacking wood. "Split," I say and he hands over the maul and throws a pair of leather gloves after it. "Where the hell did this come from?"

"Old Barker's clearing out his back property. Most of it he sold to the mill, but I talked him into a deal for this and another load that'll be coming tomorrow." He pours himself a lemonade from the pitcher sitting on the porch. "I figure we'll get six or seven cords out it."

For the wood stove and the fireplace I barely ever use. And that's in addition to the twelve cords he's already got stacked in the big barn out behind the house.

That's why he's stacking these here. There's no more room in the damn barn.

But if I say we don't need this, he'll tell me a million reasons why having a ten-year supply of firewood might save our asses one day. And more wood doesn't hurt anything, so I strip off my kutte and T-shirt, pull on my gloves, and start splitting the damn logs.

An hour later, we've got a sizable row split and stacked when I hear motorcycles coming up the driveway. Two or three.

Tensing a little, Pop looks down that way. "You expecting friends?"

"Yup."

His tension eases. "You need me to get out of here?"

"We can talk somewhere else."

"Nah, I'll head in and rest for a bit." My dad grins a little. "That way you can just keep splitting."

As long as it's not stacking. "Will do."

He heads for the stairs. "You want beers?"

"It'd be nice."

"Too bad I'm an asshole, then. Come in and grab them your damn self."

The screen door slams shut behind him, but I'm grinning when I set the next log on the chopping block. I won't go in for beers, and he'll eventually bring some out, grumbling about how I wasn't raised right without a mother.

And he enjoys it all as much as I do.

The prez rolls in, flanked by Blowback, the Riders' warlord, and Thorne, the Riders' VP—and who's also my boss at T&E. Shit. I set down the maul and pull my T-shirt over my sweaty skin, because half-naked suddenly doesn't feel serious enough.

I'm acting as the Riders' enforcer for the time being. It's a temporary role while the regularly appointed enforcer deals with some shit that went down a few months back, but it means regular meetings with the prez and the Riders' officers. I was already on the executive board, so the meetings aren't new. But meetings where we discuss killing someone?

That's something that doesn't call for casual.

Serious or not, though, I leave my kutte off, because no one's expecting me to split logs wearing a leather vest.

If I was splitting heads? That's another matter.

They're all eyeing the mountain of wood as I wave them in, then grab a few deck chairs from the porch and drag them down to the woodpile.

Good thing about cut logs is they make for a fine place to set a beer—or a lemonade.

The prez settles in, looking amused as hell. Maybe because of the pile of wood, maybe because Willie Nelson's crooning from my pop's ancient cassette player. The prez is a big motherfucker, though not as big as me, and there's few men I respect more. "Laying in for the winter?"

"A couple of winters," I tell him.

"Can't be too prepared," he agrees.

Lemonade in his big hand, Thorne takes a seat on a log instead of the deck chair. He's about as old as my dad, and is one of the men I respect even more than the prez—though partially it's because I've been riding with him a hell of a lot longer. We were both Steel Titans before we were Hellfire Riders, and a lot of what I know about being in a motorcycle club, about brotherhood, I learned from Thorne.

And he's one of the few people in Pine Valley who's friends with my dad. Not close friends—my dad doesn't have anyone that close except for me. But Thorne doesn't look at my dad like he's just some kook living out in the woods.

That goes a long way for me.

Now he asks, "Is Will around?"

"Inside."

"I got a lead on some military surplus that's off the books. I'm looking at the weapons but I hear there's gear, too. Thought he might be interested."

"Yeah, he would."

Thorne nods. "I'll head in and talk to him after, then."

Blowback doesn't say anything but I don't expect him to. Small talk isn't the warlord's strong suit. Killing is. So for now he just leans back against the porch and waits and listens.

The prez gets right to it. "What's the holdup with Osprey?"

The fucker we're trying to get our hands on. "Woodridge says he got spooked."

"Is he running?"

"Out of state? Don't think so. Word is he holed up. Probably waiting until his picture isn't flashed on the news every damn night. And Christ knows he's probably got more than enough holes to hide in. So Woodridge is setting up a new meet."

The prez's mouth flattens. Pissed. Because the longer it takes to find Osprey, the more likely it'll be the cops who find him first.

His gaze shoots to Blowback. "You heard anything on him?"

The warlord shakes his head. "If I had, I'd be bringing you his body instead of nothing."

"Fuck." The prez's gaze swings back to me. "Is this asshole Woodridge giving us the runaround?"

"I'll tell you true, boss—Vern Woodridge is the dumbest piece of shit I've ever met. But when it comes to getting what you need, he does what he says. When there's something or someone that needs to be found, he finds it."

"I agree," Blowback says, but his attention is shifting away from us. Turning toward the road. "Though I have met dumber pieces of shit than Woodridge."

I hear it now, too. The sound of a vehicle coming up the drive. Not a Harley. A car, sounds like.

For a second I think that maybe Sara jumped the gun, that she's coming to my place before I head to hers. But she drives one of those hybrid Toyotas and the engine I'm hearing isn't that quiet. This one's got some cylinders under the hood.

As a pink Cadillac comes into view, Blowback says, "New evidence says Woodridge *is* the dumbest piece of shit I've ever met."

Jesus fucking Christ. I yank the maul out of the chopping block. "I got this," I tell them.

And ol' Vern still has a tiny bit of brains, because he swings that big boat around when he reaches the clearing, like he might be driving away real fast.

Maybe because I'm coming after him with a big fucking axe.

"Wait, wait!" The stupid fucker gets out and heads around the back of the car, hands up like he's under arrest. "I got something for you!"

"If it's not a meetup with Osprey, you're two fucking seconds from having your dick shoved down your throat—and even a meetup might not fucking save you." I grab the front of his shirt and yank him in real close. "You came to my house? My fucking *house*?"

The stink of fear is pouring off him as he babbles, "I got the meetup! But, man—I couldn't get it by the time you wanted. He said in three days and I couldn't talk him down because he was getting real antsy."

"Three days?"

"Yeah, man. Three days! Thursday night at midnight I'll be meeting him behind the Baptist church on Oak. But I knew you'd be pissed so I got you something to, you know, show you that my word is good. To show you I can get you anything you want."

"I told you I didn't want anything from any other fucking dealer," I growl at him. "I gave you twenty fucking thousand dollars for crystal from Osprey. I don't want anyone else's shit product."

Don't want anyone else but Osprey. But this fucker doesn't know we're going after the dealer, not the meth.

"Okay, okay!" His head bobs with each word. "And you'll get it. But, man. You *really* want what I picked up for you—"

Fuck this. Hand fisting in his hair, I shove his face down, smashing his cheek against the pink lid of the trunk. "Let me make this real fucking clear, Vern. I don't want a single fucking thing but that twenty thousand dollars worth of crystal meth—and for you to stop showing up *anywhere* I am. You understand me?"

"Yes, man!" he says, then groans in fear as I lift the maul and place the blade close to his face.

"Let me give you a fucking demonstration of what will happen if I see you in person again. You ever watch *Game of Thrones*, Vern?"

"Oh gawwwwwd—"

I swing hard. The blade sinks through the trunk lid about two inches from his face, and he shrieks.

But it's another sound that freezes my blood. A muffled scream.

From inside the trunk.

"What the fuck?" I tear the maul from the lid, grip his head tighter. "You got someone in there?"

"I told you, man…" His body shaking, Vern's all but pissing himself. "I got you something you wanted to tide you over."

Oh Jesus. Oh fucking Jesus, *no*.

He knows what I want. He's seen me at her counter every morning for months.

"Open it," I tell him hoarsely.

His trembling hands fumble with the keys before he finally gets them into the lock and twists.

"See, man?" he says like an eager puppy as he raises the lid. "I told you."

My heart stops. Because Sara's curled up in there, her dark eyes wide—

And absolutely terrified.

Terrified of *me*.

FIVE

BULL

Among the brothers, I'm known for having something funny to say in uneasy situations. Something that'll break up the tension and make everyone relax. It's how I got my name. Most people assume Bull refers to my size, but really it's short for *bullshit*, because of the kind of stuff I say during those awkward moments.

But I can't say a single thing now. Not after I reach into the trunk to pull Sara out—

And she flinches away from my touch.

After that, there's not a word getting through the vise of my throat.

As if realizing the opening of that trunk was shit hitting a fan, Blowback's already at my back, ready to do whatever needs done. I toss him the maul, which he catches easily by the handle. His lethal gaze shifts to Woodridge and the fool finally shuts his mouth.

Her face flushed and tears gleaming in her eyes, Sara's struggling to crawl out of the trunk. Unlike the front of the car, it's not trashed, and she's not stuffed in there with a bunch of garbage. The sun's scorching, though, and it's just past the hottest part of the day. Damp patches of sweat soak through her T-shirt. She's lucky to be alive but she must not have been in there long, and Woodridge gave her a bottle of water.

Doesn't matter if he took that much care. The fucker's dead.

Sara stiffens and slaps at my hands when I reach for her again. Physically it's like being slapped by a honeybee but each blow is a hammer in my chest. Worse are the sobs shaking through her. They're a knife in my gut and I'm just bleeding to death behind this pink Cadillac.

Ignoring her struggles, I slip my big hands under her knees and shoulders and carefully lift her up against my chest, holding her securely enough that no matter how she twists and fights, she's not getting away.

But she stops fighting. Just settles against me and cries harder, her skin hot and flushed and glistening. Jesus, even her jeans feel damp against my hand, she's been sweating so hard.

I head for my front door but don't see a damn thing in front of me. My feet move automatically up the porch steps.

This morning, I held her and kissed her for the first time. Not for one second did I think it would be the last time.

Because all these fucking months, I've watched her, talked to her—hell, I *courted* her, though it was a careful kind of courting. Since the day I met her, I haven't looked at another woman, because I was waiting and hoping for the moment when Sara wouldn't be so damn scared of some motherfucker whose name I don't even know. Some motherfucker who scared her so bad, she fled across the country to get away from him.

Now she's scared of me. The second I let her go, she's going to run again. And I don't know how the fuck I'm going to stop her.

But I can make sure she doesn't go anywhere just yet.

"Pop!" I roar, ripping open the screen door and striding into the front room. "Pop! I need you out here!"

"The hell's that racket, boy?" Shirt hanging open over his skinny chest, he walks in barefoot from the kitchen, grumbling, "I told you to get your own damn—"

Pop abruptly stops, his gaze going from the devastation that must be showing on my face to the woman in my arms.

"Who you got there, son?"

"Sara," I tell him, my voice rough. He's never met her but knows I've got my eye on someone. It's not going to take him long to figure this one out. "A stupid mother-fucker put her in the trunk of his car. I gotta take care of him and I need you to look after her. Get her something cold to drink, make sure she's not overheated."

Nodding, Pop steps back and I carry her past him into the kitchen. It's a bright, sunny room with French doors that open onto the back deck, and the thickness of the log walls and the fans we've got going keep it cool enough, even on days like this.

Her sobs have already quieted, though I think it's through sheer will. She doesn't want me to see her crying.

Doesn't want me to look at her at all.

I set her down on the table and cup the side of her face in my hand. My palm engulfs her jaw and I brush away tears from her cheek with my thumb, wishing she'd meet my eyes as I say hoarsely, "I'm so damn sorry, Sara."

She averts her face. Not just her eyes. She turns her entire head, pulling away from the touch of my hand.

And there's nothing I can say now that'll make this better. There's nothing I can *do* to make it better.

It's been done.

My chest an aching mess, I straighten and look to Pop, who's at the sink drawing a glass of ice water. "You don't let her run."

"I'll watch over her."

Which isn't the same as stopping her if she goes, but with a man like my dad who respects freedom and choice more than he respects the business of a motorcycle club, it's what I'm going to get.

Woodridge, though. He's going to get something else.

I sure as fuck wish I still had that maul in my hands when I leave Sara sitting stiff and tearstained in my kitchen. Pure fury drives me through the house. I slam through the screen door, nearly ripping it off the hinges, and in the haze of anger I'm halfway to the pink Caddy before I realize the little fucker is nowhere in sight.

Turning, I look to the prez and the VP, who are still sitting by the woodpile. Blowback's joined them again, a lemonade in his hand.

My gaze zeroes in on the warlord, then to the maul propped against his leg, the heavy head resting on the ground and the handle within easy reach of his grip.

No blood on the blade. Not yet. "Where the fuck is he?"

Blowback's gaze shifts to the Caddy. It takes me a second. Then I realize the trunk's closed again.

So he shoved Woodridge in there. Keeping him warm for me.

I start for the Cadillac but the prez's voice stops me in my tracks.

"You head back this way, Bull." With a big boot, he pushes an empty deck chair into position facing him. "Take a seat."

For a moment, I think about telling the prez to fuck himself. Woodridge shoved my woman into a trunk. Scared her.

Made her scared of *me*.

But it wasn't just Woodridge who scared her. And maybe that's what's really hurting me so bad.

After what Sara likely heard me saying, she has good reason to be scared.

I wouldn't *ever* let anything happen to her. But she doesn't know that. And even if I say so, I wouldn't blame her for not trusting my word. Not now.

My blood boiling, my pulse running wild, I drag my hands through my beard, my hair. I probably look like a giant fucking savage.

I feel like one.

Dropping into the deck chair would probably shatter the plastic legs so I sit slow and easy. But there's nothing easy between all of us now.

The prez's eyes are hard and cold as steel. "That the woman from the café across from the clubhouse in town?"

"She is."

"She yours?" The prez is sitting back like this is just casual conversation but there's nothing casual about it. "I heard a thing or two about you going into the café pretty regular."

Because the old ladies' gossip circles are a little glazed donut compared to the huge motherfucking cake of rumors that feeds the brothers' big mouths. But the prez probably didn't even need to hear it from them. Thorne's my boss and I've been ribbed about Sara and her lunches more than once on the site. The VP might have told him while sitting right here.

If not for Thorne knowing better, maybe I'd have lied and said she was mine. But there's no point.

"I was working on it," I tell him.

"So it's not a done deal."

My stomach aching, I shake my head. Chances are, it'll never happen now.

So all that's left is protecting her.

His gaze shifts to Blowback. "You figure in that trunk she heard everything that we heard?"

The warlord nods. "Every word."

"She's not going to talk," I tell him. "Just this morning she asked me to get her new identification. She's not going to the cops."

"Is she an illegal?"

Looking for something to hold over her. I shake my head again. "She's American. I think hiding from an old boyfriend. She doesn't want her name out there. Talking to the cops will put it out there."

"And you're absolutely fucking sure she'll keep quiet?" Face hard, the prez sits forward. "When Maurice wakes up, are you going to be the one who tells him that Osprey is sitting pretty in the county jail, because a girl went and told the cops exactly when and where to find him? You going to tell him the motherfucker who killed his little boy is still walking around *alive* and the Riders fucked up our chance to take him out because you've gone soft over some pussy?"

I'm sure as hell not fucking up that chance. Maurice is a close brother to me. Almost as close as Duke is.

But even if he wasn't a friend, he's a Hellfire Rider. And we look after our own.

Sara's mine alone to look after. She won't like it. But she's not going to get much choice.

"I'll keep her here," I tell him. "We get Osprey, we let her go. Even if she does talk" — though I'm one-hundred-fucking-percent certain she won't — "there won't be anything left of Osprey for the cops to find. There'll be nothing to pin on anyone."

Though even if they did pin it on one of us, it's the kind of shit we'd be proud to go down for.

"And you go down for kidnapping her, instead? For holding her against her will?"

"I don't think it'll happen," I say and my voice is real fucking thick. "I think she'll just take off. Find safe waters again."

But if she does end up going to the cops, if I'm charged for holding her…fuck, I'll take it. Because the only alternative here is a hell of a lot worse.

And I won't see her hurt.

The prez nods. "All right. We'll go in and talk to her. Not a damn fucking word about Osprey or why we want him. Maurice rides with us so the cops might suspect we're gunning for him, but right now they've got nothing more than suspicion. He never shows his face again, they'll figure he ran. Let's not hand them a reason to think otherwise. All we want is the meth. That work for everyone?"

Both Thorne and Blowback nod. Then Blowback says, "And Woodridge?"

We all look toward the pink Caddy. "We'll babysit him out at the ranch, yeah?" Thorne suggests. "Until it's time for his meetup."

"Then I get him," I say.

The prez agrees, "Then you can do whatever the fuck you want with him."

That decision gets nods all around. So I've got three days with her. This morning, I had my whole damn future spread out before me. But three days is all I'm going to get.

With her looking at me like I'm a fucking monster.

Hell. Maybe I am.

The prez gets up. And maybe because he's got his own girl he's crazy about, or maybe because the Riders look out for their own and my face probably says the whole fucking world just shattered around me, he tells me,

"I'll go easy on her."

I know he will. But the prez's *easy* doesn't fit most people's definition of the word. Sara'll likely end up more scared of me than she already is.

After a morning—after months—that were the best fucking start to any time with a woman I've ever had. But it's already ended. And in three days, chances are I'll never see her again.

So I better get all my looking in now.

SIX

SARA

Blindly I look up from my ice water. The man who Bull left me with stands at the sink, rinsing a thermometer. His voice sounds unconcerned but his gaze roams all over my face, as if gauging whether I'm about to pass out.

I'm not all right, but I nod anyway. Because what's wrong with me isn't my body.

Unless you count my stupid heart. And my stupid instincts that led me so wrong again.

But health-wise? I'm great. Beyond great. Especially considering that only fifteen minutes ago, I thought I was dead. Because I was sure there was only one reason a junkie might shove me into the trunk of his car, and it didn't end up with me in Bull's bright, sunny kitchen. No, it ended with me raped or chopped up into little pieces or my body never being found again. Or all of the above.

I was *so* sure I was going to die. So sure.

This is a different nightmare. But at least it's a safer one.

Feet bare and shirt hanging open over a wiry chest covered in gray hair, the man approaches me. "Good thing. But go ahead and stick this under your tongue, anyway. Let's make sure your temperature ain't elevated."

I take the thermometer from him. It's an old fashioned one, a glass stick filled with mercury.

My throat feels rough as I ask, "You're Pop?"

"That's me."

"Is that a…a club name? Or are you Bull's father?"

His eyes are the same blue as Bull's but other than that, there isn't much resemblance. And the older man called him 'son' but that doesn't always mean a biological relationship, any more than 'brother' or 'sister' does in my religion. Family isn't always blood.

"I ain't in any club." Pop seems amused by that, shaking his head. "He's my pup."

A pup. That's not how I would describe Bull. And I wonder if that makes his dad a dog or a wolf.

A wolf, I bet. Pop's been nothing but nice since Bull brought me in here. But that doesn't mean he doesn't have teeth.

Before I can respond, he raises his graying eyebrows and gives the thermometer a significant look. Obediently I place the instrument under my tongue.

"Yup," Pop continues, "We've lived here all his life. He was born in the bed upstairs, pink all over and just screaming his lungs out. Looking at him now, you wouldn't ever guess he started out as the tiniest, baldest little thing you ever saw."

My lips curve, still clamped around the thermometer. No, I wouldn't have guessed that.

Misty with nostalgia, Pop's gaze drops to my mouth. "Hell. First time I ever took his temperature as a baby it was with that thermometer there. Stuck it right up his butt."

A laugh erupts up my throat. I sputter and choke but don't spit the thermometer out. Working in restaurants and seeing some *really* disgusting shit means I've got an iron stomach, and I saw him wash the thermometer. So I'm pretty sure that breaking the glass and spilling the mercury would be a lot worse than anything currently in my mouth.

"Attagirl," he says approvingly and heads to the fridge. "You want a beer?"

I shake my head.

"Iced tea?"

I nod, then shake my head again when he asks about sugar and lemon.

Setting the glass in front of me, he takes the thermometer and reads it. "Well, you're not dying," is his prognosis, and it's so far from the terrifying end that I thought I was heading for, I can't stop my hysterical giggle.

It's not a laugh. A real laugh isn't birthed from pain and fear. And none of this is funny.

The heavy tread of boots quiets me. The muscles alongside my spine stiffen. That's more than just Bull coming into the house. I know what's about to happen, because I'm pretty sure that I heard something I shouldn't have.

A shakedown. Except they won't be after money. They'll be after my silence.

No problem, really. If I have a choice, I won't talk to or about any Hellfire Rider again as long as I live.

I don't turn to look at them as they come into the kitchen. Instead I watch Pop's face as he sizes up the situation, his gaze lingering in one direction—I'm guessing on Bull. There's some silent exchange taking place between the two men, because Pop finally nods like he's agreeing to something unsaid.

He takes his beer and says, "I'll get that wood stacked, then." His gaze finds mine. "You give me a holler if you need anything."

"Thank you," I tell him and my voice is a tiny rasp.

Jaw clenched, he nods again and heads out.

A big man settles into the seat across from me, wearing a black leather vest over a short-sleeved gray T-shirt. Not as big as Bull, no tattoos that I can see, a short beard and cold, dark blue eyes. I know who he is. Saxon Gray. He owns the Wolf Den tavern and the gym across from Reggie's. A *PRESIDENT* patch sits below a *HRMC* patch.

So he's the one who's going to threaten me. There's a huge lump in my throat and I don't want to look at Bull, but when his giant frame moves into my field of vision, I can't help it. He leans back against the island in the center of the kitchen, inked arms crossed over his broad chest.

Concern fills the gaze that searches my face. His voice is low and gruff. "You all right?"

How does he *think* I am? I'm in a kitchen surrounded by four men who are here to scare me into falling in line. He's here to bully me and yet he's asking how I am?

Deliberately I look away from him and his bullshit concern, meeting the president's eyes.

"I won't say a word," I say.

If the president's surprised when I come right out with that, he doesn't show it. Instead he leans back in the chair and gives me a considering look. "That's what Bull told us. Said we don't need to worry about you."

Did he? I don't really care.

Except I do. And my chest and stomach hurt so much, as if I've been drinking acid. I don't say anything, though, because I'm sure he's not done.

"I do worry, though," he says, sitting forward and bracing his forearms on the table, fingers laced together like a businessman making a deal. "So let me tell you what's going to happen."

No deal, then. No negotiations. Just, he'll talk and I'll listen. Trying to ease the burning ache in my throat, I sip my iced tea and wait to see what he offers.

"You're going to stay here with Bull a few days. When the business you heard about is done, you go home. And if you stay quiet about that business, we make sure you get those papers you want."

Which sounds like a nice exchange except it's also something illegal for them to hold over me.

Something illegal that Bull gave them to use.

The betrayal shouldn't surprise me. It shouldn't hurt. But it does and I can't stop my gaze from shooting over to meet his again.

He doesn't flinch under my accusing stare. He doesn't look like he could flinch at all. His face and body are stone. He's gripping the edge of the butcher block counter, every muscle in his arms so tight that I can see the throb of his pulse through the veins threaded beneath the inked skin of his forearms and biceps.

But I don't know what I've got to lose by accepting the president's offer. I already lost everything else I wanted when I heard Bull telling the asshole who kidnapped me that he was buying twenty thousand dollars' worth of meth. And I need that fake identification.

"All right," I agree in a voice that sounds stronger than I feel.

The president nods and lightly thumps the side of his fist on the table, as if pleased by my response, then holds out his hand. "All right, then."

That's it? I shake his hand, watching him warily. "No threats of bodily harm?"

He tilts his head, an amused and dangerous glint in his steely blue eyes. "You want me to say something like—if you break our agreement, then whatever that asshole you're running from did to you won't compare to what we'll do?"

Bull makes a sound, a harsh indrawn breath. But I don't look at him. Because he gave them that, too? Not that he really knew what he was giving them.

This time it's easy to find the strength to match my voice, because there's so much rage and pain behind it. "Considering that asshole burned down my parents' house while my mother and father and grandmother were sleeping in it, I really don't think you *could* do anything to me that compares."

The president's face abruptly stills, and beneath that hard mask I see something terrifyingly lethal.

Then an explosion of shattering glass makes me jump in my seat, tearing my hand from his to cover my ears, my panicked gaze sweeping the kitchen.

And landing on Bull. He's stomping toward the deck, his back rigid, blood dripping from his hands. Glass crunches beneath his heavy boots.

As soon as he's outside, he throws back his head and *roars*, a sound unlike anything I've heard from any man before—but one I've felt. It's rage and pain and I know that sound even if I've never made it.

My heart pounding so hard it's echoing in my ears, I barely hear Pop's voice, slightly winded as if he sprinted into the house at the first explosive sound.

"The hell, David! You gone fucking crazy, boy?"

Back rigid, Bull hangs his head. His barrel of a chest expands on huge, ragged breaths and his answer is a rough growl. "I'll clean it up, Pop."

Because somehow he shattered the glass faces of an entire bank of kitchen cabinets. Throwing something. Or maybe just smashing them with his fists. Blood is dripping from his clenched fingers onto the boards of the deck.

Still seated, the president is regarding Bull with a steady, thoughtful gaze. After a moment, he turns that gaze toward one of the bikers behind me. "You want to look into that?"

"I will," the other man says.

But I'm barely following along. Because I can't stop staring at Bull. The tension in his big body is that of a man rigidly contained, yet when he rakes his bloody hands through his hair and suddenly looks back at me, nothing about him seems under control. There's just sheer primitive fury and his own blood is the warpaint.

With long strides he stalks away off the side of the deck, disappearing from my sight. All at once I can breathe again, but it doesn't feel as if I am. My chest hurts and I'm tired. So tired.

The Hellfire Riders' president stands. "You want us to get someone in here to replace those cabinet doors, Will?"

Bull's father shakes his head. "He'll be doing it."

"Then you feel free to give us the bill for the new glass."

"No. He'll be paying for it, too."

With a glance at me, the president says, "I think he already is."

SEVEN

BULL

I'VE GOT SO MUCH SHAME CLOGGING MY THROAT, IT'S like I've got a fist shoved in there. And no amount of roaring or screaming will clear it out.

It won't clear the shame—or the rage. Rage at the fucker who killed her family and made her flee across the country. Rage at myself, for adding to her hurt. For adding so much to it.

A man couldn't mistake the look she gave me when the four of us Riders walked into that kitchen. She knew exactly what was about to go down. The prez went easy on her, like he promised. He went real easy. And I knew the prez wasn't going to hurt her, even if she didn't agree to what he offered. That doesn't change how I stood behind him while he made her believe we would.

Made her believe we'd do worse than what some fucker did to her family.

I'm outside by the woodpile again when the brothers leave the house. Working alone as Pop and I often do, we can't be too careful, so we keep bandages and a First Aid kit handy wherever we're swinging axes or working with blades. Right now I'm sitting on the deck chair, taping up the bleeding gashes in my hands.

Blowback heads for the Caddy. He'll drive it out to the clubhouse on the ranch, where they'll be keeping Woodridge until the meetup with Osprey. The prez and Thorne stop by the woodpile but don't sit.

The prez asks, "You got a name for that old boyfriend?"

Tightly I shake my head.

"Blowback'll dig it up. If you want it."

"Yeah." My voice is pure gravel. "I want it."

"All right. He'll be back for his bike in a bit, probably ask a few questions."

"Ask me or Sara?" If it's the latter, I don't imagine I'll allow that. We've hurt her enough without Blowback scaring her just by looking at her with that empty, dead gaze of his.

As if he heard me thinking that, the prez's eyes crinkle

with amusement. "You, I figure."

Blowback can probably find everything with nothing but her name. But I can give him more info and a better place to start.

I nod my agreement before glancing to Thorne. "You all right with me calling in sick the next couple of days?"

"We'll make do," he says. "What about her? Anyone going to report her missing?"

Maybe tomorrow. "I'll have her call in sick, too. But her days off are Wednesday and Thursday. I can't imagine anyone'll get suspicious when she's gone those days."

We should have Osprey by Thursday night and she'll be back to work like regular on Friday morning. So this won't be jeopardizing her job, most likely. I don't know what the hell I'd do if this business with Osprey took that from her, too.

"Have her use a burner when she calls in," the prez says.

Something that can't be traced back to me. I'm still not worried about her filing any kidnapping charges, but it's the prez's job to worry about the brothers. To protect the club.

It's my job, too. And any charge against me might implicate them in this shit. So we'll use a burner.

I nod again and they leave me to my bandaging and my shame. After this, I've got to head back inside, clean up the mess I made.

But I don't know how I'll clean up the mess with Sara.

Or how I'll look her in the eyes again.

She didn't want me to hunt down her old boyfriend, even though he murdered her family. So I don't figure she'll be real receptive to the reasons the Hellfire Riders are hunting down Osprey.

I'm not the kind of man who'll hide away from responsibility, though — or the kind who'll shy away from accepting the consequences of my actions. And the simple truth is that the choices I've made fucked up any chance I had with Sara.

I can't even say I'd make different choices. I'd do anything to hold her in my arms, to kiss her again. But there's a little boy dead. I've got a brother who might never wake up. And I've got a responsibility as a Rider and as a friend to make sure the shitstain who fired those bullets gets what's coming to him.

But I can't blame Osprey for making Sara so afraid of me. I can't blame bad timing or even Woodridge's stupid ass. They weren't the ones who slammed a blade through a trunk lid or got up behind the prez to intimidate her into silence.

This shit's on me. There's nothing to do but man up and accept the consequences. Doesn't mean those consequences don't hurt, though. Like a knife through my ribs. Like a razor in my throat.

I just can't believe that on the same fucking day I got her, I lost her.

With my heart feeling like a hot, heavy ball of lead

in my chest, I finish taping my hands and return to the kitchen.

Sara's not there. Just my pop, sitting at the table, working on his second beer, and wearing an expression that tells me he's good and pissed.

"You better grab that broom, boy," he says.

I was already heading for it. "Where's Sara?"

"You telling me you give a shit?"

I turn my burning eyes his way and let him see how much of a shit I give.

He softens a bit. "She looked beat. And that ride in a trunk, sweating up a storm sure as hell didn't do her any good. So I took her up to the third bedroom, dug up some clothes for her to change into. The shower was running a bit ago but I figure she's napping now. You better grab that little hand broom and get those counters first."

Stopping in the middle of the kitchen with the push broom, I survey the damage. And yeah—I better get the hand broom first or I'll just have to sweep the floor again. Most of the glass ended up on the floor but there's shards all over the granite countertops.

"How's your knuckles?" he asks.

"About as bad as I deserve."

"Probably not that bad."

"Not even near as bad," I agree and start in on the counters.

The clinking is so loud as I sweep the shattered glass into the dustpan that I don't hear Sara's light tread. Don't realize she's there until my dad says, "I figured you'd take a nap."

Jerking my head around, I see her standing in the doorway to the kitchen. And, Christ. Jesus Christ. This is what I lost.

I'd be bawling if I wasn't staring.

I've only seen her dark hair in a braid and for months now, I've been dreaming of how those thick curls might look down. But I should have been dreaming of how it'd look up in a messy roll on the top of her head, imagining the way all that poofy weight frames her beautiful face and makes her neck seem so elegant and the line of her shoulders so pretty.

And she looks so damn fragile. Maybe because my pop gave her one of my button-up shirts to wear. Although the edge of an undershirt peeks beneath the collar and she'd have been well covered if she'd left the shirt open, all the buttons but one are fastened and her generous curves are swallowed up by the thin cotton. The tails hang to mid-thigh—and God help me, her smooth brown thighs are sweetly muscled and look as if they could wrap me up so tight.

I've never seen so much of her skin. She wears short sleeves often enough, maybe it just never occurred to me that I've never seen her legs. I've only seen her in jeans and leggings.

Just like I never thought much about her feet. She usually wears full-cover shoes because she works in food service. She's not wandering around the café in sandals any more than I'd wander around the construction site in bare feet.

But hers are bare now. Her toenails are painted bright red and it's the sexiest damn thing I've ever seen.

As if she's nervous, she's got one foot rubbing over the top of the other. The toes of her bottom foot are curling against the smooth wood floor as she stands there, biting her lush bottom lip. In her hands she holds a wad of clothes—her sweat-soaked clothes, I realize.

She darts a gaze at me and looks away before I can read anything in her eyes. "I tried to sleep. But my head won't settle."

Keyed up because she's been kidnapped by someone stupid and threatened by someone she trusted. Shame tightens my throat again but it doesn't matter. I've got nothing to say that Sara wants to hear. Her dark gaze studiously avoids me.

My dad asks, "You want a whiskey to help smooth the edges?"

"No. Thank you, though," she says.

"I don't think she drinks alcohol, Pop," I tell him quietly.

"I don't," she confirms but doesn't look my way when she does. "Is it all right if I make dinner?"

Make dinner. Even though she's basically a prisoner here and all of us know it.

We both just look at her.

She shifts her weight and begins rubbing the top of her left foot with the bottom of her right. "Cooking helps me settle," she explains.

Pop purses his lips. "Well, I'm not about to refuse. You going to, David?"

"No." I'd eat poison if she fed it to me.

"You got anything specific in mind to cook?" Pop asks. "You need any certain ingredients?"

She shakes her head. "I'll make something out of whatever you have."

Beer in hand, he gets up from the table. "All right. Run up and put your shoes on and I'll show you what we've got. That your laundry there?"

"Yes."

"Leave it for David, then. He'll put it in the wash."

She hesitates for just a moment before nodding and dropping the pile onto the kitchen table. Then she's gone.

After giving me a long look, Pop heads out, too.

My heart thundering, I set the broom aside and head for the table. There's a bit of white lace in that wadded bundle. Her bra with its generous cups and a matching pair of panties.

And here's one more thing I ought to be ashamed of—because I pick up those panties and breathe deep, getting the sweet musky smell of her pussy as far into me as I can. I'd steal them if she had any others to wear over the next few days. Instead I stop by the bathroom and wrap my hand around my aching cock, picturing the hair on top of her head, her elegant neck, the damp curls at her nape that got wet during her shower. I picture matching curls between her thighs, curls that are even wetter and smelling of the lace I'm practically inhaling.

I should be ashamed. I should be just fucking rolling in shame like a pig rolling in mud as I come, spurting into my hand and biting her lacy panties to stop the roar that's built up in my chest.

But I'm not. Instead I'm haunted. By her smell. By her pretty painted toes and her smooth brown skin. By that kiss this morning and what could have been.

And haunted by the knowledge that she'll be walking around my house without a stitch of underwear on.

If a man was ever tortured for the choices he's made…I'm sure as hell going to pay for mine.

EIGHT

SARA

They've got a garden *and* a greenhouse.

When Pop said he'd show me what they have, I expected him to lead me to a pantry. And there *is* a pantry, somewhere. Apparently a big pantry, judging by what Pop's saying about the vegetables and fruits he's canned and put away. But I barely hear him, because I've got a basket under my arm and I'm walking along the side of the garden and taking in the incredible green glory of it all.

They've got a chicken coop, too. Oh those fresh, fresh

eggs. And Pop's grumbling that the hens lay well but Bull's always skipping out to have breakfast in town, so instead of eating his share, he ends up giving away a couple of dozen to the biker widows every week.

"Just like he gave away most of Porky and Petunia a few weeks ago," the old man says.

Crouching beside a row of parsnips, I glance up. "He gave away what?"

"The two hogs we raised and slaughtered last fall. Said we need to start eating healthier, replaced it all with chicken sausage and turkey bacon. Then said if the girl at Reggie's can make that shit taste good, we can, too." Scratching his bristled jaw, he eyes me accusingly then turns a baleful gaze on the parsnips I've pulled up. "You don't want those. The woman at the seed store said they was tasty but I figure a potato got drunk and screwed a carrot to create that abomination. This was my first year planting them and will be my last, that's for damn sure."

Grinning, I shake off the dirt and lay them in the basket. "Do you have herbs?"

"Sure we do. Dried or fresh?"

I think I love this man.

I DON'T KNOW HOW TO feel about his son.

By the time I return to the kitchen with a loaded basket under my arm, the glass has been cleared from the floor and Bull's nowhere in sight. Pop heads out, telling me he's got wood to stack, and when I hear the rumble of a motorcycle engine a little later, I assume it's Bull leaving.

But it's not. That motorcycle must have belonged to another Hellfire Rider, because about a minute later Bull comes into the kitchen with an electric screwdriver.

I almost joke that he doesn't need to use that on me—I've already agreed to what they want. But every word sticks in my aching throat and I blindly focus on the cutting board in front of me.

The silence between us is thick and painful as he gets to work removing the cabinet doors.

He's sorry for what happened to me. I know he is. And I don't blame him for what the junkie did. Bull obviously had no idea I'd be a target. He didn't know I was in that trunk when he swung a blade through the lid.

I also knew that he had a dangerous side. And part of what's so confusing and difficult is trying to reconcile this piece of myself—because I didn't even blink when he offered to kill Raphael. Instead I was *glad* he offered, because it confirmed what I already believed about him. I thought I could trust my instincts again.

But I can't. Because I knew Bull had a bad side, but I also believed the core of him was decent. I thought his offer came from a place in him that needed to protect someone he cared about. From a place in him that would see justice done when someone had been hurt.

I thought he was offering to do something terrible for the right reasons. And I've been there myself. Not thinking about killing someone but contemplating something illegal to protect myself, because it didn't seem like anyone else could do it.

The wrong thing, the right reasons.

There's no right reasons for buying twenty thousand dollars worth of meth, though. Because what else are they going to do with that amount of drugs but sell them? There's no right reasons there. It's not about protecting anyone or making them pay for a wrong. It's just dealing death and addiction and preying on people's weaknesses for money.

What I thought was a bad side is just rotten all the way through.

Like Raphael was.

Except what I feel now isn't anything like what I felt then. Not even at the beginning, before all I felt was terror and grief. Raphael started pursuing me as soon as he met me, claiming that I was an exotic and fresh treat for his senses—and I was flattered by his attention. He was rich and handsome and I thought the mild attraction I felt would transform into the wild need he spoke of as soon as I had more familiarity and experience with sex.

I don't think he ever realized that I wasn't as overwhelmed by him as he apparently was by me—especially after he found out I was a virgin, and what had been pursuit turned into obsession. He thought I needed to have some great awakening and he was the man to do it.

And me, I thought it wouldn't hurt to find out. The first time was okay but I never felt what he did. I never looked at Raphael like he looked at me, as if I was some incredible creature. As if he saw something magically sensual within me that I couldn't see, even though I was always looking for that magic in me, too, and was disappointed that I couldn't find it. It took me a while to realize that I wasn't missing anything, and that Raphael was only seeing what he wanted to see—a sexual fantasy he could mold and shape. He imagined this great love, this sublime ecstasy.

I was just happy to get off now and then.

I didn't always, even though I couldn't fault his attentions. But I was too self-conscious, too aware of myself when I was with him. Too aware of how I looked and my body's responses, because he was always telling me how my appearance and responses made him feel. I was *always* too aware of how I was making him feel—and nothing I felt in return ever measured up. He could work me up physically but I never looked at him and felt everything inside me tense up and melt at the same time. I could become aroused but I never yearned for him.

I don't even have to look at Bull and I am. Yearning. Melting. Burning.

And thinking that maybe he'll come up behind me and kiss my neck. That maybe his big hands will unbutton my shirt and he'll growl against my ear when he finds my nipples already stiff and aching for his rough fingers. That maybe he'll discover the wetness between my thighs, and in a rush of need he'll bury his thick cock deep inside the slick, eager pussy that doesn't care what he's done, that just wants to be filled with him, and he'll fuck me hard with my hands braced against the counter and his fingers digging into my hips.

I think maybe Bull's feeling the same, because when I do happen to glance that way, there's no mistaking the heavy bulge behind his zipper. And he looks pained. Not just sorry, but in physical pain.

So he's aching, too.

But I don't know what there is to do except try to ignore the arousal and the hurt and get through the next few days.

At least with two men to feed, there'll be a lot of cooking to do.

The electric whine of the screwdriver falls silent—but it doesn't start up again. He'd kept a steady rhythm, unfastening the hinges and stacking the cabinet doors neatly on the counter before starting on the next. But now he's finished, I realize.

And although he's quiet, he's not looking at me. Instead he's gazing at the shelves—then abruptly he glances my way, meeting my eyes.

His voice is a deep rumble when he asks, "Am I just lazy and hoping to get out of more work, or do those cabinets really look better without the glass doors on them?"

Heart thundering, I shake my head—not a yes or a no but trying to pull my brain into a space where I can even begin to think about kitchen aesthetics.

Frowning, he turns to regard the cabinets again. "Sure, I'd have to clean it up some." He steps forward, rubbing his thumb over one of the holes left by the screws. "Fill these in with putty, sand it smooth, paint it white to match. But what do you think—doors or no doors?"

Finally I find my voice. "I don't really remember what they looked like before you broke them."

"Well, what do you think now?"

I study the cabinets. They contain the stoneware, glasses, and mugs—all mismatched but neatly arranged. As I'm looking, Bull grabs one of the doors and holds it up against the cabinet face to demonstrate the difference, then pulls it away.

"It looks better without the door," I decide.

"And what about the color?" His gaze scans the kitchen. "Because if I've got to paint some, might as well consider painting them all. The white good? Or do you think another color would do better in here?"

"It's not really white," I say and he looks at me like I've gone crazy. "It's eggshell."

His eyes narrow. "You're one of them, huh?"

"Someone who prefers to describe things accurately? I guess so."

He huffs out a short laugh. "Fair enough. So what about eggshell? Do you like it or does it need to go?"

"It's nice. It brightens everything." In a log house like this, the darkness could easily become overwhelming. But the French doors, big windows, and light cabinets provide a lovely counterbalance to the heavy wood.

Bull gives a distracted nod, as if in agreement, but the way his troubled gaze searches my face says he's not thinking about kitchen décor anymore.

But he doesn't say what he *is* thinking. Just rakes his bandaged fingers through his hair and heaves a sigh before reaching for the cabinet doors.

With the broken frames in his grip, he pauses on his way out of the kitchen. "Those parsnips?"

"They are."

"Pop hates those." He sounds sorry to tell me.

"I know."

Bull's quiet for a long second, and his voice has a harsh edge when he says, "You know he didn't have a thing to do with any of this."

Mildly I look up from the cutting board. "Do you truly think I'd cook something that tastes bad as revenge?"

Something dark passes over his face. Shame, maybe. There's gravel in his answer. "No."

"Good." I hold his gaze. "And I think you'll really enjoy the peach custard tart I have planned for after dinner. It's creamy and sweet and juicy. The perfect dessert…since you aren't getting the one you wanted to."

The way his eyes blaze. The way his fingers tighten so hard on the frames that I can hear the wood creak in protest. The stiff walk that tells me his cock's about to burst through his jeans. *That's* revenge.

But I think it's playing with fire, too. And I don't

know how we're going to get through three days without both of us getting burned.

85

NINE

BULL

I don't look away from Sara even once as I devour a big slice of her peach tart—then slowly suck the tines of my fork clean when I'm done.

Across the table, she sits watching me eat every delicious bite, her cheeks flushed, her eyes feverishly bright, and her plush bottom lip caught between her teeth. Sitting over there with her pussy as wet as my cock is hard, I just know it—and knowing it makes my cock even harder.

Sitting over there, pussy swimming in her sweet juices

and not wearing any panties.

This is the best fucking meal I've ever had.

And there's my pop, oblivious to the tension between us. He's been uncharacteristically quiet the entire meal, sliding into reverent silence after his first bite of beef that was so tender it slid right off the bone. At one point, I'm pretty sure there were tears of joy in his eyes. He even went back for a second helping of parsnips. I'm not sure what the hell she did to them, except throw in some herbs and mash 'em. But they didn't taste anything like what Pop had been cooking up.

I reach for another slice of tart—because fuck yeah, something so sweet and juicy, I'll go back for seconds and thirds and fourths—and Pop's arm shoots out.

He jabs my hand with his fork before I can scoop out another piece. "Don't be greedy, boy. You save some of that for tomorrow."

Her gaze holding mine, Sara says with a wicked little grin, "Let him eat it all up. I can just make another one."

Pop shakes his head. "That much sugar ain't good for him. Now, me—I'm an old man. Going to die sooner than later anyway. So I'll take another slice before bed, I reckon."

"You do that, Pop." I lean back, and my dick never ached so bad but felt so good all at once. "I'd rather have my slice *in* bed. Maybe first thing when I wake up."

As if picturing my mouth on her in the morning, she squirms in her damn chair.

Hell. She wants to wiggle like that, she can do it on my face.

"Who's going to serve you breakfast in bed? You can haul your lazy ass downstairs." Pop snorts, then looks to Sara. "Don't you go soft on him. If he had a choice, he probably wouldn't get up before noon."

I *do* have a choice. One I make every morning. "Some things are worth getting up early for."

Her smile fades and her thick lashes fall, hiding her gaze from mine. Hurt again. I didn't mean to with those words, but I did.

Maybe she's also hurting over what we lost. Maybe thinking I'm full of shit when I say she was worth getting up for. Because after months of getting up early and sitting at her counter, I was supposed to be taking her out tonight. Was supposed to be licking her pussy. Instead she got a terrifying ride in a trunk and me holding her prisoner.

Though maybe if losing the sweet connection we had hurts her, she'd be willing to find it with me again.

Hope is a ragged pain in my chest. She's still comfortable enough to tease me with this tart. She's still aroused by the thought of me licking her. Maybe I can still win her back. But I'm not going to push now. Earlier I went fast and she was all right with it. That was before all this went down, though.

So this time, I'll go slow.

With a contented groan, Pop leans back and rubs his belly like he's coaxing it not to explode. "That was some damn fine eating, girl. Where'd you learn to cook like that?"

"This, specifically? It's based on a braised beef dish I used to make at Sòlê—a restaurant in Manhattan. More generally, I learned from my…from my mama and grandmama." Her full lips press together and the downward sweep of her lashes conceal her eyes again. "And culinary school."

"New York? Is that where your family's from?" Bushy eyebrows raised high, Pop regards her with disbelief when she nods. "What the hell possessed you to come to a nowhere little town in Oregon? How'd you even *hear* about Pine Valley?"

Shit. I'd like to know more, too—but I don't want to hurt her by bringing up the topic of her dead family.

"Pop," I say quietly but Sara shakes her head before I can warn him off.

"It's okay. I never talk about what happened to them. Maybe I should." She pokes at her half-eaten tart before laying down her fork and folding her hands together. "I dated this guy for a while—and when I tried to break it off, he, uh…" As if she's seeing a lot more than she's able to say, her eyes go glassy. Unfocused. "He stalked me, basically. My family tried to help me. Screening my calls, riding on the subway with me to work so he couldn't just show up and hassle me. Even though it wasn't easy for them, because my dad had an app development company that took up so much time and my mama had a dental practice. But Raphael, he said"—her breath shudders—"he said *he* was the only family I needed. So one night when I was working late, he barred the doors of our house and set it on fire."

Raphael. I'm going to find him. Find him, douse him with gasoline, and light the match.

Pop whistles between his teeth. "Christ, girl."

She nods, tears standing in her eyes.

"They get him?"

"No," she says, her voice thick. "The police tried. The detectives believed me and I'd already tried filing a restraining order against him. But there wasn't any evidence. He had an army of lawyers between him and the investigators so they were never able to touch him. And he was still *always* there. Watching me. Saying he wanted to *comfort* me. How sick is that?"

"Real fucking sick," I softly growl. And he had an army of lawyers. Raphael was a rich fucker, then.

When Blowback gets me the rest of his name, no lawyers will be able to protect him.

My pop reaches out, folds his hand over her clenched fingers. Just like she did to me this morning, trying to comfort me when I was talking about Maurice and his boy. "So you ran?"

"I did. I have a little family still, aunts and cousins and—" Stopping, she shakes her head. "He'd have found me. Maybe hurt them. But I knew Minerva from culinary school and we'd kept in touch on Facebook, exchanging recipes here and there. And last year, right after my family died, her husband Reggie was killed in a fire, too. Though it was a forest fire."

I remember. One of the Hellfire Riders is a helicopter pilot who flies teams of firefighters in. Zoomie flew Reggie's team in, and later had to fly his body out.

With a soft sigh and a shrug, Sara finishes up, "So I'm helping her out at Reggie's and she's helping me out."

Pop pats her hand. "Well, if you need anything at all, we'll help you out, too."

"Anything," I confirm and the tears that were welling in her eyes abruptly spill over.

"Don't cry though," my pop immediately says. "You'll start me blubbering."

"Okay." Laughing, she nods and wipes her cheeks. "And I'm tired finally. So I think I'll clean up here and head to bed."

"I'll take cleanup tonight," Pop says. "David'll get it tomorrow."

Another watery laugh escapes her and she gives me another of those wicked looks. "Then I'll make even more of a mess tomorrow."

"Can't be worse than what I made today," I tell her.

"No." Her voice softens and her dark gaze searches my face. "I'm due at work in the morning."

"I know," I say gruffly. Her schedule's as familiar to me as my own. "You'll need to call in sick. The next two days you already have off, yeah?"

Lips suddenly tight, she nods.

"Then that ought to cover the time you're here." Three days. Maybe the last I have with her. Or maybe time to fix some of this. "I'll bring you an unregistered phone in a minute."

Her jaw clenches and she swallows hard, as if biting back a response. With another stiff nod, she stands and stalks out of the kitchen, heading for the stairs.

Maybe because in all this time, Sara's never once called in sick. Never let down the friend who helped her. Maybe never lied to her friend, either.

Now I'm making her do all of the above.

Shit. On a heavy sigh, I scrub my hand over my face, then push my own chair back.

Gathering the plates, Pop says mildly, "What you gonna do about that Raphael fellow?"

"Get the rest of his name. Probably take a trip to New York."

Nodding he says, "I haven't been to the big city in a while. You need company, you let me know."

That's my pop. Not that I'd ever risk him. But still.

I clap him on the shoulder, scoop up the half-eaten tart Sara left on her plate, then head out to get that phone.

TEN

SARA

When I enter the guest room the first thing I see are my laundered clothes neatly folded at the end of the bed, topped by a boxed toothbrush and sample-sized toiletries—the kind you swipe from hotel rooms. No doubt Pop swiped and squirreled away a salon's worth somewhere around here.

It's such a sweet gesture, but seeing my clothes and the little soaps only sharpens the ache in my chest. Because Pop and Bull are treating me like a guest, but I'm not one.

And stupid me. Until Bull told me that I had to call in sick, I almost forgot why I was here.

I'm here so the Hellfire Riders can buy twenty thousand dollars worth of crystal meth.

I'm here because it's either this or they'll hurt me.

Except I'm already hurting. And I'm angry, the rage and pain swelling hot and hard in my throat and chest.

Because sitting at that table through dinner? It was everything I wanted to have with Bull. It was everything I hoped for when I asked him to kiss me this morning and when I agreed to go out with him.

It was even *better* than I hoped for. The way Bull teased me into a squirming, needy mess with nothing more than his eyes. The way he and Pop have such a deep and easy relationship. Even the way I could talk to them about my family and, despite the pain and grief, feel safe and cared for. The way they both promised to give me anything I needed — and how I believed them.

I sat at that table and saw a future — a family — that I would love to be a part of.

But I can't be. And although I want to scream and cry and rage, I just stand silently, looking at the toiletries that say I'm a guest in this house. But really, I'm just a girl who was in the wrong place at the wrong time.

There's a fist-sized lump in my throat when Bull arrives with the unregistered cell. He's a giant presence in the room but I can't even look at him as I take the flip phone with nerveless fingers, and I don't have to pretend to *sound* sick when Minerva answers. My voice is hoarse and my chest tight.

Her immediate concern constricts everything even tighter. "Don't worry about it at all, honey. I'll cover you. Just get some rest and I'll see you on Friday, okay?"

I nod and rasp out an "Okay," in return, my shoulders hunched and my back to Bull. But I can still feel him there, standing at the entrance to the hallway, his big body as solid as any cage door.

"All right," Minerva says as if she's about to hang up, but after a slight hesitation adds, "Are you sure you're okay? You're at home, right? Because I didn't recognize the number you're calling from."

"I'm home." I press my fingers to my burning eyes. "I got one of those pay-as-you-go phones. For emergencies. This emergency was not wanting to get out of bed."

Her laugh seems a little forced. "Good. But if you're in trouble just say 'Okay' again, all right?"

My throat almost closes. We've talked about this before—about Raphael coming for me and how to signal that I need help. The weirdness of this call must have sent her alarm bells ringing. "I'm not in trouble."

"Phew." Her laugh sounds more genuine now. "Okay. Get better and I'll talk to you soon."

"Talk to you soon," I say and flip the phone closed.

Unregistered. With no GPS. No SIM card. No way to trace it back to Bull—especially after he takes the device from me, removes the battery, and snaps the phone in half.

I flinch as the case cracks in his big hands, then wait for him to go.

He doesn't. Instead he says gruffly, "You'll sleep in my room."

My heart thumps against my ribs. My gaze flies to his.

He's watching me from beneath lowered brows, his eyes shadowed, his body tense. And he's just so huge, packed with solid muscle and built like a tree. Wearing a T-shirt that stretches across his broad chest and jeans that emphasize the thick strength of his thighs, he's a bearded and inked sexual fantasy come to life.

But he's not a fantasy. He's another nightmare.

And I've had enough sleepless nights.

"No," I tell him. "I did what you wanted. I agreed to keep my mouth closed, not to spread my legs. Me screwing you wasn't part of the deal."

His jaw clenches. "I won't touch you."

"Then you can not touch me from another room."

He shakes his head, blue eyes holding mine. "It's my responsibility to make sure you stay quiet. I don't think you'll run while I'm sleeping but there's only one way to be sure, and that's if you're in the same bed with me—and my bed's bigger than that one." He nods toward the queen bed behind me. "If you're in a different room, you can take off without me knowing and be in town before dawn."

The rage and hurt are like razors in my throat. "I'm not going to run."

Bull just spreads his big hands, like he's got no other

options. Like he doesn't have a choice.

But he does.

I'm the one who doesn't have a choice. Rage clouds my vision as I turn and scoop up my clothes from the bed, then head down the hall to the next door.

His room is big and uncluttered, with thick rugs scattered over the wood floors and a window overlooking the creek, but I barely see anything ahead of me. I toss my clothes onto a bench at the end of the bed—which *is* bigger, maybe big enough for both of us to fit without touching him, despite his size—and I'm aware of him following me in, aware of the bed and how I'm so bare beneath this big shirt, aware of the slick heat building between my legs and the boiling in my blood, aware of the anger and need and pain swelling and swelling and filling my heart to bursting.

Seeing the telephone on his nightstand is like the pinprick that starts letting all of that swelling emotion out. Because it strikes me all at once—that there are landlines throughout the house, even in the kitchen, and Bull didn't watch to make sure I didn't call anyone.

And this is all such *bullshit*.

The Riders' president said that Bull vouched for me. That Bull claimed I could be trusted, that I would be silent.

He was right, wasn't he? I've been a good girl. I meekly agreed to everything they wanted.

I don't feel so fucking meek now.

"You know what?" I tell him. "I'm not sleeping here.

You're going to take me home. I'll go to work tomorrow and keep my mouth shut. You know I will."

"I know you will," Bull says but it's not agreement. He doesn't even add that he's not taking me anywhere. As if the rest was just me screaming into the wind.

Well, I can scream into something else.

Stalking around the bed, I pick the phone's receiver up out of the cradle. And yep, there's a dial tone.

"Sara?" It's a question and a warning, all at once.

A warning for what? What's he going to do?

Hurt me?

I don't think so. Despite everything, I really don't think so.

But I wonder what he *will* do.

Beige and clunky, the phone is one of those ancient, heavy ones with a rotary face. Something this old, I doubt he ever even uses it. Trembling from all the stress and emotions ripping through me, I stick my finger into the '9' and dial the number.

His quick, heavy tread crosses the room, softened by the rug beside the bed.

He's right behind me as I dial a '1'.

"The fuck?" Hard fingers stab the pegs in the receiver cradle, disconnecting the line. "What the hell are you doing?"

"I agreed not to say a word about you and your precious drug deal," I spit out. "You know I won't. There's no reason for me to be here. So take me home or I'll call 9-1-1 and get a ride back home with whoever comes. But don't worry—I'll tell them there's no real emergency, that this was a mistake."

Gently, he tries to pry the receiver from my left hand. When my grip only tightens, his heavy sigh stirs the back of my hair. "Dammit, Sara. Why are you making this harder than it already is?"

"Why shouldn't I?" A bitter laugh rips through me. "Why should I make it easy for you?"

His voice suddenly hardens, roughened with frustration. "You think this is *easy*?" Abruptly his hand wraps around the back of the phone base and he jerks it away from the wall, ripping out the line. A dull clang echoes around the room as he grits out, "I didn't fucking want *any* of this."

And he's angry now, too? Good. I toss the useless receiver and spin around to shove at his chest, which is a stupid joke. My head doesn't even reach his shoulders and his pectorals are like slabs of stone. I might as well be a mouse pushing at him.

I might as well be nothing at all to him.

"Well, what the hell do you want?" My voice rises with each word, anger and pain leaking out fast, but I'm not deflating. Instead the hurt and the rage and the need just keep growing. "I agreed to keep my mouth shut! And you *know* I won't risk putting my name out there and that your fucking meth is safe! Me sleeping in here is completely unnecessary—so what the hell more do you want from me?"

"Just you, Sara," he says hoarsely. "I just want you."

The tortured response scrapes across my heart. My gaze shoots up to meet his.

The bleak torment I see in the dark blue of his eyes steals my breath and my reply.

"Just you," he says again and palms the back of my neck, his callused thumb stroking the corner of my jaw. "I figure I've got three days before you take off running again—scared of me, scared of the Riders. I've got three days to pretend everything between us didn't get so fucked up. Three days to pretend you're in my bed because you want to be."

Pretending there's a future for us. The ache in my chest is suddenly vast. So vast, swallowing up everything else.

"Bull," I whisper on a ragged breath.

"And I'm sorry," he continues gruffly, his strong fingers pushing into my hair, tipping my head back. "I said I wouldn't touch you. But I'm a fucking liar."

The last word is growled against my skin just before his hard mouth captures mine—taking my lips as if he owns them, not slow like this morning, no testing or waiting to see if I'll push him away.

If I had any doubts about whether he'd back off, I *would* push him away. But despite everything, I don't have a single doubt about that.

Bull won't hurt me. He won't force me.

So maybe I can pretend, too. For a little while, I can pretend this will last. I can pretend there's a future for us.

But the way Bull's kiss makes me feel? There's no need to pretend. I want him so much. I want this impossible combination of security and wild, out-of-control need when I'm in his arms. I want it more than anything.

And I'm terrified that he's the only man I'll ever find it with.

Because it's never been like this. He kisses me and it's as if my next breath and the next beat of my heart depend upon the stroke of his tongue across mine. I cling to him, my arms wreathing his neck as I rise onto my tiptoes and press closer, opening my lips for a deeper taste, chasing down that incredible pulse-pounding sensation as if I'm chasing down life itself. As if I'll die without it.

My eager response is answered by a deep groan that rumbles through his chest, teasing my hardened nipples. A shiver of pleasure races over my skin.

Fingers tightening in my hair, he angles his head, deepening the kiss. Luscious peach still lingers on his lips, his tongue, but with every lick into my mouth I only taste his increasing hunger. Ravenously he feasts from my lips, as if he's starving for my touch and instead of sating his arousal, the kiss sharpens the craving.

Sharpens it like a knife's edge, a blade that's flaying me open until there's nothing left but bone-deep need, nothing left but his mouth fused to mine and the desire slicing through me.

I can't stop my soft whimper of distress when his mouth leaves mine, or my reaction when his teeth pinch my sensitive earlobe. An exquisite shudder wracks my body when he raggedly breathes my name against my ear. My blood seems molten, my nerves like fire.

Muscles suddenly liquid, my head falls back. His mouth lowers and his heated tongue slicks up the column of my neck.

I feel that lick *everywhere*. My inner muscles clench as if his tongue slicked through my pussy lips. I press harder against him, trying to ease the empty ache inside me but the need only builds the closer I am. Constrained by his jeans, his cock is a thick pressure against my stomach. Desperately climbing his big frame, I wrap my legs around his waist and writhe against that steely shaft, seeking relief—and the need simply worsens.

"Ah, fuck." As if I'm torturing him, Bull groans against my throat. "You feel so damn good, Sara."

So good. But it's not enough. Rocking against him, I plead, "Don't stop."

His entire body goes utterly still, his fingers fisted in my hair, his face buried against my neck.

That's…the opposite of what I asked for. And he's tense. So tense, his muscles locked so tight that I can feel the taut strain quivering through him.

Suddenly uncertain, I whisper, "Bull?"

A violent quake rocks through his big body and all at once he's in motion again, his left hand gripping my ass and grinding my bare pussy against his solid, denim-covered length.

"I won't stop, baby," he growls against my mouth. "Gonna give you everything you need."

He delivers the rough promise before catching my lips in another deep kiss. And I was wrong. I thought he'd been hungry. I thought he'd been starving for me.

But he'd been holding back.

Now he consumes me with this kiss, until there's nothing but his tongue, his lips, and his big body bearing me down to his bed. Moaning into his mouth, I tighten my arms around his neck, clinging as my back hits the mattress and the weight and pressure between my thighs rub against my clitoris just right, my spine arching as each rock of his hips takes me higher and higher.

Then I plummet when he breaks the kiss and lifts away. Dark hair wild, eyes savage, he looks down at me lying across his bed, my ass almost hanging off the edge and my legs trapping his waist.

My chest heaves with ragged breaths. "Bull?"

"I'm not stopping." His big hands grip my thighs just above my knees, his thumbs sweeping across the sensitive inner skin. "But I don't have any condoms. So I'm just deciding whether to get you pregnant with a big hairy baby."

My eyes fly wide. *"What?"*

His grin is quick and feral. "Just fucking with you. Mostly."

"It's not funny," I say despite the laugh that's shaking through me. Because it's really not funny, except that it's exactly the kind of crazy thing he'd say. It's exactly the kind of thing that made *me* so crazy about him in the first place.

Why I'm *still* crazy about him. Even if I have to pretend it will last.

Huskily I ask, "Why 'mostly'?"

His hands slide higher, pushing the long hem of my borrowed shirt upward. "I really don't have condoms. You on birth control?"

I shake my head.

He groans like my answer just killed him and his fingers slip higher. "It's all right, baby. I'll just— I'll... just..." His big body goes utterly still. *"Oh fuck*, you're already wet."

Wet and trembling. He hasn't done anything except run his broad palms up the length of my legs, still locked around his hips. But his thumbs are sliding along the tendons of my inner thighs and the fragile skin is slick with my arousal.

Biting my lower lip, I tilt my hips upward. Inviting a deeper touch.

But touching apparently isn't enough. He wants to see, too.

Eyes feral again, Bull grips the tails of the oversized shirt. Effortlessly he tears it apart, popping the buttons from bottom to top like ripping open a zipper. Gasping,

I curl my fingers against the quilt, watching his hungry gaze take in the skin he's exposed. I'm still wearing a thin cotton undershirt but I'm naked below my waist.

His possessive gaze lingers on my bare pussy. Except it's *not* bare. I don't have the Amazon rainforest growing down there but it's not as tidy as it would have been if I'd had time to prepare for our date.

And…I don't care. Because the way Bull's looking at me, he obviously doesn't care, either. Arousal flushes his skin and his throat works as he wets his bottom lip, like he's already preparing to taste me.

His hot gaze lifts to mine. "You got any objection to me eating your pussy?"

Breathlessly I shake my head.

"Good thing. But I'm saving dessert for last. This my pop's undershirt?"

Bull doesn't wait for my answer, just rips the cotton down the center like tissue. The shredded pieces fall to my sides and for an endless time he just stands there looking at me, and aside from a thick, low sound that he makes, doesn't seem to have any intention of touching.

No problem. I've got hands.

Feeling sexier than I ever have, I cup my full breasts in my palms. "They're all right?"

"Unnnh…" he says. Then swipes the back of his hand over his mouth as if he isn't certain whether he's drooling.

Back arching, I pinch my taut nipples. "Let me see you, too. Shirt off."

Immediately he reaches back, gripping the neck of his T-shirt and dragging it off. This time I'm the one saying *Unnnh* and maybe drooling.

But he's worth drooling over. Ink covers thick, mouth-watering muscle—but he's not lean. Just so big and solid. He obviously works hard, laboring in the gym and on the job and here at the house, but his body says he plays hard, too. His body says he doesn't follow up that labor with naked chicken and steamed broccoli but enjoys his beer and his food—especially the meals I've made for him. I've seen the pleasure he takes in my cooking. My touch was all over his incredible body long before my fingers ever got there.

"Now the jeans," I tell him. Beg him.

I catch my breath when he lets me go to squeeze the bulge of his erection through denim. His hands are huge but thick ridge he's palming overflows his grip. And Bull touching himself, even through his clothes?

Hottest thing I've ever seen. But he doesn't show me what's beneath and what I suspect is much hotter. Instead he shakes his head and strokes himself through his jeans. "My dick gets out, it'll just end up filling your pussy."

I'm trying to remember why that would be a bad thing. "It'll just fall right in?"

"My dick's a stupid, clumsy fucker." With a rough groan, he stops stroking his big cock and grips my thighs again. "The truth is, I'd probably come the second you look at me. Or touch me. And I'd rather hold off on that because I'm not even close to done with you."

I draw in a shaky breath as an unexpected pang strikes my heart, piercing the veil of pretend.

I don't ever want him done with me. But after what happened today, I'd be foolish not to be done with *him*.

I should push him away right now. I should stay away from him until the Riders' drug deal is complete and I can go home. I should tell him never to come into Reggie's again.

But the thought of doing just one of those things hurts too much. And the thought of doing all three... which I *know* I should do?

I just want to keep pretending, instead.

Maybe he sees the shadows in my eyes. Suddenly his own darken and every trace of humor vanishes from his face. His fingers tighten on my thighs and all at once he's pushing me farther onto the bed and coming down over me. His mouth claims mine and there's a new urgent edge to his kiss, as if he means to chase away my doubt with overwhelming need, as if he doesn't intend to give me even a moment to think.

And I can't. I can't do anything but desperately kiss him back, my hands roaming all over his beautiful tattooed skin. He's hot against me, flesh to flesh, the rough hair on his chest an abrasive tease to my aching nipples.

Weight braced on his left elbow, his right hand slips higher between my thighs. We both groan when his broad fingers slide through my wetness.

His mouth tears from mine and he stares into my eyes as his fingers delve deeper, slicking through my folds before returning to circle my clit.

I'm panting, hips pinned by his weight. Waiting.

His name leaves my lips on a gasping sigh when his broad finger pushes inside the tight grip of my pussy. Immediately my inner muscles clench around him, welcoming the gentle intrusion.

Groaning, he lowers his head. Hot kisses press to my throat, lower, and I'm bombarded with sensation. His hot mouth moving over my breast. His finger stroking through my clinging inner walls. His thumb slipping over my clit. His tongue flicking the taut peak of my nipple. The rumble of his groan. His skin warm and sweaty against mine. His woodsy smell and the lingering flavor of peach and the soft texture of the quilt against my back.

Sucking my nipple to a throbbing point, his cheeks hollow. His eyes are on me, watching each response. I keep meeting his gaze and then losing focus as pleasure tears through me.

My fingers slide over his heavy shoulders. Through his hair. My feet frantically rub against the back of his thighs, up over his ass before linking around his waist again.

He pushes another finger inside me and I think I'm going to—

There's no thinking. I just do. The orgasm isn't there and then suddenly it is, blasting through me, tossing my body against him like I'm trying to buck him off but my hands are gripping him tighter, tighter. I cry out his name and he groans mine in return, grinding between my thighs as if watching me come is pushing him to the edge and he can't stop his own response.

He rises up to kiss me again as I float down from the high, but instead of sinking into the kiss he leaves me — sliding down my body, his destination unmistakable.

Hands trembling, I reach for his retreating shoulders. "But I already came."

"You think I didn't feel your pussy squeezing my fingers? How much wetter coming made you?" The look he gives me sears my skin with his hunger. "Now I get to taste all those sweet juices."

He kneels beside the bed and drags me to the edge. His blue eyes lock with mine as he pushes my legs apart. He holds my gaze as his lips press to the inside of my thigh.

My muscles tremble with the aftershocks of my orgasm and new anticipation.

"You smell so fucking good." His chest lifts on a deep breath. As if in sheer ecstasy, his eyelids fall to half mast. "I just want to rub my face all—"

All over me. Because he stops talking and simply does it, his beard sweeping my inner thighs. Burying his face against my pussy, he inhales again.

I cry out and squirm but not trying to get away. I'm panting his name and embarrassed and I love it, love how he's wallowing in my scent. The way I want to be covered in his.

"I'm just going to eat this creamy pussy right up." His voice deepens. "Tell me to finish my dessert, Sara."

Pulse racing, I whisper huskily, "Finish your dessert, Bull."

Oh, he does. But he isn't in a rush, dipping his head for a long, slow taste up the length of my slit. Moaning, I tip my hips forward, seeking the touch of his tongue over my clit.

A wicked glint in his blue eyes, he swirls lightly around the aching bud, a cruel tease before licking his way back down. It feels good, so good, but he's killing me and I'm dying. His strong fingers press into the soft flesh of my inner thighs, holding me open for another devastatingly cruel slide of his tongue that feels so incredibly good and not quite good *enough*.

And he doesn't stop.

Sobbing little breaths start building through my chest. Spine arched, I cover my face with my hands because I don't know what I'm doing, can't seem to control anything. My body's a live wire, electric and jittery and burning, with an ache that's growing and growing—centered right over the clitoris that he's barely touching, yet the ache is spreading outward, my pussy clenching and my thighs shaking and everything taut and waiting.

For another hot lick. For the thrust of his tongue inside me. My flesh is so sensitive that I can feel his every whisker, every whisper of his breath, every scrape of his teeth. All the sounds wind me tighter, the slick wetness of my arousal, his pleasured groans, the smack of his lips.

And the noises I'm making. My head whips from side to side, my teeth clenched on the heel of my hand trying to hold the sounds in. I don't know if they're whimpers or screams but he's dragging them out of me with each slow thrust and slide of his tongue.

Then suddenly he decides to stop torturing me, his lips closing over my clitoris and his tongue flicking and his mouth sucking, but it's not mercy. I'm wound so tight that the direct touch is erotic agony. My entire body goes rigid, caught between pain and ecstasy.

His groan and the rough slide of his tongue push me over, the ecstasy shattering through me. And it's a scream that's been building and building, it's his name that I cry out as my pussy clenches uncontrollably.

Still he doesn't finish but slowly licks me as clean as he did his fork after devouring my peach tart. Although I'm completely spent, my body shudders with every new pass of his tongue.

Finally he rises over me again. Reaching for him, I draw his lips to mine, taste the mingling of our flavors.

But I want to taste more. "My mouth," I tell him. "Let me make you come, too."

He groans but shakes his head, his hands working between us. Unzipping, freeing his cock, and I feel him hot and hard against the folds of my pussy.

"Like this," he grits out, his face tense. "While I'm still

tasting you."

Tasting my mouth. And he feels so good against me, his weight braced on his elbows, his hands buried in my hair. His hips rock between my thighs and I moan when his long shaft glides endlessly over my over-sensitized clit. He shudders when I suck on the tip of his tongue and when my teeth pinch his lower lip, then lick my way back into his mouth again.

Abruptly he rocks back too far and his shaft slips down the length of my slit. The broad head nudges at my entrance, and we both freeze, our mouths open together.

On a shaky breath, I whisper, "Your stupid, clumsy dick is about to fall in?"

"Not so stupid." A shudder wracks his giant frame. "It knows what it wants. To fill you up."

"With a big hairy baby?"

Which is supposed to be a joke. But it doesn't emerge like one. There's too much longing and tension in my voice.

That savage look is back in his eyes. "It wants what I want," he says gruffly.

Not just inside me. *Coming* inside me. Making me pregnant.

Making a future.

The sharp edge of temptation pierces me. I want that, too. So much. And if I let him in, if a baby became a possibility, it would be an excuse to keep coming back to him. To inextricably intertwine my life with his.

It would be *so* wrong to use a child as an excuse to

stay with him. Yet the thought of him thrusting deep into my pussy, of being filled with his cum makes me ache with need, and I can't get a word out. Instead my inner muscles clench, my sensitive flesh pulsing against his thick cock as if trying to draw him in. His gaze darkens, possessive and feral, and for a breathless instant I think he's just going to do it, to fuck deep into me and take everything he wants.

And I don't want to stop him.

Then his eyes close and he groans, *"Fuck."*

Making a decision. Because in the next moment he lowers his head and his tongue penetrates my lips again, his kiss slow and deep, and the pressure increases against my slick entrance. But he doesn't push inside me, just moves subtly in time with the thrust of his tongue against mine, until I'm writhing and trying to tilt my hips, to take him in, but he draws back every time my need-swollen flesh begins to stretch around the thick head of his cock.

All at once he breaks the kiss and rides the full length of his cock through my drenched folds and over my clit. Head thrown back, neck taut with strain, he thrusts hard against me again. Abruptly his big body stiffens, his shaft pulsing between us, hot cum spilling onto my belly.

Our chests heaving together, Bull's mouth finds mine again. Still kissing me, he rolls to his side, my legs tangled with his, his thick cock wet between my thighs, my every muscle still trembling.

His big hands cup my face. His gaze searches mine. "All right?"

Overwhelmed by his sudden gentleness, by the emotions rioting through me, I nod wordlessly.

His fingers stroke through my hair. It's fallen out of the messy bun I put it up in after my shower. I'm not sure when that happened.

A broad grin suddenly widens his mouth. "Damn condoms," he says.

I laugh. "We managed okay without them."

"Yeah, we did." His eyes take on a wicked gleam. "Though there was a second there when I wasn't sure whether my little head or my big head was going to win."

"Which one's your big head?"

He kisses me for that, his mouth smiling against mine. And when he pulls away I can't stop myself from saying, "I'm surprised you don't have any here."

"Any what?"

"Rubbers."

"I'd have to bring a woman here first. But I've never done that." All the humor fades from his eyes. "And there's been no one since I met you."

That's what I was fishing for—half afraid of what he'd say. Yet even though what he says is what I hoped to hear, it still hurts.

When I don't answer right away, he adds, "I was gonna pick some up on the way to your place tonight. But that didn't work out."

No, it didn't. My heart feels raw when I tell him, "I bought some. After work, I went and picked up a box. But then—"

But then I was thrown into a trunk. But then I heard Bull arranging a time to buy a shitload of drugs. But then I got railroaded into a silence that I'd have kept anyway.

Tears suddenly burn in my eyes. He sees them. I know he does because his face whitens and his hands tighten in my hair.

"Sara—" he says but I'm already slapping at him, my palms thumping into his solid chest, not trying to hurt him or get away but needing to fight *something* because I can't fight the pain tearing through me.

Because this isn't pretend. How much I like him. How desperately I want him.

How deeply I could love him.

After all these months, maybe I already do. And he had to go and ruin it.

"Why did you have to do this?" My tears spill over and I thump his shoulder. "Does getting that meth mean so fucking much to you?"

Eyes tortured, Bull shakes his head. "The meth doesn't mean anything."

"And apparently I mean less." A ragged sob breaks from me and I weakly hit him again. "We could have been *so* good together."

"I know." His voice is hoarse. "We still can."

"How?"

He doesn't have an answer. He just pulls me closer and I wrap my arms around his shoulders, burying my face in his neck. His big hand strokes down my back. And he holds me as I cry myself to sleep.

ELEVEN

BULL

Around three in the morning, Sara stirs against me—her soft breasts pressing into my side, her hand lying on my chest, her legs tangled up with mine. Waking up every day as early as she does, her body's internal alarm clock is probably set to this hour.

Just like mine is—though tonight, I haven't slept even a minute. Not with my chest aching like it is. Because ever since I met her, I wanted to hold her through the night with the taste of her pussy on my lips.

I just never imagined that when I did, it'd be after she fell asleep crying.

But she's not crying now. I don't even think she realizes I'm awake. She doesn't shift away or untangle our legs. Instead she softly sighs, her head pillowed on my shoulder. My arm went numb hours ago but I'd have willingly sacrificed the whole damn limb to hold her like this.

Especially after she absently begins trailing her fingernails through the hair on my chest.

Petting me, exploring me, I'm not sure. And although I'd love to know what's going through her head, the last thing I want is her pulling away from me, so I keep still. My dick doesn't stay still, but at least the night's dark enough to hide the tentpole my cock's making under the quilt.

I could have stayed like this forever. But three-thirty on the dot, an electronic beep trills through the room and she stiffens beside me.

The daily alarm on my phone. Shit.

I have to let her go to roll over and silence it on the nightstand. When I turn back, she's sitting on the edge of the bed, pulling the buttonless sides of her shirt together.

"Are you going to town this morning?" she asks without looking back at me.

"To the gym? No." And I'm not sorry for it. Lifting weights and running on a treadmill is about as fun as stacking wood—but the time in the gym is necessary. Not just because I've been acting as the Riders' enforcer, though that's a big part of it.

But I've never been as dedicated as I have been since Sara came to town. Used to be, I'd drag myself in to the gym three mornings a week. Now I'm there every day she's working at Reggie's, and putting more time in. The past few months I've packed on more muscle, shed some soft inches—despite eating everything she's been setting in front of me at breakfast and at lunch.

The way she looked at me last night, I'm glad I've been taking the time.

But skipping the gym these three days won't hurt—especially since I've got a pile of wood that needs chopping.

"What time does your dad eat breakfast?"

"About six, maybe," I tell her and the reason why she's asking hits me. "You aren't getting up now to make it, are you? You ought to sleep in."

She stands. "I will. But it's almost dawn and I've got to…" Her explanation trails off to nothing as she heads for the bathroom attached to my room, scooping up her clothes along the way.

The door closes behind her, and I flop back against my pillow, rubbing my hands over my face. Shit. I don't know what's happening but it seems like she's running. She doesn't need her clothes to piss.

And if she's planning to sleep in late, why the hell is she bathing? The shower comes on and I sit up, the quilt falling around my hips.

A shower, but the fastest one I ever heard of. The

water's off a minute later.

After a few more minutes, she comes out fully dressed, dry hair piled in a bun on top of her head.

My chest tightens. "Where are you going?"

"Nowhere," she says. "I just had to wash. Because, you know"—her hand waves toward me, the bed—"I couldn't make normal wudu."

I don't have a clue what that is but her saying she's not taking off eases the tension in me. I watch as she seems to hesitate, looking around, then heads back into the bathroom. She returns a short time later carrying a folded towel and with her hair covered—in my pop's undershirt, I realize. She wrapped and neatly tucked it so the cotton looks like a scarf over her head.

"Which way is east?" she asks.

I point and she spreads out the towel facing that direction, her back to me.

Rolling onto my side, I watch her pray. I suppose the way my dick responds to her elegant movements as she bends and kneels is blasphemous as fuck, but at least I don't stroke myself while she does. I'm going to hell, I figure, but I won't disrespect her while I'm heading there.

She finishes up, kneeling and turning her head from side to side before getting to her feet. She comes back to the bed, shedding her jeans and the makeshift scarf as she does.

In her white lace panties and sparkly T-shirt, she slides beneath the quilt, mirroring my posture—on my side, head propped on my hand, elbow braced against the mattress.

Her wary eyes search my face.

Quietly I ask, "What are you looking for?"

"I don't know." Her shrug makes her tits lift and fall beneath her shirt. Her nipples are rounded like cherries against the black cotton and my mouth is already watering for another taste. "Maybe you being uncomfortable with who I am."

"Not even a bit." There's nothing about her that makes me uncomfortable. Hell, I'm just glad that it matters to her — that she wants me comfortable. That means I matter, too.

But it also makes me wonder why she had to ask. "You have any problems since you've moved to Pine Valley?"

It's a small town that leans toward the conservative. Most people are decent. But there's assholes everywhere, I figure.

She sinks down onto her pillow, turns onto her back. "Yes and no."

Tension grips me. Even knowing there's some assholes in town, I didn't figure she'd necessarily run into them.

But maybe there's asses I need to be kicking. "What's that mean?"

"That most people mean well, I think. I was a little nervous when I first moved here. It's nothing like New York. I mean, pretty much everyone is white. And there's only one other Muslim family in town."

"That Pakistani family?"

"The Lanjwanis? Yes." She laughs. "See? You know who they are, you've noticed them. They stand out."

Can't argue that. "Yeah, they do."

"And I didn't want to stand out, because I'm trying to hide. But I stand out anyway."

"So what's that mean? You've had people making trouble for you?"

"Yes and no," she says again with another shrug. "Nothing scary. Mostly just…awkward. And sometimes there's some passive-aggressive stuff about not having any pork items on the menu and how they'll go down the street to Starbucks for a breakfast sandwich where no one's trying to force them to convert. Because a single bite of turkey bacon will turn you into a jihadi, right? It's not even *halal* turkey bacon." She's suddenly laughing and I have no idea what she means, but the sound makes me grin. As her laugh fades, she rolls onto her side again, looking up at me. "But most people are okay. I always wonder if it would be different if I covered." As if in explanation, she sweeps a hand over her hair. "If I wore a hijab. But none of the women in my family did. Not even my grandmother. So it was just never an issue for me."

I frown. "You just wore something."

"Well, I was praying." She bites her lip. "I'm actually not so good at that—at praying when I'm supposed to. But since I'm always up early, I try to at least pray fajr."

"But not five times?" I know that much at least.

"No." She gives me a scrunched, rueful look that wrinkles her nose, and it's goddamn adorable. "My grandmother always did. Five times a day, seven days a week. Even in the summer like now, when praying fajr means getting up so early. My mom and dad…not so much."

Talking about her family. She never has in all the time I've known her. After what she said at dinner, I think maybe she hasn't let herself.

I don't want to stop her now. Especially if it means she feels safe enough with me to expose this part of herself—a part that she's protected until now. "They weren't religious?"

"Not really. But I think it was different for them. My grandparents on my mother's side came from Beirut in the seventies. My grandfather died when I was still a baby, but my grandmama was always observant, even though my mama wasn't too much. She said it's because she tried so hard to fit in when they first came to America, religion got pushed to the side. But my grandmama said she was just lazy," she tells me, grinning.

Fuck me. There's nothing on earth as beautiful as her smile. "What about your dad?"

"My dad's Lebanese, too, but he was born here—and my grandparents on his side are actually Christian. He converted before he ever met my mom, and I guess he was dedicated at first—enough that my grandparents approved of him—but by the time I came along, I'm pretty sure he only prayed when he went to the masjid on Fridays. And my mom never went to the masjid except for

Eid prayers." This time her smile is a little sadder, a little wry. "I guess I'm more like them. I fast during Ramadan, go to Eid prayers, but I'm not really as good as I should be. I suppose it's the equivalent of someone who only goes to church on Christmas and Easter."

Is that a bad thing? Because if it is, I'm fucked. "I don't even go then. My only church is the club meetings."

She doesn't seem to think that's unforgivable, though, because her smile widens again and her husky laugh slips right through her gorgeous lips.

Then her smile fades into something tight, her eyes darkening.

Maybe because I mentioned the club—and she believes the club business means more than she does.

And believing it made her cry.

Fuck. I've got to fix that. Somehow.

But I don't get a chance to say a damn thing. The ring of my phone has me frowning and rolling over again—and when I see who it is, dread grips my chest.

Grasshopper. The brother has been covering nights at the hospital where Maurice is—making sure Maurice's old lady has everything she needs, keeping the Riders updated on Maurice's condition.

There haven't been many updates since he got out of surgery and sank into the coma. And those updates sure as hell didn't come at four in the morning.

I don't know of any good news that ever comes at four in the morning.

Sara's watching me, and I get a glimpse of her concern as I answer the call. Shit.

I swipe a hand over my face, try to hold it together. "Bull here. You got something?"

"Yeah. Maurice woke up."

That's so far from what I was expecting, it doesn't sink in right away. "You sure?"

"Well, I haven't seen him. He's still in intensive care and they're only letting immediate family in. But Margo says his eyes opened and he responded to their questions. Blinking or some shit."

"He know about his boy yet?"

Grasshopper's voice roughens. "Not yet. He was pretty out of it, I guess. He's back asleep now. Real sleep."

"Good." My throat's tight as fuck. "When do you figure they'll let visitors in?"

The first time I go see him, or the prez sees him, no way in hell are we going to be telling him that Osprey's still running around alive somewhere. We can't give him his son back, but we can give that.

Doesn't seem like it's worth shit in comparison.

"A few days, probably," Grasshopper says.

A few days. Just enough time.

"All right. You call me if anything changes."

"Will do."

Chest aching, I toss the phone back onto the night-stand.

Softly Sara asks, "That was about your friend?"

"Yeah."

Scooting closer, she reaches for my hand, folds it between hers. "It sounds like he woke up?"

I nod.

"Isn't that good?"

"I don't know." On a ragged breath, I shake my head. "He doesn't know about Justin yet. And I keep thinking, Christ. Maybe he's better off never waking up if that news is what's waiting for him."

With a sigh, she rests her forehead against my shoulder—hiding her face. "He's going to wish he died, instead."

"Yeah." Christ knows I would.

"And he's going to blame himself." Her voice is thicker. "Blame himself for ever walking into that store. Blame himself for buying a slushie. Blame himself for not seeing Ostertag sooner, or not jumping him and wrestling away the gun instead of trying to shield his boy, and every single day for the rest of his life, he's going to wonder what he could have done to stop it. But most of all, yeah—he's going to wish he'd died instead. And he'd give anything if he could just go back and trade places with them."

Them. Not a boy. Because she's not just talking about Maurice. She's talking about her family being murdered.

It fucking kills me to think that she ever wished to die, instead. I turn and haul her up against me, bury my face in her hair. "Your family wouldn't have wanted that."

"I know." Her breath shudders against my skin. "They wouldn't have. They'd want me safe. It'd have destroyed them if it'd been me. I tell myself that a lot but it doesn't make it easier."

"I don't know anything that could."

"No. But it must be so much harder if it's your child. Someone you're supposed to protect."

Or a woman you ought to be protecting. I stroke my hand down her back.

I've never lost anyone I loved. Not loved like that. I've lost friends, brothers. And I adored Maurice's little boy. So I've felt pain, grief.

It wasn't anything close to the terror and agony I felt yesterday, realizing she was stuffed in the trunk of that Cadillac.

I don't know what it'd be like to lose her…but I've had a taste of it. Nothing that compares to what Maurice is about to go through. Nothing like Sara went through. But loss is loss, and some things are the same. Like wishing they'd done something different before it happened.

That'll be me, if Sara goes. If I let this club business get between us. Every moment, wishing I'd done something different.

I can't change what's already done. But what I'm doing now isn't going to save what Sara and I have.

So I'll have to do something different. Before it's too late. Before I'm left with nothing but regrets and wishing I was dead.

I'm just not sure yet what the hell that 'something different' will be.

ONE THING ABOUT SPLITTING WOOD, it gives you time to think. It gives you time to brood, too. With every swing of the maul, I hear her saying, *We could have been so good together.*

Instead I've been hurting her. Because she thinks a drug deal means more to me than she does.

There's reasons not to tell her what the Riders are really doing by going after Osprey. I'm not just covering our asses, but protecting hers, too. Knowledge can be a dangerous thing if the cops catch on to what's happening. Not that I'm worried about her talking. I'd be worried about her being arrested for aiding or abetting or some shit like that.

Fuck. On that end, I'm a hell of a lot more concerned with protecting her ass than mine or my brothers'. Just like if we were together, I trust that she'd do everything she could to protect mine.

Because we *would* be good together—and that's part of the reason why. I know I could trust her.

I *already* trust her. Despite her going for the phone last night, I didn't disconnect any others around the house. Because I figure she wasn't really trying to call for help—she was just pissed off and pushing me as far as she could, the same way she slapped at me before she started crying last night. There's an internet connection, too, and when she browsed through the news sites this morning on my computer, I didn't have a moment's concern that she'd try to email anyone about what's going on.

She could have called the cops a hundred damn times since she got here. But even with her outburst last night, I don't believe she would.

I *know* she wouldn't. I've known it from the beginning. I told the prez, too.

And the prez was pretty fucking clear when he told us what we're supposed to make Sara believe this is all about the meth. But if she'd been mine already, it wouldn't have been an issue. If she was my old lady, it would only be because I trusted her enough to have my back. It would only be because I know she won't fuck over me or the club.

She isn't my old lady. She isn't even mine yet. So I shouldn't trust her with this.

But maybe that's what needs to be done different.

On a heavy grunt, I swing the maul. With a thunk and a rip, the log splits clear through. The blade bites into the chopping block below.

This time I don't pull it out. Instead I wipe my brow and glance at Pop, who's got a wedge of firewood in each hand and heading toward the stack. "You need a break, old man?"

He scowls. "Do I *look* like I need a break?"

I figure he could go for a thousand years if he wanted to. But I say, "You just seem a little pale, is all. A little sickly. Like you're withering under this hot sun."

His derisive snort is followed by a shake of his head. "Not likely, considering you're so goddamn big I've been standing in your shade all day. *You* need a break, boy? Then take one. And when you're done flirting, bring me back a beer. I need it to wash away the taste of your bullshit."

Grinning, I pull off my gloves and head up the stairs. My grin fades quick, though. The house smells so damn good, like baking bread, because she's been cooking. Because cooking settles her nerves. And they need to be settled because she's been hurting. Because she thinks she means less than twenty thousand dollars of meth.

But the reason doesn't really matter. What matters is, she's been *hurting*. This has been that simple from the beginning. I don't know why I let it get so complicated.

She's been hurting.

So I need to make it stop.

And she's so damn pretty, her hair up in that fluffy roll and her small hands coated in flour. She's kneading a big pillow of dough when I come into the kitchen, her cheeks flushed and her hips swinging to some pop music on the radio.

She looks up at me, and her first response is the sweet, teasing smile that's haunted me all these months. But her smile freezes before it's all there. Her dark gaze searches my expression, which is likely more troubled than usual.

Her hands keep rhythmically working the dough but her entire focus is suddenly on me. "Is everything all right?"

"Not so much." To keep something between us so

that I don't just grab her and kiss her, I take the barstool and face her across the counter. "That bastard who shot Maurice's boy. You recall hearing about him?"

Slowly she nods, her gaze fixed on mine. "Matthew Ostertag," she says. "He's all over the news."

Yeah, he is. But not everything about him made the news.

"When he's dealing, most people call him Osprey," I tell her.

Her eyebrows knit together for an instant. I see the moment she puts it together. Her full lips round and she pulls in a sharp breath.

"Oh," she whispers, eyes wide.

Solemnly I nod. "I just wanted you to know why this deal Thursday night is so important. And I would say more, but maybe it comes back on you somehow and I don't want to risk that. So you're probably putting a hypothetical together in your head—but I'm not confirming it. I'm just saying that maybe someone on the run might be real eager to get his hands on twenty thousand dollars. Maybe he'll pop his head out of the sand long enough to pay for what he did to Maurice and his boy."

"I see," she says quietly.

And I see that she does. But maybe it's not enough yet. "The Riders don't deal," I tell her. "I'm not saying there aren't brothers who do, because some of them get into all kinds of shit. And maybe sometimes it ends up being part of club business. If the Riders want something from another club or they owe someone a favor, maybe it means handling product or making a trade. But anyone gets caught dealing while wearing the Hellfire Riders' colors gets his patch stripped and an asskicking. I've done some of that asskicking."

"Okay," is all she says but I think there's relief in her eyes. I can't blame her. Drug dealers rank somewhere near 'wouldn't piss on them in a fire' on my personal scale, too—which is saying something, because I set the bar for decency pretty low. Adults want to get high as fuck? Don't really care. But anyone who preys on kids or takes advantage of someone who's addicted and vulnerable is pure shit in my opinion. The only thing lower are kiddie perverts and fuckers who abuse women—or set her parents' house on fire.

But just in case there's any doubt left, I tell her, "And the meth doesn't mean more than you do. This business with Osprey doesn't, either. I'm not going to lie, it means a hell of a lot, though—seeing him get his due. And it's a responsibility I have."

She shakes her head. "You don't have to explain any more."

"I do." Because she needs to know I'll accept the consequences of telling her this, too. "Because if afterwards, your conscience tells you to go to the cops—"

Her frown is swift and deep. "Why would I do that?"

"You didn't want me touching your old boyfriend. Even after what he did."

Brows raised, she stops kneading the dough and stares at me. "Not because I didn't want him hurt. I didn't want *you* getting hurt or going to jail for him. He's not worth it. *I'm* not worth that."

That's about the wrongest fucking thing I've ever heard. "You're worth a couple of lifetimes in jail."

Her smile returns, but it's just a faint one, and her eyes are dark and grave as she says, "You believe your friend is worth it, too. And his son."

"Yeah," I say gruffly. "They are."

"Well, I'm not going to interfere. Or call anyone." And she's wearing her full smile when she holds up her flour-coated hands. "I'll just have a three-day vacation doing what I love."

Throat tight again, I nod. "Good."

"Boy!" Pop's boots are unusually loud on the stairs, probably using all the noise to give me a heads-up so he doesn't walk in on something he shouldn't. "You lolly-gagging in there? If she's not kissing you yet, she ain't going to! But I've got a whole pile a wood that still needs splitting."

Sara ducks her head and starts giggling. Heaving a deep sigh, I push up off the barstool and head for the fridge for our beers.

"You only need to pull one out for yourself," Pop says as he comes into the kitchen. "Thorne just called, says he's heading up to Bend to look at that military surplus, and I figured I'd go join him. Sara, you weren't expecting to visit, so maybe you just write up a list of anything you need, and I'll swing by the Walmart on the way back."

She pinches her full bottom lip between her teeth, darts a look at me that I can't read. But when she glances back at my pop and nods, her cheeks are flushed again.

"Maybe a few things," she tells him.

Pop nods and heads to the sink to draw a glass of water. He looks over at me, a wicked glint in his eyes. "That's right, boy. I'm gonna be the one buying your girlfriend's panties. What color you like, Sara?"

She doesn't answer. With her head bowed and hands braced on the counter, she's silently laughing so hard her eyes are tearing up and her entire body's jiggling.

I watch her, popping the top of my beer and taking a swig to cool blood that's suddenly overheated. That jiggle's the sweetest thing I've ever seen.

And Pop thinks he's got the better of me? Not even a bit. Doesn't matter who buys her underwear.

What matters is that I'll be the one taking 'em off of her.

"Peach," I tell him, and head out with my dick hard enough to chop that whole damn pile of wood.

TWELVE

SARA

It's mid-afternoon before I hear Pop's rattling old truck returning. The faint sound of Bull chopping wood has been a steady accompaniment to the music I've got playing in the kitchen, but now the rhythmic whack of his axe quiets. Intending to go outside and help carry in the things Pop picked up for me, I lay my knife on the cutting board, heading over to the sink to wash my hands.

I don't even have time to finish drying them before I hear Pop's truck leave again. A few seconds later, Bull comes into the kitchen weighed down with plastic shopping bags and a gallon of milk—and with his checkered shirt unbuttoned, the sides hanging open.

My breath catches in my throat and a jolt of sheer lust rips through me. The cotton frames slabs of muscle decorated with black ink and covered in dark hair. Sweat glistens over his golden skin.

But his shirt isn't soaked with sweat, though he'd been working for hours.

Because he'd been chopping wood shirtless, I realize. As the day wore on and the temperature rose, he must have taken it off.

Oh, *how* I wish I'd known before. I'd have gone outside to help him stack the logs or taken him a lemonade or sat on the porch and stared.

With my hand down my pants.

Abruptly he comes to a halt, his incredible chest expanding on a deep breath. "It smells fucking amazing in here. What is that?"

Pleasure and embarrassment rise through me in equal measure. "Well, it could be the bread." I gesture to the three loaves sitting on the cooling rack beside the stove. "Your dad said it's one of the few things you buy from the store, so I offered to bake some instead. *Or* it could be the cinnamon rolls that I prepared for tomorrow morning. *Or* it could be the plum preserves that I made, because the tree out back looked as if the branches were about to break under the weight of all that ripe fruit. *Or* it could be the sauce for the stuffed zucchini that I'm making for dinner." I gesture toward the stove, where the tomatoes are simmering, then to the cutting board, where fat zucchinis from the garden are sectioned and cored. "I might have gone a little overboard."

"No such thing," he tells me, heaving the bags onto the counter and heading for the fridge to put away the milk. "Unless you asked for a can of hornet spray and a pack of nine-volt batteries, looks like he's got your stuff mixed in with ours. Think I can have one of those cinnamon rolls now?"

"If you want to." I start sorting through the Walmart bags. "But they aren't iced yet."

"Then I'll have second one later to compare." He digs a roll out of the pan and leans back against the counter, watching me. "Just don't tell Pop. He keeps going on about sugar but really he just wants all this to himself."

Smiling, I pull out a pretty rose-patterned scarf. Not as big as I usually use, but it'll still work as a hijab. I fold the scarf and set it on the counter. "Where did he go?"

"Took all that military surplus crap he got to his bunker." A groan of ecstasy follows that answer. "Holy shit, this is so good. Do you sell these at Reggie's?"

"Yes." Iced.

"Why haven't I ever had one?"

"Because I'm too busy feeding you meaty oatmeal. Pop really has a bunker?"

"Yup. So if you ever need to survive an apocalypse, just

head out this way."

"I'll remember that when the zombies begin—" I break off when I realize what's in my hand. Suddenly overcome with giggles, I show Bull the package of underwear Pop picked up. Despite his earlier teasing, he must not have been comfortable digging through bins of panties searching for colors and styles. "It's a six pack of white granny panties."

His mouth full, Bull silently laughs, his blue eyes gleaming and his broad shoulders shaking.

Wiping tears from my eyes, I place the package on top of the scarf. "The waistband is going to be higher than the waist of my jeans."

As I paw through the next bag, Bull says, "Easy solution to that is to walk around without any jeans on."

The briefs *do* offer more coverage than some shorts I see other girls wearing. But I don't answer, because the next item I find leaves me flustered and uncertain, heat rising in my cheeks. Should I pretend not to see it for now? Bull's standing right there.

But he took a huge risk earlier today, coming in to tell me about Osprey and the real reason the Hellfire Riders want to meet with the drug dealer. I suspect he wasn't supposed to tell me, or he'd have told me earlier. But he did anyway, erasing all my fears, making me trust my instincts again. He *does* have a bad side, but he's not rotten through. I was right about him.

So I should take a risk, too.

My courage doesn't stretch to looking at him as I pull the giant box ("36CT VALUE PACK!") of large-size condoms from the bag and set it beside my little pile. Blindly I keep searching through the other items.

I hear a labored swallow, then Bull clears his throat.

"That's awkward as hell," he says. "But I suppose no one can say Pop doesn't believe in being prepared."

It wasn't Pop. "I asked him to pick them up."

There's a moment of silence. Then in a low voice he asks, "You did *what*?"

"I put condoms on my list," I say with outward calm. Inside I'm a summer storm, wet and hot, my heart like thunder.

My pulse thrums faster when I hear him move. Out of the corner of my eye I see half a cinnamon roll abandoned beside the pan but I don't turn to face him. Instead I'm trembling, remembering yesterday's fantasy—that he would just bend me over the counter and sink in deep.

Wordlessly he stops behind me. Tension holds my body in an agonizing grip, waiting, picturing the bare skin of his chest almost pressed against my back, sensing the whisper of his breath across my hair. Knowing how big he is, how tall, having him this close should make his size seem overwhelming, but instead being surrounded by his strength and warmth sends anticipation racing in taut shivers across my skin.

My eyelids drift closed when I feel a tug at my nape. Slowly Bull winds my braid around his fist. With gentle pressure he tilts my head, elongating the side of my neck.

At the first hot touch of his lips against my exposed throat, everything inside me melts and softens. Moaning softly, I try to turn my head, but his grip on my braid prevents me from seeking his mouth with mine. A sharp nip just behind the point of my jaw leaves me gasping, my nipples hardening to burning points.

His teeth tug at my earlobe, his tongue flicking inside the sensitive shell of my ear before kissing his way down to my shoulder again. Just soft kisses against the side of my throat yet it's as if my knees turn to custard.

Panting, I cling to the edge of the counter. The lush pressure of his mouth moves higher again, his tongue painting a hot trail of need along the tendon at the side of my neck, his lips tracing the line of my jaw. Trembling against him, I try to seek his mouth again, held immobile by my braid wound around his fist.

"Bull," I plead desperately and his fist tightens, tilting my chin back over my shoulder.

From behind he catches my mouth in a rough, deep kiss. Tasting me, possessing me. As if he intends to brand me with the heat of his mouth and the stroke of his tongue.

Fiercely I return the kiss—claiming him for my own, taking as much as I give. The fire builds between us, hotter, higher with each lick, each tease of our lips. When my teeth close over the tip of his tongue, he shudders and groans, a low sexy rumble from deep in his throat.

We're both panting when he lifts his head. With a

voice like gravel, he says, "You got anything cooking that you can't leave?"

Leave. So that we can go finish this in bed. Decadent need rolls through me in erotic waves, clenching the inner muscles of my pussy, swamping my senses with frantic desire. Dizzy from the powerful sensations rushing through me, my wobbling knees almost collapse but his big body presses into mine, trapping me between the counter and the thick erection against my back.

In a breathless whisper I tell him, "I should turn off the burner under the tomatoes."

"Do it."

As soon as I twist the knob to 'off,' he sweeps me up against his broad chest, where I can feel the pounding of his heart through thick muscle. My fingers delve into his coarse beard, curling and tugging his lips down to mine, savoring the taste of him, his heated flavor sweetened by brown sugar and warmed by cinnamon. I don't know how or why every kiss with Bull is so different from every kiss I've ever had before. It's all lips and teeth and tongue, nothing's changed in the mechanics, but with him every taste soothes some deep need inside me—and makes me want more, so much more.

Makes me desire and feel and breathe nothing except him.

Even with our mouths fused, his stride is swift and sure as he carries me toward the stairs.

He abruptly stops halfway up.

With a tortured groan, his lips release mine. "I forgot the condoms in the kitchen."

Softly I laugh against his mouth. "I'm glad I'm not the only one losing my head."

"I lost mine months ago," he says and swiftly kisses me before setting my feet on the step. "Now you wait here for me."

I do. But only long enough to watch him descend the stairs and turn toward the kitchen. Then I race up to the second floor and into his room.

A few moments later, his boots thunder up the stairs. I'm standing at the end of the bed when he crashes through the door, his thick hair a finger-tousled mess, his chest rising on deep breaths, mock anger roughening his voice.

"I told you to wait, woman," he growls.

"So you did," I respond with a cheeky grin. "What are you gonna do to me for disobeying?"

Danger glints in his eyes. "I'm gonna fuck you."

Heart banging against my ribs, I whirl and jump up onto the bed. His big hands snag my hips before I can run another step, and I start laughing wildly as he drags me back to the mattress's edge. Admitting that I'm caught—delighted to admit it—I turn and throw myself at his chest, hooking my arms around his shoulders, pushing my hands into his hair.

"I love being with you," I impulsively tell him.

All that mock anger instantly stiffens into a tortured mask of determination and need. "I love being with you, too," he says hoarsely. "So let me start this all over again. Whether it takes a month, a year, or ten years…let me fix this, Sara."

My heart swells. Cupping his cheeks in my hands, I ask softly, "What's left to fix?"

"You and me."

The big lunk. Doesn't he realize this was all fixed when he explained what was really going on with Osprey? "What do you think these condoms are?"

"You tell me." His voice is still rough, his gaze boring into mine. "What are they?"

A risk. Maybe. Because the way he looks at me, I don't think there's much risk at all.

"They say I want to give this another go," I tell him, and my throat tightens as I watch wonder and relief crack his tortured mask. "And if it works out between us, maybe one day we'll throw away the condoms."

"It'll work out," he vows gruffly. "It'll be so damn good."

"Of course it will be good for you. You're a guy." I catch my tongue between my teeth but can't stop my teasing grin. Arching my brows, I add, "I guess we'll find out if it'll be good for me."

His eyes narrow at that blatant challenge. In the next moment we crash together, hungry lips and hurried fingers. I drag off his shirt, worshipping the heavy muscles beneath my hands. Our wet panting kisses are broken as he tears my shirt over my head, as I back up to shimmy denim over my hips and kick away my jeans, then crashing together again. Softly I moan when his lips leave mine to skim the lace edge of my bra, as his fingers unfasten the hooks at my spine. Not wasting any time, his left hand delves down the front of my panties, and my gasp of pleasure becomes a strangled cry when his mouth claims my nipple at the same moment his broad fingers press into me. I shudder wildly against him, the sudden acute pleasure bordering on pain, my inner muscles clamping down on his softly thrusting fingers.

His mouth an erotic furnace, Bull groans against my breast. "You're so fucking tight, baby. I'm gonna make you come first. Gonna make you so damn wet. You'll need to be real wet to take my big cock."

Another shudder rips through me. What his mouth does to me, his lips—it's pure pleasure. Yet that ecstasy is almost nothing compared to what his words do, the frantic arousal they stir deep inside me.

Desperately I shove my hands into his hair and bring him in for another kiss, moaning as his slippery fingers slick through my folds to circle my clit.

I can't bear it. Gasping, I break the kiss, my head falling back, my hips working against his hand.

His mouth latches onto my throat, suckling the tender skin before growling, "You like me teasing your clit, baby? Or you do you like my fingers inside you?" His thick fingers pump deep again. "Or maybe you want my tongue on your clit while I'm inside you? You want to come with me eating you up while my fingers fuck your sweet pussy?"

My only response is a stuttering moan as my sweet pussy clenches hard on his fingers.

"Hell yeah." Satisfaction and arousal deepen his voice. "That's what you want."

A laugh breaks from me because I want *everything*. My hands buried in his hair, I kiss him again, then launch all of my weight against his chest, knowing that my attack will only have any impact if Bull wants it to.

He must. Because he lets me shove him backwards onto the bed without resistance—though there's some reluctance when I grip his wrists and push them up, his fingers slipping from inside me.

But I have to make him stop touching me. Or I won't be able to focus on what I want.

Which is right in front of me, wearing nothing but his jeans—a sexy combination of thick muscle and inked skin and his gorgeous grin.

That grin widens as I crawl over him, straddling his heavy thighs, my hands braced on his iron hard pecs.

A moan of sheer visual pleasure rises through me. "You're just so…yummy."

My fingernails scrape through the coarse hair on his chest, my gaze following the narrowing trail that leads down his stomach and disappears beneath his belt, where the thick bulge of his erection looks as if it's about to burst through denim.

Poor thing. I really need to let it out.

"Yummy?" Watching me, his eyes are intensely blue

as he sucks my arousal from his glistening fingers. "I'd say that's you."

"What description do you like better, then?" I tug at his belt. "Rugged? Masculine?"

He's tensing up now, the muscles in his stomach and arms more sharply defined. His gaze locks on my hands as I slowly drag his zipper down.

"Yeah," he says gruffly. "Those are all right."

"What about 'massive'?" I ask breathlessly, freeing his dick from the straining prison of his navy boxer briefs. The exquisite ache between my legs intensifies as I take a long, *long* look. His cock's more than a match for his size, his heavily veined shaft standing rigid and flushed a deep red, as if angry it had been trapped inside his jeans for so long. My voice is hardly more than a moan as I tell him, "You should have been named Goliath, instead."

A shudder wracks his body. I'm not sure if it's from laughter or pleasure, as my fingers firmly grip his heated length.

His response is a thick rasp. "David's better. Goliath got a rock to the head."

My gaze holding his, I bend over him. "And it's not so easy to bring you down?"

"I hope not—"

He breaks off, his big body turning to stone at the first touch of my mouth. His eyelids fall to half mast. His hands fist in the quilt, the tendons in his strong forearms standing in sharp relief.

Watching his response from beneath my lashes, I take a long, slow lick up the steely length of his shaft.

"*Fuuuuck*," he says on a groan that deepens as my tongue swirls around the head of his cock. Breath hissing through his teeth, he grates out, "I'll come if you keep doing that."

"Are you telling me to stop?"

"Hell, no." A tortured laugh shakes through him. "I can't. I've dreamed of your lips wrapped around my cock for too damn long."

And I've dreamed of this, of Bull enthralled by my touch, overcome by need. But none of my imaginings ever prepared me for the thrill of touching him, tasting him.

Of holding him in the palms of my hands.

From a bed of dark hair, his heavy shaft rises in a proud curve, the veins soft beneath velvety skin. Beaded with a pearl of precum, the bulging crown is smooth and taut as a plum.

With a flick of my tongue, I lick away that salty drop, savoring the flavor, the clean musky scent of him, the groan from deep in his throat.

"I love how thick you are," I tell him huskily, stroking his length with my right hand and wedging my left beneath his loosened jeans for a good grip of his tightly muscled ass. "Just thick and meaty all over."

So thick, and so long, he's too much for my mouth but I still give him as much as I can, what he dreamed of, wrapping my lips around his shaft and taking him deep.

It must be enough, because as I begin to suck his cock, his eyes glaze over and a tremor rocks through his strong form.

He makes a choked, guttural sound. His hips jerk once, shoving his dick to the back of my throat before he freezes.

Struggling for control. And losing that control as I slowly, deliberately wreck him with my mouth.

His groans deepen, his words nearly unintelligible as he growls *suck me* and *harder* and *oh fuck please baby*. He reaches for me before abruptly drawing his hands up to fist in his own hair. The muscles of his stomach contract with his every ragged breath.

Watching him unravel, *making* him unravel is the sweetest pleasure I've ever known. And the moment he breaks, abruptly gripping my hair and fucking into my mouth, as if he's taking control—but he's completely lost it, his restraint destroyed by the stroke of my tongue—I've never felt so sexy, so powerful.

Suddenly he stiffens, grinding out through clenched teeth, "I'm going to— Ah fuck. Sara…" With another groan he releases my hair. "In your mouth— You need to pull back or I'm going to—"

I dig my fingers into his ass and suck harder, my gaze locked on his, silently urging him to come.

He does, looking utterly savage with his lips pulled back in a grimace, as if he's in pain. But it's sheer feral pleasure glittering in his blue eyes as his cock pulses against my tongue. Hot salty cum fills my mouth, and I barely have time to swallow it down, to take another lick before he's dragging me up over his bellowing chest and raising his head to capture my lips.

Greedily he kisses me, then lets his head drop back to the bed, looking up at me with almost sleepy satisfaction.

But there's nothing sleepy about the amusement in his voice when he says, "I don't taste nearly as good as you do. I got the better end of this deal. You get bleach and I get peaches."

His palate needs some refining. I giggle against him, my body splayed over his chest, my thighs straddling his stomach. "If you were squirting bleach into my mouth, I'd spit. And I don't taste anything like peaches."

"No? I remember your cunt being pretty damn sweet. Guess I'll have to go down and refresh my memory while we're waiting for my cock to recover." Though that heavy, satisfied look is still in his eyes, so is the glittering feral hunger. "Maybe your pussy is more like cake."

"Cake?"

"Because I get to have it and eat it, too."

So bad. I start laughing, but it transforms into a startled gasp when Bull abruptly flips us over and slides down, pushing my thighs wide.

"Oh," I breathe, then he's on me, mouth open and hot, his tongue dragging over my pussy in a long, slow lick. Back arching, I cry out when he stops to suck on my clit, each pull of his mouth fraying every nerve inside me with devastating pleasure.

Groaning, he lifts his head and presses a kiss to the inside of my trembling thigh.

"Still ripe and juicy and sweet," he says gruffly, his hands slowly spreading me wider. "But you're right. Not peach. You're so much more delicious."

I don't know if I am. I don't know anything, because he dives in again and his hands join his tongue. Though we're not in a rush, there's no teasing like last night. Instead his tongue goes directly to my clit, his fingers thrusting deep as he relentlessly drives me straight toward orgasm.

Then doesn't stop at one.

When he finally lifts his head again and moves up over me, I'm completely wrung out, my body still shuddering with the aftershocks of the third climax he dragged from me.

His glistening mouth hovers over mine. "All right to take me after all that?"

"Yes," I whisper and he rewards that answer with a long, slow kiss.

Everything seems long and slow now, time stretching out endlessly. As if in a dream, he pulls away from me again to shuck his boots and jeans, then shoves his shorts down his heavily muscled thighs. My body in a languid sprawl, I watch him sheathe his cock, and lift my arms to welcome him back when he returns to the bed.

My hands slide over his heavy shoulders as he dips his head to kiss me again.

Roughly he says, "After coming so hard in your mouth, I'm going to last a long damn time. It gets too much, you tell me. I'm too heavy, you tell me. You're just a tiny thing."

Not that tiny. Only compared to him. And he's big all over, completely surrounding me, but he's not really *on* me. His inked forearms braced by my shoulders, he's bearing all of his weight as his knees urge my thighs wider. Burrowing through my folds, his thick cock lodges against my entrance, the sheathed crown slick with my arousal. His mouth covers mine as he bears down.

Building pressure becomes a burning stretch as his cock slowly pushes inside me, and I knew he was big, could see it, but had no idea how overwhelming he would feel. Not painful, though tears sting my eyes. Just filling me *so* full. With a shuddering little gasp, I break the kiss to bury my face in his neck, breathing shallowly as he pushes deeper.

Until there isn't any deeper, and he stops. His heavy shaft feels like a hot length of iron wedged inside me.

Holding his big body immobile above mine, the tension in Bull's muscles feels like steel. His voice is hoarse as he asks, "You all right?"

I nod against his neck.

That must not have reassured him. "Is it too much?"

I shake my head.

"You aren't talking, though. My dick isn't so big it's clogging your throat, is it?"

It was emotion clogging my throat, but my laugh

opens it up. The way he always makes me laugh has opened up so much of me the past few months.

It's no wonder I fell in love with him.

Huskily I confess, "It's just never been like this before."

He's still tense against me. "For me, either, but I can't see your face so I don't know if we're talking about the same thing. So what's this like?"

Intense. Fun. Sexy.

How is it that sex was never *sexy* before? Instead it always felt as if I was reaching for something I couldn't see—and I was never even sure what it was. I just knew that no matter how much effort I put in, I wasn't finding it.

But I've found something better. Something effortless. Because it's so easy to be with him.

Easing back, I meet his eyes, intensely blue and looking down at me with concern. My throat tight, I whisper, "As if I'm losing myself and finding myself, all at once. As if I'm discovering where I'm supposed to be."

His gaze darkens. "I know where I'm supposed to be. I've known since the first day I sat at your counter. And that place is right here with you—preferably real deep inside you. Like this."

Subtly he flexes the muscles in his back, his cock shifting only slightly deeper but I can feel every thick inch caressing my interior walls.

A jolt of pleasure rocks through me. "Bull," I breathe his name and bury my fingers in his hair.

"All right?" he asks again.

"Yes," I gasp.

Then even better when he slowly pulls back and thrusts deep. Fingernails scoring his shoulders, I lift my hips to meet his endless stroke. After three orgasms, my pussy is excruciatingly aroused and sensitive, and he feels *so* big inside me, my inner walls slick and swollen with need, hugging his thick shaft.

And he's not in a rush as he slowly begins to fuck me, but soon I'm frantic, crying out on a sudden, hard thrust.

His labored breaths hot against my ear, Bull rasps, "That feel good, baby? You like it hard?"

"Unnnh." It's all I can manage but it's enough of an answer for him.

"Fuck yeah," he groans, wedging his hand beneath my ass and tipping my pelvis up. His cock shoves deep, striking high and hard inside me, some magic place that has me throwing my head back and writhing beneath him.

"Like that, baby. Fuck." Roughly he shoves a pillow under my hips and sinks deep again. "You're so goddamn beautiful. And you feel *so* fucking good."

He feels so fucking good. So thick and heavy inside me, driving me wild with each long, hard thrust, taking his time as if I'm not dying beneath him. My fingernails dig into his skin and my every breath urges him on, because now he's going hard but slow, not hard and fast. Sweating, my breasts swaying with each leisurely stroke of his cock, I pull him down for a hot ravenous kiss.

Groaning into my mouth, he fucks deeper into me,

then pulls back, his gaze feral as he lowers his head to my breast. Hungrily he sucks my nipple into the heated cavern of his mouth, still pistoning into me, but shallowly, the broad head of his cock breaching my entrance with every thrust. The sensation is exquisite and maddening, and I'm all but screaming with frustration as he releases my nipple and licks a bead of sweat from between my breasts.

Then he rises over me and buries his full length inside me, and suddenly it's all so much more than it was before. His open mouth meets mine and we're joined everywhere, his skin slick, his cock deep, his tongue thrusting past my lips as if he's branding me all over again with his kiss.

He groans into my mouth as my inner walls tighten around him. I'm not coming yet but it's building and building inside me, until I'm helplessly clawing at his back and writhing on his thick cock.

With a grunt, Bull grips my left thigh and pushes my knee up toward my shoulder, and fucks into me deep and hard and fast.

I cling to him as the orgasm bursts through me on a guttural scream. The clenching of my pussy seems to break whatever control Bull has left, and he pounds into my convulsing sheath before stiffening.

He groans my name as his cock pulses deep inside me, then everything's long and slow and dreamlike again, his kiss sweet and hot and perfect.

Our chests heave together when he lifts his head, a wry smile curving his mouth. "I didn't last as long as I figured. I thought I'd be fucking you for an hour or two. I didn't know how good you'd feel."

With a grin, I shake my head. "You'll get no complaints here. It was just long enough."

He kisses me for that, then says, "You know who's going to be complaining? Pop. Because I don't know how I'm going to be cutting any wood when I'm in here with you all the time."

All the time? "We'll have to take a break now and then."

That feral glitter returns to his eyes, and his big hand slides up my ribcage to cup my breast. As my nipple tightens, I feel the stirring of his thick cock inside me.

"You think so?" he softly asks.

Maybe not.

THIRTEEN

BULL

I'D HAVE BEEN HAPPY TO STAY IN BED UNTIL THE NEXT morning, but around six in the evening Sara sensibly reminds me that we'll need food to fuel all that exercise. And the thought of her cooking is worth getting up for.

After putting my clothes back on, I head out to the woodpile, feeling so damn rugged and masculine and massive that splitting logs didn't ever seem so easy.

Over the next two days, I make a good dent in that woodpile. I've never had two days that felt filled so full.

When she's not in the kitchen, Sara comes out to help us stack. In the house, every breath I take is perfumed with the scent of her bathing there, baking there, living there. She seems half in love with the garden and greenhouse, and I'm jealous of the time Pop spends with her there until I get her back in my arms again and keep her close to me all night.

Thursday comes too fast. I spend some time at the woodpile after breakfast, then help Sara pack up a picnic lunch and put her on the back of an ATV. The intention is to ride around the property and show her the size of our spread, but as soon as we get the picnic laid out beside the creek, I just end up showing her the size of my dick.

Best picnic I ever had.

When we head back to the house that afternoon, I don't even bother with the damn woodpile. I just carry her upstairs and don't come down again.

Then night falls, and I never hated the thought of dragging myself out of bed so much. Sara's warm, soft body is all tangled up with mine, her lips still red and swollen from all the kisses we've shared, her brown skin glistening with sweat after another wild fucking, her hair spread out all over my pillow and tousled by my hands.

Pulling away from that is the most difficult thing I've ever done. I sit up, reaching for my jeans.

Her hand strokes down my back. In a soft voice, she asks, "You're heading out?"

So she hasn't forgotten what's happening Thursday

night, either.

"Yeah, I am." We want to be in place near the church long before midnight so Osprey doesn't see us coming and spook again.

"Be careful," she tells me and I hear her worry. Maybe because she knows Osprey carries around a gun. After all, he shot Maurice and his boy with it.

Maybe because she knows that what I'll be doing might get me in serious trouble. If I'm caught.

The plan is that I won't be.

Jeans on, I bend down and cup her pretty face in my hands. "I'll be as careful as I can. You think I'm not coming back to this?"

Sweetly she clings to me when I kiss her, and I head out to my bike with her taste on my lips. Funny how some men complain that women make them weak. With Sara, I never felt stronger.

But I figure those fuckers who whine about women making them weak? Those bastards were probably just weak to begin with. Because a strong woman only makes a man more of who he already is.

And me, I never felt so fucking ready to take on the world so I can get right back to her arms.

God help anyone who tried to stop me.

SNAGGING OSPREY AT THE CHURCH is the easy part—and that part of the plan goes as easy as easy ever does.

Away from the church is where the real shit will go down, which is how I find myself behind the wheel of that fucking pink Cadillac, driving through the night with Osprey hollering and banging around in the trunk. Vern Woodridge played his part real well at the church. Now a prospect is taking the little weasel back to the Hellfire Riders' clubhouse until I figure what I'm going to do to him.

In the passenger seat, Duke tells me he's hoping I figure it out soon, because he's one of the unlucky bastards saddled with babysitting the little fucker.

"I've *never* heard so much stupid shit come out of one person's mouth." He cranks down his window, and the rush of cool midnight air helps muffle the noises coming from the trunk. Sometime in the past few days, the trash has been cleaned out of the Caddy, hopefully courtesy of a fire hose. "And you've met my brother-in-law, so you know that's saying something."

"I've met your sister, too," I tell him, and he nods because there's no arguing that she and her husband don't possess a donkey's worth of brains between them.

His lips twist. "You know he actually asked me what my opinion was regarding some teenybopper being cast as Mary Jane in the next Spider-Man movie?"

"We talking Woodridge or your sister's husband?"

"Woodridge."

I glance at him. Duke got his road name because of John Wayne—which is Duke's real name, poor bastard—but he doesn't look a bit like the movie star. Long and lean, he's more like a young, blond Eastwood playing Dirty Harry, maybe. Except without the squint or the Smith & Wesson Model 29. The bad temper and the square jaw, though, he's got on lockdown.

Not that his temper fires often around me. Probably because he's got a lot of tolerance for bullshit. What sets that temper off usually involves women, and the mistreatment thereof.

Right now disgust is etched all over his face, so I ask, "What *is* your opinion?"

"That any man my age with an opinion about a girl that young ought to have his fucking balls chopped off."

A man his age. Yeah, he's got one foot in the grave, all right. Just past thirty this year—same as me. "How old they got to be?"

"Old enough to drink, at least. Why?" He throws a narrowed glance at me. "You cradle robbing with that girl from Reggie's? She looks twenty-five or so, but is she really sixteen or some shit?"

"She's twenty five or twenty six, I guess."

"You guess? You never got around to asking?"

"No." Got around to other things, instead.

"I thought you were serious about her."

"I am." Dead serious. I just never figured her age mattered as much as other shit does. "I gave up bacon."

His forehead creases with confusion, like I spoke Latin. "What?"

"I gave up bacon," I say again. "Pork bacon, anyway."

"The hell you did." Now there's horror mixed up with the confusion. "She ask you to?"

"No." I don't think she ever would. Sara doesn't want to change me any more than I'd change her. But just because I don't believe what she believes, that doesn't mean I can't respect who she is in my own way. The same way she accepts what I'm doing tonight, and why I'm doing it, even though it's not a route she'd normally take. She threw her old boyfriend into the path of a police investigation, but she's keeping quiet for me. "But what if something I eat makes her feel like maybe she shouldn't be kissing me? Even bacon's not worth that. And if I ever suspect the alcohol's making her uncomfortable, I'd also give up beer."

"Shit," Duke says and starts laughing his damn head off. He's wiping away tears when he adds, "Giving up bacon and maybe beer. That's *love*, brother."

No doubt about that.

He sobers as I swing the big pink boat onto the old quarry road. Grasshopper's waiting at the gate marked with a big NO TRESPASSING sign leading to one of the gravel pits. He swings it open for us, then pauses to chain it closed and secure it with a padlock before following on his bike.

The pit hasn't been used for a while and the road's all but washed out. Between two deep ruts are tall dried grasses, and as we slowly drive over them, it sounds like there's a straw broom sweeping the Caddy's front bumper.

Bouncing around in the trunk, Osprey's still yelling but it's a silent, bumpy ride for Duke and me.

There's a ring of Harleys in the gravel pit, their engines off but headlights shining, creating a pool of light. Not every Rider is here—mostly just the executive board. Because God love my brothers, but some of them run their mouths when they've had too much to drink, or feel some need to boast. Small shit, it don't matter so much. They get an asskicking and a fine. The worst offenses, maybe they get their patch stripped.

But this isn't small shit.

The front of the Caddy closes the circle of bikes, the headlights illuminating the prez, who's standing in the center with a sledgehammer in his hands. Thorne and Old Timer are right next to him, along with the four Dubs—all original Riders from way back when the club was founded. Everyone looks grim as hell, because although we finally caught the baby-murdering bastard, this is no celebration.

Grasshopper rolls up behind me. He and Duke go join the brothers while I haul Osprey out of the trunk.

Out of the light are Blowback and Zoomie, Gunner and Spiral. Looks like Stone made it back for this, but although he's wearing the enforcer's patch, he defers to me and the role I've taken on with him gone, letting me bring Osprey to the prez and finishing what I started when I first contacted Woodridge.

The fucker goes quiet, the fight going out of his body the second he sees what's waiting for him. Maybe he's tired of running. Maybe he realizes there's no use trying.

No speeches are made. There's no bullshit here, no posturing, no ceremony.

The prez simply looks over at Grasshopper and asks, "The boy was your godson, yeah?"

His jaw tight, Grasshopper nods.

The prez holds the sledgehammer out to him. "Then you get the first swing."

And although the fight went out of Osprey, there's plenty of screaming left. When it comes round my turn, last in the circle, the sledgehammer's dripping red. But it's not the blood I'm seeing. I see Justin and remember how many rides that little boy took on my shoulders, how wildly he'd laugh. I picture Maurice in that hospital bed wishing that he'd never woken up, wishing he could take his boy's place, wishing he were dead. But it's not Maurice who's dying tonight.

My swing is the one that quiets the screaming.

FOURTEEN

BULL

At the clubhouse, I shower and change clothes before riding home. Sara will probably notice. Different T-shirt, darker jeans. She's smart enough to figure out without my saying a word that the others were splattered with blood.

Maybe that's why some men prefer the dim bulbs. If a woman's not too bright, then there's fewer questions, no judgement, no explanations to give.

And there's no worrying that she'll be done with you

when she realizes what you really are. Because accepting a hypothetical and accepting a reality are two different things.

That reality's about to come home.

Though it's well past two in the morning, both she and Pop are waiting up, sitting at the kitchen table with coffee and a pack of cards. As soon as I come in, Pop gets to his feet and grumbles something about going to bed. But I'm hardly even listening, watching Sara's face as her gaze seems to slide all over me, maybe looking for injuries or just noticing the different clothes and processing what it means.

She's changed her clothes, too. The past few days she's been borrowing my shirts, which are so long on her she didn't always bother with pants. But now she's back in the T-shirt and jeans she arrived in.

Because that's what she'll be wearing home.

A sick nervous ball rolls up hard in my gut. The past few days with her here were better than I ever dreamed—but she wasn't exactly allowed to leave. Now Osprey's dead and she's free to go.

And if she's done with me? I don't know how I won't turn into the same crazy fucker she's running from.

Not that I'd ever hurt her or anyone she loves. But I don't know if I could let her walk away without chasing after her.

As Pop heads out, she carries the coffee mugs to the sink. "I have to be at work in about an hour, so I'll need a ride into town soon. But take a seat at the table and I'll warm up your dinner so you can eat something before we go," she says. "Unless you ate while you were gone?"

I didn't. And I take a seat but—"I can't eat a fucking thing."

Her eyebrows draw together and concern darkens her eyes. Setting a mug in the strainer, she dries her hands while studying me. "Are you all right?"

I suppose that will depend on her. And maybe I shouldn't say anything at all, but keeping my mouth shut didn't work out so well between us before. What did help was talking. Not giving details, but still offering the truth. "What I did tonight, a lot of people would say a good man wouldn't do. They'd say it's something that can't ever be right, can't ever be justified. Some kind of primitive, caveman shit."

"Did you enjoy it?"

Her question's so unexpected, I can't answer right away. From her post by the sink, she watches me work it through, her gaze unwavering.

"No," I tell her and can't keep the hoarse note from roughening my voice. "There's no pleasure in it. There's satisfaction because I did what needed to be done, but I'd be lying if I said it wasn't some sick ugly shit and that it doesn't leave a stain. But I also can't say I'm sorry."

"I know," she says and crosses the kitchen toward me.

I frown, not following her meaning. "What do you know?"

"This. About you." She settles her supple weight on my lap, straddling me on the chair. Her arms link around my shoulders. "I always knew this about you—that you had this side of you. The bad side that can do some terrible shit and not apologize for it."

Not sure if I'm relieved or worried. "Did you?"

"Mmm-hmm," she confirms and leans back a bit, looking up at me. "What would you do if I'm in trouble?"

I don't even have to think about it. "Protect you."

"And if a friend of mine needed help?"

"I'd help her."

"If someone hurt Pop?"

"Fuck 'em up so bad they never could again."

"Would you ever hurt me?"

"Not in a million fucking years," I vow.

"See? I already knew all that. And knowing how you might solve those problems didn't bother me. Instead I liked knowing how far you'd go to take care of yours." A wicked little smile curves her full mouth. "Why do you think I was always swinging my ass in front of you?"

Putting on that sexy walk she has? I figured her ass just naturally swung like that. "Were you?"

She nods and tugs playfully on my beard. "Maybe I was hoping you'd just lose control, let some of that primitive caveman out."

"And show you my big caveman club?"

A laugh shakes through her, jiggling her soft tits. She's wearing her bra but the lace is thin, and her little T-shirt doesn't conceal the tight buds of her nipples beneath the cotton.

"Did you ever think it?" she wonders.

Think about fucking her after watching her swing that curvy ass? I can't believe she has to ask. "You want me to show you?"

Breathlessly she says, "Yes."

Her answer's barely out before I have her facedown over the table, my right hand working the fastening of her jeans, my left hand cupping her chin. Bending over her, my rigid cock right up against that curvy ass, I growl against her ear, "The counter where I always sit is too high for anything but eating you out, but all those little tables? I imagined having you on every single one."

Though I couldn't have fucked her properly on the spindly café tables at Reggie's. Here, though, the table's good solid wood that can stand up to a pounding. Roughly I drag her jeans and panties halfway down her thighs, hobbling her with denim and lace.

Falling to my knees, I bury my face in her hot cunt.

"Bull!" It's a half gasp, half muffled scream.

Then a wild moan as I lick all the way up the seam of her pussy in a long, broad stroke. She's already so fucking wet, then wetter as I suck on those pretty pussy lips and take another long lick from her clit to her ass. Christ, she's got the sweetest rounded cheeks. I press my thumb against her puckered little entrance.

She trembles and I softly nip the tender skin at the

bottom curve of her right cheek.

"You're too small to take my cock here," I tell her gruffly. "But maybe we'll get a few toys. You like how thick I am, but I'll feel even thicker inside you when you're filled up everywhere."

And I'll be buying those toys soon, because simply talking about filling her up has her rocking her hips and moaning, her pussy glistening with more of those sweet juices.

Hungrily I lick them all up, then fill her cunt with two thick fingers. Her inner walls are like hot wet velvet clamping down on me. Groaning, my dick so fucking hard I'm about to come in my jeans, I pump my fingers deeper, and her sleek thighs start shaking when I get my mouth up in there again, sucking on her clit. She's getting real close but I want to be in her when she goes over. I ease up, withdrawing my fingers, and when she moans in frustration I slide my tongue up and tease her entrance until she's begging me for more and desperately rubbing her pussy all over my face.

Fuck yeah. I give her what she wants, feasting on her cunt with my hungry mouth and thrusting tongue. She's shaking again when I unbuckle my belt and ease my aching dick free of my jeans. These past couple of days I've been carrying a handful of rubbers around in my pockets, and it takes me about two seconds to rip one open and roll it on.

Rigid with need, I align my stiff cock with her slick entrance. A single hard stroke sinks every thick inch deep inside her.

Sara cries out, her eyes squeezed shut, her face flushed and pillowed in her arms, her full lips parted in ecstasy. For a long second, I can't even move, looking at how beautiful she is when she's lost to her need.

Fuck, I'm all but lost, too. She's so damn tight and burning hot. I could heat up a peach and drill my cock through it, but that sweet flesh still wouldn't feel as juicy or as luscious as her cunt does. Her plush inner walls take my cock in their voluptuous grip, hugging my thick shaft as I begin stroking deep and hard.

Already shaking again, she turns her face into her arms to muffle her ragged cries.

And I can't get deep enough. Gripping her hips, I tilt her ass up higher, lifting her up off her toes so I don't have to crouch so low, and fuck her harder. The new angle drives her fucking wild. Moaning helplessly, she thrashes her head from side to side, her hair flying, then pushes up against the table, bracing her hands and throwing her hips back against me, giving as good as she's getting.

When she comes, her pussy's a velvet vise squeezing my cock, drenching me in a rush of hot juices. Feeling that, I can't hold back. I load up the condom with what feels like gallons of cum, pumping into her lush cunt until I'm completely spent.

I collapse over her, bracing my forearms on the table beside her shoulders to take my weight. She gasps as I rock gently against her, her plush walls clenching at me again. I need to pull out, to get rid of the condom, but I don't have the strength yet.

Burying my face in her hair, I tell her, "I'm real glad I didn't stick my thumb up your ass."

A giggle works through her. Fuck, that feels good. From now on, I'm always going to make her laugh when I'm inside her.

Through her giggles, she asks, "Why are you glad? Seems like *I* should be."

"Well, it'd be real awkward if my thumb was up your ass the first time I tell you I love you."

Her giggles abruptly stop as she catches her breath.

Is she surprised? Or just feeling awkward, anyway? Gruffly I say, "I know I move fast."

"Yeah, you do," she whispers. "Let me up?"

I do, then drag off the condom as she turns around and pulls up her panties and jeans. All the sudden, she looks real fucking wary.

With her dark eyes watching me so carefully, that hard ball of nerves sits heavy in my stomach again. I trash the rubber and rake a hand through my hair, try to smooth my beard. This is the part where she leaves. And I've got to act like I'm not going to turn into some fucking stalker. "You heading straight to Reggie's or to your place first?"

Stiffly she says, "My place. I need to change and my car's there. I can drive to Reggie's from my house."

Does she think I'm just going to dump her at her house and take off? "I'll still follow you in to work. But I likely won't be at breakfast. I'll probably come back here after, get some shut eye before heading out to the job site."

As if I'll ever sleep again without her beside me.

And it seems like she's still stepping real careful when she asks, "Do you want me to warm up that dinner before we go?"

"No." Though maybe I should have said yes, kept her here longer. I rake my hands through my hair again. "Fucking hell."

Something softens in her face—and suddenly I realize the wariness she wore before was nerves stretched as taut as mine. And she's still not steady as she whispers, "Will you kiss me, please?"

Hell yes. I cross the distance between us in two long strides. I kiss her hard, loving the way she rises up on her toes to meet me, loving the sweetness of her mouth and the warmth of her skin.

Loving her.

Her breath is coming quick and shallow when she draws back, looks up into my eyes. "You do move fast. But I haven't been going any slower."

My throat's tight. "No?"

"No," she echoes huskily. "After all these months of knowing you, even before you kissed me that first time, I was completely crazy about you. Why do you think it hurt me so much when I thought we wouldn't have any kind of future?"

The same reason it ripped me apart to think I'd lost

her. "Are you hurting now?"

"Not at all." She rises onto her toes but can't get high enough. Bending my head, I kiss her smiling lips until she slowly lowers to her heels again. Her hands smooth down my chest as if she's reluctant to stop touching me. "If you're not coming into breakfast, maybe you can take me out to dinner? And we can try it all again—and see how good we are together when we've got work and real life always intruding."

"We'll be so damn good together. Christ, I love you."

So damn much. Overcome by the feeling, I wrap my arms around her waist and pull her up against me. And she's a hell of a lot better at this than me, because I'm holding her and her mouth is against mine the first time she says, "I love you, too."

Not a bit fucking awkward. Just fucking perfect.

Just like she is.

FIFTEEN

BULL

We take my bike, and Sara holds onto me tight all the way into town. Though she was nervous about riding behind me at first, by the smile on her face when we roll into her driveway, I think she ended up enjoying it.

Shutting down the engine, I help her with the buckle on her helmet. Her skin's soft and smooth, her face flushed—but as I move in for a kiss, something suddenly changes, her expression going tight and wary.

Her eyes aren't on me. They're on her house.

Softly I ask her, "What are you looking at?"

"The living room curtains are closed." She bites her lip, tearing her gaze from the house to meet my eyes. "I always leave them open. But I guess maybe Woodridge closed them."

It's not Woodridge she's afraid of, and her fear is like an iron fist squeezing my heart. "Tell me his name."

Expression suddenly fierce, she shakes her head. "He's not worth risking you."

She's worth risking me. But I won't argue. Blowback will get the name and then I'll be taking a trip to New York.

Gently I tip her chin up so she meets my gaze again. "Are you always afraid?" I ask her.

"Not afraid, exactly."

"So what are you, *exactly*?"

"Careful." Nervously she wets her lips, her gaze darting down the street, and I figure the real answer is closer to *completely fucking terrified*. "I try to be aware of my surroundings. Like I notice when there are new cars around. Such as that one."

I look where she's looking, at a vehicle parked at the curb a few houses down. The dim streetlight doesn't penetrate the darkness of the tinted windows. "That black SUV?"

"Yes."

"You want me to go check it out?"

"No." Her fingers clamp around my wrists to stop me

and she offers a shaky little laugh. "It's not necessary. The woman who lives there has overnight visitors sometimes. So she keeps me on my toes."

She's real jumpy on those toes. But I nod, easing back. We're not staying here now, and I can make certain she's always got someone watching out for her when she gets off work.

"How about this for a solution? You won't be sleeping alone again. And you likely won't be sleeping here."

Most of the tension seems to bleed out of her. "That sounds like a good solution," she says softly. "That and a new name."

"You still want that, you'll get it." Taking her hand, I tell her, "We'll go check out your house together. Then I'll follow you in to work. All right?"

The relief in her eyes almost kills me. How many months has she been coming home terrified like this? I shouldn't have been so damn patient, waiting for her to become comfortable around me before asking her out. I should have been with her, protecting her before this.

But I can't change the past. I'll just do what needs to be done now.

Abruptly she stops. "Oh shit. My keys." Her wide eyes meet mine. "I dropped them in the garage that day."

When Woodridge attacked her. Come the end of the day, I'm going to beat that little weasel's ass for sure.

"I don't see a problem," I say, leading her up to the front porch.

"I do. I can't unlock my front door."

"Not a problem," I say again.

"Why? Are you just going to break in?"

"Something like that. Because you know I've got my bad side." Grinning, I pause to kiss her sweet lips. "And I think you're about to like that bad side a hell of a lot more than you already do."

SARA

I DO LIKE BULL'S BAD side. I like all his sides. I like the side of him that patiently waits while I dress for work. I like the side of him that follows my car to Reggie's and looks around the kitchen—to make sure there aren't any perverts waiting, he says—then shoves me up against the door and kisses me. And I especially like the side of him that presses into me when he does, because that's the side with his thick yummy cock.

I'm still floating a few minutes after he leaves, listening to the radio and practically dancing around the kitchen.

Until a surprised "Oh!" and heartfelt "Thank freaking God!" freezes me in place.

I glance over at the kitchen entrance, where Minerva's standing and looking at me as if she's stunned—and pleased—to see me.

Which is a little odd, considering that I was scheduled for work today. And she's not supposed to be here until later in the afternoon.

I eye her carefully. "Are you okay?"

She *looks* okay. But she always looks okay. Great, actually, because she works the retro look like a pro, with sleek black hair and ruby red lipstick, and her eyeliner game is on point even at three thirty in the morning.

"Am *I* okay?" Now she laughs, hanging her big polka-dot purse up on the hook by the door. "That's what I was going to ask you! I wasn't even sure if you'd be here. Were you with Bull? *Please* tell me you were with Bull."

I can't see any reason not to. The silence the Hellfire Riders demanded only included their deal with Osprey—and somehow she already knows where I was, anyway.

"I was with Bull." It won't be the last time, either.

"Oh thank God!" She pretends to collapse with relief against the counter. "Because that call Monday night was so *weird*. And I tried to call you back on that number but got nothing. So I kind of freaked out and went to your house to check on you."

My lips round with realization. "Oh."

"Yeah, oh." She gives me a baleful look. "So I found your car there, and your purse spilled all over—with some condoms right by it, which was *extra* weird. But I didn't find you sick in bed."

Heat climbs my cheeks. I really hated lying to her. "Because I wasn't in my bed."

"Yeah, I figured that out. *After* calling up every hospital in the area, because I thought maybe you collapsed in the garage. And then I freaked out for the rest of the night, wondering if I should report you missing. Because you *did* call in sick. Then in the morning, Nancy mentioned that she saw Bull kissing you behind the counter."

The nurse who walked in on us. My face gets hotter. "He did."

"Well, since Bull didn't come like usual on Tuesday morning, either—even though he couldn't have known you called in sick and weren't going to be working—I put two and two together. I figured he dragged you off to take care of you." She arches perfectly pencilled eyebrows. "And do other things to you after you got better."

I press my hands to my burning cheeks. "It was something like that."

"Good." Still half-sprawled across the counter, she sighs and props her chin on her fist, looking at me with an expression caught somewhere between embarrassment and worry. "I have to tell you… At first, I put two and two together and got five."

I give her a quizzical look.

"I called Raphael's office on Tuesday morning," she says and my heart begins thumping against my ribs. "Because I hadn't talked to Nancy yet and I was still freaking out, and I wanted to find out whether he was there or out of town. But he was there so I figured he couldn't have grabbed you."

My stomach feels tight and sick. "Did you talk to him?"

"No. Just a secretary. I pretended that I had a boss with an unexpected layover in New York and hoping to meet with him. But of course she said Raphael was too busy, blah blah blah. And I thanked her and hung up. I figured that would be okay."

It probably will be. Even Raphael can't monitor *every-thing*. Or follow up on every odd call.

I hope.

Watching me, Minerva bites her lip. "You don't think a call from here would tip him off?"

"I don't know." I really don't. "Worrying that it might sounds crazy. But—"

"Raphael's crazy, too."

"Yes."

And now I'm thinking of that black SUV. I told Bull it was probably nothing. It probably *was* nothing. But should I have let him check it out?

No.

Because either it was nothing, or it was Raphael. And I don't want Bull anywhere near him. I still don't think Raphael would hurt me.

But he'd kill someone who loved me and who tried to protect me from him.

And there *was* someone who drove by when Bull followed me into Reggie's back parking lot. I didn't think much of it then, or really notice what kind of vehicle it was, because there's not much traffic this early but there's still a car now and then — and because I'd been focused on Bull. I hadn't been thinking of Raphael at all.

Maybe I shouldn't be thinking of him now. It's probably just paranoia.

Unless it isn't.

Hesitantly, Minerva asks, "Do you think everything is okay?"

I'm not sure. I'm still working it through. Slowly I say, "When I got home, my purse was on the kitchen counter." At the time, I assumed Woodridge had picked it up and gone through it after grabbing me, but Minerva just said that she found my purse in the garage after he'd already taken me to Bull's place. "Did you put it there?"

"Yes."

That should ease my mind, but it doesn't. Because — "And you said you found the condoms, too?"

"Yeah. I put them by your purse. Along with the razors."

And the razors had been there.

The condoms hadn't been. I'd assumed Woodridge had swiped those. But he couldn't have.

Which means someone was in my house after Minerva left.

Sudden fear skitters like an icy spider down my spine. My voice is thin and high when I ask her, "Can I use your phone?"

"Of course, honey." She hands it over and watches me, her eyes dark and worried.

I don't have Bull's cell number. And I spend a few frustrating minutes trying to look up David Masters or William Masters in the online white pages before I abruptly realize that their home number is probably an unlisted one. Pop would never make it that easy for someone to find him.

Which might also help protect them from Raphael. Unless that SUV *had* been his. Then he could just follow Bull home.

I'm probably panicking for nothing. But suddenly all I can see is their beautiful log house going up in flames. And Bull can take care of himself, I know it—but he wouldn't expect Raphael to go after him. He'd expect Raphael to come after me.

My heart thundering, I look up from her phone. "Would you mind taking over here for an hour or so? I just want to run out to his place and warn him to keep an eye out."

A frown pulls at her red lips. "You'd go by yourself?"

"I'll be in my car with the doors locked. I'll be fine. Can I take this?" I hold up her phone.

That eases some of her worry. "Of course. You call here if you have any trouble, okay?"

"I will." I shove the phone into my back pocket and head for my purse. "Maybe I'm overreacting. But I know I'll be worried sick if I don't at least tell him."

Minerva follows me. "Maybe you *are* overreacting," she says. "But after what Raphael did to your family, maybe it's better to overreact than not to act at all."

That's my feeling, too. I pause at the door, glance back at her. "Will you watch to make sure I get to my car?"

"You know I will." Her teeth flash in a quick grin. "You should take one of those, too."

She nods toward the wall above the prep counter, where an assortment of long steel knives hang on magnetic strips.

"Good thinking," I tell her, and select a chef's knife with an eight-inch blade that I hone to a fine edge every morning.

Minerva grabs her own knife as we walk to the door, then stops to watch me cross the dark lot.

"Remember!" she calls after me. "If you run into Raphael, cut downward and *away* from your body. Safety first!"

I truly couldn't be more fortunate in my friends. As tense and worried as I am, I'm laughing as I unlock my car. And maybe checking the back seat to make sure Raphael's not lying in wait is also overreacting.

But safety first.

BULL

IF GOOD NEWS AT FOUR in the morning is rare, then I figure the odds of hearing good news at three-thirty is a hell of a lot worse. And when that call comes from the

Hellfire Riders' warlord, who was responsible for making every trace of Osprey vanish, the chances that it's good news sink straight to zero.

I'm on my front steps when the call comes in, but I don't continue on into the house. His calling means I'm probably about to leave again.

But the call's not about Osprey, as I assumed. And Blowback's first question has my balls shriveling with cold dread.

Without any preamble he says, "Is your girl with you?"

"No." I'm already heading back to my bike. "Why?"

"His name's Raphael Wainwright. You ever hear of him?"

My heart's a jackhammer against my ribs. "Fuck no. Should I have?" Because he says it like maybe I should have. And I remember Sara mentioning his army of lawyers. "He a big name?"

"If you're on Wall Street. I only ask because I wanted to know if you'd recognize him. I'm texting a picture."

"Why do I need a goddamn picture?"

And my jackhammering heart just fucking stops when he says, "Because he flew into Bend yesterday. So where's your girl?"

"At Reggie's." Thanks to the meetup with Osprey, I've got more weapons than usual stowed in the saddlebags on my bike, but I'm not taking any chances of being caught without a gun on hand. I tuck a semi-automatic pistol into the back of my belt. "I'm heading there to get her now."

"Do that. You'll be taking her to your place?"

"Yeah."

"All right. Me and Lily are coming your way. You get her home and we'll plan the rest from there."

A plan to hunt down fucking Raphael Wainwright. I swing my leg over my bike and fire up the engine.

I give a second's thought to calling Reggie's and warning her, but looking up the number will take too fucking long. No doubt Sara's all right. I just left her and she's so damn wary. Even if Raphael showed up at Reggie's, she wouldn't open the door for him.

So I'll just get there as fast as I can.

My engine's a thundering roar as I hit the road. I open up the throttle, racing along the dark ribbon of asphalt, my bright headlamp the only light in sight.

That's why I don't see him coming. Don't hear him coming, either, not over the thunder of my engine. A faint gleam of red in my side mirror—the glow from my tail light glinting off a chrome grill—is the only warning I get that a big vehicle's right behind me.

There's no avoiding what happens next. The fucker hits my back tire—

And I go flying.

SIXTEEN

BULL

A man my size isn't supposed to fly. But landing's even harder.

So hard I don't remember much of it. Just some tires screeching. Feeling something pop in my right shoulder. Hearing steel drag over asphalt and seeing a shower of sparks. Agony shooting through my left ankle like something took a bite out of it.

Now the fucker turns on his headlights. His rig's about a hundred feet down the road from where I'm sprawled in a ditch—all the way over beside the lane opposite the one I was riding.

I don't know how the hell that happened, considering that in the split second between realizing he was behind my bike and him hitting me, I bailed out of my seat—but I was aiming for the ditch on the other side of the road. Somewhere in there I must have been whipped around and tossed in this direction.

And I'm not moving real fast now, because not everything's working like it should. I manage to sit but I don't get much farther upright. My right shoulder's out of joint or broken. I'm not sure which because everything from my neck to my fingers feels like it's been through a shredder. My ankle's throbbing like a son of a bitch and I'm not sure what's going to happen when I put some weight on it.

But bailing probably saved my life. Because as his reverse lights flare and the SUV starts backing up along the road, he's dragging my Harley with it. If I'd still been on the motorcycle, I'd have been dead for sure. My beautiful FXR is nothing but a broken wreck wedged right up against his front tires.

Fuck. I spent three years restoring that bike. Seeing her twisted up under that rig hurts more than my shoulder does.

And if I didn't already have reason to kill him, I would now.

As he stops the vehicle even with where I'm sitting in the ditch, it's clear the murderous intent is mutual. Wearing a fucking suit and tie, he climbs out of the rig—and there's not much to read on his face, but he's carrying a tire iron. Thank fuck it's not a gun, because I don't think I can move fast enough to dodge a bullet—and my own weapon went flying when I did. I can see the pistol lying farther down the road, right at the edge of the blacktop. About fifteen feet away.

Close enough to see but not close enough to reach. And my hurting isn't over yet.

Because that tire iron means it's real damn personal. You don't beat a man to death when it's not.

That he's making it personal might give me my only chance, though. I can take a few hits from a tire iron, use my arm to block the blows. It'll likely break some bones, but better a few busted bones than a bullet to the head. I just gotta last long enough to get to my weapon.

I could use a distraction in a big way, though. Something to give me a few extra seconds to reach my gun.

But his focus never wavers from me when he stops in the middle of the lane. He's a smooth-looking, handsome fucker, that's for sure, like he might have just stepped out of a magazine spread. Good thing I know that Sara prefers her men rugged and massive, with a dick the size of a redwood tree. Otherwise I might be feeling real insecure right about now.

Without a word, he swings his arm like he's throwing an underhand pitch, and a small box comes flying my way. A package of condoms lands at my booted feet.

The *fuck?* Shaking my head, I eye him again. "Is this foreplay? Because I gotta tell you, man. You've got that rich city boy look down pat, but you're still not pretty enough for me."

"These were in her home." His voice is as smooth and cold as he is. "Did you have her?"

Did I have *Sara?* It takes every fucking bit of my control to keep from lunging at him simply for referring to her in that possessive way. And knowing he was in her house?

Gives me just one more reason to kill him.

But I only say easily, "I figure that's her business."

Because I'm not sure whether to piss him off or not. Some men, that's the way to go. They lose their shit, they open themselves to attack. But some men, they lose their shit, and it's like trying to take down someone on PCP. You can break their legs and they'll keep on coming.

I can't tell what he is. Except fucking unhinged. If someone goes looking into his life, I bet they're going to find pieces of people in his freezer.

"Did you have her?" he asks again.

Yeah, I think I want him pissed. Might as well be two of us. "You mean, did I kiss that little mole on the inside of her right thigh before I licked her pussy until she came all over my tongue? Or do you mean, did I fill her up with my fat cock and ride her while she screamed for more? Yeah, I had her. I had her mouth, I had her cunt, and I had her tight virgin ass. But I sure as fuck didn't use any rubbers.

I pumped my cum deep inside her and I figure in about nine months, she's going to be having a baby with pretty blue eyes just like mine."

That doesn't piss him off. Or it does, and he doesn't show it. Either way, that's bad fucking news. Someone that cold is going to be a lot harder to goad into losing his focus.

But maybe I won't need to.

Two headlights appear down the road, swinging around the curve about a half mile away. Someone coming from town. Not Blowback and Zoomie, though that would be the best-case scenario. But even they don't ride fast enough to have gotten here yet, and from this distance I can tell it's a car, not a pair of motorcycles.

Grinning, I ask him, "You figure that's a cop?" because I doubt he'll know that budget cuts in the county mean there's only one deputy on duty this time of night, and that deputy sure as hell doesn't patrol these back roads. "You better get on with killing me or get going."

Unless he's crazy enough to kill whoever's coming, too. Because no doubt, that person's going to stop. What they're about to come upon will look a hell of a lot like an accident, and there's one thing that's certain about back roads and small towns: anyone driving by is going to pull over and try to help.

Maybe a city boy doesn't realize that. Or maybe he does, and when they pull over he'll go after them with the tire iron.

It's a shitty thing to hope for. But it might give me time to go for my gun and save us both.

I'm thinking Raphael's intending to kill them, too, because he doesn't step out of the lane, even though he's right in the path of that oncoming car. The driver's already slowing and dimming the high beams.

And he's smiling.

He's smiling, and my stomach fucking turns inside out when I realize what he's already seen. The SUV's headlights are shining through the car's windshield, illuminating Sara's frantic expression. Everything goes abruptly silent, her hybrid engine shutting off as she slows to a stop a few yards from where he's standing. She's not looking my way, because my bike's smashed up under his front bumper, and her face is crumpling with grief and terror even as she throws off her seat belt and opens her door.

Fucking hell. She's only ten feet away from him—closer to him than I am to my gun, which is in the other direction. To go for it, I'd have to move farther away from her—maybe allowing Raphael a moment to get his hands on her. "Get back in that car, Sara!"

My harsh shout swings her wild gaze in my direction. It takes a second for her to find me in the ditch.

"Bull?" she whispers my name in horror. "Are you—"

"Get back in the fucking car!" I get my good foot under me—then freeze when Raphael hefts the tire iron and takes a warning step closer. In a lower voice, I tell her, "I'm just fine. You get back in the car and get the hell out of here."

She doesn't move. Because now she's looking at Raphael, too. There's no mistaking the threat in his posture and her pretty face is a frozen mask of fear.

His triumphant gaze on me, he says to her, "He's just fine, my love. And he'll *remain* fine if you come with me now. He'll remain fine for as long as you stay with me."

Jesus fucking Christ. If that's her choice, I know what she'll decide.

He knows it, too.

"Don't you even think it, Sara," I say hoarsely. "You get in your car and go."

She rips her gaze from Raphael to find me in the dark. And my heart shreds to nothing when I see the tears filling her eyes.

"Don't," I beg her. "Don't."

"I'm not risking you, Bull," she says on a shuddering breath, then straightens her shoulders and looks to Raphael. "I'll go with you. But we're obviously not going anywhere in your vehicle. We'll take mine."

Without another glance at me, she gets into the driver's seat and pulls on her safety belt.

I look to Raphael. "I'll come for you."

He grins and takes a step back, still holding the tire iron high. "You do that. And when you find us, you'll see who that pussy belongs to. You'll see the only baby filling her belly is mine—"

And I didn't hear him coming because of my loud

fucking engine. He doesn't hear Sara because her engine's so damn quiet.

On a soft whir, her car shoots forward. His eyes widen but he only has a moment to glance toward the oncoming headlights before she rams into his legs.

Even through her closed up windows I hear her scream as she hits him. Immediately she slams the brakes. Raphael bounces off her hood, the tire iron sailing out of his grip. It clatters to the asphalt about the same time he rolls off her car and lands in a heap in front of her tires.

For a stunned moment, I think maybe it was an accident. I think that maybe in her terror and distress, her foot slipped and she didn't mean to punch the gas.

Until she gets out of the car again with a long fucking knife in her hand.

She starts toward Raphael, who's groaning and crawling across the road toward the SUV, dragging his right leg.

Fuck. Although a part of me wants to roll around laughing, I can't let her do this.

"Sara," I say gruffly and shove to my feet. White bursts of pain flash behind my eyes as I feel the bones grinding in my ankle. Probably the only reason I can even stand on it is the support of my boot. "Stop, baby."

She stops but doesn't lower the knife.

"I'm not letting him take anyone else," she says thickly. "I'm not."

"He won't." I hobble over to my gun, pick it up with

my left hand. My right's not working too well.

Tears are streaming down her cheeks as she turns to me. "I can't lose you, too."

"You won't." And I'm not going to let her finish him off. We could call the cops now, and every jury in the country would say what she did was justified after he tracked her across the U.S., and after he mowed me down. Killing him while he's crawling across the road is another matter. She doesn't need that stain on her hands.

Not when mine are already covered with blood.

Gently I take the knife from her. Down the road, there's headlights approaching. Two motorcycles. I can hear the rumble of their engines from here.

They'll be the cleanup crew.

I would use his own tire iron but my shoulder hurts too fucking much. Instead I hobble over to where Raphael's rolled over onto his back, blood dripping down his temple from a gash over his eye.

Yet the crazy asshole is grinning. Somehow, he still thinks he's won. Maybe because he's got an army of fucking lawyers. Maybe because he knows that after the cops show up, he'll be taken in—but his money will get him off and he'll come after her again.

But we're not calling the fucking cops. Because the Hellfire Riders take care of their own.

And Sara's mine.

I return his grin with a feral one of my own. "Tell me again who that pussy belongs to?"

"Me," Sara says before the fucker can answer.

All right. I'll give her that.

"The soon-to-be Mrs. Masters," I tell him, then pull her close and tuck her face against my chest. She needs rid of him but she doesn't need to see this.

I aim right between his eyes. Her body flinches when I squeeze the trigger. For a long second she stands rigidly against me, then I feel her shudder and soften as she begins to cry.

My throat aching, I hold her closer. "You okay?"

"I don't know," she whispers brokenly. "Is it really over?"

Not quite yet. Raphael's a big name, so his disappearance will raise questions.

No one's going to find any answers. An hour from now, there won't be any sign that anything ever happened on this stretch of road. And by the time the sun rises, there won't be anything left of Raphael Wainwright—or the vehicle that brought him here.

But that's what Blowback and Zoomie will take care of. It's nothing she has to worry about.

"Yeah, baby." I press a kiss to the top of her hair and lead her around the side of her car, where she won't see the mess of his head. "It's really over."

She abruptly halts. "You're limping."

"Because I broke my damn ankle. And dislocated my shoulder, I think." I squeeze her hand, stopping what I know will be coming when her mouth drops open. "We'll head to the hospital after I talk to them."

Her brow furrowing, she turns to look at the approaching motorcycles, and when she glances back at me I catch her chin.

"You saved the fucking day," I tell her, just in case she hasn't realized it yet. "Running your car into him."

I meant to distract her from worrying about me by telling her that, but her eyes fill with tears again.

"I thought I was too late." Her voice is a hoarse rasp. "When I pulled up and saw your motorcycle, I thought he'd killed you. And I just wanted to die."

My chest is suddenly aching worse than my arm. "No, baby—"

"Then when I saw you hurt…I'd have done anything to stop him." She looks up at me, and despite the tears glimmering in her eyes, her expression is fierce. "You said 'the soon-to-be Mrs. Masters.'"

"Yeah, I did. Was that too fast?"

She's shaking her head. "I want to know *how* soon? Because I'm not losing you."

Just like that, the ache is gone. "As soon as you like," I tell her.

"Then I want *very* soon," she says and hesitates for a brief moment. "Though I'd like to keep my name, too. It's all I have of my family. I'll add Masters but not get rid of Abu-Hamdi."

"I don't care what you call yourself," I say. "As long as I can call you mine."

Christ, her happy smile. It's so fucking beautiful.

"You can call me that forever—which is as long as I'll be loving you," she says softly, then rises up on her toes. "Now will you kiss me, please?"

And I do.

EPILOGUE

BULL

Two years later...

Even with Sara snuggled up against me, getting out of bed in the middle of the night has become a hell of a lot easier. Because the longer I lie here, the more likely she is to wake up, and for the past few months sleep has been a luxury for both of us. So better to let her rest a bit longer.

And what's waiting for me down the hall is someone

I'll always be happy to get up for.

But the crying that woke me up quiets before I'm halfway there. By the faint yellow light shining beneath the nursery door, it's easy to guess why.

In the rocking chair by the window, Pop's cradling Nadia's tiny form against his chest. Pride gleams in his eyes when he looks over at me. "Just needed a diaper change," he says in a hushed voice. "She took a shit that weighed almost as much as she does. That's a sign of a healthy appetite if I've ever seen one."

She's definitely a hungry little bug, spending almost as much time on Sara's tits as I'd like to. Grinning, I ask, "You want me to take her?"

"Hell no." Gazing down at her sweet face, my pop says, "You want a baby to hold all the time, you better go back to your pretty wife and get busy making another one."

Can't argue with that. Still, I don't immediately go, watching him rock my sleeping little girl.

After meeting Sara, maybe I should have been prepared for how such a tiny female could wrap herself around my heart. But I wasn't. And every single day, I'm fucking staggered by the sheer amount of love I have for that little girl and her mama.

And maybe we will have another baby. I'm not real certain yet. We tossed the condoms the night of our wedding, but it still took almost a year of frequent trying before she got pregnant.

Sara took to pregnancy real well. She spent the whole

time glowing. But me, I watched her belly grow bigger and bigger, and began worrying that she was too delicate to survive what I put in her.

And I was close to right.

Nadia's got a full head of dark hair now, but she arrived bald and she sure wasn't big. Because Sara fainted one day when she was a little over eight months along, the baby came early, and in the few hours between seeing Sara fall and watching her wake up in a hospital room, I learned what true terror was, fearing I was about to lose them both. It all ended up well, Sara was fine, the baby was strong—but we're five months past that, and I don't know how many times I've sat where my pop is now, holding my little girl close, simply watching her breathe.

But in my pop's arms, Nadia's as safe as safe can be. And I've got a wife to hold. Chances are, I'll spend the next hour watching her breathe, too.

Pop's voice catches me as I head back out the door. "You did real good, marrying that girl. I got plenty of reasons to be proud of you, David. But out of all those, setting your eyes on Sara was the best thing you ever did."

My chest is suddenly real fucking tight, my eyes burning. "Yeah, it was. 'Night, Pop."

"'Night, boy."

Moving silently through the dark, I return to my room and ease into bed. But all that effort at being quiet was for nothing. As soon as I'm under the covers Sara turns to me, pillowing her cheek on my bare shoulder. I pull her closer, wishing we were skin to skin from head to toe. But since we're up and down the hallway so often at night, we've both taken to wearing a pair of pajamas to bed. Half a pair, anyway. I take the bottoms, she takes the tops—which are more like a nightdress on her—and it all works out in a Jack Sprat fashion.

In a drowsy voice, she says softly, "Is she sleeping again?"

"Yeah. Pop's in there with her." I bury my face in her hair, breathe in her clean, sweet scent. Since we've been married I've been using her shampoo on my beard just so I can smell her all through the day. "He's going to have her hunting and fishing and building her own underground bunker before she's five years old."

She turns her face against my shoulder to muffle her laugh. Then with a heavy sigh, she pulls away and sits up.

It's too early for her to be praying. "You all right?"

"Just leaking a bit." In the faint moonlight filtering through the curtains, I see her cup her breasts in a way that's become familiar the past few months—as if she's trying to staunch a flow. "Since she's sleeping, I should go pump."

"You don't have enough milk stocked away?" I ask. "Seemed like there was plenty when I fed her a bottle earlier."

My casual tone doesn't fool her. The first time after we got the doctor's go-ahead to resume marital relations, Sara was straddling me with my cock deep inside her, and I was nuzzling her full, ripe breasts when her milk let down and squirted all over my face. The past two years I've been real good about making her laugh almost every time I get into her, but it wasn't any effort making her laugh that night. As I was blinking milk out of my eyes, she cracked up, her inner muscles rippling the length of my cock. And I had no idea what to do, because the milk kept dripping from her nipples in a steady stream, and I knew that when she's full enough to leak like that her breasts ache, but after two months without being inside her, there was no chance I'd soon be leaving the warmth of her cunt. So I latched on and began sucking to ease the pressure — and between the creamy sweetness of her tits and the rediscovered heaven of her pussy, I started coming while she was still laughing.

Each time since then I've lasted longer, but I can't resist sneaking a taste once in a while.

Now she giggles and pushes at my shoulder. "You're depraved."

I strive for a woeful expression. "Where do you think my bad side comes from? I was abandoned by my mother as a pitiful little baby. I never got enough time on her tits. But you can turn my life around, make me good."

Her laugh is a sparkling flash in the dark. "I'd rather keep you bad."

"And depraved isn't bad?"

Her nose scrunches up in that adorable way she has. "You're such a caveman."

Yeah, I am. And she likes that, too. Because depraved

or not, she sure is quick to pull off her nightshirt and nursing bra before straddling me, her mouth all over mine.

And as sweet as her pussy is, as sweet as her tits are, they'll never compare to the sweetness of her kiss and all the love that spills from her lips. Two years or two decades or two centuries, I'll never have enough. I'll crave this woman until I die.

Then probably keep on craving her after, too.

With her face flushed and her nipples fat as cherries, she rises over me and impales herself on my thick cock, moaning as she fills her pussy as deep as she can. It requires all my control to simply let her take what she wants, rather than flipping her over and fucking into her. Instead I slide my hands up the sleek length of her thighs and help her along, working her slippery clit with my thumb. Her head falls back, the ends of her long hair sweeping my thighs in a rhythmic tease. Slowly she rides me, a curvy light in the dark—my light, my life.

I know she's close when her leisurely movements quicken. When her sleek thighs begin to shake.

When her pussy begins clenching around me, that's when I break.

And I'm not nearly as civilized as a caveman when her cunt's squeezing my cock. On a feral growl, I slam her back onto the bed and shove deep, consuming her ragged cries with a ravenous kiss. And she's still coming, then coming even harder as I fuck relentlessly into her lush depths, until her cries become muffled screams of pleasure, my name over and over. Primitive need drives me deeper into her even as I spill my cum and her pussy milks me dry.

Her full breasts are still heaving when I lower my head and latch onto her nipple, and that's when she starts giggling again, her cunt rippling around my cock.

Threading her fingers through my beard, she whispers tremulously, "I finally have my big hairy baby."

And I discover I can't suckle her tit when I'm busting a gut laughing. I can kiss her, though, and her lips are just as sweet and loving whether she's grinning or moaning.

"Your big hairy *man*," I growl against her mouth. And since my cock is still hard inside her, it's easy to punctuate that point with a rock of my hips that leaves her gasping.

"My baby, my man, my husband," she responds breathlessly, her dark eyes shining as she loops her arms around my neck, pulling me tighter against her soft body. "It doesn't matter, as long as I can call you mine."

"You'll be doing that forever," I vow. "Because we'll always be so fucking good together."

And every kiss, every breath—it just gets better.

So I breathe her in deep and kiss her again.

THE END

DUKE

ONE

DUKE

You'd think a man would learn. Wednesday night, I'm riding along the road toward the Hellfire Riders' clubhouse without a care in the damn world. The last time I can remember feeling this good, I was fourteen years old—and that was when my whole world went to shit. One minute, not having a care and being so fucking *careless*… and the next minute, losing everything.

So you'd think I'd know better. Feeling this fine, I should have known something was coming for me.

I should have known it wouldn't be long before I lost everything again.

But that's how it always starts. Some stupid fucker doesn't open his eyes and recognize what's in front of him. This time that stupid fucker is me. Because when Bull and I ride into the clubhouse lot and I spot the two black Mercedes-Benz SUVs parked near the entrance, I assume it's business as usual.

I know Bull assumes the same, but he's not being stupid. For that big bearded bastard, the world is all unicorns and roses—and has been ever since he hooked up with his girl, Sara. Nothing's coming for him. Mostly because he put a bullet in the head of the last man who did.

Now he cuts his engine, eyeing the SUVs. "Looks like someone's delivering your baby."

"Looks like." And I hope like hell it doesn't whine as much as the last one did. "You hear any word about who it is?"

He shakes his head. "Nothing aside from Widowmaker's email."

That's all I got, too, and those messages are about as helpful as snot on ice. Every Wednesday before the Hellfire Riders' executive board meeting, Widowmaker sends out an agenda to the attending brothers. Today we got two emails, and the second included a last-minute addition—"Babysitting"—which told me a job had abruptly come up. And that single word was all the information given about it.

But the meeting starts in two minutes so I'll find out more soon enough. I head across the lot and Bull falls in beside me.

"Did you read the rest of the agenda?" he asks while pulling his fingers through his black beard. On a weekend ride a few years back, a bumblebee got caught in that thick bush and he nearly took down the whole goddamn club swerving and trying to get it out. I doubt there's any bugs in there now but there's a reason I shave every day. "Item number three was 'A DUMBSHIT ASSHOLE.' So whose skull do you figure the prez is going to crack?"

"Could be any of us." We're all assholes. But some of us are dumber than others. "I'll put my money on Burnout."

Bull's snort says he's got no argument there. But my mind's quickly changing, because standing at the clubhouse entrance is—or is *supposed* to be—one of the brothers. Everyone works security for the club now and then, though truth be told, there isn't much need for it. The clubhouse sits in the south corner of an old ranch spread, twenty miles outside of the nearest town and about a mile off the main road. A few pine trees grow along a stream behind the clubhouse, but beyond that, there's no real cover. The landscape's flat and there's little chance of anyone sneaking up on us. Securing the clubhouse usually just involves giving directions to civilians who got turned around while trying to find the brewery on the opposite side of the ranch, or holding back pissed-off old ladies who suspect their men are inside screwing other women.

But a job is a fucking job. And the dumbshit who is *not* standing at that door deserves a fine, an asskicking, or both.

Luckily for Bottlecap, he's only a few paces away from the entrance when we walk through. No one can say the kid wasn't at his post. But judging by the slack-jawed way he's gazing deeper into the clubhouse, he apparently got real distracted.

One hard look sends Bottlecap hauling ass back to where he should be. As the prospect passes Bull and me, he says to us, all goddamn giddily, "Did you see who's hanging out in our clubhouse?"

No one I give a fuck about.

Not until someone's paying me to give a fuck, anyway. By the time I leave the executive board meeting, I'll probably give all the fucks. A lot of motorcycle clubs run drugs or guns or hookers to make their money, but the Hellfire Riders prefer not to get mixed up in that shit. Not because we're goody-goody—we're far from that—but because that shit brings in a whole lot of trouble not worth dealing with. We just want to ride and fuck and fight. So a good portion of the Hellfire Riders' income flows in from fighting, in the form of the security a few dozen bikers can provide. Sometimes that means escorting cargo along the highways. Sometimes that means guarding a building or standing in line, forming a wall of muscle that anybody with a brain won't dare to cross. And sometimes that means providing personal protection—babysitting—here on club property or at another location.

Me, I'm the head babysitter. Which gives a lot of people a chuckle, the first time they hear it.

When they see what happens to anyone who comes after our clients, they stop laughing.

And it doesn't matter to me *who* I'll be sitting. All that matters is doing my job, because fucking it up will smear shit on the Hellfire Riders' reputation.

A single glance deeper into the clubhouse tells me this job's already a little different. The club's property sits on an old dude ranch, and the guest lodge was renovated into the clubhouse. Most of the brothers hang out in what used to be the big open lobby, lounging on the leather couches and watching sports or playing video games, or shooting pool. Farther back, the former dining room is a big open bar with more seating.

Everything's mostly empty now. Wednesday nights are board meeting nights, and most brothers have work in the morning. By the weekend it'll be loud as hell, with brothers drinking and partying and fucking the girls they bring. But except during the summers, the weekdays and weeknights stay quiet.

And the half dozen people waiting in the bar area aren't patchholders. Instead of kuttes, most are wearing black suits—and most look like hired muscle.

Which is damn strange, if someone's here to hire the Hellfire Riders' muscle.

I can't tell who put the stars in Bottlecap's eyes. There's two standing at the bar who probably aren't muscle—which means they're most likely the clients. One's a slick-looking fucker in a gray suit who eyes Bull and me as we start up the open staircase to the second level. The other's a blonde. Her back's to me, her elbows on the bar, honey-gold hair hanging past her shoulders. She's wearing a short white dress, and I can't see much of her except for a pair of long, long legs and a sweet ass, but my immediate impression is that she sure as hell doesn't belong here. Girls with knockout figures that harden your dick, we see plenty of. Girls with the kind of money she and the slick fucker obviously have, they aren't so common.

Hell, girls who end up with that kind of money, the first thing they do is hightail it out of places like this. She won't be staying, either. As soon as this job's done, she'll be gone.

So I don't know why the hell I take another look. Her body's worth a second and third glance, easy. But that's not what I'm looking for. Instead I'm hoping for a glimpse of her face. As if her face matters.

It shouldn't. Especially since she's paired up with that slick fucker. I've never touched another man's woman—or wanted to—and I'm not starting now. Yet still there's something in me that's silently urging her to look over her shoulder. Still there's something in me that's resenting the thought of him touching her smooth golden skin. Still there's something in me that's hoping he's her brother or gay cousin or some shit.

She doesn't turn around. Then there's nothing to see anyway, because we hit the second floor and head to the conference room.

Bull and I are the last of the executive board to show. The entire club meets every month, and that's where all the general business and voting is conducted. The executive board meets every week, and that's where the nitty-gritty shit gets done. The board's headed by the prez, Saxon Gray, whose word is law around here. There's also a seat for each of the club's officers, and a few more seats for the handful of Riders appointed by the prez to serve on the board—brothers who have something worth saying or who have their fingers on the pulse of the club. Since we're not ranking officers, Bull and I fit in that latter category.

Everyone else is already settling down at the big table, loaded plates and foaming pints in front of them. The VP's old lady normally provides a big spread for the board meetings, but Molly must be doing something else tonight. Instead of her usual homemade feast, there's boxes of pizza.

Though Bull will likely have dinner waiting for him at home in a few hours, the hollow-legged bastard goes straight for the pepperoni. Me, I just snag a beer. Having babysitting on the agenda means I'll need to talk. I'd rather not be stuffing my face at the same time, and pizza tastes just as good cold. I grab an empty chair between Spiral and Zoomie and sit my ass into the plush leather seat. All the furniture in here looks like something out of a fat cats' club, a holdover from the old lodge. Makes me feel almost classy.

Almost.

Never one to waste time, the prez starts the meeting while Bull's still piling slices on his plate. The first item on the agenda is "money"—that never changes. Neither does our treasurer, Old Timer, whose gray grandaddy of a beard puts Bull's black bush to shame, and who takes his sweet time chewing and swallowing before giving a rundown of the club's finances. Which are solid, if running tighter than he'd like.

"Although," Old Timer says, "depending on how long this new babysitting job lasts, those numbers might loosen up."

Wearing a broad grin, Knucklehead pipes up, "Let's hope we're babysitting a long time. Because *damn*."

A laugh of agreement ripples along the table. Frowning, I eye the brothers sitting across from me. Laughter at these board meetings isn't unusual. Except nothing Knucklehead said was funny. Nothing Knucklehead *ever* says is funny.

So I must have missed something. "How much are we charging them?"

The prez answers that. "Twenty grand."

Fuck me. That's not twenty thousand for the job. That's twenty thousand a *day*.

The Hellfire Riders don't babysit at set rates. Instead

the prez factors in the risk to us and the client's ability to pay. Which means my impression earlier was wrong. I thought that slick fucker probably had money. But he must have some real fucking *big* money.

It also means the prez thinks there's a hell of a risk involved.

But now's not the time to ask what it is. Babysitting is fourth on the agenda, and if there's one thing I've learned about these meetings—skip ahead and you'll get shut down hard.

The next item I don't want to skip, anyway. In the email, it's simply listed as "Updates." Every item is an update of some sort, but this one is specifically about the brothers. Anyone in trouble, anyone needs help, the Hellfire Riders look after their own.

Several patchholders go on and off that list, but there are two brothers we discuss every meeting. We have for a while now.

The prez's gaze zeroes in on Grasshopper, who's sitting across from me. "How's Maurice holding up?"

"He's not," Grasshopper says bluntly. Though he's not a member of the executive board, he's the brother closest to Maurice. So he's been a regular at these meetings ever since Maurice and his little boy, Justin, got caught in the crossfire at a convenience store robbery. Maurice survived. His boy didn't.

The Riders hunted down the fucker who shot up the store. A sledgehammer meted out our brand of justice.

But we couldn't bring his boy back. And we don't know if Maurice will make it back, either. Physically, yeah. Mentally and emotionally is another story.

I don't know if any parent can come back after losing a kid. When my sister Holly disappeared, my dad didn't come back from it emotionally, and before long he was gone physically, too. My mom tried to hold on, taking care of Sandy and me as best she could, but she didn't really come back, either. Not as the mother I'd known the first fourteen years of my life. Losing Holly changed them both.

Hell, it changed us all. Everything I am, everything I think and feel can probably be traced back to a movie theater, the empty seat where Holly should have been sitting, and a spilled bucket of popcorn.

And Maurice, whether he comes back to the Riders or doesn't, he won't be the same man. But whoever he ends up being, he's still our brother. We'll still have his back.

"He says he's fine," Grasshopper continues. "And that his doctor cleared him to return to work, start riding again."

"That's news to me," our VP says, and considering Thorne owns the construction company where Maurice works, that information's of double interest to him. "He hasn't called in or said a damn thing. What's his old lady say?"

"That he's not sleeping and he's eating Percocet like candy."

"Fuck." On a heavy sigh, the prez scrubs his hand over his face. "We get the word out, then—here and up in Bend.

No one better sell him anything stronger than grass or we'll come down on them like the fucking wrath of God. And the brothers need to act hard up if he starts looking to them." He looks to Grasshopper again. "But get him all the weed he wants. What are their bills looking like?"

"Like there's a gaggle of medical professionals building their luxury vacation homes on Maurice's back."

"Before or after insurance?"

"After."

"Shit." The prez shoots a glance at Old Timer. "You've been putting some aside?"

The Riders' treasurer nods. "They need help, we've got it covered."

"All right." The prez's gaze sweeps down the table and lands on the vacant spot beside Gunner. That spot belongs to the Hellfire Riders' enforcer, but it's been months since he's filled that seat. "I got word from Stone. He has no idea when his shit will be settled or when he'll return to Pine Valley, so I'm stripping his rank."

That announcement rips through the executive board like machine gun fire. Stone's still a brother, still a Hellfire Rider. But no longer the enforcer, though I'd have laid down money that he'd carry that rank all the way to the grave. Stripping his enforcer's patch is like the prez saying there's a damn good chance Stone's not coming back.

Feeling like my gut's been punched full of hot lead, I look to Gunner. He and Stone go way back, serving in the Marines together, joining the Riders together—hell,

Gunner's even marrying Stone's sister. Blood brothers aren't any closer than those two are. Right now Gunner appears grim as hell, but not surprised. Maybe he knew this was coming.

Maybe we all did. Because the rest of us are surprised, but we're not arguing that the prez should wait a little longer or change his mind.

"I'll appoint a new enforcer at the club meeting next month," the prez continues and immediately all eyes go to Bull. Given that the big bastard has been acting as temporary enforcer in Stone's absence—and doing a fine job of it—he's the obvious choice. Obvious to everyone but the prez, maybe. Because he says, "What do you think of that, Bull?"

I've known Bull a long time. Usually right now he'd be cracking a joke. But today he strokes his hand over his beard, his expression thoughtful. "I think you aren't appointing me."

"I might if you want it. Do you?"

Bull shakes his head. "Not permanent."

"That's what I figured." The prez leans back. "So I'll be choosing someone who does."

I want it.

I want that enforcer's patch real damn bad. But I'm the last asshole who'll ever get it. Because I walked away from the Hellfire Riders once. And the prez, he isn't ever going to forget that.

His steely gaze lands on me now. A hard little smile

touches his eyes—like he can see how much I want it, and knowing that I'm not getting it pleases the hell out of him. Because I never paid for leaving the Riders six years ago, when they patched in a woman. I turned in my colors, joined up with the Steel Titans and rode with them until last summer, when the Hellfire Riders folded the Steel Titans into their club.

Reinstating the three Riders who walked away six years ago—me, Valentine, and Maurice—was part of the deal. Valentine's dead now, and no one's sorry about it. And the prez is a mean motherfucker who isn't in the habit of showing mercy or offering forgiveness, but what happened to Justin wiped Maurice's slate clean. No one will ask him to pay more than he has.

I'll be paying for long time, though. In the prez's eyes—in a lot of Hellfire Riders' eyes—walking away marked me as a disloyal fucker. There was plenty of grumbling when the prez gave me a seat on the executive board, but that wasn't out of the goodness of his heart. I figure Thorne—who's VP now and used to be the Steel Titans' VP—threw his weight in for me. Because in the five years I was a Titan, I was the one who started this whole babysitting gig, which is now the Hellfire Riders' largest source of income. And I'm damn good at my job. I'd be a damn good enforcer, too.

But no disloyal fucker is *ever* going to be appointed to that position.

That knowledge eats at my chest like acid, but I can't

even argue and claim the prez is in the wrong. Because I turned my back on the club. I walked away, thinking the Riders were becoming everything I hate. When Zoomie patched in, I watched brothers go up against her, fighting her, making her bleed. She pulled through, won every fight and got her patch, but the whole fucking time I was sick to my stomach, thinking that shitshow was what the Riders had become. I thought we were turning into assholes who beat on women instead of protecting them.

But that wasn't what happened. If it was, I wouldn't be wearing the Riders' colors so proudly today.

And Zoomie sits beside me now. No one protects her—no one needs to. Hell, I'd have her protecting *my* back any damn day. I've told her so, too. There's no hard feelings between us now, no bad blood. Six years ago, I didn't want her in the club, but it wasn't anything personal. I never doubted her capabilities.

But like I said. Everything I am and everything I do can be traced back to that theater and that empty seat. Back to the day when I took my eyes off my sister for a few seconds. My decision to walk away from the Riders six years ago—the reason I won't be appointed as enforcer—can be traced there, too.

I can accept that I'll be paying forever for failing to protect Holly. But damn if losing an opportunity like this doesn't burn in a man's gut.

Beside me, Spiral sits forward, tattooed forearms braced on the table, eyes hard and eager. "Did you already pick out your man, boss? Or are you still deciding?"

"I've got someone in mind," the prez says. "But I'm willing to consider alternatives. So spread the word among the brothers. If they're interested, they can come to me, and we'll have a conversation. *Now* is not that time," he adds when Spiral opens his mouth again.

The brother grins, holds up his hands. "I'll wait."

Nodding, the prez looks to me, and for a brief second I think he's going to ask whether I'll be asking for a conversation, too. Then his face hardens, his expression like a wolf scenting blood. "Next item on the agenda, Widowmaker?"

Farther down the table, the club's secretary looks at the paper in front of him. He's wearing his wire-rimmed glasses like he does every meeting, which makes him look like a badass Santa Claus. "A dumbshit asshole, boss."

That steely gaze never leaves my face. "You got any idea who that is, Duke?"

I've got no fucking idea. Still that burning knot in my gut twists tighter. "Not specifically. But I could make a long list of people who fit that description."

There's a few chuckles at that, but just as many uneasy glances. And the prez, when he smiles it's like that wolf's baring his teeth.

"Why don't you put Corey Harris at the top of that list," he says.

Corey Harris. My brother-in-law belongs at the top of *every* list of dumbshits. Right alongside my sister Sandy.

Fuck. "What's he done now?"

The prez hands that over to the Riders' warlord. "Blowback?"

The warlord's sitting on the other side of Zoomie, who sits back in her chair to give me a clear line of sight.

Nobody wants to be in Blowback's line of sight. Though I don't think the warlord's as crazy as some of the brothers do, there's no denying he's a cold, lethal fucker whose head simply doesn't work the same way as most people's heads work. He's not the kind of sick fuck who grew up pulling wings off flies or skinning cats or shit like that. But if a threat comes for the Hellfire Riders, he won't stop until that threat's eradicated. Not just dead, but minced into little pieces and scattered across the county. And he won't break a sweat while doing it.

The way he's looking now, my brother-in-law is damn close to becoming fertilizer. And no lie, the world would be better off if he was.

The world would be better off. Sandy, I'm not sure about. My sister loves the idiot. But then, she's almost as foolish as Corey is.

Almost, because there's no one as stupid as someone who does what Blowback says next.

"The Blue Coyotes gave him product to move. They got half its worth in return, and your brother-in-law told Howler no one was paying the prices the Coyotes were asking so he had to discount." The warlord's mouth twists. "Then he told Howler that if the Coyotes had a problem with the money going missing, they need to take it up with you. Called you out by name. And added that the Hellfire Riders would fuck up anyone who touched him, because he's related to you and under our protection."

Around the table, brothers are shaking their heads, half looking pissed and the other half disbelieving. Stealing the Coyotes' money is stupid enough. Using my name is stupider. But speaking lies about the Riders, issuing threats in our name and potentially damaging our relationships with other motorcycle clubs—that's fucking suicidal.

The prez leans forward, his stare burning the length of the table and into me. "The Coyotes only want their money. As it was the Hellfire Riders' name he whored out, they're allowing our club the courtesy of letting us deal with him. And as he's your relation, I'm giving *you* the courtesy of handling it."

Corey Harris isn't my relation. He's just the dumbshit who married my sister. It's fucking shameful that his name is even connected to mine.

But that's not the answer the prez is looking for. "This club's name won't pass his lips again," I tell him.

"You see it doesn't. Or next time I'll send Blowback."

To kill him—or at least make Corey wish he was dead. I wouldn't be sorry. Not until my sister started crying. So I'll take care of it.

I nod. "I'll see it done."

"Make sure Howler gets his cash, too."

There's no fucking hope that Corey will have it. But I nod, because this isn't the first time I've bailed that asshole out. At least with this babysitting job, I should be able to afford it. "I'll do that. How much?"

The prez looks to Blowback, who says, "Eight thousand."

Jesus. I see a few of the brothers wincing, because they know where that cash is coming from, too. Me, I'm just thinking that my brother-in-law isn't the only dumbshit. Someone in the Blue Coyotes must be, too, trusting him with that much meth.

But on that point, I keep my trap shut—and hope this damn job lasts a while. The longer it runs, the bigger my cut.

The prez finally eases back, looks to Widowmaker. "Next item?"

"Babysitting," the old man says, then looks up at me over the rims of his glasses. "A movie star."

I frown. "That slick asshole downstairs?" I've seen a lot of films in my day and I'm sure I've never seen his face before. "Or is 'movie star' a nice way of saying he's in porn?"

You rarely see those guys' faces. Thank fuck.

"His wife's the movie star," Thorne says, grinning as if he didn't just say *wife* and blow my whole day to shit.

Blow it to shit worse than it already is. And hell if I know why. All I had was one look at her long hair and longer legs and golden skin. Hearing she belongs to someone else shouldn't make my gut clench like I'm on the verge of puking. But it does.

I do my best to ignore it. "So she's in porn?"

With that ass, probably raking in the cash. And not just her husband touching her. A whole army of men fucking her.

And now my gut's twisting tighter.

Beside me, Spiral's laughing, shaking his head. "Not porn, brother."

"Well, what the hell is any other kind of movie star doing *here*? Whoever she is, whoever her husband is, they're not the type to look at the Hellfire Riders to babysit." I can't imagine how they even heard of us. The Riders don't advertise our services. People come to us by word-of-mouth, and that word doesn't exactly reach to Hollywood. It doesn't make any sense. "If they're paying twenty thousand a day, they've got cash to burn. And they've already got professional muscle. So why are we being hired to babysit the two of them?"

"Not both. Just the wife," Thorne says.

That makes even less sense. "So you're telling me a Hollywood actress is hiding away at our clubhouse by herself? You're saying her husband is leaving her here alone with a bunch of bikers?"

If she were mine, I wouldn't leave her alone with any of us.

Especially not Knucklehead, who throws in, "Fuck, man. You're complaining about watching a looker like that? Put me in charge of babysitting, then. I'll take *real* good care of her."

"Not a woman on this planet has ever said anything

you've done to her is 'real good,'" I tell him, and while the brothers are getting a laugh out of that, I look to Thorne again. "I don't give a fuck what she looks like. I'm saying that shit isn't adding up. And when shit doesn't add up, that means I'm missing critical info that might make the difference between me doing my job well or fucking it up."

The VP nods. "You aren't wrong. There's details we'll fill in for you after the meeting." He flicks a glance at the prez and at Blowback before sliding his gaze around the table. "Right now Molly's airing out the suite on the other side of the lodge. I don't expect our guest will venture out much, not with that face. She's too recognizable, and in this particular job, the most important thing is keeping her whereabouts a secret. So what everyone here needs to know is that mouths better be zipped tight. I hear any whisper about Keri Bishop being in town, any hint that she's out here on the ranch, I'm not stopping until I track down who opened their fucking mouths."

The bottom drops out of my stomach. "Did you say Keri Bishop?"

Thorne nods, his eyes gleaming with amusement. "That's right. So maybe you care what she looks like now?"

Not like he thinks. Not like any of the brothers are thinking as chuckles and grins start spreading around the table. Because these assholes don't have a lot of patience for bullshit, especially the kind of artificial bullshit that Hollywood serves up, but I'd bet half of them have jerked off to an image of Keri Bishop at one time or another.

Because, yeah. With her big blue eyes and soft full lips, she's a hell of a looker. A walking wet dream.

But although I know her face better than my own, I can't say my hand's ever strayed near my dick while looking at it. Because that face means something else to me.

A younger version of that face sang and danced her way through one of those Disney kid shows while my sisters were growing up. I didn't pay any attention then but Holly and Sandy did. A poster of a young Keri Bishop was hanging over Holly's bed the day she disappeared. And the movie we were at, that was Keri Bishop's, too. Holly begged me to take her, because she wanted to be just like Keri Bishop. So that girl's face was up on the screen while I was frantically searching every row of that theater.

And I saw that girl's face grow into a woman's face in other theaters, because I had the crazy hope that the sick fucker who took Holly would repeat what worked so well for him before. I had the crazy hope that I'd find him. That I'd save some other girl from the terror Holly must have lived through.

Now Keri Bishop herself is here—downstairs in the Hellfire Riders' clubhouse—and she'll be under my protection.

Some people might look at this as a second chance. Holly disappeared on my watch and now I've got an opportunity to make amends, protecting the woman Holly wanted to be. But I don't believe the universe gives second chances. Instead it lines you up for a second kick in the teeth, reminds you that no matter how much you've already paid, it wasn't enough. Soon you'll be paying again. And if I fuck up a job like this, I won't have anything left.

So Keri Bishop coming here isn't a second chance. Somehow, she'll be my punishment.

And I don't have a single damn hope she could be anything else.

TWO

OLIVIA

My teeth are *so* white.

Whenever I catch a glimpse in a mirror, I have to stop myself from staring at how dazzlingly bright they are. Two days ago, I considered my teeth fairly white. Or at least ivory. But now they could light up a room—or a biker gang's clubhouse, like the one I'm in now. I'm sitting at the bar facing a mirror and the flash of my teeth in the reflection keeps surprising me.

I thought my new eye color would be the hardest to

get used to. Contact lenses have transformed my irises from hazel to Keri Bishop's famous sky blue, but although the difference was startling at first, I've already become accustomed to that change.

But I can't get over my teeth. Maybe it's not because of how white they are, though. Maybe it's because I can't stop smiling.

Maybe because I've never had so much to smile about.

I *shouldn't* be smiling. The threat to Keri Bishop's life must be serious. Her husband, Ivan Tataurov, is spending a fortune to keep her safe—and that includes the small fortune he's paying me to impersonate her.

Not that I'll see a cent of that million dollars. But I don't care.

I don't care about the money or the suitcases full of designer clothes and shoes that I'll keep when this is done. I don't care about the jewelry—including the wedding and engagement rings adorning my finger—that I'll be able to sell for another small fortune.

I care about the custody agreement that Ivan's lawyers are drawing up—and I care about my stepfather's promise to sign it as soon as I hand over the million dollars.

And finally, *finally*, I will take Erin and get as far away from him as we can.

Just the thought of escaping my stepfather fills me with so much emotion, so much relief and joy, that I'll either laugh or cry. But crying would ruin the carefully applied makeup that subtly contours my nose and reshapes my eyes to more perfectly match Keri Bishop's. So instead of crying, I've been smiling more than I should.

More than *Keri* should, considering the circumstances. And of course Ivan notices that I'm not playing my role.

His grim look immediately wipes away my smile. Softly I bite my bottom lip, trying to appear as a woman like Keri would appear at this moment, when a psycho stalker is bent on killing her. I don't really know the details. But I know she loves Ivan, and he's supposedly leaving her in the protection of these bikers so that he and his security team can hunt down the threat. So I should appear apprehensive—not particularly worried for my own life, because I've been assured the psycho won't find me here— but terrified for Ivan. I should be clinging to him, milking every drop of emotion from these final moments together because I love him so desperately.

The truth is, though…I'm not a very good actor. I don't think Ivan is, either.

I don't really know *what* he is, aside from ruthlessly driven to protect his wife. Which is admirable. Beyond that, however, there's not much information out there about him.

Not that he doesn't show up on a Google search. He does. But every article and photo relates to Keri, not Ivan. Before they started dating—and before their marriage— he might as well not have existed. He owns a hotel and casino in Las Vegas, but an online search doesn't reveal much else. Just that he's a wealthy businessman.

A businessman I recognized when he showed up at my stepfather's door five days ago. Nothing Keri Bishop does passes me by, though not by my choice. If she hits the gossip blogs or releases a new movie, half my customers at the diner will mention it at some point during my day. So when she got married, pictures of Ivan and the happy bride were constantly shoved into my face.

I used to amuse myself thinking that Ivan was kind of a lookalike, too, because in all of his photos there's a strong resemblance to Alexander Skarsgård. That resemblance fades away in person. Not that I've seen the actor in person. But I don't really think Ivan looks like Skarsgård anymore.

Instead Ivan has started to remind me of my stepfather. Not violent, necessarily—Ivan's not, as far as I've seen. But just that I feel safer when his attention is somewhere else. And I don't *ever* want to find out what his reaction might be if I mess this up or if I cross him, because I have a feeling it won't turn out so well for me.

But I won't mess this up. I can't. My stepsister is counting on me to protect her. And I will, just as I always have. No matter the cost.

If everything goes as it should, that cost will only be a million dollars.

And I *really* need to stop smiling whenever I think about that custody agreement.

A quick glance at Ivan tells me he didn't notice this time. His focus is directed across the clubhouse, where it sounds as if a herd of buffalo is tromping down the stairs.

I look over my shoulder—carelessly, as a glamorous movie star would, though the small-town waitress I really am burns with curiosity.

Not a herd of buffalo. Just a dozen bikers. They were having a meeting upstairs but apparently that's over. Earlier I was briefly introduced to a bunch of them, but there are a couple I haven't met yet heading this way now. One's a bearded giant who appears mightily amused as he looks me over, which is preferable to the hungry, measuring glances a few of the others gave me before. The second guy is tall, too, though not as massive as his companion. Nor is he as hairy. His angular jaw is clean-shaven, and his dark blond hair is cut short. And he's not looking at me hungrily, either.

Instead he looks as if he wants a sinkhole to open beneath my feet. His pale green eyes rake the length of my body, his expression set like stone, his mouth thinned into a grim line.

A shiver races over my skin. Instinctively I shift closer to Ivan, which is crazy, because I don't exactly feel safe with *him*. But no matter how much disdain Ivan sometimes aims toward me, the bare fact is that he needs me to do this job. He might not like me but I'm necessary. So Ivan doesn't look at me as if he wishes I didn't exist—or as if he'll help me along to a state of not-existing.

The biker's jaw clenches as my bare arm brushes Ivan's sleeve. Razor sharp, his green gaze slices over to meet my fake husband's.

"You're Tataurov?" His voice is like a glacier, all slow-moving ice and gravel, and another shiver raises goosebumps across my skin. His big hand shoots out to shake Ivan's. "Duke. I'll be in charge of looking after your wife."

He says the last word like he's chewing a bite of something that he'd rather spit out.

Ivan doesn't notice or he doesn't care. Instead he frowns. "Your club's president is not in charge of her security?"

"He's in charge of deciding who we watch. I'm in charge of how we watch them." Duke withdraws his hand, not looking at all bothered that Ivan didn't take it. "And the prez is a busy man. Whereas me, this is all I do. But if you want someone with a thousand other demands on his time to look after your woman, just say the word and I'll go see how he feels about spending the next few days babysitting."

I've met the Hellfire Riders' president, who seemed steely cold and unimpressed by Ivan—which is a far cry from the regimented deference Ivan's own security shows him, and a far *far* cry from the fawning obeisance shown by the bevy of stylists and aestheticians who've spent the past three days transforming me into Keri Bishop. Indeed, all of these bikers have seemed unimpressed by Ivan, as if they don't give a single damn about him or his wealth. With me—with *Keri*—some of their badass attitudes have cracked a little, but still their responses are nothing like the overwhelming reactions I've gotten from strangers who mistook me for her before.

Yet this biker, Duke—his attitude goes beyond *unimpressed* and straight into *wouldn't spit on you if you were on fire*. Because Duke basically just told Ivan that if his being in charge is a problem, then Ivan can take his twenty-thousand-a-day and go screw himself with it.

I'm not sure if the best person to protect me is someone who doesn't give a flying flip about me. But apparently this guy's response satisfies Ivan.

"No distractions, yes?" he says.

Duke nods. "None."

"That is very good." Ivan's fingers lace through mine and gently squeeze, which probably appears affectionate, but his voice is stiff and his faint Russian accent deepens as he adds, "My beautiful Keri must be kept safe."

A noncommittal grunt is Duke's response to that. His attention shifts to the bearded giant—Bull.

I really appreciate how all of these guys wear their names on their vests.

"Will you see her settled in?" Duke asks him. "I'll round up the brothers I'm bringing in on this."

The giant nods easily. "I'll do that."

Duke's gaze skips over me and lands on Ivan again. "Bull will take care of her. Anything else I ought to know before you hand her off and head out?"

"Only that I do not tolerate failure." Although it sounds like a line from a villain in an action movie, I don't think Ivan's acting.

I also don't think his message is only for Duke.

A sardonic smile twists the biker's mouth. But he doesn't respond to the implied threat. Instead he simply gives a short nod before turning away, his long strides carrying him past Ivan's hulking security guards as if he doesn't notice—or care—that they're there.

As soon as he goes, the tension tightening my skin eases, but I still can't tear my gaze from his retreating back. Over the years, I've developed a sense about some men. Guys like my stepfather, like Ivan—my gut warns me to tread warily around them. Now my instincts are screaming that Duke's a danger to me, too…but it's not the same kind of danger. I don't know *how* to categorize it because I certainly haven't felt it before. Because with my stepfather, with Ivan, I feel a lot safer when their attention is else-where. And Duke…

I *want* him to look at me.

But he doesn't glance back. Instead he stalks through the clubhouse's front door and the night swallows him up. Faintly I'm aware that Bull's saying something to Ivan— that maybe Ivan would like a few minutes alone with his wife before leaving.

His wife. That's me. And I'm supposed to be in love with him, not staring after another man.

So I gaze adoringly up at Ivan's handsome profile. "A few minutes alone would be lovely, Bull. Thank you."

And I screwed that up. Because Ivan's fingers tighten

on mine and faint disapproval firms his mouth. "We will take a moment out by the vehicles. Walk with me outside, love."

He doesn't finish talking before tugging me forward, and I have to race-walk to keep up with him—not easy to do in these shoes. The Jimmy Choo sandals are more comfortable than any heels I've worn before, but I'm still adjusting to the height of them. Keri is about an inch taller than I am, so every bit of footwear Ivan bought for me increases my height by that difference, plus two or three more inches. And although I'm used to spending all day on my feet, it's usually in sneakers, not peep toe sandals with needle-thin heels.

Outside, the chill night air immediately sinks through my thin silk dress. I don't remember which designer label was sewn into the inside seam, but whoever made this white silk sheath obviously pictured summer days in Los Angeles, not September evenings in central Oregon. When we arrived at the clubhouse late this afternoon the air was much warmer, but now it's a little too brisk for my Louisianan blood.

Even before Ivan stops, though, I realize my Louisianan blood is the problem, because it spills out in my accent. Try as I might, I can't speak in those flat tones that the California-born Keri does. We've already concocted a story as cover—that Keri is practicing her Southern accent for an upcoming film—but if Ivan had his way, I'd spend the entire time here with my lips sewn together.

"Give us space," he orders the security following at our heels, and they immediately back off. Ivan keeps going, past the SUVs that brought us here, almost to the end of the clubhouse building, where the angle of the vehicles and a pool of shadows conceal us from the men standing back near the entrance. Probably everyone thinks that he's giving me a passionate good-bye in private, but I know he won't kiss me. The one good thing I can say about him: he's devoted to his wife. In all this time, he's only touched my hand, and only does that for show.

Now he pivots to face me, his voice low and dangerous. "There's only one thing you need to remember while you're here, and that's to keep your stupid mouth shut. Can you do that?"

Anger spits fire through my veins but no matter what Ivan believes about my brainpower, my mama didn't birth a stupid baby. I keep my mouth shut and simply nod. Because he's not just talking about my accent—he's talking about the warning he drilled into me over and over the past few days: *No one can know you aren't Keri. If you tell a single person or do something to reveal yourself, the deal is off. No money, no custody agreement. Nothing.*

I can't afford to ruin this deal. Erin can't afford for me to ruin it.

And he's not done. "You are *Keri Bishop*," he reminds me. "You are a goddess who walks red carpets. Men crawl at your feet. Women dream of being you. You have *nothing* to say to this biker trash and nothing in common with them. Can you remember that?"

Again I nod. This time it's not enough.

His eyes narrow. "Let me hear it, then."

I can't keep the acid off my tongue. "I've got nothing in common with this trash," I say in my accent that gives lie to every word.

Because I've got nothing in common with Keri, except a face. And even though I'm more than two thousand miles from Winnfield, Louisiana, these bikers are a lot closer to home than my new Jimmy Choos are.

"So you don't cozy up to them and you don't run your mouth, and everything will work out as it should. Understood?"

"Understood," I echo woodenly.

His cold gaze searches my face. Finally he nods and calls out to his security team that he's ready. "You had best head back in," he tells me and looks toward the clubhouse entrance, where Bull is waiting for me to return.

"I will in a minute," I say sweetly. "As your loving wife, I ought to see you off." *And say good riddance when your tail lights vanish down the road.*

I don't add the last, but the warning in his final look tells me that my tone said it clearly enough. Hugging my bare arms to my chest, I paste on a smile and wait in the shadows while he and his security team load into the SUVs. As soon as the engines start, I let out a huge, relieved breath.

Then suck it in again when the rasp and flare of a

lighter comes from behind me.

Duke. He's standing in the darkness just around the corner of the building, shoulder casually braced against the side of the lodge, his hand cupped around the end of a cigarette. The flame highlights the strong planes of his face and reflects like a demon's glow in the sea green of his eyes.

Suddenly all the tension's back, my spine so stiff that my neck muscles begin aching. How much did he hear? Did Ivan or I say anything that exposed me as a fraud?

I don't know. He's looking straight at me as he lights the cigarette but I can't read his expression.

Then he flicks the Zippo lighter closed and all but disappears into the shadows again, invisible except for the glowing tip of his cigarette. I can still feel him watching me, though.

And because I don't know what else to do, I smile at him. There's no way he can miss it. Not with these teeth, as bright as the sun.

A chuckle rumbles out of the dark, but it's not a nice sound. Neither is what accompanies it. "No matter how pretty your feet are, Mrs. Tataurov, I have no intention of crawling at them. So you pack away that sweet smile. It's wasted on trash like me, anyway."

Oh, dear Lord. So focused on wondering if my identity was discovered, I forgot Duke might have heard that part, too. Dismayed, I shake my head. "I didn't really—"

"Save it for someone who gives a shit." His cigarette

drops to the ground and a moment later even that soft glow is extinguished. "And get your ass back inside. When your husband returns, I sure as hell don't want to tell him that you froze to death the first fucking night."

I don't think Ivan would care, because when he comes back, it means the danger to Keri has been eliminated. And it's not *that* cold out there. Just chilly.

But there's nothing else to say—and even if there was, Duke obviously doesn't want to hear me say it. So I lift my chin, square my shoulders, and let my Jimmy Choos carry me back to the clubhouse. And as far as impersonating Keri Bishop goes, at least now I'm doing one thing right.

Because I'm not smiling anymore.

THREE

DUKE

Something about this babysitting job feels real fucking *wrong*.

Not just the way my dick hardens every time I look at her. She's married, for fuck's sake. And my cock sure as hell has never reacted that way before, seeing her onscreen or her pictures. Instead I always only saw Holly.

In person, though… Christ. Nothing about her seems the same. Keri Bishop's a big name and everything I've ever seen of her says she's got boldness to match her fame.

But instead of swagger, I see vulnerability. I see a sweetness and a tartness all at once, and hell if something in me doesn't want to taste both.

Not that trash like me would ever get a chance.

Shaking my head, I crush out my second cigarette of the night and head back inside. I don't smoke much. But I need to do something with my mouth, my hands. Something that doesn't involve touching a married woman.

A married woman whose husband treats her as if she's a stupid child.

And there's the other bit that's wrong. A woman like that and her asshole of a husband didn't even kiss her before leaving. Didn't drag her into the shadows and get that short skirt up and her legs wrapped around him. If she were mine, I'd fuck her so hard she'd be feeling me inside her until the day I returned. Except if she were mine, I wouldn't leave her here under another man's protection in the first place. Especially knowing that man is me, and that I get real hungry every time I look at her.

None of it makes any damn sense.

Inside the clubhouse, Zoomie and Gunner are racking the balls at the pool table. Knucklehead's settled down on one of the couches, the television tuned to a game. Most of the others have already gone home—and Bull must have taken Keri to the suite because they aren't here now. I'll be following them over to that side of the lodge soon, but first I head upstairs. Thorne said there's more details about this job to fill in.

I find him, the prez, and Blowback still in the conference room—with Spiral just leaving, no doubt after putting in his first bid for that enforcer's patch. I bump his fist on the way in. Spiral would serve the club well.

I'd still rather be the one wearing that patch.

That's not why I'm here, though. And I don't waste any time before getting to it. "So how the hell did Keri Bishop end up *here*? And am I right in thinking that when the first agenda was sent out this morning, you had no idea she was coming?"

We've had some jobs come up on us quick, but Tataurov doesn't strike me as a man who does anything without planning for a while.

But the prez has a question of his own first. "Who are you bringing in on this?"

Because I'll essentially be looking after her twenty-four seven, but I've still got to sleep—and there's that shit with Corey to take care of, which will pull me away for at least a couple of hours. Plus the clubhouse's general security will be heightened, and I can't look after Keri and keep an eye on the property's security cameras at the same time.

"Bull's with her now," I tell him. But although the giant biker used to sit a lot of these jobs with me, now that he's settled down with Sara, he won't want to stay at the clubhouse for extended periods of time. "But he'll only pick up a couple of hours a day. I'm bringing in Picasso, Scarecrow, and Grasshopper—and I put a bug in Grasshopper's ear about bringing in Maurice, too."

Waiting for Grasshopper to come out and have that conversation was why I was outside when Tataurov dragged his wife over to my corner of the clubhouse and didn't kiss her good-bye.

The prez's eyes narrow as he slowly nods. Probably thinking the same thing I am—the job will not only earn Maurice some cash to help with those damn medical bills, but also give him something to do besides popping pain pills.

Then he says, "You'll likely want to add a few more."

A few more. Four men means high security on a job, which I figured a Hollywood actress warranted. I've never pulled in more. Never needed more. Not out here. Nobody's ever been stupid enough—or crazy enough—to attack the Hellfire Riders' clubhouse. While babysitting on someone else's property, it's happened plenty of times. But not here.

"All right." With tension suddenly knotting my gut, I glance away from the prez's face to Thorne's and Blowback's. Both appear grim as hell. "So who's coming for her?"

"Pyotr Alekseevich Zhuk," Blowback says flatly. "Does that mean anything to you?"

I've never heard that name before. Hell, I'm not even sure I could spell it. "Not a damn thing."

"There's three reasons for that. Number one is that Zhuk is a member of the Suvurovskaya bratva and you'd be lucky to find his name or photo anywhere. Number two is that he operates out of the Eastern European block and Russia. Number three is because most people who hear that name end up dead, so it doesn't get around."

Number three could be said about Blowback, too. I don't know what exactly he did for Uncle Sam before joining up with the Hellfire Riders, but the stories he's told and some of the shit he knows makes me real glad he's on our side.

It's also why any information he gathers is a hell of a lot deeper than a motorcycle club might usually get.

"So why's a Russian mobster gunning for an actress?" Unless he's not after her. *Ivan* is a Russian name if there ever was one. "Or is he really after Tataurov?"

"Zhuk's after her," Thorne says. "The story Tataurov gave us—and Blowback verified—is that she starred in one of those public service videos to raise awareness about human trafficking. This one was aimed toward Eastern Europe, and it showed pictures of girls sold into sexual slavery, crime photos, that kind of thing. One of the photos also showed Zhuk's brother in the background. So his face got out there, he was recognized, and now he's rotting in some Russian shithole prison."

"And now Zhuk wants revenge."

"He's gotten it." Thorne starts ticking off his fingers. "The video's director, producers, cameramen—all gutted in their homes. And they were all based in Europe, but Tataurov got word that Zhuk entered the U.S. a week ago."

"'Got word?'" I echo, shaking my head. "If this fucker

is so deep under that no one knows his name, how'd Tataurov hear he was coming? Or is her husband mixed up in that bratva shit, too?"

"Born into it." Blowback grabs one of the pizza boxes and drops it onto the table before sitting and digging in, as if this discussion rates the same level of worry to him as watching a football game. "Word is, he's gotten out of the business and keeps his hands clean."

Word doesn't mean shit. "Are they clean?"

The warlord shrugs. "Depends on how you look at it. A cop wouldn't find anything to pin on him. But any business he's involved in seems to go real smooth."

"You think his connections pave the way for him?" I ask and his nod confirms it. "So he keeps his hands clean by paying someone else to dirty theirs."

"Maybe not paying money. Maybe trading favors." Blowback polishes off his first slice and reaches for another. "They do something for him, he opens up a path to do business with his family."

"And that family's how he heard Zhuk was coming?"

The warlord nods. "And those favors were how he got here."

"I got a call around noon from the prez of the Iron Pagans, the Las Vegas chapter." The prez leans back in his chair, appearing relaxed but the intensity of his gaze on me is anything but. "He told me Tataurov needed somewhere to hide her away, with someone who didn't have any connection to his family or his business associates."

So there would be no trail leading Zhuk to her. "Is Tataurov worried about a leak?"

The prez's response is dry. "I think more worried that Zhuk might make even a loyal man talk."

By torturing him. But if no one knows anything, then there's no one who can give information.

Except someone always knows something. "What about the security team that was here? Or the Iron Pagans?"

"The security team will be with Tataurov. Of the Iron Pagans, their prez is the only one who knows. So if one of them is compromised while she's here, we'll know it quick."

"And meanwhile, Tataurov's men are hunting down Zhuk?"

"Trying to lure him out," Thorne says. "Apparently they'll be posting fake info to fan sites online. Saying she has a reservation at a restaurant, maybe—or a hotel maid will supposedly say on a message board that she spotted Keri hiding out. Then they'll hope Zhuk shows up."

"And her husband thinks that shit will work?"

The prez simply nods, but an amused gleam in his eyes has me glancing at Blowback.

"You're doing a little hunting, too?"

"Watching and listening, right now." His flat, empty gaze holds as much emotion as a dead man's. "Watching to see if that online shit is what Tataurov actually does. And if Zhuk is searching for her, he'll leave a trail. Even if he tries to cover it up, a pattern will start forming. So I'm keeping an eye out for that pattern."

A trail of bodies, most likely. Keri's won't be among them.

But making sure of that means taking steps we don't usually take. "You got any issue with me putting the clubhouse on lockdown? No one but brothers in and out."

The prez nods. "I'll have Widowmaker put the word out."

"And I'll want every brother's cell phone left at the door." Getting a signal out here is all but impossible, but it's not a connection I'm worried about. Just one brother sharing a picture of Keri might bring Zhuk straight to us. I glance at Thorne. "What about Molly? Do you want her to stay home and we pick up our meals from there?"

If the Hellfire Riders had a den mother, it would be the VP's old lady. Molly oversees the housekeeping around here, and is queen of the lodge's big old kitchen. That's where she cooks up the food for the meetings and anything else we need while babysitting. Most of the time we're looking after assholes who we don't even want near her, so we stick them out in one of the cabins and just bring in the meals she whips up for them. But Keri Bishop's staying in the lodge's big suite and it'll be damn hard to keep Molly from crossing her path.

"Molly ought to be all right," Thorne says with a faint smile. "She already knows Keri's staying in the lodge, and I'm not sure I could keep her away if I tell her that you'll be the one cleaning up after Ms. Bishop."

I wouldn't be doing any cleaning. I'd be delegating

that shit to the brothers I'll be bringing in on this job. Unless it's her laundry. If anyone's going to be handling her panties, that'll be me.

Christ. And here I am, thinking about jacking off into a married woman's underwear.

And despite all this talking about Zhuk and hiding her away with a club that has no connection to Tataurov, that's the part of all this that still doesn't make sense. Because Keri Bishop is a married woman. Yet her husband dumped her here, left her surrounded by people he didn't know could be trusted—as if he didn't think she was worth more than the trash he called us.

Maybe I'm a pathetic sap, believing a man wouldn't do that to the woman he loves. But I don't think so. I look to the prez. "Would you ever leave Jenny here like this? Not with the Riders"—he'd trust us to look after her—"but, say…with the Blue Coyotes?"

Something fires in his eyes at the mention of his woman. Something dark and dangerous, as if he's imagining someone like Zhuk coming after her. "Not a fucking chance."

Yeah. "What about Molly?"

Thorne shakes his head.

And although it's treading a tight line, suggesting a Hellfire Rider might run up against any danger she couldn't handle herself, I ask Blowback, "And Zoomie?"

He just looks at me.

That's all right. I know the answer. "You'd keep her

with you."

Because when you'd die to protect the woman you love, when you'd kill anyone who tried to come after her, when you'd tear the world apart before seeing her hurt, there's nowhere safer for her than right by your side.

And that settles it. "But Tataurov left her? Something about this whole setup is simply fucking *wrong*."

"Yeah, it is," the prez agrees. "But Blowback will keep his eyes on that and unravel whatever Tataurov's lying about. You keep your eyes on Keri Bishop, because as far as we can tell, Zhuk *is* coming after her."

Maybe. He sure as hell won't get to her, though. Because she might not be mine, but I know what to do with a woman who's depending on me—I'll keep her by my side.

That's where she ought to be now. Pushing back my chair, I stand. "You got anything else for me before I head over to the lodge?"

"The second Blowback has more, you'll know it." The prez tilts his head, eyeing me. He's a hard man to read, but I'd say he was looking expectant. "You got anything else for me?"

What else is there? Something about my dumb-shit brother-in-law? Or about putting in my bid for the enforcer's patch?

One isn't settled yet. The other I don't have a hope in hell of getting. "Not tonight, boss."

His steely gaze holds mine for a long second before

he nods. "We're done here, then."

Yeah. I'm feeling as if I fucked up that answer, but the second I'm out of the conference room, my head's already over in the opposite end of the lodge.

When the club took over the old dude ranch and transformed the guest lodge into the clubhouse, a good portion of the original rooms weren't touched. They weren't used much, either. I don't know what Red Erickson—the Steel Titans' president who owned the property up until he died this past year—had in mind when he divided up the building, but it might just be that the club didn't need all that space and he didn't want to deal with the upkeep of the entire lodge when the old lobby and a few other rooms and offices served the club's needs.

So the clubhouse and the rest of the lodge are closed off from each other, but access is easy enough. From the second floor, I just follow the hallway to where a wall addition serves as a partition between the two sections of the building. We don't even keep that door bolted, normally—though that will change while the clubhouse is on lockdown.

Second floor of the lodge's side is where all the old guest rooms were. Most of them are empty, but for these babysitting jobs there's a couple of suites that we keep stocked and cleaned—and locked, because if we didn't, the brothers would start using those big old beds to fuck their women in. They can use the empty rooms for that shit and save Molly the labor of cleaning up after their asses.

For the next while, though, aside from Molly and Keri Bishop, anyone who isn't a patchholder won't be allowed through the gates at the head of the driveway leading here. Those gates will be closed up, too—everyone entering will be required to stop and use the intercom, so that someone here at the clubhouse can let them through. Normally those gates are always open. Some of the brothers will bellyache about the hassle—and the lack of women—but if they need pussy they can always ride into town.

At the very end of the hall, a door opens to the rooms Keri Bishop will be staying in—though she's not there now. A pile of luggage is stacked in what used to be the lodge's high-end suite. She'll have a private bedroom and bath, along with a sitting area. And while she's here, I'll take over the adjoining room that opens up off the suite's foyer, so that no one can pass through the entrance to her rooms without going past me.

And she won't be able to do a damn thing without me knowing. I'll hear her bathing, knowing her golden skin's glistening and bare. I'll hear the quiet that means she's sleeping alone in that big bed.

My dick's already aching, just imagining it. No doubt living through the reality will be pure fucking torture. If she's my punishment, the universe did a damn fine job picking one.

Because I've never reacted like this to any woman. Now when I do, she's a married woman. A woman under my protection. And even if those two factors weren't part of the equation, she's still a woman who'd never want trash like me touching her, anyway.

But the only factor that matters is: she's under my protection.

Telling myself that doesn't ease the ache in my cock, though, and my mood's running hot and irritated as I head down the stairs to the kitchen. The air smells fucking amazing, so the VP's old lady apparently worked her magic in there.

This part of the lodge is Molly's domain. The old lobby and dining room have been taken over by the clubhouse, but she's got a restaurant-quality kitchen that opens up into an area she calls the day room. Big windows overlook the creek, and a pair of French doors open up to a wide porch, which I know from experience serves as a damn fine place to greet the morning with a coffee in hand. When it's too cold to sit outside, a pair of overstuffed chairs and a sofa face a stone fireplace. And just off the kitchen sits an oak dining table with benches running along either side like a fancy version of a picnic table.

That's where I find the brothers I've already called in, sitting around the table like they're at a church social. Each one has a foaming pint of ale sitting in front of him.

Grasshopper's facing me, so he notices me first, tipping his glass toward me with a wide grin. Either he already talked to Maurice and got an affirmative response or he's just feeling damn good about this job. Maybe both. Because when Picasso and Scarecrow look over their shoulders at me, they appear pretty damn pleased with themselves, too.

I don't see the two people I'm expecting to see. "Where's Bull and the woman?"

"The *woman*"—herself comes sailing out of the kitchen, loaded down with four steaming plates—"found out that Bull has a wife he was eager to get home to, so I told him to go. And since these kind gentlemen were here to look after me, he left me in their tender care."

As she's speaking, she's setting a plate in front of each of the brothers as smoothly as if she does it every damn day of her life. But no waitress ever wore a dress like that, creamy silk hugging every slim curve and barely long enough to cover any panties she might have on under there. Miles of tautly muscled, sun-kissed legs are supported by a pair of ridiculous heels.

Married. Woman.

My cock doesn't care. It just sees those bare golden thighs and imagines sliding between them.

Teeth grinding, I swing my gaze back to the brothers. "Why the fuck are you assholes making her wait on you?"

"Oh." With a single plate still in her left hand, she stops all at once, eyebrows raised as she looks the brothers over, her sultry red lips rounded in an O of surprise. "I didn't realize you were *all* assholes. I didn't intend on serving *him*"—she nods toward me—"because I thought he was the only asshole here. Ah well. Too late, I suppose."

Gracefully she places a plate next to Grasshopper's

and takes the seat beside him. I can't see Picasso's and Scarecrow's faces but Grasshopper is on the verge of losing it, lips mashed together and his head bowed, shoulders shaking.

She slants an innocent look at me through her thick lashes as she picks up her fork. "We didn't know how long you'd be, so Molly left another plate for you in the oven's warming drawer."

"Left?" Frowning, I head in that direction.

Picasso's answer follows me. "We told her not to worry about cleanup."

These fuckers wouldn't volunteer to scrub any dishes. Which means a certain actress must have suggested it and they fell over themselves agreeing.

"Duke?" The sweet Southern accent she's been faking rolls over my name and into me like a cannonball. "I left my wineglass on the counter. Would you be a darling and bring it out with you?"

Yeah, I'll be a fucking darling. Even though the fragrance of the red wine tells me exactly how her mouth would taste.

The ruby liquid sloshes around in the glass when I set it in front of her a little too forcefully. Now I have to decide between the torture of sitting across from her and watching her face, the sensual slide of every bite between her full lips—or the torment of sitting right next to her, all that golden skin only inches away.

I take the seat across from her, where I can't just see

her face, but get a continual eyeful of the giant sparkling rock on her ring finger.

That goddamn bastard didn't even kiss her good-bye.

Didn't kiss her good-bye and just left her here. For all her bravado, all the confidence she's displaying by sending Bull home and herding the brothers into a dish-washing troupe, she must be unsettled by all this shit, too. Because I can see it, hear it. Her voice is different—and that's not just the damn accent. It's deeper, huskier. Like maybe her throat's been roughed up from crying. And her expressions are just slightly off. I don't expect Keri Bishop onscreen to appear exactly like she does in real life, but still. Even acting, some things don't change. Her smile's different. Her wide-eyed innocent look is different.

And the only thing I can think of that accounts for that difference is she's more rattled by the threat to her life—and her husband dumping her here—than she's letting on.

But, shit. If Zhuk was after me, I'd be rattled, too.

Grabbing my fork, I dig into the roasted red potatoes piled beside sliced steak and peppers. I manage all right for myself in my kitchen at home, but no lie—I look forward to babysitting and Molly's dinners.

And now that we're settled in, there's no use putting this off. "Starting tonight, the clubhouse will be in lockdown. I'll also be bringing in four more brothers. They'll be doubling up at the entrances and sweeping the property line on the regular."

All the brothers' good humor vanishes. They know that means the threat coming is a hell of a lot bigger than any that's come before. And although our guest couldn't know what the Hellfire Riders' usual babysitting operation looks like, she's obviously no slouch when it comes to reading faces. Quietly she examines Picasso's and Scarecrow's grim expressions before turning to me.

A little frown pleats her brow—and that's different, too. Keri Bishop shows her worry with her lips, not her forehead. Go onto any online message board any day of the week, and a gif of that full mouth curving downward will pop up somewhere.

"Is that an unusual amount of security?" she asks quietly.

"It is." I meet those big blue eyes, see her worry has deepened. "You want to fill them in about Zhuk or you want me to tell them?"

She blinks as if in confusion, her gaze searching mine. "I…don't know any of the details. Just that I've got a stalker—and that there's no chance he would find me here."

A *stalker*? That's what Tataurov told her?

How the fuck is that protecting her? No one was *ever* better off for being ignorant about a threat coming after them. Especially a threat like Zhuk.

Anger has a grip on my throat, roughening my response. "Whether that bastard finds you or not, he's not going to get to you." I pause while the brothers offer up their agreement and reassurance on that point, then continue. "But keeping you safe means you follow all our rules. Did Bull lay them out for you?"

Silently she nods, her full red mouth looking soft and vulnerable as she nervously traps her bottom lip between her square white teeth.

"I want to hear them," I tell her. Not because I don't think she listened or remembers, but because I want to hear that throaty voice and gliding accent again.

She rolls her eyes. "No calling or texting anyone. No accessing any of my accounts online. No going anywhere outside without an escort. No leaving any room without telling someone where I'm going."

Good. To the others I say, "I want one man watching the security feeds and manning the driveway gate at all times. You'll rotate in four-hour shifts, and I don't care how goddamn boring it gets, there better not be any dicking around or watching porn. Eyes on the screens."

His narrow face grave, Scarecrow asks, "Who are we watching for?"

"He goes by Zhuk. We don't have a goddamn clue what he looks like. The only thing we've got is a picture of his brother—and from that, I'd say he's white, maybe thirty to forty years old, and connected to some bratva shit, so he'll probably have tats visible on his fingers and his neck." Elsewhere, too, but unless he's coming naked, we wouldn't see them. "So that means no one comes in who isn't wearing a Riders' patch, because for all we know he can pass for a girl and sneak in on the back of a brother's ride."

"And why's he after her?" Picasso asks me before looking across the table. "You don't know?"

She shakes her head, still wearing that pleated brow and that soft, vulnerable expression. Her eyes meet mine. "Did they tell you?"

"They did." So I give them what I know, and watch her face grow paler, her eyes bigger, her teeth digging deeper into her bottom lip.

"Jesus." Grasshopper whistles between his teeth when I finish up. "All because of a video trying to help some girls?"

Picasso stabs a spud with his fork. "No good deed goes unpunished, and all that shit."

"I guess not," she says softly, and her fingers are nervously clenching the wine glass like it's the only thing keeping her at the table instead of bolting away, searching for a place to hide. "Do you think he'll find me here?"

I'm not going to lie to her. "Your husband made sure there was as little trail as he could. But there's always a trail, so it's possible."

"Unlikely, though?" Hope lifts through her voice.

"Yeah," I tell her. "Unlikely."

Her smile is sweet and blinding. Beside me, Picasso goes still—then abruptly starts laughing.

"Christ Almighty. Keri fucking Bishop is sitting right across from me, and she's even prettier and sexier in person."

Her cheeks go scarlet. Something in her gaze flickers, her smile faltering, then suddenly she's laughing, too.

And fuck me, that laugh. Just as throaty and rolling as her voice.

"Now, c'mon." The asshole leans forward, taps his cheek. "You going to give me something to dream about? Lay one on this ugly mug. Be the princess who turns the frog into a prince."

"You hush," she says, still laughing, but her hand comes up—with that fucking diamond winking—and she cups his jaw, lifting up out of her seat to touch her lips to his cheek.

"Shit," the joker says as she sits back, running his hands over his crooked face. "Am I pretty again? Because that felt like magic. Tell me I'm pretty."

"You still look like a junkie kicked in your face while you were passed out drunk in the county jail," I tell him dryly, and under the table my hands are fists. But I'm not punching a brother just because he got a kiss that I'd kill for.

Just because he got what I shouldn't even be wanting.

"Is that what happened?" she asks, her gaze sliding over his busted features.

"Yeah." He sounds abashed, as if he's embarrassed by it, but I know for a fact that the junkie getting the jump on him bothers him more than what the fucker did to his face. "If that hadn't happened, this mug would have taken me to Hollywood for sure. I'd be a big movie star, too. Probably kissing you after I save the day."

She tilts her head, a teasing glint in her eyes. "I'm sure I'd prefer that to kissing Shia LaBeouf."

"I don't know who the hell that is," Picasso says, "but I can guarantee you it'd be better with me."

"You don't know?" Her hand flattens over her chest in mock-astonishment. "But *Her Serving Grace* is my most popular film. And I really was a princess in that. Though I didn't kiss any frogs. Just Shia."

"A duchess, actually. And you also kissed that smug fucker McAvoy at the end when you decided to stay married to him."

Every eye turns to me.

I don't know what the hell they're looking at. Because, sure—I saw it a couple of times at different theaters, hoping to spot the pervert who took Holly. But any man who has known, fucked, or been related to any woman has been forced to sit down and watch that flick sometime in the past ten years. "You assholes say you haven't seen it, you're goddamn liars. It's the one where she runs away from her new husband"—after entering into an arranged marriage with some stiff-necked duke—"and goes slumming in a diner, pretending to be a waitress and screwing around with the cook."

She's giving me a funny look I can't read. "That's the one," she says faintly.

"Ah yeah," Picasso says while Grasshopper and Scarecrow nod, indicating they're finally remembering, too. "I fucking hated that one."

Me, too. But I hate all of her movies. And I can't watch them without feeling all over again how I failed Holly.

Looking at her in person, though. That's real damn easy.

Especially when that sweet smile appears again, as if she's not the least bit bothered by Picasso hating a film she was in. Instead she asks him, "So if you'd have been a movie star, does that mean you're an actor? I thought you might be an artist."

He gives her blank look. "An artist?"

"Well, yeah. Or is your biker name more like, 'I'll paint the walls with the blood of my enemies?'"

Oh shit. I start laughing, and Picasso's finally catching on, too.

"No, duchess," I tell her. "Think about it."

Her brows knit together when she frowns. I see the moment she gets it, puts the name together with the crooked arrangement of his features, and how she's not sure whether it's funny or horrifying. By her expression, a little of both.

By her response, she intends to pretend that she never asked. "So you're not an actor?"

"Nah, not me." Grinning, Picasso shakes his head. "Not pretty enough. Now our boy Gunner—you met him?"

She nods, sipping her wine.

"He could."

"Maybe." She sets down her glass. "Looks are only part of the reason someone would be successful in Hollywood. Or anywhere else."

Beside her, Grasshopper snorts. "Easy for you to say."

"It *is* easy for me to say." For a moment she bites her lip, then continues, "About seven years ago, *People* magazine ran this series of articles about celebrity lookalikes. They found mine—she was this sixteen-year-old girl in a tiny Louisiana town—and so I flew there, we had this big photoshoot where they made her up, did her hair, everything to erase the little differences between us. The whole time she was so excited, and you could just see in her eyes, her face…she thought it was the moment that would change her life. There she was, being told she's as beautiful as one of the most popular actresses in the country, so something in her horrible little life *has* to change, right?" Her voice goes thicker, her accent deeper. "But all she had was that face. No talent. Couldn't sing, couldn't act. She was smart enough, but nothing special. And so she'll never get out of that damn town where everyone knows every sin she's ever committed, and because of that she'll never be anything more than a waitress in a greasy-spoon diner—no matter how pretty she is, and no matter how hard she tries."

"Jesus fucking Christ, you're a real piece of work." Blood thundering in my head, I drop my fork to my plate. *This* was the woman Holly wanted to be? Thank fuck my sister never met her. Not this woman who'd have labeled her a talentless waste of space. "Sitting here in your thousand-dollar dress, shitting on some girl for dreaming of having just a little bit of what you've been lucky enough to get."

Her eyes narrow. "You think it's just luck?"

"I have no fucking idea. But I'll tell you what, duchess—I'll take that no-talent girl who works her ass off and who keeps trying to improve her life over the woman who's so damn full of herself she can't see how fucking fortunate she is to be where she is now."

Those blue eyes regard me for what feels like a long damn time, though she should be looking away, ashamed of herself. Instead a soft warmth fills her steady gaze and her smile spreads again.

With a lift of her glass in my direction, she replies, "If you'd take a regular girl over a movie star, I guess you aren't an asshole, after all."

Yeah, I am. And chances are, I'll prove how much of an asshole I can be before the night is through. But for now, her unexpected response has me so turned around, I don't know what the hell to say.

So I shut up and eat.

FOUR

OLIVIA

My rooms are big, and more elegant than I really expected from a defunct dude ranch. I expected elk heads on the walls and handwoven blankets on the beds. Instead the dark paneling and heavy furnishings seem better suited to the luxury hotel in Charleston where Ivan hid me away with his team of stylists.

Apparently Keri was briefly at the same hotel, though I never saw her. I suspect she went in as herself and those stylists transformed her into someone else before she left—

so that anyone stalking her wouldn't know the person still there was just a lookalike.

A lookalike who left with Keri's luggage.

I don't know whether I should unpack everything. The way Ivan talked about this job, it wasn't going to last more than a few days. A week at most. Surely not long enough to wear two extra-large suitcases' worth of brand-new designer clothes.

But after what Duke said about this Zhuk guy, I can't imagine the threat being eliminated so quickly. It sounded as if Zhuk is good at flying under the radar. And it's great that he probably won't find me here…but if finding *him* is just as difficult, this might take a while. Maybe a month or two.

And that worries me.

I've already been away from home for four days. Erin knows that I might be gone a couple of weeks—and she should be safe during that time. As messed up as it is, my stepfather has a certain code that he follows regarding his punishments. Younger than thirteen, harsh words are enough. Older than thirteen, all bets are off.

Erin's only just turned twelve, and she's good at reading his moods—and when he's in a bad one, good at making herself scarce. It breaks my heart how good she is at it.

I hate knowing that she learned it from me.

But this job—and the custody agreement my stepfather will sign when I hand over the money—will change all of that. It has to. And if it doesn't, I'll do whatever it takes to get her away from him, no matter the consequences. I've tried taking her away before and it backfired in a big way. But if I have custody, legal custody, everything will be okay.

So for now…for now I'll just travel this route. No matter how long it takes.

I end up unpacking everything because I don't have anything else to do, anyway. I don't feel like watching TV, and I don't have a computer with me. A grand piano takes up one corner of the sitting room, but I don't play. Books are stuffed into a small case, but I can't imagine settling down long enough to read. Not tonight.

So instead I fill the closet with my clothes and shoes, then I start in on the cases full of makeup and beauty products. The past three days, pretty much every inch of my skin has been waxed, my teeth bleached, my blond hair recolored with lowlights and highlights and restyled—all so that I can maintain a Hollywood-level appearance when I'm on my own. Working with the team of stylists that Ivan provided was kind of fun, at first. Now it feels like more of a chore. Usually I just pull my hair up into a ponytail, but now I'll be spending almost an hour every morning on my hair alone.

But I guess it doesn't matter. I don't have a job to rush to in the morning. Instead my job is looking like Keri. So I'll put on the scads of makeup and style my hair for hours and wear my thousand-dollar dresses.

Or five-hundred dollar dresses, which was the price listed on the tag I snipped off the label this morning. Duke disappeared into the room off the entrance to my suite about an hour ago, and a little part of me wants to knock on his door and let him know that the white silk sheath was only half as expensive as he thinks. But since a five-hundred dollar dress is just as ridiculous, it wouldn't be much of a victory.

Especially since my shoes are fifteen-hundred dollars and my underwear is another couple of hundred. Which is *beyond* ridiculous.

So instead I kick off my Jimmy Choos and leave Duke alone.

My mind doesn't leave him alone, though. As I pin up my hair and step into the shower, I'm thinking of his light green eyes. Before my dad died, and before my mom married James and when we still lived in our house on Magnolia Lane, a framed print called "The End of the Storm" hung over the bed in the guest room—a painting of a boat plowing into a towering ocean wave. Set at night, the water was dark except at the crest of the wave where the light shone through, and there it was a pale green. The same stormy green as Duke's eyes. Maybe that's why I like them so much—they remind me of that painting and of happier times.

Or maybe it's because he's obviously one of the good guys.

I suspect he wouldn't agree. But he doesn't have to. I

learned a long time ago that there are two kinds of men in the world—the ones who will hurt you and the ones who will help you. And no matter how gruff and angry he sounds, no matter how irritated he seems by my presence, Duke intends to help me.

Wrapped in a towel, I stand at the sink and finish getting ready for bed. With the makeup off, with the contact lenses out, I'm Olivia Burke again—except for my shiny highlighted hair and my blinding white teeth.

I'm brushing those teeth when the ring of my cell phone trills through the suite. For a second I stand there with my toothbrush hanging out of my foaming mouth. Who'd call me?

Only one person.

Erin.

Heart leaping, I spit into the sink and race for the crystal-studded Prada bag I left on the table near the suite's entrance. I dig the phone out and hit the answer button just as the door to Duke's room opens. Shirtless, he stalks into the foyer, his light green eyes lasering toward me and landing on my phone.

Oh shit. Turning my back, I head toward my bedroom, clutching the towel to my chest.

"Erin?" I whisper into the phone. "Honey, is everything okay?"

"Livvie? Is that you?"

She's whispering, too, not because she's worried that Duke will overhear her sister's name but because it's two hours later in Louisiana and she's supposed to be in bed. But I know where she probably is—huddled on the floor of our bathroom with the lights turned off, so James most likely won't hear her or realize that she's up.

"It's me, honey. Is everything okay?"

"Yes. I…all ri…"

All right. Relief fills my chest. "Erin, honey, you're breaking up."

Because the network connection out here at the clubhouse is terrible. Bull told me that, just before he told me I wasn't supposed to use my phone at all.

But Zhuk would be looking for Keri Bishop's phone, not Olivia Burke's. Even Ivan let me use this phone, because—as he said—if someone knows to ping my phone then that person already knows I'm not really Keri. So the jig would be up.

Now that Duke's seen me use it, the jig is up, anyway. For my phone, at least.

"Just… know when co…home?"

"I'm not sure. Soon, I hope."

I glance over my shoulder—and oh my god. I thought Duke's eyes were stormy? *Now* they are, hot as lightning, his face thunderous.

And he's coming after me.

My pulse racing, I veer sideways, trying to get some furniture between us, keeping my back to him because all my makeup's off and my eyes are hazel and *oh shit oh shit*, I can't just hang up on her.

"Honey, I have to go," I whisper fiercely, jumping up onto the sofa then leaping over the back, and Duke's not slowing down, just steadily coming after me. I head for the piano. "I don't know if I can use this phone again. But if anything happens, I'll let you know, I swear. I love you so much. I miss you."

"I miss you, too."

My heart squeezes. "I'll be back soon and then we'll be together, okay?"

"Ok—" The call drops.

As soon as the disconnection tones beep in my ear, I freeze. No more running. Instead I stand in place, shaking, my eyes squeezed shut and ready for Duke's rage to come down on my head.

But there's nothing. He's silent, and I can feel him moving closer, yet he's not saying a word. I can't turn around, can't look at him—my face might pass for Keri's but my eyes won't. I can still picture him, though—that glimpse when he came out of his room, when he was bearing down on me, wearing nothing but a pair of low-slung sweats, his chest and stomach packed with muscle, his big hands fisted at his sides.

Suddenly it's not fear pinning me in place. Anticipation spears through me, hot and sharp and unexpected.

I don't even know *what* I'm anticipating. Just…something.

A gentle tug on the sagging back of my towel sends my heart jumping into my throat. My head jerks around to look over my shoulder before I can stop myself—but it doesn't matter. Duke's towering over me, his broad shoulders like a solid wall, yet he's not looking down at my bare face or my hazel eyes.

He's staring at my back, his jaw clenched, cold rage filling his gaze.

Oh my god. I know what he's seeing.

On a shuddering breath, I face forward. My grip tightens on the edges of the terrycloth tucked around my breasts when he pulls the oversized towel lower, exposing more of my spine—and more of the bruises striping my skin.

"Where else?" he rasps, his voice low and lethal.

"My ribs," I whisper. "But I'm not showing you those."

Technically, I'm not *showing* him these. Not deliberately. But holding the phone and my toothbrush while running around the suite trying to avoid him meant I didn't have a good grip on my towel. And I'd forgotten about the bruises, truthfully.

"He made certain to hit you where your clothes would cover it up, yeah?" His rough laugh holds no amusement. "And he called me trash. But a man who does *this* is about as low as it gets."

True. But I can't correct his assumption and tell him it wasn't Ivan. I can't say that my stepfather was enraged when I offered him a million dollars in exchange for his signature on a custody agreement—enraged because of the insolence and disrespect I showed by suggesting he'd ever sell his daughter.

So he beat me with his belt. Just like I knew he would.

Then he agreed to my terms. Just like I knew he would.

I can't tell Duke that. But I can tell him something almost as important.

"I don't think you're trash," I say softly.

"I know. Your piece of shit husband made you say it." His voice is gruff now. "But it's better for me if I believe that you think I am."

That makes no sense. But I can't look over my shoulder, can't try to read his face. "Why is it better for you?"

He doesn't answer. Instead he carefully pulls my towel back up, waits for me to readjust and retighten my grip. "Power off your phone."

I do, then don't wait for him to tell me to hand it over before holding up the device. His long fingers cover mine for an instant before he lightly lifts the phone from my hand.

"Do I have to search through all your shit to make sure Zhuk doesn't have any way to trace you?" he asks quietly.

I shake my head. "I don't have anything else."

Considering that I don't even have my identification with me, the phone is literally the only thing here that's mine. And Zhuk would have to trace Olivia Burke to find us through it.

But I can't say that, either.

"Good." His tone hardens. "Are you going to break the rules again?"

"No." Then because I can't stop myself, ask—"But what happens if I do?"

Silence falls between us. All at once I'm breathlessly aware of his hard, bare flesh looming behind me, and my mind begins providing suggestions of what he can do to me. Despite the warmth that pours through my body when I imagine his touch, a shiver races over my skin, tightening my nipples into aching points.

But his mind goes somewhere else. Voice harsh, he says, "You don't have to fear another beating. No one here is going to touch you. What you have to fear is Zhuk finding you."

And fear anyone discovering who I really am.

Closing my eyes again, I bow my head. "Right."

"Yeah, *right*." The edge has returned to his voice and I can feel the moment he moves away from me, as if a fire at my back has been extinguished. "Sleep well, duchess."

"You too, Duke," I tell him softly.

But I suspect neither one of us will tonight.

FIVE

DUKE

YESTERDAY I DIDN'T WANT TO DEAL WITH THE MESS MY brother-in-law stirred up. Now I'm looking forward to it. I'd rather beat the shit out of Ivan Tataurov. But Corey will do.

For now.

Because I'm not letting what that rich bastard did to her pass. I don't give a fuck how much money he's paying the Hellfire Riders or that his ring's on her finger. Some-one's going to teach him a fucking lesson. When he shows his face again, that someone's going to be me.

And I'll enjoy every second of it.

This thing with Corey, I'll only enjoy the first part. That part lives in the two-bedroom house at the end of Hamilton Drive. On paper the house belongs to me, though the place I call home—despite rarely being there— is a farmhouse out in the country, and not far from the Hellfire Riders' clubhouse. But this place, I own because my sister and her stupid fuck of a husband are so damn lazy and irresponsible, they can barely take care of themselves.

They don't live in the house, though. Instead they've got a fifth-wheel trailer parked out back. Parked out front is a '14 Camaro that wasn't there two days ago.

No question where the Blue Coyotes' money went, then. Corey didn't smoke it all; he bought himself a car. And I'm glad to see it, because it means I won't be forking out the eight thousand to pay his debt to the Coyotes. I'll just be paying the difference between the eight thousand and whatever I can get for that damn car.

I cut my bike's engine as I pull up onto the concrete apron in front of the garage. Even before I start up the walk, a towheaded six-year-old comes flying out, her pale hair in two buns at either side of her head and a red cape flapping from her shoulders.

"Uncle John!"

Jessie throws herself at me—and if there's any sweeter feeling in the world than a little girl's arms wrapped around your neck, hell if I know what it is. I spin her around to make her scream with laughter before tucking her under my arm like a piece of luggage and carrying her up to the front door, while she's kicking and laughing for me to put her down.

Joyce Harris stands behind the screen door. Just past fifty, her hair's threaded with gray and she's got steel in her spine but a soft welcoming smile. How this smart and snappy woman birthed a shithead like Corey will forever be a mystery to me.

Sometimes I think it's a mystery to her, too. "John," she says warmly as she pushes the screen door open. "Come in. We've just made some lemonade."

That's not what I'm smelling. "And cookies, too?"

"For the school bake sale, so hands-off," she warns, though I know she'll pack away at least a dozen for me before I leave.

I set Jessie down at the kitchen table, where she's got crayons and papers all over. "There you go, squirt."

"I'm not a squirt." Immediately she gets to scribbling, her voice as superior as a queen's. Or if not a queen's, then—"I'm a princess general."

"Princess general, huh?"

"We were watching the new Star Wars together," Joyce tells me. "She wants to be Leia."

"This girl's being raised right." I take the icy glass of lemonade she gives me. "How you doing?"

"All right."

Mindful of Jessie and her big ears, I say, "Any trouble with anyone?"

Her gaze sharpens. "Should I expect trouble?"

"Not after today."

She sighs.

Yeah, I suppose there's not much else to say on that topic. "You got everything you need for the month?"

"Even if I didn't, you give more than enough to cover anything that comes up."

That doesn't mean her son doesn't take what he can. That's why there's not a valuable in sight, and I've bolted down everything he might try to sell—or that my sister might.

But I won't mention that in front of their daughter. Instead I say, "I've got a job that'll keep me out on the ranch for a week or more. So you need me, call that landline direct instead of trying my cell."

"I will," she says and pulls a cookie sheet out of the oven. "Your mother came by this morning to see Jessie."

That's a surprise. After Holly went missing and my dad took off, she quit her full-time position as a music teacher in Hood River, and we moved here to Pine Valley, where she got a job part-time at the high school, supplemented by giving piano lessons on the weekends and afternoons. For years, she held what remained of our family together—until Sandy and I made it to adulthood, then she simply checked out of our lives.

She still works, still goes through the motions of

living, but she doesn't spend much time with her children. Maybe because we remind her of how she lost Holly and it's too damn painful to be around us. Or maybe because it's easier to push us away than lose us, too.

Though she lives a five-minute drive away, I can count on two fingers the number of times she's spoken to me in the past year. Sandy sees her even less. And Jessie…usually she just receives a card on her birthday and Christmas.

"What'd she want?"

"She spent some time chatting, then asked Jessie if she'd like to take lessons."

Huh. "How did she seem?"

"As if she genuinely wanted to get to know her granddaughter better."

And the lessons are a safe way for them both to do that, I suppose. "What do you think, Miss Princess General? Do you want to learn to play piano?"

Without looking up from her coloring, she replies, "Only sissy girls do."

"Who told you that?"

Her shrug tells me exactly who it was—and that just gives me another reason to pound Corey Harris's face in.

"Well, he's wrong," I tell her. "Girls play, boys play. *I* can play."

That gets her attention. She looks up, eyes wide. "You can?"

"Sure. Your grandma gave me lessons, too. I was even younger than you when I started." And fourteen when she stopped. Right before he left, my father blamed her for turning me into a sissy—and said that was the reason Holly was gone. Because his sissy son couldn't even protect a little girl. "I'll tell you what. If you take a few lessons and learn a song, we'll play it together."

"Really?"

"Yup. I'll get you a big keyboard to practice on. And if you stick with it, we'll get you a real piano, like the big one at my house." I sink to my heels beside her chair so that I'm on eye level with her big baby blues. "And you listen to me. There's nothing wrong with being a sissy girl. It's as fine as being a princess general or anything else you want to be."

"I'm a sissy girl," Joyce puts in. "And I rather enjoy being one."

Jessie makes a face. "You're not a girl. You're old."

Joyce snorts out a laugh and shakes her spatula in Jessie's direction. "Don't put me in the grave yet, young lady."

"She's not old," I whisper to Jessie. "She's mature."

"Oh," she whispers back. "Are *you* mature, too?"

I wink at her. "Only when other adults are looking."

Joyce gives another snort and starts sliding cookies from the baking sheet into a big plastic baggie.

Hell, yes. Though now I'll have to be careful to hide that baggie from the brothers babysitting with me at the clubhouse. I'll share with the duchess and Molly, though.

I'm not a completely selfish asshole.

"Maybe hold off on putting another batch in the oven," I tell Joyce before looking to Jessie again. I flick her button nose with a folded twenty-dollar bill before slipping it into her front jeans pocket. "How do you feel about taking Grandma Joyce out for some frozen yogurt while I go talk to your daddy?"

"Frozen yogurt?" Eyes big and hopeful, she looks to Joyce. "Can we?"

Joyce eyes me. "Go put on your shoes, then."

We wait in silence until she scampers off.

Then Joyce sighs again. "Do I want to know what he's done?"

I shake my head.

She turns off the oven. "Does it have to do with that car out front? He's already come asking for gas money."

"He won't have a tank to gas up much longer," I tell her, then decide to warn her about the rest. "I'll be roughing him up some. Nothing that will put him in the hospital or make it hard for him to get around." Nothing that will add to Joyce's burden.

Her lips purse. "Maybe I oughtn't say this about my own son—but I hope you give him a boot in the ass for me. Maybe your sister, too."

Shit. "Has Sandy been after you?"

"Not me. She doesn't give us the time of day unless there's groceries she wants me to pick up. Just the same old…" She trails off as Jessie comes running back in. "You know."

I do. All of Sandy's attention and love is directed toward Corey. But even though she won't spend any time with Jessie, she resents the bond between the little girl and her grandmother.

Not that Sandy says a damn word to Joyce. Instead it's Jessie who suffers from that resentment, her mother running hot and cold with her affection. Hot when Joyce is right there with Jessie. Then Sandy's all over her, hugging her and claiming to love her and saying she's mommy's little girl—but never bothering with her otherwise, unless she's reminded to. That's why we ended up with this arrangement with Joyce and this house, back when Jessie was still an infant. Sandy just wouldn't even bother feeding or bathing her until Jessie's crying reminded my sister that the baby was there.

And I can't fucking understand it. Even if Jessie was the snottiest little shit in town, I wouldn't understand that kind of neglect any more than I'll ever understand how a man can take a belt to a woman's back.

I can't understand it—and can't help thinking that Jessie's life would be a hell of a lot better if my sister and her husband took that fifth-wheel and just fucking left town. But every time that suggestion comes up, every time there's a hint that we'll cut off their groceries or stop paying their bills, they threaten to take Jessie with them. They wouldn't know what the hell to do with her, but they know they've got us by the balls.

So I just hope that, between me and Joyce, we can

give this little girl enough love that it'll help make up for the shit hand her parents dealt her.

"All right, princess general. You've got your money?"

Jessie digs her fingers into her pocket and pulls out the twenty.

"That's all yours, all right? So you treat yourself to your yogurt. And when you get back home, ask Grandma Joyce to put the change away for you, so you don't lose it."

"And so my daddy won't take it from me?"

That's exactly fucking why, and it rips at my chest that she knows the reason without me or Joyce ever saying it in front of her.

For now, I avoid talking shit about her father by ignoring the question entirely. "You think about those piano lessons. When it comes to filling your head, knowing more is always better than knowing less, even if you never use what you learn. All right?"

"Yes, Uncle John."

"Give me a hug, then."

She does, clinging tight. Every time I visit, she clings a little tighter. So do I. At some point, I figure I won't be able to let her go. But my big empty farmhouse is no place for a little girl.

I can't imagine that house filling up any time soon, either. Not when the only woman who has ever made me want something beyond a night in bed is already fucking married to another man.

And although Joyce and I have discussed the possibility of her and Jessie coming to live at my place, we both know what would happen. It wouldn't be long before Corey and Sandy would park their trailer in my backyard—and spending that much time around the dumbshit my sister calls a husband, it wouldn't be long before I'd kill him.

I wait until Joyce's car is halfway down the street before heading out of the house and across the small lawn. Even before I arrive at the trailer door, the sound of Corey playing Grand Theft Auto reaches my ears. No doubt he's in there, picturing himself as some badass motherfucker in his new Camaro. In reality, he'll never get off the goddamn couch.

The noise goes silent when I rap my knuckles against the door. After a long pause during which the window curtains twitch, Sandy opens it. She's looking as pretty as always, her blond hair falling in waves and the tails of her sleeveless shirt tied in a bow beneath her breasts, showing off her tanned belly.

I won't ever think less of her for taking as good care of herself as she does. I sure as fuck think less of her for not taking nearly as good care of her girl.

"John!" Her face lights up. "Come in!"

She waves me inside, her long fingernails carefully painted in a sparkling diamond pattern—and that's where most of their income comes from. She paints her friends' nails and uploads tutorials to YouTube, which pull in a few advertising dollars.

They'd pull in more if she worked at it. But she doesn't.

She doesn't put effort into anything except pleasing her husband.

I figure that's why their trailer's clean instead of trashed. Growing up, she didn't ever bother with cleaning her room and couldn't be persuaded to help with chores even when our parents bribed her, but the inside of the fifth-wheel is spotless. Spotless and cramped. There was never much space to begin with, but they've replaced the compact table and seating at the front of the trailer with a full-sized sofa. Mounted across from it is a sixty-inch flatscreen and a cabinet full of game consoles.

Normally that wouldn't piss me off. People can spend their money however the hell they want and on whatever makes them happy. But a lot of this shit came out of Joyce's purse—which means it came out of my pocket—but paying for it doesn't piss me off as much as knowing Corey stole it from his mother, and that he sees it as just taking what she should have given him.

Standing at the small fridge toward the rear end of the living area, Corey looks over at me, lifts his goateed chin in greeting. For all that he's as lazy as shit in every other respect, he's a big fucker who visits the gym regularly and who takes as good care of himself as my sister does. "Nice to see you, man."

I can't say the same. His smile falters when I tell Sandy, "You want to head outside for a minute? Your husband and I have business to discuss."

"Well, give me a second to say hello first." Smiling,

Sandy sits on the arm of the sofa, though she doesn't give a fuck about saying hello to me. Because she can be foolish but she knows damn well I'm not here for a friendly visit. So she'll try to smooth everything over and protect him as best she can. "Corey and I were actually just talking about you."

"What were you saying?" Something stupid, most likely.

She proves me correct by sharing, "I was saying that he ought to go and talk to you about these guys who are hassling him."

"That right?" I eye the shithead, who's grabbed a beer out of the fridge and is twisting off the top, his eyes twitching like he's real fucking nervous.

He should be.

"They keep asking for money, but we don't have any."

"You must have had some cash if it went into buying that Camaro."

With a wave of her hand, she laughs that off. "No, no. The car's an investment—so he can get a job. Isn't that right, Corey?"

"Yeah." He's not nervous anymore. Instead he's wearing a sullen frown. "No one in this fucking town will hire you if you can't get around. But how the hell can you afford to get around if you don't have a fucking job? It's all cyclical, man."

"As in, what goes around comes around?"

He grins as if I just said something clever and tips his

beer in my direction. "Yeah. That."

Yeah. I don't need a crystal ball to know that Sandy's never going to step out of this trailer. Which is a real fucking shame, but one I'll live with. Because between them, they share about half a brain—and if I can't get through to his half, then maybe it'll sink into hers.

And this dumbshit starts sauntering past me in the narrow space, heading toward the sofa. Maybe realizing that he ought to hide behind her.

Too fucking late.

My hand shoots out and clamps around his throat. The whole goddamn trailer shakes when I slam him into the wall beside the door.

Behind me, Sandy's shrieks and pulls at my arm as if she could haul me off him. I tune out her screaming and get into his face.

Each word is low and lethal. "The way I hear it, you skimmed off the top of what you were selling for the Coyotes." My hand tightens until he's choking for air, his face turning red. "I also fucking heard that you claimed I'd come to your rescue. That the Hellfire Riders would come to your rescue."

"Because he's *family*!" Sandy screeches.

"And if that means a damn thing to you, then you better start thinking about family," I warn him. "Because you're real goddamn lucky it was Howler you were doing business with. But he sure as hell won't do business with you again. And the next person you steal from might take it real fucking personal. But if they kill *you*, you can't pay them back. So instead they'll come after my *sister*."

I punctuate that with a fist to his stomach. What breath he has left wheezes out between his clenched teeth.

"No, John!" With a wail, Sandy stops trying to pull me away and begins scratching at me, ripping at my arm, my face, opening up burning streaks of pain. "Let him *go!*"

Fuck. My sister's more dangerous than her husband is. I'm going to lose a goddamn eye if she keeps this up.

Gritting my teeth, I back off just enough to swing Corey around in her direction. In the narrow space, his big body blocks her path to me. She throws her arms around him from behind.

I pound a fist into his face. His knees give out and I release his throat, grabbing the front of his shirt.

"They'll come after Joyce." My fist smashes lips into teeth and his head snaps back. "And they'll come after *Jessie.*"

I snatch his hair and land another satisfying blow— but not satisfying enough. Not considering what's at stake. Groaning, he slumps to the floor. He's done and so am I.

Except one more warning. Chest heaving, I watch my sister cradle the stupid fucker in her lap.

"You *ever* speak the Hellfire Riders' name again, it'll be my brothers who come to shut your mouth—and I won't say a word to stop them. You understand?"

"He's family!" she shrieks at me again.

"He's no family of mine," I say coldly. "Now I want the

keys to that Camaro. I'll send someone to pick it up. You give them any shit and your husband will find out what real pain is."

Her eyes glitter with rage. "He needs that car for his job."

"Get the keys."

"I won't! You think you're so much better than us, always tossing your money around? You don't know how hard it is when everyone in this town won't hire you!"

"I know that no matter how hard it got, I wouldn't be so stupid as to steal from the Coyotes." Fuck, the side of my face is on fire where she scratched me up, and I don't want to start tearing this place apart looking for those damn keys.

But she keeps this trailer real clean and organized, so it only takes me a second to spot them on a little key hook near the door.

I lift them as I head out.

"Put those back, John! Or…I'll call the cops on you!"

Shit. That actually makes me laugh. "You sure you want to do that, Sandy? The Riders' goodwill sent me here. You might not think it, but I'm doing you a hell of a favor—because if he pulls this shit again, you won't have much of a husband left."

"It's all your fault." She's sobbing now, just like she always does when she doesn't have any arguments left. "People are afraid to hire him because he's related to an unemployed outlaw biker who's doing god knows what illegal shit!"

For fuck's sake. I leave without answering because that stupidity doesn't even deserve a reply.

And because I've got a job—and it's time to get back to it.

After I pick up my baggie full of cookies.

SIX

OLIVIA

Aside from Erin, my boss is the only person from home who I miss—the woman who put the Barb in Barb's Diner. When no one else in town would even accept a job application from me—some of them were friends of my stepfather's, and some were just afraid of him—Barb hired me to work tables.

Sometimes I think she hired me to spite him. She's never said so, but little things she's said and done make me wonder if I'm not the only one my stepfather has tried to hurt or control. But whatever happened between them, she fought back and did well for herself—and gave me hope that I could, too.

In a way, Molly reminds me of her. Not physically. Where Barb is short and curvy, Molly is tall and lean. But they both have a no-nonsense, take-no-shit attitude that's awe-inspiring, considering what they're up against. Men like my stepfather—or these bikers—would probably roll right over anyone with less steel in their spine, but Barb and Molly simply won't put up with any of that shit. I can't emulate that attitude, but I sure can admire it.

And try to learn from it.

I'm chopping carrots for dinner and listening to her describe a big horse she's training—a process which sounds a lot like the way she deals with the guys around here—when Duke's voice comes from behind me.

"Everything all right while I was gone?"

Tension stiffens my body, stilling my hand on the knife. I haven't seen Duke since he left my room last night after discovering the bruises on my back, yet I spent most of the day thinking about him. Thinking thoughts I shouldn't be having. Thinking about his gravelly voice and the way he tugged on my towel and how he towered over me, all hard muscles and bare skin. The past hour I've spent talking with Molly has been my brain's first respite from my obsession with him.

Yet here he is again.

"Why? You think we can't manage for an afternoon

without you?" Kneading a ball of bread dough into the floured countertop, Molly glances toward the kitchen entrance. "How were Jessie and Joy— Dear god, Duke. What'd you get into?"

The rising note of worry in her voice breaks my stillness. I look over and my breath catches in my throat. From his temple to his jaw is a sheet of crimson, as if someone slopped red paint down the left side of his face.

"What?" His frowning gaze catches my horrified one and he wipes a big hand over his mouth. "Do I have chocolate all over? I only ate a few. I saved the rest for you both. Better take one before the brothers see them."

Moving to the center island, he sets a bag of chocolate chip cookies onto the counter next to me—and now that he's closer, I can see three deep furrows from his eyebrow to his hairline. Similar furrows score his left biceps and the inside of his elbow, and more streak his neck, though they aren't as deep.

Does he really not know? "You've got blood all down your face," I tell him.

He touches his bloodied cheek and looks at the tips of his fingers. "Shit. I figured it wasn't any worse than the one on my arm."

Molly suddenly laughs. "Let me guess. Sandy?"

A strange little pang strikes my chest. "Who's Sandy?"

A girlfriend? Who else but a lover would ever get mad enough at a man to scratch him up like that?

"My sister." He angles his face to catch his warped

reflection in a stainless steel pot hanging from the overhead rack. "Ah, fuck me. Those goddamn fingernails. I better go clean up."

His *sister* did that? He heads out of the kitchen and I stare after his back, until Molly says, "There's a first aid kit beneath the sink. Do you mind running it up to him?"

Not at all. I grab the kit and trot up the stairs. The door to my suite is open—as is the door right off the foyer. I stop at the entrance to Duke's room and knock softly on the doorframe to announce my presence.

His room looks more like a traditional hotel room than my suite does—just a double bed, and a sink-and-vanity combo separate from the bathroom.

Duke's standing in front of the vanity, his kutte in hand—carefully wiping blood from the leather.

Taking care of his club vest before taking care of himself.

Though without the vest, the extent of the damage becomes clearer. He's wearing a white T-shirt and the collar is soaked with red. So is his shoulder, where she must have scratched the hell out of him, too, though I can't see any furrows corresponding to the blood—as if she was ripping at his shirt and vest, her nails gouging his skin beneath the shirt as she pulled. Maybe trying to drag him away from someone.

He sees the first aid kit in my hands and gestures toward the bed. "Just throw that there."

I come farther inside but don't toss it and leave. Instead

I open the kit and begin searching for the antiseptic gel. He's finished with his kutte, and when I glance back he's dragging the T-shirt up over his head, hissing out a breath when the cotton sticks to the wound on his shoulder.

Most of the blood is dried. That won't come off easily. Grabbing another washcloth, I head into his bathroom and soak it beneath the hot tap. He's moved to the bed and is picking through the first aid kit when I return.

The knuckles of his right hand are bloodied, too.

"So your sister did this to you," I say. "But who were you hitting?"

"Not her."

"I didn't think you would." Though it's a relief to hear him say it. "Sit on the bed and we'll get this cleaned up."

He scowls over at me. "I can do it."

"But I can do it better. Especially those scratches on the back of your neck and shoulder. It won't be easy for you to reach those."

His scowl deepens.

I just look at him. Really, I've got nothing else to do. So I can wait forever.

With a muttered curse, he sits on the end of the bed.

I offer him a blinding smile and move in closer. He's sitting with his knees apart, so I step in between them, looking down at his shoulder and aware of his pale green gaze locked on my face.

"Well, she really got you here," I say softly, laying the warm wet cloth over his thickly muscled shoulder. "Most of the blood is dried so I'm going to put this here a minute. That should make it easier to wipe away without scrubbing and making the scratches start bleeding again."

While it's doing that, I take a look at his face, gently tilting his jaw to get a better angle. With a sigh, I shake my head. She got him good there, too. I was hoping that it looked so bad only because she got some of his scalp, which bleeds more freely. But, no. She ripped the hell out of his skin.

He regards me steadily. "Will I live?"

"I think the question is: Did the other guy?" I say lightly.

"Unfortunately."

"Who was he?"

"Sandy's dipshit of a husband."

I lift the washcloth. Most of the dried blood has softened and liquified again, so I begin softly dabbing the skin around the deep furrows. If I didn't know his sister had done this, I'd have thought a wildcat had attacked him. "Did he hit her or something?"

"If he did, my answer a minute ago would have been different."

The answer about whether the other guy lived. Remembering his rage when he saw the belt marks on my back, I can't say I'm surprised.

I reach for the antiseptic. "Why did you beat him, then?"

"Because he did something real fucking stupid"—he

sucks in a sharp breath as I spread the gel over the gouges—"and if he does it again, it'll come back around on him. But it'll also come back around on my niece, my sister, and his mother."

Protecting them, then. "But your sister didn't see it the same way?"

"No." A deep sigh expands his chest. "No, she didn't."

Ripping open a sterile bandage, I place it over the scratches and tape the dressing into place. His face is next.

"Don't you move now," I tell him and return to the bathroom to soak the washcloth again. When I head back, he's holding his arm out in front of him, twisting it around to check out the scratches scoring his triceps.

And I could never be a nurse. Not when my bedside manner includes ogling the taut cut of his muscles. His bulging biceps and heavy shoulders are sculpted works of art, his hands and forearms a marvel of sinewy engineering. Golden hair dusts the broad planes of his chest, and I've never seen a stomach as ripped as his in real life. Only in movies and magazines—and I'm pretty sure a lot of those are Photoshopped. But there's nothing fake about the corrugated ridges that define his abdomen.

My breathing is a little unsteady when I step between his legs again. "Tilt your head back."

He does, and I try to pretend that I'm only looking at his scratches when I lay the soaked terrycloth against the side of his face. But I'm not. I'm looking at his eyes, that stormy pale green surrounded by thick, dark blond lashes.

I'm studying the angle of his cheekbones and the firmness of his lips. His jaw is sharply cut, and that chiseled edge is only more pronounced when his head is tipped back.

A shallow cleft dents the center of his chin. I can't stop looking at it, and I'm so, so very glad that his gaze is focused on my face, because it means he has no idea what my body is doing, that my nipples are prodding the soft cotton of this stupid designer T-shirt and pointing right at him—as if to say, *Here we are.*

I don't know how a girl like me—a girl who goes out of her way to avoid attention—ended up with brazenly flirtatious nipples. But clearly my entire body has issues, because my usually reclusive pussy seems to be clamoring for Duke's attention, too. That intimate flesh is so hot and slick that I clench my thighs and shift my weight, trying to ease the building ache.

A distraction would be good. Gently I begin cleaning away the blood from his face. "How old is your niece?"

His voice seems deeper, with a taut rasping edge. "Six."

"That's a sweet age."

So sweet. I remember Erin at that age—she in her first year of elementary school, me in my last year of high school. That was the year she began to see all the pain I'd been trying to hide from her. That was the year she began creeping into my room at night to hold me, and I'd tell her about a future where we'd be together and free, and we wouldn't have to be afraid.

I tried to give her that future less than a year later...

and it fell apart before we got twenty miles away from my stepfather's house. But I won't fail this time.

God, I miss her so much. And I worry so much. She's smart and strong but it's been almost a week now. We've never been apart for so long—and everything about Zhuk suggests that I'll be here for at least another week. At *least*. It could be much longer.

Those pale green eyes suddenly narrow. "What are you worrying about, duchess?"

I shake my head. "Nothing."

"Your face says otherwise. It doesn't hide much. Makes me wonder how you ever got through a single film."

I give him a sour look. "And *your* face says that your sister won. Makes me wonder how you made it back here in one piece."

A heart-stopping grin suddenly appears on his lips. "I had those cookies motivating every step."

"They must be amazing cookies if you didn't realize she'd done this."

"Wait until you taste one." His smile fades as I begin spreading the antiseptic over the gouges, but not because the medicine stings. Instead he adds quietly, "If you were worried that I beat him in front of Jessie, I didn't. I wouldn't scare her that way."

That's not what I was worried about, but I don't mind if he thinks it is. "Even if she doesn't see it, she might be scared to see the damage you did to him."

Erin rarely saw James actually hit me. But the bruises

he left still frightened her—and that fear hurt me more than he ever did.

"She probably won't see him. They don't bother with her much."

I frown. "They neglect her?"

"She lives with her grandmother. And is a hell of a lot better off for it."

"Sometimes we are better off without our parents." I wouldn't have been better off without my mother or my father, just my stepfather. And I never knew Erin's mother—James's first wife, who died giving birth to her—but Erin would be better off without James, too. "And a mother doesn't have to be the woman who gave birth to you."

"That's true enough. Still, Jessie deserves better than the mother she got."

"The way your voice sounds when you talk about her, I'd say she got a loving uncle and a grandmother who'll make up for it."

"I hope so." He shakes his head when I pick up another sterile bandage. "No need for that on my face. Just wherever I'll be wearing clothes that might stick when it starts scabbing over."

Nodding, I put away the bandage and start cleaning the gouges on his biceps. "I think I'll amend what I said before. Maybe it would scare her to see her father beaten up. But now I suspect it's better that she didn't see what happened to *you*. It looked really bad, Duke. And little kids pick up on more than we think they do.”

"I know it." It's a grim reply, as if he worries about what else his niece has picked up on. Then his brow creases and his gaze intently searches my face.

Wondering how much my expression is giving away now, I ask warily, "What?"

"I was just thinking that everything about you is different onscreen."

Oh god. My belly knots up but I do my best to shrug as if it's nothing. "I'm acting then. This is really me."

He makes a soft, noncommittal sound. As if he doesn't quite buy that explanation. "Why aren't you wearing that big rock on your finger, duchess?"

"Oh." I glance at my bare hand. "I was helping Molly in the kitchen, and needed to wash a few dishes, so I took my rings off."

That sounds plausible, at least. The truth is…I think they're still in my bathroom, where I left them last night. I'm not used to wearing any jewelry.

A muscle in his jaw works. "Your husband's paying us a hell of a lot of money to take care of you, not to put you to work in a kitchen."

"So I should just sit around, bored out of my mind? I'm not used to doing nothing."

"Yeah, it's a far cry from what you're usually doing." His voice roughens. "Who's Erin?"

I freeze with the washcloth against the side of his neck. "Who?"

His stormy eyes ice over. "You were talking to him last night. Saying you missed him, that you'd be together."

Him. Not Erin. *Aaron.*

Duke thinks I was talking to a man…who obviously isn't my husband.

I'm not sure whether to laugh or cry. One explanation is a stepsister I shouldn't have; the other suggests Keri is cheating on Ivan. Which one is better to confess to?

Neither one is good. But the confession that might lose me custody of Erin is worse.

"He's no one," I say softly and hope Keri won't ever find out that I just turned her into an unfaithful wife.

Duke's expression closes, leaving nothing to read except his unyielding hardness. "Your husband doesn't seem as if he'd tolerate you being with another man. It that why he beat you?"

It seems wrong to let him continue believing that. "That wasn't Ivan. It happened on a movie set. I was doing a stunt and I just…uh, slipped and fell. You know."

"Sure," he says flatly.

I wouldn't have believed my shitty lie, either. I sigh and continue washing the blood that dripped into the hollow of his clavicle.

"Listen." The command in his tone draws my gaze to his again. His eyes are still hard and cold, but steady on mine. "I have a job to do, protecting you from Zhuk. But when the job's done, if you don't ever want to worry about another beating, you just say the word."

My heart clenches painfully tight. My fingers tremble against his skin and my voice sounds faint and breathless, like a lost little girl's as I ask, "You're saying you'd help me escape him?"

His expression softens. "I'm saying that if you don't want to leave with him, you don't. And if you want me to make sure he can't hurt anyone again, I will."

He's talking about killing him. But he's not talking about my stepfather.

I shake my head. "If you're saying what I *think* you're saying—"

"I am."

"It wasn't Ivan who beat me. Truly it wasn't," I say, my gaze holding his. He easily recognizes my lies; hopefully he'll recognize the truth. "You'd be killing a man who doesn't deserve it."

"Then was it this Aaron fucker?"

"No," I say automatically before realizing I should have lied. Blaming a man who doesn't exist wouldn't hurt anyone.

"Not Ivan, not Aaron. So who else would be doing this shit to you?"

"No one." And that's clearly a lie. Those bruises didn't appear magically.

"Duchess." Long fingers catch my chin and make me look at him, his gaze almost tender as it searches mine. Gruffly he says, "Let me help you."

My heart is suddenly full. So full, expanding to enormous proportions in my chest, clogging my throat, stinging my eyes. How many times in my life have I prayed for someone to just *help*? Someone who'd believe me instead of believing my stepfather's lies; someone who'd risk everything to help me and Erin escape him.

Raw emotion thickens my voice when I say, "I wish I'd known someone like you before all this."

His brows draw together as he frowns up at me, then tension seems to pull his skin tight when my thumb brushes the corner of his mouth. Overwhelmed with wonder and longing, softly I cup his hard jaw in my palm.

Then I bend my head and press my lips to his.

His mouth is firm and unmoving beneath mine. His breath smells faintly of chocolate and cookie. My heart beginning to pound, slowly I increase the pressure of the kiss, trying to coax his warm lips to part. He doesn't open for me.

Because I don't really know how to kiss. I'm probably doing this wrong.

But I want—*need*—one taste of him. Just one.

I tentatively lick his lower lip, and hear his deep tortured groan, feel the rumble of it against my mouth. It's all the warning I get.

And Duke knows how to kiss. He must, because his mouth opens beneath mine and suddenly the rest of the world is gone, swept away by the hot thrust of his tongue, by his hand fisting in my hair and dragging me closer so that he can devour my mouth with rough hungry licks.

Whimpering low in my throat, I cling to his shoulders and fall with him as eases back until his upper body's lying flat on the bed, my thighs straddling his hips and my knees sinking into the mattress, and I'm bent over with my mouth fused to his.

I moan softly when Duke breaks the kiss and his lips skim along the edge of my jaw. His fingers tighten in my hair.

His voice is pure gravel in my ear. "You're…fucking… *married.*"

Oh my god. Splayed wantonly over his big body, I go utterly still. Shame floods my face in a hot wave.

Cold and mocking, he adds, "Did you forget?"

I did. I forgot I was supposed to be Keri Bishop.

Instead I was Olivia, kissing the man I can't stop thinking about.

My throat hot and thick, I sit up. His body goes rigid under mine, every muscle like steel, but I can't even look at him. Everything that was sweet and pleasurable a moment ago is suddenly sour and painful, because there's so much wrong in what what I just did.

Risking mine and Erin's future. Risking Keri Bishop's reputation.

Stiffly I climb off him. "I'm sorry. I shouldn't have done that."

With a short, hard laugh, Duke sits up. "Sure as hell took you long enough to remember that. But maybe you forget a lot, huh? Maybe you've just got a string of men dangling from your pretty fingers. Your husband, this Aaron sap—and fuck knows how many others. Just don't plan on adding me to their number, duchess."

"I won't," I whisper, the pain of his rejection and my stupid hopes crushing my chest.

I've never wanted a man like I want Duke. Never admired another man like I do him. Never dreamed of being with any other man.

But I can't touch him again.

"Don't fuck with any of my brothers, either. We've got a job to do. If you're bored, read a goddamn book. Don't start thinking of screwing us as a way for you to pass the time."

In shock that he'd think I would ever do that, my gaze flies to his. Anger burns in the storm of his eyes. "That wasn't why I kissed you. I was just…caught up in the moment."

Caught up in a dream where someone would fight for me. Where someone would believe in me.

But his short laugh tells me he doesn't believe a single word now. "Just get the hell out of here," he commands.

I do, racing for the privacy of my bedroom, tears full of shame and heartache blurring the way.

SEVEN

DUKE

THREE FUCKING DAYS AND THE TASTE OF HER WON'T leave my tongue. I can't forget the feel of her sweet weight lying over me. I can't get the sultry sound of her moan out of my head.

But I try, goddammit. Every day, I try.

Then I spend every fucking night stroking my cock while remembering how she looked at me with such hope, as if I was the answer to every question she ever had. Remembering her gentle fingers tending to my wounds, her soft laugh and beautiful smile and teasing replies. Remembering her worry for a little girl she'd never met and the sadness that kept darkening her eyes.

And when I come into my fist, it's while remembering the softness of her lips pressing into mine. Remembering the innocent touch of her tongue.

Innocence from a married woman. A woman who was in the public eye for years—and Ivan sure as hell wasn't her first lover. I don't pay attention to that gossipy shit but it's not something anyone who ever stood in a grocery checkout surrounded by tabloids can escape knowing.

Yet she kissed like she was new to kissing. I tell myself that she was just playing a role. That she's been playing me from the first day.

Except that she's a shitty actress and a shittier liar. And her innocence seemed as real as the shame and pain that shadows her beautiful face every time she looks at me now.

And it's fucking tearing me apart, knowing she's hurting. I'm not the kind of man who'd touch someone else's woman. But I'm beginning to wish I was.

That's reason enough to stay the hell away from her.

So except at night when she's in her room and I'm in mine, except at the dinner table where I can't avoid her, I've been leaving the clubhouse and working outside every chance I can—letting my brothers watch over her directly, while I oversee the whole operation.

Usually they'd rather do anything than watch over the

people we're babysitting. But with her, they're practically lining up to volunteer for a shift. Hell, even when they aren't assigned to her personal protection, they're hanging around wherever she is. Because everyone she talks to, she makes them feel real damn good. Asks them all kinds of questions about their lives, as if they're the celebrities instead of regular bikers, and she gives them such sweet and friendly attention that they walk away feeling more interesting and a hell of a lot more important than they felt before.

She's so damn easy to talk to, I don't think they even realize how much they're saying. Like me, sitting there telling her about my sister and Jessie and my dumbshit brother-in-law. She's the one with the life everyone ought to be asking about, but whenever the talk turns in her direction, she always deftly turns the conversation around. Almost like she's avoiding talking about herself. But if it's deliberate, it's also real natural. More natural than her lies or her every attempt to hide her emotions.

Like I've been hiding mine.

Every damn day has been an exercise in holding in my temper, as if I'm a bomb ready to blow. Every damn hour they spend with her, my jealousy has been running hot, though I don't have a right to be jealous about a damn thing.

So I've been keeping busy—doing extra runs around the perimeter, hitting the weight room morning and night to burn out the frustration. And spending most of my downtime in the old stable, working on my motorcycle.

Which is where I am now, repacking my steering head bearings with fresh grease about six months ahead of schedule. It's hot as fuck outside, the last gasp of summer, so the big doors at either end of the old building are wide open. I shed my kutte about an hour ago, and my sweat-soaked T-shirt's about to follow when Picasso's voice comes over the two-way radio we use to keep in touch while we're out on the ranch, since our phones are fucking useless.

"Molly's riding this way."

Which means it's one of the few times that "riding" refers to a horse instead of a bike. Thorne's property backs up against the ranch so Molly doesn't always come by the road—but our cameras pick her up as soon as she comes through the gate separating the two spreads of land.

"Keep an eye on her," I radio back. Zhuk likely won't find the ranch but that doesn't mean we're taking any chances.

"Will do. And our duchess wants to know if she can take a walk outside."

Radio in hand, I have to grit my teeth to stop myself from responding as I'd like. They all picked up on me calling her "duchess" real quick—and it's a usual thing for us to give our clients a nickname and avoid saying the name of the person we're babysitting. A nickname makes it easier to not let a real name slip when it shouldn't. Still, she's not *our* duchess.

She's mine.

I'm silent too long. As if she's standing right by Picasso waiting for an answer, another message comes through. "She says she'll go crazy cooped up one more day."

Fuck. I press the transmit button. "Grasshopper, take her around."

His reply comes through his own radio. "Pleasure."

Yeah, it would be. Pleasure and torture. Despite the way she walks around in those fancy clothes and expensive shoes, she isn't the least bit pretentious. And she doesn't have a malicious bone in her. Even when she's tart, such as expressing surprise that I'm not the only asshole or telling me that my scratched-up face means that my sister kicked my ass, there's a sweet, teasing humor to it. She helps Molly without being asked and cleans her own suite and patches up fuckers who got their asses kicked by their sisters.

Nothing about her makes sense. How can a woman who's so sweet and generous be the same woman who fucks around behind her husband's back with this Aaron asshole?

Though the cheating might better explain the tension between them when Tataurov left—and why he didn't kiss her good-bye. Though he obviously still loves her enough to spend a fortune protecting her.

Now *that* makes sense. I can easily imagine a man loving her so much that he'll keep on loving her after she stabbed a knife into his chest.

But she just doesn't strike me as a woman who'd stab a man in the first place.

Grasshopper's voice floats through the open door nearest to my bike's stall. "And this is our garage. Mostly we work on our rides here."

"Mostly you do?"

Christ, her accent. A single fucking word and my cock's twitching against my zipper.

"Yeah, well. When we've got girls out here and the clubhouse is packed, it's a good place to come and get your dick sucked."

Her throaty laugh in response changes *twitching* to *hard as a fucking stone.*

And what the fuck is Grasshopper doing, bringing her out here? If she wanted to take a walk there's a hell of a lot of other places on this property to show her. And why the fuck is he mentioning his dick?

"I'll show you around. I think Duke's in here—there he is." Grasshopper appears at the open front of the stall, his expression saying he's damn pleased with himself. "Looks like he's changing out his steering head bearings."

"Just repacking them." I straighten, my whole fucking body on alert when she steps into sight, wearing another one of those ridiculous getups that show miles of golden skin. "Duchess."

"Duke." Instead of her full-watt smile, there's only a hesitant curve of her lips. It fucking kills me to see how wary she is around me now, but it's for the best. She gestures to the motorcycle jacked up in the center of the stall, its disassembled front end laid out on the worktable behind me. "This is yours?"

I grunt an assent and move around behind the bike's raised frame, hoping like fuck that the erection trying to rip through the front of my jeans doesn't knock the damn thing off the jack. "Yeah, it's mine. I'm not in the habit of touching what belongs to someone else."

Her gaze skitters away from the bike and meets mine, color flushing her cheeks. Softly biting her bottom lip, she averts her face.

Yeah. She didn't misunderstand me.

But it flies right over Grasshopper's head. "You've got to understand how it is, duchess. A man's bike is his freedom and you don't fuck with another man's freedom. And when you've got one of these rides, you don't need much else. Just a beer, some pussy now and then, and a place to sleep."

She rallies with a wry smile. "That's all you need? Yet you have a big clubhouse, dinners made for you, and free liquor anytime you want it."

"We don't *need* all that," Grasshopper says with a wide grin. "But it sure is nice to have it."

Over the radio, Picasso breaks in, "Maurice is at the gate and coming through."

Grasshopper's eyebrows shoot up in surprise. "Holy shit, he actually came. You want me to field this?"

I nod. The business of bringing Maurice in on this job

will be kept real casual. No man likes being led around by the nose, even if the person—or the whole damn motorcycle club—doing the leading is only thinking of what's best for him.

"You stay here with Duke, then," he tells her.

She nods. As soon as he leaves, there's nothing but quiet between us, with her leaning back against the side of the stall, watching me clean the old grease from the top of the headstock with a rag stinking of solvent. Despite the heat she looks cool and pretty, wearing tiny checkered shorts paired with a loose tank top. Her shoes are a mile high, toenails painted a cherry red. Grasshopper must have taken her down behind the lodge before coming this way, because a fine layer of orange dust the same color as the dirt by the creek is all over her feet.

Seeing her dirty is sexy as fuck—and irritates the hell out of me. I'd like to get her dirtier.

I'd like to carry her around so her feet never touch the ground.

Arms crossed over her chest, she starts walking the length of the worktable, absently looking at all the parts laid out there. "Maurice is the one who lost his little boy?"

I frown over at her. It's one thing if the brothers tell her all about themselves. It's another thing if they're running their mouths about another patchholder's business. "Who told you that?"

Something in my tone must have alerted her. She looks my way, studying my face. "Will it get him in trouble if I tell?"

"No."

She knows I'm lying. Her red mouth curves. "No one did, then."

That answer just irritates me more, but I have to admire it. She doesn't have any reason to protect the brothers. Yet she does.

Christ, and I can't think of one damn thing about her that I don't admire. Especially those stems. She's not all that tall. But she's got legs for fucking *days*. Like she's been made to wrap them around my waist. Or my face. It's all good, as long as she's squeezing tight and screaming my name.

"Why does Maurice use his real name?"

"What?"

"Maurice." She's standing in front of my kutte, which I draped over the top of the stall wall. Her slim fingers trace the shape of my name patch. "Everyone else has these nicknames."

"A road name. That's his." I drag my gaze away from her taut thighs and turn back to my bike, grabbing a socket wrench from the tool cart beside me. "You don't choose your own, but he tried to. He was a prospect maybe a month before he announced that he'd like to be called the Space Cowboy. So of course the brothers weren't having any of that shit—but we also never let him forget it."

"But how do you get Maurice from…? *Ohhh*. That song. What is it called?" She hums a few bars, as if mentally singing the lyrics until she hits the chorus and the line that includes the title. "Ah! 'The Joker,' right?"

"Yeah, that one," I say, eyeing her. That was about as off-key as any humming I've ever heard. And if there's one thing Keri Bishop can do, it's sing. It's how she got her start in those Disney kid shows.

And as bored as she claims to be, I've never heard her pass the time on the piano in her room, though I know she can play. Even I've been known to sit down at the keys from time to time during these long jobs.

"What about yours?"

"What about my what?"

"Your road name. Duke." She says it in that sweet accent and it's the sexiest damn sound, like her tongue gliding up the thick length of my cock. "Is it because you hit people? Like, 'Put up your dukes?' Or maybe like the Dukes of Hazzard?"

That'd be fucking shameful. "It's because my real name is John Wayne."

"Like the actor in those old westerns? I remember watching those with my dad." Something in her voice softens. "It's a good name."

It's a name. I grunt an answer, and I don't even know what the fuck I'm loosening with this socket wrench. Instead I'm just remembering the taste of her mouth, the sound of her sexy moan.

"You don't look anything like him."

"Maybe I did as a baby."

She laughs. "I guess your parents couldn't know what you'd look like grown up. But still, how did you get Duke?"

I frown at her. "You really don't know?"

She seems to hesitate. "Should I?"

Yeah. Considering that she dyed her hair brown and played Ella Raines in a John Wayne biopic. But even if she hadn't, I can't fucking imagine how anyone working in Hollywood wouldn't know that much about one of the greats.

I continue eyeing her, with my gut telling me that something's real fucking *off* here. It's different than the wrong feeling that first hit me about this job, a man leaving his wife without kissing her goodbye, but more like something's off about *her*. Like she's not who she says she is.

Or maybe it's just wishful thinking. Because it fucking pisses me off that she gave me a taste of what I can't have. But if she wasn't Keri Bishop, I could take more.

I'd take everything.

Looking suddenly nervous, she turns her back to me, sliding her fingers around the chrome rim of my front wheel. Her shorts are so damn short. Hardly more than panties. I wouldn't even have to get them off her. Just move aside the scrap of fabric between her legs and slide so fucking deep.

Instead I begin lubing up the bearings, my palm and fingers slippery with grease.

She faces me again as I'm working, and when her silence continues I glance over and catch her longing gaze locked on my hands, her lips soft and parted, her eyes wanting.

And she's not even fucking hiding it from me. Instead she's letting me see all that hot need.

As if that ring on her finger doesn't mean a goddamn thing.

"Duchess."

At the rough sound of my voice, her gaze jerks up to meet mine. She's breathing hard, her skin flushed.

Slowly I reach for a towel and begin wiping away the grease. "What're you looking at?"

"Your hands. Your knuckles healed up well."

She was looking at my hands for another reason. Maybe picturing what I'd do to her. "You're not a very good liar."

"No." It's a breathless agreement.

"So what are you thinking?" Only a short distance separates us. I cross it in two steps and her head tips back, her eyes still holding mine. "Maybe that I'm going to dirty you up some. Maybe get my greasy hands all over you."

She sucks in a sharp breath between her teeth. Her lips are so full and red and I want to taste them again so fucking bad.

"You're bored inside the clubhouse. So maybe you thought you'd fuck around with me, is that it?" Pushing up the bottom of her loose tank, I circle her bare waist with my slippery hands. Even as she's gasping, her fingers clutching my forearms—that goddamn ring shining like the sun—I lift her up and set her ass on the worktable, then spread those taut golden thighs and push in between. "Maybe we'd do it right here. I'd fuck you deep and hard, my big cock filling you up while I suck on these pretty tits."

Her stiff nipples are like fat diamonds against my palms, her breasts soft handfuls. Under this clean tank top, I know I'm leaving my dirty, greasy mark all over her golden skin but she doesn't seem to care, moaning as she arches her back, seeking a firmer touch. Her eyes are glazed with arousal, her breath coming in soft pants, as if she's already lost to her need.

After a mere touch. As if she has no experience with desire and how overwhelming it can be.

But, fuck. It's never been this overwhelming for me, either.

If it weren't for the big, shiny ring that keeps reminding me that she's not mine, I'd have already lost my head and started fucking her.

Instead I lower my mouth to hers and grate out against her lips, "Is that why you wanted to wander around outside? Were you looking for me? You heard Grasshopper say we'll bring girls out here to suck dick. Maybe you think you won't be so fucking bored if you wrap your lips around my cock and start stroking me off with your husband's big rock sparkling on your finger. Is that what gets you off?"

Her eyes fly wide. "No. Oh my god. I— *No.*"

Suddenly frantic, she pushes at my chest and I let her

shove me away, because I don't know if I could back off of my own volition. And I'm not sure if what comes out of my mouth next is a warning or a promise. "If you ever find me out here again, I'll take it as a sign you want to get down on your pretty knees and suck my dick until I come on your tongue."

"That's not…I didn't—" She chokes to a stop. Hand flying up to cover her face, as if she doesn't want me to see the tears suddenly glittering in her eyes, she jumps down from the worktable and rushes past me.

And past Grasshopper, who's stopped at the entrance to the stall, frowning darkly at me.

"What the fuck is wrong with you, man?"

Shaking my head, I tear my hands through my hair, fighting the desperate urge to race after her. My cock's hard as steel, aching with need. But it's doesn't hurt as much as the ache in my chest. Because there's definitely something real fucking wrong with me.

I'm falling for another man's wife.

EIGHT

OLIVIA

WHAT AM I DOING?

Blinded by tears, I stumble through the garage doors and out beneath a glaring sun. The lodge looms to the right, separated from the garage by a big open asphalt lot. Beyond the lodge, a dirt road leads toward the creek and across the broad field that stretches out as far as I can see.

Down that road comes Molly, riding toward me on a tall brown horse. Desperately I try to get the tears under control—smiling instead of crying so I won't ruin all this stupid makeup that took an hour to apply this morning.

But what am I doing? This attraction to Duke is easy to understand. I desperately want him to look at me. What woman wouldn't? Not just because he's gorgeous. For all his gruffness, he's a good man.

I can't say the same about myself. What kind of person am I, letting Keri Bishop's name be stained this way? I'm painting her as unfaithful every time I look at him with all the longing I feel shining from my eyes.

And I know what it's like to have your name shit on, for people to think you've done something you haven't. My stepfather's got everyone in town believing I'm a thieving whore who'll ruin any man I get my hands on. And everyone believes it because, five years ago, I did something terrible in the eyes of the law.

If I *was* sleeping around with every guy in town, I wouldn't be ashamed. But to have a lie spread about you, that's something else. Especially if it's a lie that jeopardizes a relationship.

I've had one boyfriend in my life—and our relationship lasted all of one date before my stepfather ran him off with lies. Since then, men don't even get past flirting with me before someone in town is warning him. Of course, it's not just that I'm supposedly a slut. Not a lot of men would run if they're promised easy sex. No, what sends them running is that I'm supposedly a thief, too.

The only thing I ever stole was my little sister.

The only thing I regret was getting caught.

"So they let you out?" Molly's grinning as she reins the horse to a stop and slides from the saddle.

"They did. Is this the new horse you mentioned training?"

"This is him." She pats his heavy brown shoulder. "Corsair."

Beautiful. "Can I pet him?"

"Be my guest."

He's huge. Tentatively I reach out to stroke his sleek neck. His head swings around as if to see who's touching him and I stiffen, trying not to freak out when his mouth comes near my shoulder.

"You know," Molly says, "I could see about bringing one of my trail horses over here for you to ride. It might be a little more exciting for you to go around the property that way."

"I wish I could. But I don't know how to ride."

Molly frowns and I realize my mistake almost immediately. Of course I know how to ride. I'm Keri Bishop, star of that movie about outlaw cowgirls…I don't even remember the name of it. Before I got here, I thought I'd still have my phone and access to Wikipedia or streaming video if I ever needed to fill in gaps. So I've been forced to dredge the shallow depths of my own knowledge—and thanks to this face, I *have* heard a lot about Keri Bishop, but it's all background noise. I haven't even seen most of her movies.

Hastily I try to cover with, "What I mean is, I didn't

bring any clothes to ride in."

Her gaze flicks over my shoulder—probably at Grasshopper, coming out to show me more of the property. "My daughter Iris is about your size. A little bigger. I could bring some of her things."

Oh no. This is the problem with lies. They just roll and roll and become bigger and stickier. "I can't anyway. The contract for my next movie says I can't do anything risky."

I'm pretty sure I've heard something like that before. Contracts that say actresses can't eat certain things or participate in dangerous activities.

"Horseback riding is risky?"

"I'm sure your horses are very well mannered. But it's on a list of prohibited pastimes. Like skydiving, bungee jumping, motorcycle riding—"

"Making videos about human trafficking," a voice behind me adds. "That turned out to be damn risky."

I stiffen. It's not Grasshopper. It's Duke. But I don't glance back, because although I can feel him looking at me—although I want him looking—it's not *me* he's seeing.

He's seeing the woman I'm supposed to be. A woman who shouldn't care what he thinks.

Lightly I say, "They'll probably add that to the next contract."

"Maybe they'll throw in some clothes and shoes that aren't so fucking ridiculous."

My throat tightens. They *are* ridiculous. Beautiful, but

ridiculous. I know I look stupid traipsing around in the dirt and a garage in these shoes. "Well, I had no idea where I was going before I actually got here. So I apologize if my wardrobe offends your…your…whatever it offends."

"Don't apologize, Keri. He can take his offense and shove it where the sun don't shine," Molly puts in, her voice hard. "Now, why don't you come with me over to the corral, and we'll get Corsair settled."

"I'd like that." My response wavers with the strain of *not* turning to look at Duke. Because then he'd just see how hurt I am.

Even though Keri Bishop shouldn't be hurt. She *wouldn't* be hurt.

And for the first time in my life, I wish I really was Keri.

I DO LIKE TENDING TO the horse, though I can't do much—because as Molly points out, brushing a twelve hundred pound horse while wearing strappy high heels is just asking for a crushed foot.

So I stay near his head, holding a bucket with a handful of oats tossed into the bottom, and by the end I love everything about Corsair. I love his thick mane and silky muzzle, his big hooves and the way he smells up close.

Erin would love this even more. She's been pony mad for a while, and every time we go to the library, she brings home a stack of horse books, fiction and nonfiction.

When I get custody of her, I'm going to make sure

she takes riding lessons. My ridiculous clothes will pay for that. And seeing her on the back of a horse will make every stupid step in these heels worth it.

Grasshopper stays back near the corral fence—as he says, the only riding he'll do is on a steel horse—and between him and Molly, my mood has lifted by the time we return to the lodge. There's a shift change between my babysitters, and as Grasshopper heads off to watch the security feeds, Scarecrow—fresh off eight hours of sleep— seems content to put his feet up in the day room while Molly and I head into the kitchen.

She starts washing her hands, and nods toward my feet—which are filthy. "Even if you don't get up on a horse, I'll still bring you some clothes tomorrow—if you want to wear something different."

I do. But part of my job is dressing like this. "I can't."

She eyes me without saying anything. Just levels that perceptive gaze on my face.

I don't want that much attention on me. "You said the clothes belong to your daughter, Iris?"

"That's right."

And Molly is married to Thorne, the Hellfire Riders' VP. From what I've gathered from conversations with her and the bikers, Molly is the head "old lady"—which is apparently not an insult but something to be proud of. Certainly all of the guys here look at her with the highest respect.

I haven't seen any other women, though, aside from

the first meeting when I was introduced to the blonde who wasn't an old lady but a member of the club. Every other woman has been banned from the property while the clubhouse is in lockdown.

"Is your daughter an old lady, too?"

Molly snorts. "No. She couldn't run away from the life fast enough. Not away from us—my husband or me—but all this. She's in Corvallis now, at Oregon State. She just entered their animal sciences graduate program."

So about the same age as me. But several years younger than Keri. "She doesn't want to end up with a biker?"

"No." Molly pauses, glances at me. "She had her eye on Duke once."

Something in my chest squeezes tight. "Did she?"

"About five or six years back, just before she took off for college. He'd left the Riders and joined up with the Steel Titans—that was who my husband used to ride with before they folded the clubs together—and after a year or so more, he bought the old farmhouse on the ten acres across from our place, so he was always around."

Confused, I shake my head. "So Duke was a Hellfire Rider, then a Steel Titan, but is a Hellfire Rider again now?"

"That's right. But back then, he was a new and shiny Titan and caught her eye."

"But he didn't look back at her?"

Molly shrugs but her voice is troubled when she replies, "I don't think he'd have seen any woman then. He was going through a rough patch."

"What kind of rough patch?"

"The kind we don't run our mouths about," he answers.

My heart jumping, I look over at the kitchen entrance, where Duke's standing and watching Molly, his lips in a wry twist.

"I think you've got truth serum in that accent of yours, duchess, because Molly sure isn't the type to be going on about a patchholder's private concerns."

She braces her hands on her hips and gives him a challenging stare. "I'm just making conversation with our guest. I wasn't going to offer any details. Of course she's curious about the people protecting her."

"Is she?" He doesn't wait for her to answer but shifts his pale green gaze to me. "Here's what you need to know about that rough patch: it's none of your fucking business."

A thick ache builds in my throat. "Okay."

"And if you've got something to ask, ask me personally. Don't go sneaking around talking about any brother behind his back. You understand?"

That's fair. Silently I nod.

Molly rolls her eyes. "She's not an old lady. You can't expect her to know—or care—about the damn rules. And the person we were *really* gossiping about was my daughter. Will you forbid me to talk about her?"

"Just keep it about your daughter and we won't have a problem."

After another hard look at me, he leaves. Molly frowns

after him.

"Did something happen between you and Duke?"

Something like kissing him while I bandaged him up? Something like drooling over him in the garage? But I can't say either of those things. "You mean, aside from him thinking my shoes are stupid?"

She shakes her head. "I've never seen him like this with any woman. If you asked me who would always treat a girl with respect, it'd be him. Yet the past few days, every time I see you two, he's getting onto you about something."

My chest tightens. "I guess I'm special, then."

A laugh erases her speculative frown. "Honey, that's the understatement of the year." She eyes me, smiling. "And I'll tell you what—he's not wrong about that truth serum you've got when you talk."

Funny. Because just about every word out of my mouth is a lie.

EXCEPT FOR THE WORDS I'M about to say, though I have to work up to them. After a dinner where Duke barely spoke—though I'm not sure anyone noted his silence because I was talking so much to everyone else—I retreated to my suite. He wasn't long behind me, entering his room without a word and snapping his door shut decisively.

I'm standing there now, hesitating. Though I don't know what I'm hesitating for. If it's one thing my mother taught me, it's to apologize when an apology is due.

I think one is due.

I rap on the door and back up until I'm all the way across the foyer, my shoulders pressed up against the opposite wall. Ready for bed, he's only wearing his sweats again when he opens the door—and when he sees me standing here, he braces his palms against each side of the doorframe and simply looks at me. He fills the entire doorway, his arms roped with muscle, his big body in a long, taut line.

Carefully I avert my gaze, because I can't hide how beautiful I think he is. I can't hide how much I want him. And I know he's watching me but I can't meet those pale green eyes.

"What is it, duchess? You want to finish what we were working toward earlier?"

With his dirty hands under my shirt, lubricated fingers cupping my breasts, teasing their aroused tips. At the memory, my nipples immediately stiffen.

Crossing my arms over my chest to conceal my reaction, I rush right into it. "I wanted to say…I'm sorry for prying. I know you don't like it when the guys talk about each other's personal business. And I know what it's like for people to stick their noses into your private life, talk about you behind your back."

"I bet you do." His voice has roughened. "And that's the only reason you knocked on the door?"

"Yes. I just…hope I didn't make you uncomfortable by asking Molly about a difficult period of your life."

He doesn't answer right away. Tension gripping the

back of my neck, I dare a glance at his face—and he's regarding me as if he's not certain what to make of my statement. "You came to apologize because you worried you made me uncomfortable?"

"Yes."

His expression softens. With a deep, heavy sigh, he asks quietly, "What am I going to do with you, duchess?"

Nothing. That's the only possible answer.

My throat aching, I just shake my head.

His hands drop away from the doorframe. With the slow, purposeful tread of a predator, he begins crossing the foyer. "How about we make a deal? You tell me who put those bruises on you, I'll tell you about my rough patch."

"I already told you it wasn't Ivan."

"I didn't ask who it *wasn't*. The deal is, you tell me who it *was*." His voice flattens. "But, hell—I'll go first. I was fourteen years old when I took my two younger sisters to a movie. *Your* movie, in fact. That first one, *Play Acting*. Halfway through, Sandy needed to piss, so I left my twelve-year-old sister Holly in her seat while I took Sandy to the bathroom. When I came back, Holly was gone—and everyone was so busy watching you up on the screen, not one person saw who'd taken her."

My gaze riveted to the harsh lines of his face, I can only shake my head in silent horror.

His eyes full of remembered torment, he stops in front of me, arms crossed over his broad chest. "Then a little more than six years ago, a couple up in Hood River starts renovating an old house, and find sixteen girls buried in the basement. One of them was Holly."

Tears sting my eyes. Without thinking, I reach up to cradle his jaw between my hands, trying to offer that poor comfort. "Duke," I whisper.

He plows ahead without stopping. Maybe because that's the only way to get through it. "Turns out the bastard who previously owned the house died peacefully in his sleep, and his kids who sold the place never had any idea of what their old man had gotten up to all those years they lived there." The edges of his lips whiten. "For ten fucking years I'd dreamed of finding him. Of killing him, of saving Holly or maybe some other girl unlucky enough to catch his eye. But I never saved Holly and she never got justice. The pervert died real easy and there wasn't a goddamn thing I could do about it. So, yeah. I went through a bad patch."

One that I dug up again by prying into his life. "I'm so sorry. And I'm sorry for bringing it up and reminding you."

A hard laugh escapes him. "You didn't remind me of anything, duchess. It's *always* here"—he taps his knuckles against the side of his head—"right at the fucking surface. I think it and live it every single goddamn day." Against my palms, his jaw works as if he's trying to contain all the emotion raging inside him, then he gives a short nod. "Anyway, what's done is done. Now it's your turn."

To tell him who beat me. To tell him about my stepfather—a stepfather who isn't Keri's. To jeopardize my deal with Ivan and admit who I really am.

If it was just my future at stake, I would. But I can't risk losing Erin.

Drawing my hands back, I avert my face, hugging my arms to my chest. On a broken whisper, I tell him, "I can't."

"Why? Are you afraid of him? You don't have to be." His big body presses closer, fingers tangling in my hair and forcing me to look at him. His eyes are dark and stormy, his gaze searching mine. "I'll help you. You want to get away, I'll get you away. You want him never to touch you again, I'll do that. Anything you need."

And here's this sweet dream again. Because as I stare up at him, my lips trembling and my heart filled with so much hope—so much longing—he gives a tortured groan and leans in, his head lowering.

Warm lips claim mine. His kiss is sweet and searching, his big hand cradling my face as he gently coaxes my lips apart. Slowly he takes over my mouth in long, slow licks, and I can't stop myself from clinging to him, pleasure mingling with the growing ache in my chest and the burning in my eyes.

I'd have given anything for Duke to have come along before this. I'd have given up anything in the world to have this.

Anything but Erin.

A sob shudders through me and he breaks away, mouth still close to mine, his thumbs wiping away my falling tears. "Shh, baby. No," he groans the denial. "It'll be all right. We'll make it all right."

I don't know how we can. "I just don't want to hurt anyone. I just want everyone to be safe."

"I'll do that," he promises. "Just tell me what you need, Keri. I'll make it happen."

Keri. I stiffen against him as reality crashes over me.

He's not kissing me. He's kissing Keri.

He's not making promises to me. He's making promises to Keri.

And he's such a good man, I think he would help *me.* Regular old Olivia. But I don't dare risk telling him who I really am.

Not without risking everything.

I jerk my head to the side, away from his warm touch. "I don't need anything from you." Raggedly spoken, it's such an obvious lie. And I can feel him looking at me but if I look back, I won't be able to stop crying. But he's not moving, not answering, so I add desperately, "The only thing I need from you is for you to do your job!"

And I'll do mine.

For a long second Duke doesn't react, then abruptly he pulls away. Without a word he stalks to the suite's exit.

The door slams behind him. Hands covering my face, I slide to the floor in a sobbing heap.

I didn't look at him. But I can't stop crying, anyway.

NINE

DUKE

"Rough night?"

At the sound of the prez's voice, I jerk my head up from a hard pillow of green felt—and immediately regret it. There aren't quite two Saxon Grays floating in front of me, but the one who's there is damn blurry and in danger of getting his boots puked on.

That'd be a fine capper to all this shit—the half bottle of whisky I downed last night coming up on the prez's feet.

Not that he looks worried. Instead he looks damn

amused as he snaps his fingers at Bottlecap and tells the prospect, "Get this brother a bloody eye. And maybe a bucket."

A hangover remedy. Just the thought of an egg yolk swimming in tomato juice sets my stomach roiling again, but if the prez orders it, I'm fucking drinking it.

Stifling a groan, I scrub my hands over my numb face and stagger to my feet. At some point last night I must have passed out—and by some miracle, flat on my face on top of the pool table instead of in a puddle of piss some-where. I don't know *how* the fuck I ended up on the pool table, but obviously I wasn't ever intending to go farther than the clubhouse's front door, considering that I'm wearing nothing but the sweats I dragged on last night.

Last night before I kissed her. Before I made her cry.

And that shit was all on me. The first time she kissed me, the day she was taking care of the scratches on my shoulder and my face, I could tell myself that I was just trying not to hurt her. That letting her kiss me was better than shoving her off me. Which is all fucking bullshit—a tiny thing like her, I could have stopped her easily and without hurting her. But I didn't. I wanted her to kiss me, married woman or not, so I didn't stop her from doing it.

But last night, that was all me. Putting my mouth on a married woman—and not giving a fuck that a ring was sparkling on her finger.

The prez grabs a bottle of water from behind the bar counter, then sets another one in front of me as I drag my ass onto one of the stools. "I got a message from Howler, thanking me for taking care of that shit with Harris so damn fast. Said he got his eight thousand yesterday. Is that the reason for all this?"

For getting wasted? No. Though I sure as hell wish I could use it as an excuse.

But you don't disrespect a brother by lying to him. Either your answer's the truth or you don't answer. Except *don't answer* isn't an option with the prez.

Evasion is an option, though. "That eight grand didn't hurt as much as it could have. Beaver turned over his Camaro for me. That covered most of it."

"So you getting piss-drunk isn't because you bailed out your piece of shit relation?"

My jaw tightens. "No."

"Grasshopper said Maurice will be taking a shift here at the clubhouse, securing the perimeter. Since that's good news, I'm guessing that isn't the reason, either."

I shake my head.

"It's this actress, then?"

Shit. "If she *is* the actress."

He frowns. "What's that mean?"

"Truth is, I don't know what the fuck it means." I scrape my hand through my hair. "Just a feeling."

Or wishing. Because to my mind, any man who beats his wife forfeits any claim on her. But that doesn't make her mine. And maybe all of this suspicion is just me wanting to believe that she doesn't really belong to anyone else.

"You talking about something beyond the general shit feeling that this job is all wrong?"

Is it really different? Because that wrong feeling started when Tataurov dropped her off here. That didn't make any fucking sense, abandoning his wife in the company of a bunch of bikers.

Unless she wasn't really his wife. That makes *more* sense.

What doesn't make sense, then, is why the hell he'd hide away someone who wasn't his wife and pay twenty grand a day for her protection.

"Yeah," I say gruffly. "Something beyond."

"You know for sure or just your gut?"

"My gut. Though there's things she's said and done…" I take a swallow of water, thinking through all the things about her that just don't fit.

Thinking about her reaction last night when I called her *Keri* instead of *duchess*. It was the first time I said her name and she responded like it was a fist to her heart.

"I'm pretty fucking sure," I finally say. "But maybe it's just what I want to hear and see."

"You usually trust your gut?"

"Yeah." I do.

The prez nods, his gaze thoughtful. "You ever going to put in your bid for the enforcer's patch?"

I stiffen, trying to read him. I can't. "Would I have a chance of getting it?"

Unlike the rest of us, the prez doesn't have to answer

the question asked. "Tell me why you walked six years ago."

Shit. "Does it matter? I walked."

"You let me decide if it fucking matters." His expression doesn't change but his voice sharpens to a razor's edge. "You've got no issue with Zoomie now. Did you then or was it some other shit going on?"

Some other shit? How much shit does he want me to name?

A little more than six years ago, I was desperately trying to round up enough cash to set up a home for Joyce and Jessie, because my stupid fucking sister never remembered to feed her baby.

A little more than six years ago, they discovered Holly in a basement and I found out that the perverted fucker who killed her died real easy in his sleep.

Because everything *still* leads back to that theater. To Holly going missing. To my family falling apart.

And that led to the other shit, too. The shit with Zoomie and me walking away from the Riders, which happened right in the middle of the emotional storm I was living through.

I pinch the bridge of my nose, trying to ease the throbbing ache in my head, and tell him, "I originally joined up with the Riders because Lucifer was fucking my mom." She and my dad had just broken up, we'd just moved to Pine Valley—and she was floundering, searching for something to hold on to. So she grabbed on to the biggest badass around. "She was feeling real low in those days. And you know how Lucifer was."

The prez nods. Neither of us will talk shit about the Hellfire Riders' former prez. Hell, once upon a time I admired him. But a more selfish fucker doesn't come along often. He sensed my mother's vulnerability and got right in there, larger than life, taking care of her. Taking care of me and Sandy. And it was a few years before I saw Lucifer for what he was.

"I was sixteen, seventeen when they started up," I continue grimly. "And I knew all about his other women. Especially his wife, his daughter—though Zoomie was already over in Afghanistan. I never even met her until she came back and got her prospect patch. But some part of my head, I don't know. I started thinking of her as a little sister. Someone I needed to protect."

At that, the prez starts laughing.

Yeah. I take another swallow of water and continue, "Before I met her, I pictured her as someone like your woman, maybe. A fighter but not"—I raise my fists to indicate the kind of physical fighting that Zoomie does—"so I had no fucking idea what she was really like. Or that she sure as hell didn't need a big brother looking after her. And that day she was patched in, watching our brothers going up against her and beating her down…it just fucking snapped something in me."

"Even though she won?"

"Even though she won. I just didn't want to be a part of that shit anymore."

To this day, I don't even know if she knew about her dad and my mom and what I was carrying around in my head. Lucifer died before she returned, but he and my mom had cooled off long before that.

Then I joined the Steel Titans and it wasn't something I'd ever tell Zoomie after the fact. Because looking back, it's all damn stupid.

Didn't feel like it then, though.

Something hard gleams in the prez's eyes. "You all right with watching Zoomie get beat down now?"

"As all right as I am watching any brother get beat down." Which means that I'd step in and have her back. "But over the years, I figured out most women are a lot stronger than I gave them credit for."

Even if they can't kick ass like Zoomie does. But muscle isn't everything.

He nods in agreement and gets that look in his eyes that says he's thinking of his woman, Jenny.

And no more dancing around this now. "If I put in for the enforcer's patch, am I going to get it?"

"No. I like you doing what you do now." As I'm processing that blunt answer, he asks, "You really want it? Or you just want people to stop saying you're disloyal?"

There's not much difference. "It'd settle the matter. You'd never make me a ranking officer if I was."

"True." He leans forward. "But what's also true is that nobody's saying it anymore. There was some grumbling when we folded the clubs together, yeah. There was more grumbling when I appointed you to the executive board, because everyone was whining about everything then. But after that, if anyone called you disloyal, that shit got shut down."

The hell? I always figured that when I stopped hearing it, it just meant the brothers were saying it behind my back—because they'd have been spitting teeth if they'd said it to my face. "What changed?"

A hard little smile touches his mouth. "Maybe there was a point I considered walking, too. It didn't come to that. But it might have given me another view on the matter."

I can't imagine what might have made him think about walking…except one thing. His woman, Jenny. She was the daughter of the prez of a rival club. Would he have walked away from the Hellfire Riders to have her?

The way the prez looks at her, I think he would.

He rises from his stool. "Maybe I'll reconsider if you tell me this: do you really want to be sent out alone doing an enforcer's work instead of continuing to oversee the jobs with the brothers here? You don't like babysitting?"

"It suits me." Suits me real well. Everything in my life was leading up to this. Watching over people, keeping them safe.

"And it makes you good money, yeah?"

Good enough to support Joyce and Jessie, and have plenty left over. "That it does."

"And it makes good money for the club. So I'm content

to leave things as they are."

Huh. I am, too.

The prez must read that realization on my face. He leans in, his gaze hard on mine. "So you keep this job. And when your gut settles, you listen to it. You figure out this girl. If she's not who she claims to be, then we'll figure out what the hell Tataurov's trying to pull."

I nod. But I'm not thinking of Tataurov.

Instead I'm thinking that if she's not who she claims to be, then I'll be making a claim of my own.

And I'll be making her *mine*.

TEN

OLIVIA

I suppose I'll earn the diva label today.

I woke up with my eyes so swollen from crying that attempting to put my colored contact lenses in—a chore that takes forever on good mornings, which this morning was definitely not—just irritated my eyes more. So instead of getting ready and heading downstairs, I'm lounging in bed with a cold gel mask over my eyes, waiting for the sensitivity and puffiness to subside.

Except I'm not really *lounging* like a movie star should.

Curled up in a miserable ball is more accurate.

I become a stiff and silent ball when I hear the door at the main entrance to the suite open. Duke. He's the only one who'll enter without knocking.

He never returned last night. Which is probably best because he'd have heard me sobbing through half of it.

Now I remain quiet and motionless, hoping he assumes I'm already downstairs.

My tension eases when I hear his bedroom door open and close, followed by the sound of his shower running. The past few days, that's the sound I've woken to and there was something wonderful—and so deliciously hot— knowing that he was naked only a few yards away.

It's not so wonderful today. Today I curl up tighter, ignoring the flame that sparks through my body. Because I can't deny that I want him. That I'm falling for him so hard and so fast.

But I can't risk losing this chance to get legal custody of Erin. It'll be the only time I have any power over my stepfather—by dangling a fortune in front of him.

Otherwise I just don't have any sway over him. As current mayor and former chief of police in our small town, his word always holds more weight than mine—and he has friends in all the right places. So every time I tried to report his abuse and remove Erin from his custody using legal routes, it was turned around so that I inflicted my own bruises. So that I've been lying.

Maybe, once upon a time, someone in town would

have believed me. Except that when I was eighteen, I tried to run away with Erin. I didn't have a license or a car, but I got her on a bus and we attempted to escape.

We didn't get far. And although the kidnapping charges against me were dropped—at my stepfather's insistence, as a public act of benevolence and forgiveness—afterward, my word meant nothing to the police in town.

But in addition to giving me money, Ivan has lawyers who will draw up an ironclad custody agreement. She'll be mine, and she'll be safe, and if the law comes to my door, I'll have legal guardianship.

I think that if he knew the truth, Duke would help me. I *know* he would help me. But the kind of help he'd offer wouldn't be much different from me boarding a bus. It wouldn't be legal or permanent. I'd always live in fear of someone coming and taking her away—taking her back to her father. So I absolutely cannot risk losing this chance with Ivan. I can't tell Duke who I am or how much I want him.

But it kills me to know I have to make a choice between him and Erin. So instead of listening to him shower with my fingers between my legs stroking that flame hotter, the only thing I feel is the weight of that choice.

And I feel as if it will crush me.

I stiffen again when the door to his room opens. Curled up on the bed, I listen for the sound of him leaving the suite.

But all is quiet. My tension winds tighter.

Then he speaks, the gravel in his voice rasping over my heart. "You all right, duchess?"

"Yes." My throat's raw, my response hardly louder than a whisper. "Just a headache."

"Hell, if a headache is reason to be lying in your bed, then it's a good thing that I've got one, too."

I don't realize what he intends until his hands abruptly grip my ankles. Even as I cry out in surprise, he drags me out flat and pulls my feet to the end of the bed, my nightshirt bunching up over my hips and exposing my tiny thong. Then he quickly moves up onto the mattress—and over me, his body covering mine.

Oh my god. My fingers grip his biceps, brush the soft edge of a short sleeve. I smell shampoo and toothpaste and the leather of his vest, then I'm gasping when his heavy thigh wedges between my legs and deftly spreads them wide.

With a groan, he settles into the cradle of my thighs and I can feel his erection against me, rigid and thick behind his jeans. Nothing separates us but denim and the scrap of silk I'm wearing.

Panting, blinded by the gel mask, I struggle to calm my rioting senses. He's got his weight braced, his upper body lifted away from mine. I can feel the depression beside my shoulder, as if he's propped up on his hand or his elbow and looking down at me.

His voice is low and intimate. "So what's this mask for?"

Breathless, I can only shake my head. Until I feel his fingers at the edges of the gel mask and my hands fly to stop him.

Too late. The cooling mask eases up above my eyebrows and he goes quiet. My lids are closed—I don't dare open them without the blue contacts in—but I know he sees my reddened and puffy skin.

A soft brush of his thumb beneath my swollen lids is followed by a gentle, "Fuck me, duchess. Did you spend all night crying?"

"No. It's nothing." My whisper is strained. "Just allergies."

"Oh, yeah? Then open your eyes and look at me."

Lips pressed tight, I shake my head.

"Why?"

I search for a good lie.

A new urgency fills his voice. "Why wouldn't you want me to see your eyes, duchess?"

"Because…because they're bloodshot."

"Probably not worse than mine are, considering the shit night I had." Although there's humor in the reply, it's still low and intense. "What are you hiding from me?"

I squeeze my eyes tighter. "Nothing."

"And you're a fucking *terrible* actress," he growls.

I get no warning. His mouth covers mine and this isn't the sweet, searching kiss of last night. Instead it's fierce and possessive, his tongue thrusting between my lips as if staking a claim, his fingers tangling in my hair to anchor me in place.

But I couldn't have pulled away, anyway. Instead overwhelming need sweeps through me and I pull him closer. I've got no defense against this. I can't even *think* of defense. Only the heat of his mouth. His weight, the delicious weight of him that isn't crushing me but somehow lifting me against him, my body desperate to be even closer to his. The kisses before couldn't prepare me for the onslaught now, my entire being taken over.

Taken over by Duke.

Hungrily he feasts from my lips and it's different from every touch that came before. As if he previously held himself behind a barrier but that barrier has been torn away, and in this kiss I'm cherished and worshiped and wanted. I don't want it to end. I never want this to end—it feels too good and too right.

But it's not right. And when he lifts his head and gently says, "Look at me, duchess," the weight of the choice I have to make drops onto my chest again. But it hurts more now, because now I know what it feels like, for just a moment, to have him.

Throat aching, I try to avert my face. But he brings me right back, strong fingers tangling in my hair, his mouth gently brushing my closed eyelids.

"I shouldn't be doing this," I whisper thickly.

"And 'shouldn't' is different than 'you don't want to.' But you also don't want to hurt anyone, is that right? That's what you said last night."

Lips trembling, I nod.

"And you're thinking if word got out that a famous actress was messing around with a biker, then it might end up in some tabloid and hurt her reputation—or hurt the people she loves."

My heart aches. "It would."

"It wouldn't," Duke says firmly. "Because no one outside this room would ever know. And even if they did, none of my brothers would go yapping about our personal business to anyone outside the club. You believe that?"

I do.

Hope rises in me. Maybe I can have this now. Not forever. But while staying here at the clubhouse—

And while lying to Duke the entire time about who I really am.

The crushing pain in my chest thickens. A sobbing little breath shudders from me. "I can't."

"You can. Duchess, *look at me.*"

It's almost impossible to resist the authoritative command in his voice. But I can't risk losing Erin. I'll do anything to keep my little sister from living through the hell that I have.

Even if it means sacrificing my heart.

"All right, sweetheart. We'll play it your way." Firm lips skim down the side of my jaw. "You can keep those eyes closed tight, even though it means you won't see what I'm about to do to you."

My breath catches. "What?"

His answer is a scrape of his teeth in the hollow of my throat, followed by the rough glide of his big callused hand up my left side, dragging my nightshirt higher. Cool air kisses my exposed breasts a moment before his hot mouth captures my nipple, drawing a strangled gasp from my lips.

Sheer pleasure rips through me. Desire sears across every nerve, tautening every inch of skin.

"Duke." My back arches as if to press my breast deeper into the fiery heaven of his mouth. My fingers dive into his short thick hair. The exquisite suction increases, my nipple almost painfully hot and hard.

Then abruptly bereft when he lifts his head to groan, "You're so fucking beautiful. If you could just see what I see now, your nipples so pink and stiff."

I dare not look. But even without seeing, I *feel* beautiful when he immediately latches on to my other nipple, as if desperate to taste me again.

And desperate to touch me. Rough fingers slide between us down the front of my belly. He doesn't hesitate at the waist of my panties but goes straight in, delving into silky wetness and heat.

Duke stiffens even as I'm reeling with sensation and surprise. The only fingers that have ever touched me there are my own, and mine never incited this exhilarating pleasure.

A tortured groan rumbles from his broad chest. "Duchess," he rasps against the soft swell of my breast.

"Your pussy's *so* wet for me."

I don't know what to say to that. On a breathless laugh, I tell him, "I can't help it."

"Good, because I sure as fuck can't help how hard I am for you." His voice deepens and a tremor shakes through me as his fingers subtly rub against my clit. "Are you going to open your eyes and watch me eat this juicy cunt?"

Oh god. Swamped by need, by the image of his head between my thighs, of his mouth on me, I can't even form a response.

His fingers begin moving faster. "You want that?'

A whimper escapes me and I squirm against the luscious torment that is his touch. I'm wet, soaking wet, but the pads of his fingers are callused and the friction is robbing my brain of every coherent thought.

"You want to watch me lick these sweet pussy lips? You want to watch me suck on this pretty little clit?"

His thumb flicks that sensitive bud as he says it and I can't stop my needy cry, though my hands fly to my mouth to stifle the sound. Instead my desperate moans fill my cupped palms, my hips rocking in frantic rhythm against his hand.

"Open your eyes, duchess."

"I can't!" It's torn from me on a ragged sob of frustration and misery. "I want that so much. But I *can't*."

Instantly his firm lips are against mine again, his voice gruff. "It's all right, baby. Whether you open your eyes or not, I won't leave you needing. Nothing on this earth could stop me from tasting you."

Starting with my mouth. His kiss is long and slow, but still not sweet. Instead he's taking me over again, staking a deeper claim with every leisurely thrust of his tongue. His broad thumb strokes my clit to the same slow beat, his fingers slipping through the slick folds of my pussy, teasing at my entrance until I'm pushing back against his hand, tilting my hips and trying to urge him to fill the hollow ache.

But Duke doesn't claim me there. His slow torture continues, kissing and licking his way down my neck, strong teeth nipping at my shoulder before tugging the stiffened tips of my breasts to throbbing points. My fingers rake through his short hair, gripping tighter when the burning pleasure of his mouth rises to a taut peak, my nipple a fiery diamond against his tongue—then moaning as he abandons my breast, lips tracing the outside curve on a path to my ribs.

Lost to sensation, I'm desperate to touch him but he's still completely dressed, denim rough between my thighs, cotton and leather covering his torso. I slide my palms down over his wide shoulders. Heated by his body, the leather of his kutte is warm and smooth. I love the feel of it, of the heavy muscles beneath. My fingertips trace the edge of the Hellfire Riders rocker sewn to the back, then abruptly he moves lower. I gasp and my fingers curl, nails scraping through his hair again when his tongue dips into my navel.

His fingers slide out of my panties to grip the waistband. "Lift up your sweet ass, duchess."

Heart pounding, I do as he commands, my body suddenly trembling as the fabric drags slowly down the lengths of my legs.

"Holy hell." The gravelly curse is followed by a soft kiss to the inside of my thigh and a deep inhalation. "Look at you, so pink and wet for me, your little clit just begging for my tongue. And you smell *so* fucking good."

Embarrassment and pleasure war within me, heating my cheeks, lifting my breasts on panting breaths. I turn my head against the pillow, biting the heel of my hand in a mindless attempt to control my responses.

But there's no control. Not when his tongue flattens against the lips of my sex. At the first touch, his ravenous groan underscores my wild cry, then his tongue parts my folds and slowly slides all the way up to my clit, as if trying to devour me in one long lick.

Hungrily he licks the length of my slit again, then with a suckling kiss, his tongue swirls around my throbbing clit. Involuntarily my body bucks against his mouth and his hands catch my hips, holding me in place.

"Don't you try to take this pussy from me, duchess," he growls against my greedy flesh. "Because now that I've had a taste of you, I'm not letting you go."

I don't want him to. And as his mouth begins devouring me again, I let myself believe this incredible dream is true—that I'm his, that he'll want me despite the lies, that this could last. That he won't let me go when he learns what I've done.

Instead I let myself believe that Duke could come to love me, that every slick stroke of his tongue is a promise of a sweet and wild and wonderful future—giving myself over to this dream as if my heart is never going to break, as if I don't have to keep my eyes closed to conceal who I am. At this moment, I'm Olivia.

And the man I'm falling in love with is eating my pussy as if he'd die without it. As if he'd kill anyone who tried to come between us.

My head turning frantically against the pillow, I cry out in delirious pleasure when his lips close around my clit, his tongue stroking harder, faster across that oversensitive bud. Every muscle in my body draws taut. His fingers tighten on my hips, as if to brace against an explosion, but I don't think I can come like this. I've gone beyond anything I've ever felt before, my arousal so keen it's approaching agony, and a scream builds in my throat with every merciless lick across my clit. It builds and builds and abruptly shatters, but I'm not screaming, not doing anything but splintering apart against his tongue, my breath trapped in my lungs and my back bowed, my legs shaking as if electrified, a shock that seems centered inside me, my inner muscles clenching wildly.

A deep groan against my pussy sparks another convulsion, and his hot tongue abandons my clit to lap away the flood of wetness the orgasm wrings from my body.

As I'm still shuddering, he kisses his way back up, more quickly than he went down. His mouth finds mine and my flavor clings to his lips, and it seems so erotic and wonderfully dirty and arousing all over again.

Leisurely he draws back before leaning in for another kiss, then says against my mouth, "How's that headache doing?"

I laugh and feel the curve of his lips against mine. "Better."

"That's because an orgasm is even better than aspirin." He stretches out on his side next to me and slips his arm around my waist, tucking me in against his chest. "So why don't you try to rest a bit now."

Wait. We're done? I don't have a lot of experience but I still know that I'm not the only one who is supposed to come. "But you didn't—"

"Yeah, I did." His voice is gruff and amused. "If you'd opened your eyes, you'd have seen me stroking my cock while I sucked on your clit."

Oh. "I'm sorry I missed that."

His quiet laugh rumbles through his big body. "Next time."

Next time. There shouldn't be one…but I don't want this sweet dream to end. Not yet. Not ever. But it will. And until then, I'll take what I can get.

Pillowing my cheek against his hard chest, I let myself believe that it's me—Olivia—he's holding so tight. As if he'll never let me go.

But that's only because he doesn't know how many lies I've told.

ELEVEN

DUKE

She's not Keri Bishop. Of that I'm certain. I'm not sure about much else—her name, where she's from, how old she is, or even her eye color. Except they must not be blue. I can't think of any other reason she'd be so afraid of opening them. Keri's sky blue eyes are as famous as Jolie's lips or JLo's ass.

But I'll find out what color they really are. As soon as I can get her to look at me.

That won't be today. I heard her frustration when she

refused—but I also heard her fear.

Maybe she thinks I wouldn't be holding her so close if she wasn't Keri Bishop. When the truth is, I wouldn't be holding her like this if she *was*. Because my reaction to her makes a hell of a lot more sense now. Keri Bishop is nothing but a woman who always reminded me of the pain of failing Holly.

This woman eases that pain.

So the question of who she really is doesn't matter. She's mine now. And if she's afraid of revealing her identity, I'll take that fear away. I'll love her so damn well she won't ever fear that I want Keri Bishop instead of her.

But the secret identity raises a hell of a lot of other questions about this job and why Tataurov is hiding her here. That accent tells me she's from somewhere down South. Most likely Tataurov is paying her to pose as his wife. Probably a hefty sum, considering how much he's paying the Riders to watch her. He's not sparing any expense.

Where he found her, I don't know. Maybe she's a stunt double or someone who regularly impersonates celebrities. But she's not an actress herself.

And I can't think of any other reason she'd take this job except that the money's good enough.

Unless she didn't have much choice. Someone took a belt to her. She insisted it wasn't Tataurov who beat her and I'm starting to believe it.

But if he's paying her, maybe when he put his offer

on the table, someone forced her take it. Maybe that Aaron fucker she was talking to, although if he was the one beating her, she likely wouldn't promise to be with him forever. Unless she was trying to placate the fucker, and hopes to take whatever Tataurov's paying her and run from him.

She won't have to placate Aaron—or anyone else—ever again. She says she wishes she'd known someone like me all her life. I can't go back in time, but I can make up for all the years I missed. Starting with whoever took a belt to her back.

Those bruises are all but gone, yet I know I'll see them for a long time to come. She's been through hell.

I won't add to it. I already did enough. Her swollen eyes are testament to that.

Now I hold her as long as I can, loving the sensation of this woman sleeping in my arms, the sweet taste of her pussy lingering on my tongue. I don't want to leave her, but I need answers—and I won't be getting them from her. Not today.

So I'll find them.

HER EYES ARE A BEAUTIFUL, gold-flecked hazel.

Now that I know what I'm looking for, finding her is easy. A few searches on the laptop in my room is all it takes. Hell, she all but told us who she was, mentioning that lookalike contest held by *People* magazine, and talking about a no-talent girl who never got anywhere no matter how hard she worked.

That girl is Olivia Burke.

In the photo that accompanies the feature in the magazine's online archives, she's only sixteen. Which means she's twenty-three now, five years younger than the woman she's impersonating.

Side by side, she and Keri are pictured with wide grins—and those smiles couldn't be more different. One is the smile I've seen onscreen a thousand times. The first time I saw the other smile was out in the dark, flashing so bright she lit up my whole fucking world.

It's the smile that I intend to see the rest of my life.

And I'll wake up to those beautiful hazel eyes every morning. But before there's any future, I need to make sure she's safe now.

Because this job never felt quite right, but now I'm real fucking uneasy. Why hide away a double of his wife unless Tataurov thought the trail leading here wasn't as invisible as he claimed? By dressing her up as Keri Bishop, he put a target on Olivia's back. But even if Zhuk got to her—*he never fucking will*—but if he did, what the fuck did Tataurov expect would happen then? Eventually Keri would resume her public life and Zhuk would just come after her again.

So there's something else going on. And maybe it's as simple as what struck me from the very first: that a man who loves a woman will keep her by his side, because there's no safer place for her.

I'd lay down good money betting that the real Keri Bishop isn't too far away from Tataurov now. Hell, an actress with access to the best makeup and wigs—she could be right beside him without anyone being the wiser. Except they wouldn't want Zhuk looking too closely. They'd want to divert his attention in another direction. Maybe they dressed up Olivia and hid her away so that Zhuk would search futilely for her hiding place instead of looking where Tataurov is.

Because everything else has happened exactly as Tataurov claimed it would. They've been leaving those stupid lures online—the ones where Keri's supposedly making reservations at restaurants or holed up in a hotel room. Blowback's found a couple of those lures—and said Zhuk could probably easily find them, too—but nothing's come of them yet.

So maybe it's all that simple. Maybe it's not. But I won't be the one figuring that out.

I e-mail Blowback the link to the *People* article. No need to send anything else. He'll start digging and looking at Tataurov from this new angle.

Because figuring out what Zhuk and Tataurov are doing is Blowback's job. My job is to protect the woman sleeping in the other room.

Except protecting Olivia Burke is not just a job anymore.

Now it's the reason I'm breathing.

* * *

I'VE NEVER KNOWN A WOMAN to take so long putting on makeup and doing her hair. But now I know why she does.

It doesn't matter anyway. I'd wait a long damn time for Olivia Burke. And today the waiting gives me a chance to think over how I'm going to handle this. Because it's real clear that she doesn't want anyone to know that she's not Keri Bishop.

But there's two problems with allowing Olivia to continue thinking that I don't know who she is. One is that I sure as fuck don't want her believing I'm the kind of man who will mess around with a married woman. Because I don't know how any woman can trust a man who does. I don't know how she could fall in love with me, thinking I would. And I aim to make her fall for me.

As a reason, it's selfish as hell, maybe. But I don't give a shit. I'd rather have her thinking I'm selfish than have her thinking I've got no respect for marriage vows. Because I do. And down the road, when it's time to make her mine, I don't want her feeling any doubt about whether I'll always honor those vows.

And the second reason is that I don't want her to spend another minute thinking that *I* believe she's Keri Bishop. I want her to know that when I touch her, I know exactly who I'm touching.

I'd sure like to be touching her now.

To pass the time, I open up the piano in her sitting

room. And, yeah—I know what I'm really doing: luring her out here a bit faster. Because there's something magic about this instrument, and nothing draws people in like someone playing. Like moths to a flame. Doesn't matter where it is. People will stop and watch and listen.

Thanks to all those years of lessons—and the years since, playing on my own to keep from getting too rusty—I've got a decent repertoire memorized. Almost all classical. My mother is nothing if not traditional.

It doesn't take long. I hear the door to the bathroom open as I'm warming up. Most likely Olivia poking her head out.

I don't turn around but slide right into Beethoven, starting with the first movement of "Moonlight Sonata" because I know she'll be familiar with it, then the "Appassionata" because it's a hell of a lot more dramatic and fun.

More impressive, too, if there happens to be a girl to impress.

And it draws her, just as I hoped it would. I can feel her coming quietly closer, as if she doesn't want to distract me. Then I glance back and my fingers strike all the wrong keys.

That's Olivia Burke—and she's so fucking beautiful. And I don't know if she's more beautiful now simply because I know her name, know her taste, know she'll be mine. But knowing all of it now, it's as if I'm seeing her for the first time—and it's like a kick to my chest.

The piano falls silent.

"Oh no." Blue eyes wide, she freezes in place, her hands flying up. "Sorry. I didn't mean to make you stop."

"You didn't," I say gruffly and slide over a bit. "Come park your ass beside me, duchess."

Shyly biting her bottom lip, she does, parking an ass that's barely covered by a short denim skirt. Her red heels are like little boots—and must be the most impractical, sexiest boots ever made—and her top is a loose flowing thing with rips in the sleeves that expose her shoulders and arms.

She's not wearing her rings. Maybe in her rush to finish getting ready and come out here, she forgot all about them. Forgot all about another man's ring.

I'll make her forget about more than jewelry. I'll make her forget every other man but me.

My touch will erase every other man's touch. Fuck, I want to kiss her now and obliterate every other kiss she's ever had. But if I start, I don't know if I'll stop.

And the next time I kiss Olivia, I want her to know I'm kissing *her*.

Maybe because I don't immediately kiss her, though, she looks shy and uncertain. Or maybe it's morning-after nerves. Or afternoon-after nerves, considering it was only this morning that she came against my mouth.

The memory of burying my tongue in her sweet, sultry pussy instantly hardens my cock, but that has to wait, too. This woman is mine to take care of and that will always come first. "You hungry? I told Molly you were sleeping late, so she left a lunch for you downstairs. I can have Bottlecap run it up."

"Maybe in a bit." Lightly she touches the ivory keys in front of her. Not hard enough to strike a note, but as if she was wondering what they felt like.

Keri Bishop would have known. And I'm going to try to take this slow and easy. With my right hand, I tease out the melody for "Heart and Soul."

"You want to take the bottom?" I ask her.

Her gaze shoots to mine, her cheeks flushing. "The bottom?"

I grin. No doubt where her mind is. In the same place mine would like to be.

But we're not going there yet.

"The bottom," I say again, and demonstrate by playing the chords with my left hand. Her lips part when recognition strikes. Because of course she's heard this before, and is realizing I'm asking her to play a duet.

Then her expression freezes. "Oh," she says lightly, with a laugh that's probably supposed to sound careless but sounds as if it's being pushed through a cheese grater. "No. I can't really play."

"Really?" With my right hand, I start in on the melody from the theme song of Keri Bishop's Disney show. As often as my sisters watched it before Holly was abducted, the song will probably still be echoing in my head when it's nothing but a brainless skull in a grave. "I could have sworn you played the piano all the time on that TV show of yours.”

"Not me." Flustered, she twists her fingers together and looks everywhere but at me. "That was, you know—a stand-in. And camera angles. Like, I'd be at the piano but when they showed my hands playing, those were someone else's hands. So it's all faked.”

I catch her chin, bring her gaze back around to meet mine. "Do you fake everything?”

Her floundering stops. Hurt seems to draw up within her eyes, hard and tight. Lips trembling, she shakes her head. "No," she whispers.

I don't want to hurt her. Or scare her. So I'll still try to ease her into this but I think the hurt and fear are coming.

Releasing her chin, I play a bit of Chopin, allowing her to settle. She's quiet beside me as I finish up.

"You're really good," she says softly.

I don't mind if she believes that. "If you want to learn, just ask. It can help pass the hours while we're waiting to hear about Zhuk.”

And we can pass the other hours in bed.

Her face brightens. "I'd like that.”

"I'll have you playing 'Mary Had A Little Lamb' by the end of the week, then.”

That brilliant smile flashes and she glances back at the keys again. "Who taught you?”

"My mother.”

"What's she like?”

"Before or after Holly?”

She sucks in a breath, her gaze searching my face as if making sure that this topic doesn't hurt me too much to discuss. "Before."

"That's when she was laughing all the time. And full of fire. And…fancy."

"Fancy?"

I nod, thinking back. "It's not something I realized at the time. Because she was a lot like what I saw on movies, on TV. I thought it was just the way mothers were. That sort of…tough, feminine elegance. You said your dad liked John Wayne movies?"

She nods.

"My mother was like Maureen O'Hara—that redhead who starred in a couple with him. Like *Rio Grande*. Or *The Quiet Man*."

Recognition fills her expression. "Oh yeah. Okay."

"So she was like those women who grow up fancy, but end up somewhere a lot rougher. Yet they still make a place for themselves. And I suppose that's what happened to her. She grew up back east in Boston—even went to one of those fancy girls' schools—then fell for my dad and moved out here to Oregon."

Which isn't the Old West anymore but is still a long way from Beacon Hill.

"And then Holly went missing?"

"Yeah."

As if in response to the sudden roughness in my voice, she slips her hand into my palm, her fingers threading through mine. "Does she still live here?"

Not asking what my mother is like now. Maybe for the best. Or maybe it's too easy to guess. "Yeah, she's in town."

"Is she the one who takes care of Jessie?"

"No. Her other grandmother does."

"Oh." She looks back at the piano. "So what's Jessie's favorite song?"

Christ, what she does to me. Taking me somewhere painful but realizing exactly when to pull back into something easier.

And I want to see her smile again. I spend a few seconds running through the beginning of the Star Wars theme in my head before I start laying a simplified version down on the keys, and within a few more seconds, she's laughing and nodding.

"Your niece has good taste."

"Yeah, she does. Now come here, duchess." I don't wait for her to figure out what I mean, but grip her waist and lift her closer, turning her around so she's straddling my lap and facing me, her ass almost level with the keys, her lower legs and feet dangling over the back of the piano bench.

Her breath shudders, her eyes softening with immediate arousal. And it's so fucking hard not to draw her mouth to mine. So fucking hard not to just unzip my jeans and drag her forward over my cock and take her right here.

Instead I cup her beautiful face in my hands, looking

at her. Trying to figure out where to start. Because everything I planned just doesn't fit now.

And she's realizing that I didn't put her on my lap so I could kiss her. She doesn't realize yet that I did it so she can't run away…but still, she's biting her lip, looking wary and hesitant as her gaze searches my face.

Whatever she sees there must worry her. "What are you thinking?" she whispers.

"About Maureen O'Hara," I tell her. "And this other movie she was in that my sisters used to watch all the time. You probably know it. *The Parent Trap.*"

"Oh. Yeah." Her brow pleats into a frown. "But I'm pretty sure that was Lindsay Lohan, not…not me."

"No, this was the original movie." And because I know it's coming, know it's going to hit her, I run my palms up and down her bare thighs—distracting her or soothing her, it doesn't matter, as long as she knows I'm here for her. "But the premise is the same. A pair of twins switch places."

She stops breathing. Stops everything, except staring at me, her face deathly pale.

Then she starts shaking, and looks away from me, her gaze darting around the suite but I don't think she's seeing a thing. Just frantically thinking of a way out of this.

Finally she says, "You've seen a lot of movies."

As if she can continue on, pretending I didn't suggest anything.

"Yeah, I have. And until six years ago, I saw every one of Keri Bishop's movies. Most of them more than once."

Her eyes close. "That's great," she whispers shakily. "You must be my biggest fan."

"No, sweetheart. Holly was. And I always hoped that the asshole who took her would try again in another theater and that I'd find him that way. So I went to every one I could."

That brings her gaze back to mine. "I'm sorry you didn't find him."

"Me, too." And she does it again. Flips the conversation away from herself. I still don't know if it's deliberate or if it's just her curiosity and compassion for other people, but it's damn effective. I can't let this get derailed, though. "But watching those movies meant I have a real good idea of what Keri Bishop is like. And I know damn well that you're not—"

Her palm claps over my mouth, stopping me—then she holds her hand there, her eyes filled with glittering tears. "Don't," she tells me hoarsely. "Please don't. You're wrong."

Her frantic gaze implores me to agree. I nod—but the only thing I'm agreeing to is not finishing what she stopped me from saying.

Her palm falling away from my mouth, she curls forward, her shoulders hunched. "You're wrong," she says again.

"Duchess," I say softly. "You don't have to hide this from me."

Full lips pressed tight, she shakes her head. Uncontrollable shivers are overtaking her body, and her misery and fear are ragged claws digging into my chest.

Gently I cradle her face in my hands and wipe the tears from her cheeks. "Why are you so afraid? You must know you can trust me."

Her breath shudders. "I do."

"But you still feel as if you have to hide from me?"

"It's not…" Swallowing hard, she averts her face, trembling as violently as if she was stranded naked in a snowstorm. Utterly vulnerable. Utterly terrified. "It's not about trust."

"Then tell me what it's about."

Her trembling intensifies. "If it was just about me, I would tell you. I would risk it. But…"

"It's not just about you." I finish for her. "Who is it about?"

She shakes her head.

"All right," I say to her softly because I can't fucking bear the way she's quaking so hard, as if her world is falling apart. "But you have to tell me one thing: Have you been forced to do this? Is someone going to hurt you if the Hellfire Riders find out you aren't—"

"No." Her lips are stiff, barely moving. "No one's forcing me. Or threatening me."

On a heavy sigh, I pull her in close—expecting some resistance but she wraps her arms around my neck and clings, her tearstained face buried against my throat.

"I'm sorry," she whispers brokenly. "I'd tell you. I

would. But…I did something wrong for the right reasons once and everything became so much worse. This time I'm trying to do it right, to follow the rules I was given. But I didn't expect to meet you. And I can't tell you what you want to know." Her voice cracks on a sob as she adds, "And it's tearing me apart."

Her pain and fear are tearing *me* apart. Throat thick, I shake my head. "Don't let it, baby. This is easy here, all right? You don't say anything you feel you shouldn't. And I won't say a damn thing, either, or ask questions that you can't answer. You've got a job to do, yeah?"

Her response is a shuddery breath against my neck. "Yes."

"Then you keep doing it." I stroke my hand down her spine. Her trembling is easing now. "And no one else needs to know a damn thing."

Though Olivia isn't even aware of how much I already know. Which isn't much, because except for a picture and a caption, that lookalike article was fucking worthless. I just know her name and where she's from, and her age.

And I've got a feeling that if I said her real name now, it would break something in her.

"You have to believe I'm Keri," she whispers.

"I can't do that." When she stiffens, I add, "But with everyone else, with the brothers, I'll fake it, too. All right?"

She nods against my throat.

"Now I've got something for you," I say, because I knew this might be rough. And I wanted to see her smile after.

This time it's a giggle that shakes through her. "Another aspirin?"

Shit. My cock had been behaving, because there's no part of me that finds her tears or her fear arousing. But now that she's softened against me, now that she's teasing me, the only thing that matters to my dick is that she's straddling my hips and in the perfect position to fuck.

Then her soft lips open against my throat, her hot tongue gliding over my skin, and every nerve in my body joins my cock, coming to swift attention.

With a reluctant groan, I pull back a bit. "You hold off on that a minute." Because if she doesn't, this will never get given. I reach back for the phone in my pocket. "I'm returning this to you."

She lifts her head, her makeup a dark, tearstained smudge around blue eyes. Those eyes widen when she sees her phone, gaze snapping to mine. "Are you sure?"

"Yeah," I say gruffly. "If Zhuk's looking for this phone then he already knows he's looking in the wrong direction."

"Yes," she agrees softly.

"You aren't likely to get much of a cellular connection, but we've got the wireless. So if you need to research, watch a few of her movies—this'll come in handy, won't it?"

"Yes." Her gaze searches mine. "Can I check my e-mail or should I stay away from my personal accounts?"

Is she expecting a message from that Aaron fucker? My jaw clenches while I wrestle for an answer. Because I know she's not going to tell me a damn thing about him.

Not that it matters who the hell he is. Because my gut tells me she's not the type of girl to kiss one man if she's with another. So maybe this Aaron is an ex or some shit. Part of her past.

I'm her present. I'm her future.

Although if Aaron is the one who beat her, he's more than her past. He'll be goddamn history.

Studying my rigid expression, she withdraws from me a little. "I don't have to. I just…wanted to make sure that someone's okay."

And she's been away for a while. She might have friends, family to check on. Fuck.

"Go ahead," I tell her, then possessively clamp my hands over her hips. "But you're *mine* now. You understand? When this is all over, I'm not faking a damn thing anymore. Not for anyone."

She blinks. Then smiles, so bright and wide that I'm fucking stunned by how beautiful she is. A second later those lips are on mine, her hands fisting in my hair, and she's kissing me as if she's been waiting to kiss me her entire life.

And this time I don't stop myself from kissing her back, because Christ knows that I've been waiting for her all of mine.

But I'm done waiting.

With a ravenous groan, I push my hands up under that short skirt, gripping the soft bare curves of her ass. She's got a pair of those barely-there panties on, the kind where the back's nothing but a string that I can twist around my fingers and tug a bit, knowing it'll snug the fabric in front tight against her clit and tease those sweet pussy lips.

One sharp tug, and she fucking catches *fire*. Not just kissing but rocking against me on a full-throated moan, grinding against the thick bulge of my cock.

Needing me inside her. Ah, fuck. That's where I need to be, too.

With my palms cupping her ass, I rise from the piano bench, carrying her up with me. Her long legs tighten around my hips, her arms clinging to my neck. The noises she's making low in her throat as she strokes her tongue over mine are the hottest sounds I've ever heard, desperate and hungry whimpers, and I just want to feed that need.

Just want to make her mine.

Every intention I had of taking this slow, of worshiping every inch of her skin before sinking my cock deep into her, is blown away like ashes in the wind before I reach the bedroom. I can't bear to abandon the lush heat of her mouth, can't even fucking make myself stop kissing her long enough to lay her on the bed. Instead I go down onto the mattress with her, catching my weight on my hands, my hips settling between her thighs and her legs circling my waist. She's still rocking and rubbing her pussy up against my cock as if she's going to rub straight through my jeans and fill herself up, and her moans have taken on a pleading note. As if begging for more.

I'll give it. Because fuck knows, I'm about to beg, too.

At the edge of control, I break the kiss and grate out, "We'll take it slow next time, yeah?"

She nods, and her ragged panting breaths paint my lips with heat. "Next time."

But fast this time. Claiming her mouth again, I reach between us to tear open my belt, groaning as I free my erection from the prison of my jeans. Then groaning again as I turn my wrist, fingers sliding down to find her panties soaked through, her inner thighs slippery with her juices.

Beneath me, Olivia shudders. Her fists tighten in my hair and she pushes up against my hand, a wordless demand. I immediately give her what she needs, pulling aside the crotch of her panties and sinking two broad fingers into the tightest, hottest heaven I've ever known.

Her muffled cry of pleasure against my mouth joins my harsh groan, and all at once she's moving again, writhing against my hand, fucking herself on my fingers. Like a dancing flame under me, and I stoke her hotter, sliding my thumb up through her slippery folds to tease her clit with firm strokes.

I can't fucking wait any longer. Teeth clenched in a feral grimace, I force myself to lift away from her—my right hand still between her legs, my left hand desperately seeking the condoms I shoved into my back pocket after discovering who she really was, praying this moment would come. And the sight of her, sweet Christ. Her golden hair in wild disarray, her eyes glazed and lips parted, skin flushed as she's completely lost to her need. Her shirt's pushed up haphazardly over her chest, baring her smooth belly and exposing one breast, her nipple rosy and stiff. Her little skirt is in a crumpled band high around her waist, panties twisted to the side and the gusset trapped between her plump labia and the crease of her thigh, my fingers buried in her glistening cunt. Her shoulders are braced against the mattress and her body undulates in supple motion, rocking her hips, fucking my hand to the same rhythm as my thumb rolling over her juicy clit.

With my teeth I rip open the condom packet. A goddamn eternity passes as I roll it on, my dick so fucking hard that every second I'm not inside her is pure agony. She softly moans in despair when I drag my fingers from the fiery clasp of her cunt, then catches her breath when I push her left knee up and to the side, spreading her wide so that I'll have a real good view of my cock sinking into her when I stake my claim.

I press closer, gritting my teeth at the first gliding touch through her soft, slippery heat. She feels so fucking good.

"Duke." My name is a desperate plea from her lips. Her right leg hitches up higher around my hip, opening herself even wider to me. *"Now."*

Fighting for some measure of control, I fist my shaft and guide the fat head of my dick up and down the length of her drenched slit before lodging against her tight entrance, watching her pink pussy lips part around the thick tip. Welcoming me in.

"Don't stop," she gasps, though there's no chance I might. Her fingers twist in the sheets, as if she's anchoring herself in preparation for the first thrust. "Don't stop."

I won't. Except I can barely get into her. She's tight, so goddamn tight, and where she took my fingers all right, the delicate ring of flesh around her opening is resisting the greater width of my cock, giving way to the broad crown in a slow, slow stretch.

Olivia makes a whimpering sound of frustration, arching her back, hips pushing up against me as if to force me in. "Please. Oh god, please, Duke. I need you in me. All the way in me."

Jaw clenched, I snap my hips forward in a short, sharp thrust, and when the resistance abruptly yields I keep going, until my cock's completely buried in scalding velvet grip of her pussy and luscious heat surrounds every inch of my shaft.

And sweet fucking Christ, the *feel* of her. The hot, wet, tight feel of her cunt.

The tense, silent feel of her slender body beneath mine.

"Duchess." I hoarsely rasp her name, my voice taut with sudden worry. "You all right?"

"Yes," she says, but her tone is strained and her head's turned, her cheek flat against the mattress. And her eyes aren't glazed with passion now, but clear and bright.

So bright.

"Did I hurt you?" Fuck, fuck. Slowly I begin to withdraw.

Swiftly both her legs wrap around my waist and tighten, as if to drag me back down. But I'm twice her size and instead of moving me, she just pulls herself up the length of my cock, until I'm once again buried in that luscious heat.

"It doesn't hurt," she answers breathlessly. "Not really. You're just bigger…thicker than I thought. And…so deep."

So deep. I bite back a groan. She feels so damn good that my brain's moving real slow through a fog of pleasure.

But something in my head's still working because the pieces begin to fall into place. Even though I can't believe it. But it all fits.

Feeling completely fucking stunned, my gaze locks on her face. "You're a virgin?"

A funny little smile trembles across her lips and she looks down between us, to where she's got me trapped inside her with her legs wrapping me tight.

"No," she says with a note of pure feminine satisfaction, and there's a wickedly pleased gleam in her eyes. "I'm not."

Not anymore, I realize. Because I've taken her. Claimed her.

And I'll be the only man who ever does.

Possession swells within me, hot and fierce and primitive. Tangling my fingers in her hair, I lean in for a kiss— and my cock moves deep inside her. Her lips part on a soft gasp.

Voice rough, I ask again, "Are you hurting?"

"No." It's breathless again. "It's just…strange. Uncomfortable. Like I've got a big dick shoved up there."

Her reply invites me to find humor in this but I can't. Not yet.

And uncomfortable is better than painful. But not much. "You should have told me. I could have hurt you."

"You didn't." Biting her lip, she gingerly rocks against me, my cock sliding back and forth inside her in tiny increments. Fuck, she's so damn tight and hot and her moving like that is sweet torture. "And I was afraid you'd be honorable or something and stop."

"Stop?" Head hanging low, I bark out a short laugh. "I'm not that honorable."

"I think you are," she says, then moans low in her throat as I reach between us to tease her clit.

"I'm not," I tell her, my voice harsh with need and the effort of staying still while the slick inner muscles of her virgin cunt are holding every inch of my cock in their taut grip. "But I'd have made it special for you. Took it slow and easy. Undressed you, kissed every inch. But I didn't even get your fucking panties off."

Or her little boots. But maybe I'd have left them on. Those heels are hot as fuck.

With her eyes shimmering, her hand comes up to cup my jaw. "This *is* special. I can't think of anything I'd want more than a man who looks at me like you do—and who can't wait to make me his."

Make her mine.

That primitive need surges through my blood. But I have to be sure first. "And you're not hurting?"

Her beautiful, laughing smile flashes. "*No*," she insists. "I swear. And it's not so uncomfortable now, either."

Thank fucking Christ. Still stroking her clit, I capture her lips in a long, leisurely kiss until the tension in the slender form beneath me changes, no longer stiff with discomfort but taut with anticipation, and her inner channel is softer, wetter, hotter.

When she's moaning uncontrollably with each slippery caress over her clit and her pussy's tightening around me, as if she's on the verge of coming, I finally surge deep— and she's right there with me, clinging to my shoulders, red heels digging into my ass, urging me harder and deeper with every frantic cry. I give her what she needs, what *I* need, fucking harder and deeper with every stroke, until she suddenly stiffens again. She comes with her head thrown back and a wild, keening moan, her inner muscles clamping down on the length of my cock.

The sensation is like lightning shooting up my shaft, and I try to make it last, but each convulsive squeeze of her pussy just shoves me closer to the edge.

Then Olivia breathes my name in that gliding accent and it's all over. With a thick groan I bury myself in her sultry depths and come harder than a kick in the balls, teeth gritted and my hands fisted in the sheets, thinking that I'm going to die, just fucking fall over dead because a man can't survive this kind of sweet pleasure, and I'd be happy in my grave except that I wouldn't be able to do this with her again.

Chest heaving, I hold myself over her still-trembling body. Aftershocks keep quaking through her—and around my cock—and I'm not going anywhere soon. Lowering my mouth to her panting lips, I kiss her sweet and slow.

When I look down at her again, she's smiling that gorgeous smile—but I can't mistake the mischievous glint in her eyes that accompanies it. Even if those eyes are blue. But I'll see the hazel soon enough.

With a narrowed glance, I ask her, "What's that look?"

She giggles. "Just thinking…that I ended up playing the bottom part, anyway."

"You sure did, duchess." I grin. She played it real damn well. "And you know what that means now?"

Without waiting for her answer, I roll over onto my back, carrying her with me. Olivia sits up in surprise and then gasps as the change in position pushes my hardening cock up deep inside her again.

Biting back a rough groan of pleasure, I grip her hips. My voice is hoarse with need when I tell her, "Now you learn the top."

And my woman…she's a hell of a quick learner.

TWELVE

OLIVIA

I wake up to warm lips caressing my shoulder and callused fingers traveling over the curve of my ass.

"Good morning, duchess."

Duke's voice is a low, sleepy rumble against my ear, his chest a steely furnace against my back. Softly I moan as his roaming fingers dip between my thighs.

He muffles his groan against my hair. His cock is a heavy steel rod against my backside. "You're so fucking wet, baby. How long have you been awake?"

I arch against him. "Thirty seconds, maybe."

His voice deepens. "You must have been having a damn good dream, then."

I was. But this is better.

And *this* is even better, when Duke lifts my thigh and pushes deep inside my dream-drenched sheath. The delicious feel of his thickness stretching my inner walls draws another low moan from my throat, and I rock back against him in helpless need when he begins a slow, steady rhythm. Endless pleasure rolls through me, building faster and higher with every long stroke.

Then I'm suddenly gasping when he pushes me over onto my stomach and drags me up to my knees, and it's not slow and sleepy sex now, but a hungry and rough fuck that hurtles me straight into orgasm, screaming into the pillow. Duke groans behind me as my pussy convulses around his pistoning shaft, and his fingers tighten on my hips, pounding deep, deeper, until his big body goes rigid and his cock pulses against my inner walls as he comes.

Boneless and sated, I collapse against the mattress. Duke stretches out next to me, chest heaving and grinning in satisfaction. "That'll give you something new to dream about."

Arrogant jerk. I swat at him in answer, because I won't tell him that I *was* dreaming of him.

But he probably already knows. I don't think there's anything I can hide from him.

I just wish I didn't have to hide so much.

The sea green of his eyes is calm as he leans in to drop a kiss to my mouth. "Shower?"

"I'll just be a minute. I want to check my e-mail first."

That green isn't so calm now. But he only kisses me again—hard, possessive—before grabbing his sweats from the floor and heading to my ensuite bathroom.

I admire the muscular flex of his naked ass and thighs before rolling over and reaching for my cell on the nightstand. Nothing from Erin this morning, but I didn't expect anything. In the week since Duke returned my phone, she's been e-mailing me in the afternoon after school, using the computer in the library. It's Monday morning now, though, so she hasn't been at school or e-mailed in the past two days. Only if she were desperate would she use James's computer at home—and if she were that worried, she'd probably try to call, instead, even though she knows the call might not go through.

My chest tightens. I know she's fine. But not having Erin here with me feels as if I'm missing a piece of myself.

Especially since she would love everything here as much as I do. She'd love Molly and her horses. She'd love the lodge. She'd love my babysitters—especially Picasso and Grasshopper.

She'd love Duke, too. But not as much as I do.

I head into the bathroom, where Duke's already standing under the steaming spray. A quick glance in the mirror tells me my contact lenses haven't come out while I was sleeping. I don't like sleeping in them—although the instructions say it's okay for up to a week, I have this terror of waking up and finding that one of the lenses has stuck to the inner side of my eyelid—but now that Duke's in my bed every night and morning, it's either facing my fear or making him sleep in his room.

So facing my fear it is—because I'd face a lot worse to have him.

Pinning my hair up, I slip into the shower cubicle. Duke greets me with a kiss before angling the shower head lower, making certain I don't get a face full of water. Soap in hand, he pulls me flush against his chest and begins lathering my shoulders and back.

I've never imagined my life could be this sweet, this good. And I should be waiting for the other shoe to drop.

If there's one thing that my life has taught me, it's that the ups are always followed by the downs. My childhood was one wonderful up; then my dad was killed in a car accident. My mother's remarriage began as an up—when James hadn't yet shown his true colors and his sweet infant daughter became my little sister—and then my mother got cancer.

That was the start of a long, long down. There were ups along the way—almost all of them because of Erin—but until Ivan Tataurov came along with his million dollars and his lawyers, I'd lost hope that downward trajectory would ever change. And I've been so conditioned to watch for that moment when everything goes sour, when indifference transforms into violent rage, I can't remember the last time I've gone through a day happy and unafraid.

Until now.

When I realized that Duke figured out I wasn't Keri, I thought it was the end of every hope. But it wasn't. Instead it feels like it was the beginning of everything.

Perhaps I should be wary and preparing myself for the inevitable down. But when he holds me, when he kisses me, it's almost impossible to believe that anything can go wrong.

And the only thing wrong right now is Erin not being with me…and this endless waiting.

As he steps under the spray again and scrubs shampoo into his short hair, I ask, "Any news yet from Ivan?"

"No." He tilts his head back to let the water rinse away the lather, and my gaze follows the soapy rivulets flowing down over his chest, over his stomach, around the base of his thickening cock. "Blowback says they put up another fucking lure at some new restaurant opening."

I sigh. If Zhuk hasn't taken the bait yet, I don't know why they believe he ever will.

"Why?" There's humor in his voice but his gaze is intense as it searches my face. "You ready to get out of here? Maybe getting tired of Molly's cooking?"

"Never," I say truthfully, then sigh again. "But it feels like the longer this takes, the less likely it'll ever be resolved."

"Speaking as a Hellfire Rider, I don't care how much time it takes as long as Tataurov's twenty thousand keeps showing up in our account every day." His thumb skims down my jaw. "But speaking as the man who's aching to tell the whole fucking world who you really belong to, yeah—I'm pretty damn tired of waiting."

My heart swells, sweet and painful all at once. "I don't think the whole world cares who I really am." Maybe about…five people do.

"Their loss," he says gruffly. "But I don't mind not sharing you with the world. Bad enough I have to share you with these assholes here."

Smiling, I let my hand drift down his chest, forefinger tracing the narrow line of hair bisecting his abs. He's fully erect now, his cock thick and long, the flaring crown flushed a dark red. "You know what I'm not going to do with any of *them*?"

He knows. But he still asks in a voice hoarse with need, "What?"

My gaze locked to his, I sink to my knees. And the way he looks at me, with hot lightning flashing through the storm of his eyes, is better than any dream could ever be.

So is his taste. With a hungry moan, I take as much of him as I can, all at once.

It'll never be enough.

THE ONLY THING I'M TIRED of is spending half of every morning doing my hair and makeup. By the time I head downstairs, it always feels as if everyone else has been up and at it for hours, while I've been indulging myself upstairs and avoiding the real work. And although my appearance *is* part of my job, they can't know that.

They can't know it, and they probably wouldn't care. I could spend the entire time eating grapes in bed and they wouldn't blink an eye as long as Ivan's money is coming in.

Still, I'm not very good at being waited on. Or at letting other people do things for me.

I find Duke in the day room going over the schedule with Grasshopper. Here in the lodge, the Riders watching over me have remained the same, but since the clubhouse is still on lockdown, they've been rotating in other club members to stand guard at the doors.

Duke glances up as I come in, his gaze heating as it skims from my head to my toes…and lingers on the sparkly sandals I'm wearing.

Maybe when all of this is done, I won't sell the shoes.

"Duchess," he says simply, as if I hadn't slept in his arms all night and swallowed his cum an hour ago.

"Good morning, Duke. And to you, too, Grasshopper," I add breezily on my way to the kitchen. "Anyone else want a cup of coffee?"

If they do, they don't get a chance to say so. Picasso's voice comes over the radio. "Head's up, Duke. Sandy's at the gate."

His sister? I stop at the entrance to the kitchen, my gaze flying to the faint streaks still marking the side of his face.

A worried frown creases Duke's brow. "Did something happen to Joyce or Jessie?"

"I asked if it was an emergency, or something that she could tell you over the phone. She said it was a *family* emergency, and that if I didn't let her through, you'd kick my ass." Picasso's amusement bleeds through the radio.

Duke doesn't look as entertained. "For fuck's sake. What's she driving? I sold their Camaro."

"Looks like she hitched a ride with that Fowler girl."

"Who?"

"The girl who banged Burnout for all of a week before going *Fatal Attraction* on him."

"A knife-wielding psycho. At least it's not the dumbshit husband," Grasshopper says.

Duke pinches the bridge of his nose as if warding away a headache caused by the mere mention of his brother-in-law. "Tell her I'll ride out and talk to her. Christ knows she'd camp out at the gate otherwise."

"All right, man. Watch out for those nails this time."

Grasshopper snorts out a laugh. "She's like the fucking Wolverine."

"I wish she was half as reasonable." Duke glances over at me. "You'll look after the duchess?"

The other man bumps his fist. "I've got her, brother."

After another look in my direction, Duke nods and heads out.

Grasshopper turns to me. "Grab your coffee and let's go."

I blink. "Where?"

His grin is broad and quick. "To watch the fireworks."

Which means we head for the room with all of the camera feeds up on a dozen flat screens. Leaning back in one of the chairs, Picasso's got his feet up on the desk, a bag of chips in hand.

He holds out the bag to me. "Dorito?"

I shake my head, my gaze going to the screen in the lower left corner. The gate camera must be up on a post just beyond the metal barrier, giving a view of the gate itself and the road leading to it. Duke hasn't arrived yet. About twenty feet from the gate, a dark-haired woman is sitting on the hood of a parked Trans-Am, smoking and poking at her phone, her posture a picture of boredom. Standing beside the intercom housing must be Duke's sister—a pretty blonde who's staring through the metal slats in the gate, her arms akimbo, looking as if she intends to make Duke appear on the road ahead by her willpower alone.

"That's Sandy?"

"Uh huh," Picasso confirms, munching.

Another voice comes over the radio. "Camera five check."

He glances at another screen—one of the perimeter camera feeds. In the left top quarter of the screen, Maurice is holding up three fingers, an empty field behind him.

"Three," Picasso replies through his two-way, the releases the transmitter to tell me, "That's so if anyone tries to loop the feed, we'll know it on the next perimeter check."

And they make a circuit every hour. "Has anyone ever tried to?"

"Nah," Grasshopper answers. "Though one time, an elk knocked out a camera by scraping his antlers on the tree where it was mounted." He reaches for the Doritos bag and Picasso swivels out of his range. "You selfish fucker."

Unperturbed, Picasso tosses another chip into his mouth and crunches away.

"There he is," Grasshopper says and Picasso leans forward to flip a switch.

Immediately the rumble of a motorcycle engine comes through the speakers—the audio from the open intercom. Which means we're not just watching, but will also hear everything Duke and his sister say to each other.

Suddenly uneasy, I glance at Picasso. "Won't he be upset?"

"At what?"

"Because we're listening."

The biker shakes his head. "He'd be pissed if we didn't. Our brother can take care of himself, but a) we're on lockdown and if Zhuk rode up now we'd feel like real dicks when we didn't see him coming, and b) there's no fucking telling if that Fowler girl's got a weapon in that car of hers. So we watch and listen and that's how we have his back."

"So he knows you're listening?"

"Yup."

"Can they hear us?"

"Nope. Not without using that." He points to a microphone on the desk.

"Okay," I say, then fall quiet when Duke's engine does. Sandy's transformation is incredible. All at once she's smiling, waving at him through the gate.

"John!" She beams at him. "I knew you'd come."

Duke doesn't bother pretending to be glad to see her. "What the hell are you doing out here? Go home."

With only his back visible, he walks into the frame, and from this angle he looks huge and dangerous, all thick muscle in a leather kutte.

"No." Sandy's smile disappears and she crosses her arms over her breasts. "Not until you return Corey's car."

"You're going to be here a long time, then, because it's gone. Is your husband still breathing?"

A confused little frown furrows her brow. "Yes."

"That's because I sold the fucking car and paid the people who needed to be paid." Duke's big hands grip the top of the gate and he leans in to tell her, "He fucked up, Sandy. He got thumped for it. If he doesn't learn his lesson the next time he'll get a lot worse than a few loose teeth. And you acting like he didn't deserve that thumping isn't helping him."

"*You* are the one who isn't helping him!" She tosses her hands up in the air. "You know he needs that car. How's he supposed to get real work when he can't drive?"

Exasperation fills Duke's voice. "Pine Valley's not a big town. Plenty of people use their feet to get around."

"There's no jobs in Pine Valley! He wants to go looking up in Bend. But Joyce won't let us borrow her car—"

"Because she's a lot fucking smarter than that."

"Let us use your truck, then. Unless it's snowing, you don't have any use for it."

"Sure I do. It makes a real classy lawn ornament."

"So why can't we use it?" Her voice rises on a piercing note. "You don't drive it. Instead you ride your bike around, spending your time with all these criminals. Fucking all your whores."

"Hell, yeah," Picasso says and raises his fist.

Grasshopper bumps it. "We're fucking *all* the whores."

Though I can't see Duke's amusement when he replies, I can hear it. "Seems to me that Corey hung around the old clubhouse once upon a time, trying to earn a prospect patch. You'd have been all right with him fraternizing with criminals and whores if he'd gotten in?"

"He *would* have gotten in if you hadn't turned the club against him! But do they even know how much of a pussy you are?"

"Shit," Grasshopper mutters. "If *he's* a pussy then I don't know what I am. What's a weenier version of a pussy?"

"A dick," I tell him, then suck in a horrified breath when Sandy's next statement rings shrilly through the speaker.

"Do they even know you were supposed to watch over Holly and you were too much of a sissy to protect your little sister?"

Though they'd been laughing over my dick response, Grasshopper and Picasso fall silent. Angry and horrified, too—or maybe thinking the same thing that I am: that *this* is the moment someone needs to have Duke's back. Not because of Zhuk or a gun, but because his sister's utterly poisonous.

But as if it didn't even touch him, he says easily, "And now you sound just like Dad."

Oh my god. My gut twists even tighter. His *father* had said he was weak—or that he failed his sister?

Yet Duke *could* throw it back in Sandy's face. Point out that she was the one who'd had to visit the bathroom and was why they'd left Holly alone. I know plenty of people who would toss the blame right back, no matter how undeserved the blame is. But he doesn't do to her what she so carelessly does to him.

Which is just another reason I love that man.

Sandy's entire body is a stiff, angry line. "Better to sound like Dad than like you! For god's sake, Corey can't even be a real father because of you! Because you're always pushing into his place. You think I don't know how jealous you are of him? You try to take what's his, bribing Jessie with all your gifts, so that nothing he gives her seems good enough."

"You think that's jealousy?" Now Duke's starting to sound pissed. "You think making sure she has good food to eat and clothes to wear and a roof over her head is about me sticking it to your stupid fuck of a husband?"

"I know it is. Because you know what Jessie told him the other day?" Sheer outrage has each word rising to a shout. "She wishes Uncle John was her daddy!"

His voice roughens. "I wish I was, too. Then she'd have a father worthy of the name."

"One who'd leave her alone in a theater to be raped and murdered by an old man!" Sandy snaps, then slaps her hands over her mouth, as if shocked by herself.

A long, cold silence follows. Then Duke turns away, saying over his shoulder, "I think you'd best get home. And if you're thinking of stopping by my place and borrowing my rig, you unthink it."

"Then I'll trade you for it!" she yells after him. "If you want to be her daddy so bad, I'll trade Jessie for your truck!"

Duke freezes at the edge of the screen. I can't see his face, can't see anything but his steely arm—and the clench of his fist.

"Oh holy shit," Picasso breathes. "You'd better run, you stupid girl."

Slowly, Duke turns back. "What did you just say to me?"

Though I know he'd never hurt her, I flinch at that tone. And although a metal gate separates them and Sandy hadn't shown any fear—or sense—before this, even she takes a step back. Sullenly, she says, "You're the one taking care of her, anyway. We might as well make it official."

Not exactly what she said before. And a little more

palatable. But only if you pretend to forget what her first offer was.

Duke doesn't pretend. "For a truck?" he says flatly.

In a small voice she says, "Corey says he really needs it. And I promised I'd get it for him."

"Then I'll tell you what. You and your piece of shit husband sign legal guardianship over to me and Joyce, and I'll give you the truck."

Her mouth sets in a mutinous line. "I'm not giving her to Joyce!"

"Just me, then. Then you'll take the truck and haul that fifth-wheel as far as you can. Because he won't find work in this town. You think I've been ruining his chances? He's been ruining his own. But that'll change. Anyone in Pine Valley who hires Corey Harris is going to find out real quick that they can't afford to have him on their payroll. Not if they want to stay in the Hellfire Riders' good graces."

Anger pinches her face. "You're an asshole, John."

"Yeah, I am. But I figure if you'll trade your little girl for a truck, it won't be long before he's stealing from someone else and trading her to pay off his debt. So I'm going back to the clubhouse and calling a lawyer who'll draw up the paperwork. And aside from the day we sign those papers, I never want to fucking see you again." Radiating menace, he steps closer to the gate and she shrinks back. "And if you give Jessie over to me, that means she's mine. So if you have any thoughts about taking her with you when you go, as far as I'm concerned you'd be kidnapping her—and you know how I feel about people who abduct little kids. I'd track you down, and you'd find Corey skinned in your bed with his cock shoved down his throat. Now get the fuck off the Riders' property before I send my brothers to chase you off."

I watch him walk out of the frame again, my stomach roiling. Picasso's staring at the screen, his jaw clenched. Grasshopper's just shaking his head in disbelief.

Her lips flat, Sandy stares after Duke, then suddenly turns and skips back to the Trans-Am—and just before the roar of Duke's bike engine drowns out everything else, she crows, "He gave us the truck!"

Picasso's hand snaps forward and he silences the audio. "That was a fucking—" His gaze lands on me and he abruptly stops. "You okay, duchess?"

Whatever he's seeing on my face must tell him I'm not, so there's no point in lying. In a strained voice I whisper, "Just…sickened."

But Sandy's not the only reason I feel as if I'm about to throw up. Because I should have known the other shoe would drop.

You know how I feel about people who abduct little kids.

And that shoe just did.

THIRTEEN

DUKE

I spend most of the afternoon talking to Joyce and tracking down a lawyer who can get started on that paperwork right away, because I'm not giving Sandy time to change her mind.

Maybe I've given her too much time already. Waiting for…I don't know. For Sandy to grow up. For me to stop thinking that losing Holly fucked her up just as much as it did everyone else in our family, and so I ought to keep helping her along. Maybe it did fuck her up, maybe it didn't. But Jessie isn't going to pay for it another damn minute.

Olivia's real quiet throughout the evening, and the uncertainty I keep glimpsing in her eyes has my gut all twisted up. Everything I had to offer her this morning is different from what I'll be offering her now. A girl is a huge responsibility. And I won't be going it alone—I'll still be relying on Joyce to help me out—but I won't ever be just Duke again. I'll be a package deal, Duke and Jessie.

That's a lot to ask a woman to take on.

Though maybe I'm worrying for nothing. Maybe it was just the ugliness of the scene she witnessed that's bothering her, because when bedtime rolls around and we get to her suite, not a second passes before she's on me, kissing me and clinging to me as if she thinks I'll be walking out the door in the next second. But I carry her to the bed, and she holds nothing back with me there, her every touch so sweet, so fierce.

Yet still I wake up with a heavy knot in my chest, and I hold her against me until I feel her stirring. Usually right now I'd be parting her thighs and easing my cock into her warm pussy, greeting the morning with a leisurely fuck— but this time she just lies quietly against me. As if content to stay in my arms…or thinking of a gentle way to extricate herself from them.

I can't put it off any longer. "You think I did right yesterday?"

Olivia blinks and looks up at me. "With Sandy?"

"Yeah."

"Absolutely." She comes up on her elbow, her gaze searching my face. "Are you worried about whether you'll be a good father to Jessie? Because you shouldn't. There's no doubt you will."

That makes my pride swell about ten times bigger. "I'll sure as hell try. Though I'll probably fuck up a few times."

"We all do. And it'll be a big change for you. Unless she's going to continue living with her grandmother?"

We're still working that out. "For a little while, maybe. Not long. Just until we figure out the logistics. I have a house near here, but I'd have to adjust my schedule so she can stay there. Because she's too young to be left by herself after school. And some of these jobs require me to be gone overnight."

A wry smile curves her lips. "Like this one?"

"Yeah." Though this is lasting a hell of a lot longer than most. Usually they're one or two days. But she's been here almost two weeks now. "But it means Jessie might still be spending a lot of time with Joyce."

"Does Joyce mind?"

"No. She's always been happy to take care of her." My throat's real fucking tight again. "But she thinks this will be best for Jessie in the long run."

"Maybe she's right." Her fingers trace circles on my chest, her gaze following their path but her focus seeming far distant. "I know it's a lot to take on, though."

A hell of a lot. "But worth it."

Olivia nods her agreement. "Definitely worth it."

I'm glad she thinks so. Because it feels as if the difference between living and dying hinges on her answer to, "So would you do it, too, if the need ever came up? Take on that responsibility?"

"In a heartbeat," she immediately responds, and I don't know what to make of the funny little expression that flits over her face when she says it, but I don't take the time to tease it out. Because her answer's everything I hoped it would be, and in the next second I'm kissing her hard and deep, and she's holding me so tight, as if trying to slip right up beneath my skin.

She's already there. Beneath my skin, in my blood, and taking up the whole of my heart.

Then she stiffens, because she hears the same thing I am: someone poking at the piano keys in the suite's sitting room.

The suite with the door that I locked last night.

"Stay here," I tell her, rolling out of the bed and scooping up my jeans. I drag them on and grab the semi-automatic from the drawer in her nightstand, tucking the pistol into the waistband at the small of my back.

And it's just goddamn Blowback. The Hellfire Riders' warlord is standing at the piano, playing a halting "Frère Jacques" with his forefinger.

Real fucking funny.

I glance back at Olivia, who's sitting up in bed with the sheet clutched to her chest, her eyes wide and face tense.

"It's nothing," I tell her. "Just Blowback. I'm going to close this door, but holler if you need anything."

"Okay," she says softly, but although some of her tension eases, the worry doesn't leave her gaze.

Because now she's thinking that Blowback knows I'm fucking her—or fucking Keri. She hasn't wanted anyone to think Keri Bishop is a cheater. So I don't know if she'd be relieved or even more worried if she found out that Blowback probably knows more about who she really is than I do.

So I just quietly close the door and head across the suite, setting the gun on the end table by the sofa. "You got news about Zhuk?"

Because Blowback wouldn't be breaking in here unless there was something important to tell me.

The warlord turns away from the keys and reaches into his pocket. His dark eyes are empty of emotion, as if there's nothing living behind them. But if he sounds like he wants to kills someone, he's got good reason.

Because he tells me, "Tataurov pointed Zhuk in our direction."

Icy tension grips the back of my neck. "What the fuck are you talking about?"

He hands over a folded printout and says, "I found that on Chopper Forums. Posted anonymously."

Like members of motorcycle clubs sometimes do when they share something they shouldn't. Most of the time, it just means they're real fucking stupid, because there's about nothing easier to trace than an IP address.

The paper shows a screenshot of a message board post, which is bullshit all the way through.

Was leaving a business meeting at a local club when I saw this HOT girl by the bar. I fucking swear it's Keri Bishop. No clue why she'd be hanging out at this joint, but maybe she's preparing for a role? I'd pay good money to see her dressed up as a biker bitch and taking it from a brother, that's for goddamn sure.

Accompanying the post is a badly composed picture, off center and partially blocked by something in the foreground, as if the person taking it was being careful that no one saw him snapping a photo on his phone. There's nothing to identify the location but I recognize the bar in our clubhouse—and the woman in the white dress standing with her back to the camera. It's exactly the same place Olivia was standing when I first saw her, except I didn't see her face then. And here she's got her head turned to the side, showing what looks like Keri Bishop's famous profile.

"Someone on Tataurov's goddamn security team took that," I grate out, rage shattering the ice that was gripping me. "She was wearing that same fucking dress the first day here."

And hasn't worn it since.

Blowback gives a short nod. "This was posted yesterday. Used a Starbucks in Bend so he looks local—and he didn't strip the metadata, but they edited the date so it looks as if it was taken two days ago."

Didn't strip the metadata, which is a fool's mistake—or made to *appear* like a fool's mistake. Because changing the date is the work of someone who knows what he's doing.

But the date is the least of my worries. "And GPS?"

"Shows it was taken right here."

So they might as well have given Zhuk our address. But it doesn't make any sense. They've been trying to lure the bastard—and this bait is a hell of a lot tastier than any they've dangled before—but the plan then was to wait for Zhuk to show up and take him out.

Jaw clenched, I stalk over to the window and back. "Is Tataurov here in town?"

Because he'll need to be if he hopes to intercept Zhuk. Except the reason I'm asking is so I can go and pound his slick face to a pulp for pointing Zhuk at Olivia.

"He's in New York," Blowback says grimly.

I frown. "You sure?"

He nods.

"So he's not going to warn us—but just let Zhuk come and kill her? But even if Zhuk gets to Olivia, thinks he's done, Keri still has a career. Is she going to hide forever?" I rip my hands through my hair, determination replacing the rage. "Well, let the fucker come. He's not getting to her."

"That might be what Tataurov's counting on," Blowback points out.

Eyes narrowing, I process that—remembering how Tataurov supposedly got out of the Russian bratva shit, yet his businesses still run so damn smoothly. "Because he keeps his hands clean, yeah? He lets someone else handle the dirty work. So send Zhuk straight toward a motorcycle club, let the bikers there take care of the bastard." I won't have a single fucking problem doing that, but the way Tataurov's jerking the Hellfire Riders' chain is some real disrespectful bullshit. "So we're on assassination duty, not just protection duty. Fuck. We should have set our fee at fifty grand per day."

That gets a twitch from Blowback's lips.

All right, then. The news changes shit up a bit, but my priority is still protecting her. "You find out anything about Olivia?"

Blowback shrugs. "I looked some but didn't see any reason to dig deep. She's got a Facebook page but she doesn't post much, and only has a handful of friends. She works tables at a diner in Winnfield that has about thirty Yelp reviews. The ones that mention the waitress are mostly of the 'she's fast and friendly' type. A few call her a slut and a whore."

That'd be a neat trick, considering that she was a virgin up to a week ago. "You see anything in connection to her about a guy named Aaron?"

Those flat, dark eyes sharpen. "Don't think so. Why?"

The *why* burns in my gut like poison. "Someone beat the shit out of her just before she came. I want to know who it is. She got a father, brother?"

"Her parents are dead. In her Facebook feed, she posted on their birthdays a few times over the years, usually about how much she still missed them. She was the only child listed in the father's obituary. I didn't find the mother's obit but one of those Facebook posts included her date of death and it was only two years after the father's—and there weren't any other Burkes in town. But I can expand the search, look at the mother's side."

Her parents dead. Christ. Aside from Jessie, my family isn't nothing to crow about. But still I like knowing that they're alive. "Can you look into police reports? See if there's some domestic violence involving her. If a man takes a belt to a woman, it's probably not his first time."

Probably not his first time beating a woman.

Probably not the first time Olivia got a beating.

Just the thought of it makes me fucking sick.

Blowback nods. "I know someone who can look."

"Good. You got anything else before I go update the brothers?"

He shakes his head. "You want me and Lily to stay here nights until this is finished?"

"Yeah." The more Hellfire Riders keeping an eye, the safer Olivia will be. I tilt my head to indicate the gun on the end table. "Let's make sure the brothers are carrying at all times, too."

He nods. "I'll tag Gunner."

The Riders' sergeant at arms, who'll dispense weapons

from the club's armory to anyone who isn't already packing their own. "All right. And you'll let me know if you get a bead on Zhuk?"

"I won't waste time letting you know." He starts for the door. "If get a bead on him, I'll bring his body to you."

Shit. No need for that.

"Just his head will do," I tell him.

Easier to carry, too.

FOURTEEN

OLIVIA

I'M BAIT.

Wrapped in a short silk robe and sitting on the end of the bed, I listen as Duke tells me what Ivan's done. All day yesterday, I could hardly think of anything but how I'm going to lose Duke as soon as he finds out who I am and everything I've done. And now…this.

I don't know if something's broken in me, because I don't know how to feel. I don't know if I'm feeling anything. I know what I *should* be feeling—the same rage that Duke is so carefully containing—but instead I feel like a hollowed out doll.

When I agreed to this job, Ivan told me I'd be safe. I wouldn't have taken the risk otherwise, because I can't protect Erin if I'm dead. Better to stay with my stepfather forever, acting as her shield and enduring every blow, than not being there at all.

But now Zhuk knows where I am. A Russian mobster who's already killed everyone else attached to that video… along with heaven knows how many other people in his career. A man so dangerous that Ivan's gone to these crazy lengths and expense just to divert Zhuk's attention away from his wife.

I guess that expense might not be so crazy, though. He won't need to pay that million dollars to a dead woman.

A big, warm hand cups my cheek. "Duchess?" Duke is leaning over me. Concern fills those sea green eyes. "Are you still with me here?"

"Yeah," I whisper, trying to pull it together. "So what does this mean? Since Zhuk knows where we are, are we leaving the lodge?"

He shakes his head. "We've got all the advantages here. He's not getting on this property without us knowing. And once he's here, we've got a secure clubhouse and an army of brothers standing between you and him. We take off running, we lose those advantages. He could be right on us and we'd have no idea he was there until it was too late."

Staying makes sense, then. And there'd be no point now in saying who I really am, trying to tell Zhuk that he'd be killing the wrong person—because if I were him, I'd just assume it was Keri Bishop lying and trying desperately to save her life.

Breath trembling, I say, "Do you think he'll come? Or will he ignore this lure like he did the others?"

Duke's strong jaw clenches and for a second it looks as if he won't answer. Then he says gruffly, "I think he'll come. I also think those other lures were deliberately stupid—so that this one would appear legit in comparison."

Deliberately stupid? Oh god. "So you think Ivan planned this all along?"

The expression in his eyes suddenly lethal, he nods. And when I look blindly away in despair, his hands tighten in my hair and he brings my gaze back to his. "He didn't send you here to die, you understand? He was counting on us being able to take Zhuk out. And that's what we're going to do. So you've got no reason to look so scared."

No reason? That makes me laugh, and the sound is just as hollow as I feel.

"Duchess," he says, his voice low and rough with emotion. "Do you think I'd ever let anything hurt you? Do you think I wouldn't lay down my life to keep you safe?"

My heart swells up tight and hot, and suddenly I'm feeling *everything*, anger and fear and so much love for this man. "No," I say hoarsely. "I don't *ever* want you to lay down your life for me."

"Then that'll be the one thing you want that I won't ever give you." His thumbs stroke my cheeks. "But if we're ready for him, this won't be an issue. No more walks outside, all right? And you'll need to say good-bye to Molly this morning, because when we send her home, she's not coming back until this is done. Her going in and out every day makes her a real easy target, and we don't want to give Zhuk anyone to get his hands on."

"No, we don't," I say softly, feeling the pang of that loss already. "But I'll miss her."

"I'll miss her cooking," he says. "Because the brothers will be taking over in the kitchen."

"I can take over, instead." When he appears on the verge of rejecting that idea, I cut in, "I've got nothing else to do—and I have to eat, too. And would you rather eat what I cook or what Picasso does?"

He grimaces. "You got a point there."

I really do. But I think we both know what it really is—just a swift distraction from the topic of Zhuk.

But only a distraction. He sighs and leans in, kissing me softly. "I've got to update the brothers, let Molly know she'll need to stay home from now on. You all right here?"

I nod. "I'll get ready and come down as soon as I can."

"No rush. Molly won't leave until after lunch." His mouth claims mine again—then with a groan, he pulls away.

Chest aching, I watch him leave, then look blindly around the suite. I'll be safe here. I *know* I'll be safe here.

And I have to believe that Duke's right about Ivan not intending anything to happen to me, because the Hellfire Riders will stop Zhuk—and I also have to believe that Ivan still intends to follow through on our agreement. But there's always the other shoe…and if this all goes wrong, I need to make certain that Erin's safe. Duke might never forgive me when he finds out about my past—but if I can't protect Erin anymore, I know *he* would. No matter what I've done.

My gaze lands on the rolltop desk in the corner of the sitting room. Quickly I cross over to it, pulling stationery and a pen from the cubbyholes. Molly won't leave until after lunch.

That gives me more than enough time to write the letters I hope she'll never have to deliver.

FIFTEEN

DUKE

"How'd the sit-down with the judge go?" Picasso asks through the intercom while I'm waiting for the driveway gate to open. "Are you a daddy now?"

The closest thing to. The lawyer I retained turned out to be a bulldog in heels, and she pushed my petition through so hard and fast I imagine the court clerks' heads are still spinning. I suppose it didn't hurt that I look damn good on paper. A steady security job, and I own the house where Jessie's been living and paying all her expenses for the past six years—but in the end I figure it was Joyce's and Jessie's interviews with the judge that sealed the deal. Either that, or it was his interview with Corey and Sandy. Their special kind of selfish stupidity can't hide itself for long. The judge might have preferred offering legal guardianship to a clown rather than leaving Jessie in their care. As it was, no one even attempted to counsel them against withholding the right to revoke their consent—so if they ever want her back, they'll have to go to fucking war with me. And we all know they won't put that much effort into anything.

So Jessie's mine now. But I'm still Uncle John. And for a few days, nothing will change for Jessie except her parents' fifth-wheel won't be in the backyard anymore. We'll figure out the rest over the next couple of weeks.

Or sooner. Joyce told me that Jessie is already packing up all of her things in anticipation of moving to my place. But the *when* depends on this job coming to an end.

It sometimes feels as if the whole damn world is on hold, waiting for this job to end.

Waiting for Zhuk to show.

Waiting for the moment I don't have to pretend that Olivia isn't mine.

Waiting for her to say what's got her so scared that she won't risk me knowing who she really is.

The gate creaks open, and I ride on through, heading for the clubhouse. There's an executive board meeting in a couple of hours, and Old Timer will likely have the time of his life reporting the amount of cash gracing the Hell-fire Riders' accounts. Another few days and we'll hit a half million earned on this job.

I sure as hell don't mind the money. My cut's edging toward six figures. No one else is complaining about the cash they're earning, either. But just about every brother is running hot and tense, and it's only getting worse the longer this job continues. Some of them are just assholes, whining about the clubhouse still being on lockdown and pussy-free after three weeks, though there's plenty of joints in town where they can fuck around. For the rest of us, it's because we know that the longer Zhuk takes, the longer he can plan. The longer he can watch the brothers coming and leaving. The longer he can study the lay of the land, scoping out our security and looking for holes.

I've been running as hot and tense as the rest. Partly because of Zhuk.

Partly because Olivia's put up a wall of quiet reserve between us and I don't know what the hell is going on in her head.

I know when it started, though—the same day Sandy came to the gate. I noticed how quiet and uncertain she was that night and figured it was because she wasn't sure whether she wanted the responsibility that comes with a little girl. But it turned out that wasn't what she'd been worrying about. And although Tataurov setting her up as bait rattled her pretty good, she didn't learn about that until the next morning. She went quiet before Blowback delivered that news.

And she hasn't really come out of it. She's still sweet and generous with her time, taking over most of Molly's duties though no one has asked her to lift a finger. She's still tart and teasing, knowing just how to make a man laugh at himself without ever making him feel like a fool. She's still hot as hell in bed, holding nothing back—but that's the only time I ever seem to break through the wall she's got up between us now.

As if she doesn't trust that what we've got will last, and she's steeling herself for when it comes to an end.

But there's never going to be any fucking end. And since that quiet reserve drops away the second I touch her, there's not a night that I haven't made her mine, not a night that I haven't made her come screaming, her pussy squeezing tight while my cock's pumping deep. Hot and rough, slow and easy, over and over again.

Every night, every morning, and most afternoons.

Not this afternoon, though. Not while I was in town.

So I'm thinking of how it'll be tonight. Thinking of pinning her hands over her head and slowly feeding my thick cock into her hungry cunt, making her hold my gaze. No hiding her emotions. No looking away. Just feeling me over her, feeling me inside her, and fucking her so long and good that she'll still be feeling me when I'm not touching her. So hard and deep that there won't be anywhere for her to go when she tries to withdraw from me, because I'll still be right there beneath her skin.

Maybe I won't wait until tonight.

My cock like molten steel, I reach the clubhouse and find a spot next to Maurice's ride. It's another hot fucking day and the grasshoppers are stridulating away in the tall dried grasses past the edge of the lot—those are some damn smart bugs, playing music to draw the females in—but not much else is going on outside. Probably the only brothers out in this heat are the unlucky bastards on the perimeter sweep.

Just the kind of long, hot afternoon when a woman might be persuaded to take a nap.

Not that I'll let her sleep.

I unclip my two-way from its mount beside my handlebar grip. "Who's looking after the duchess and where is she at?"

Scarecrow comes back, "I've got her. She's in the kitchen."

Shit. There's not going to be any fucking her now, then. She takes her cooking pretty seriously, and if she's starting this early, she must have something special planned.

Something as Louisianan as her accent. The woman can cook, for certain. Spicier than I'm used to. But a man can get used to heat real easy when food tastes like hers tastes.

A man can also get used to watching her sashaying around the kitchen in those heels she's always wearing. So I'll head over that direction, too, and watch her until the executive board meeting starts.

Before I take a step away from my bike, Picasso breaks in. "Camera four is compromised."

A camera on the east end of the property. Instantly I'm hauling ass around the side of the clubhouse, heading east so I can get eyes in that direction. "Is it blacked out or looped?"

"Looped. Burnout just called in a check and he isn't on the feed."

"How long?" Since hearing that Zhuk is coming, we've begun staggering the time between perimeter checks but they're never more than thirty minutes apart.

"Not more than ten minutes."

Shit. More than long enough for a determined fucker to run the distance from the property line to the clubhouse. "Scarecrow, move the duchess into the clubhouse and get her secured in the safe room."

"Moving her now—"

The quiet afternoon rips open in a barrage of machine gun fire and shattering glass, the sound amplified through the two-way—along with Olivia's scream.

Scarecrow's radio cuts out.

Shattering glass. Fuck no. There's only one room with that many windows—the room Olivia would have been crossing as Scarecrow escorted her from the kitchen.

I dove to the ground at the first sound of gunfire. Now I'm on my stomach in the dirt and snarling into the two-way, "Get to the fucking day room!" even as I surge to my feet again.

Then there's no talking, not as I'm racing to the southeast end of the lodge. Statuses and commands burst from the two-way—Picasso trying to get eyes on the fucker, Zoomie going for her rifle and heading for the roof, the prez demanding a sitrep from Scarecrow.

Olivia's breathless, trembling reply comes over the radio instead. "We're back in the kitchen, on the floor behind the center island."

Thank fucking God. The island and the appliances installed beneath the counter will help shield her from any bullets flying in from outside.

It won't help her if he's *inside*.

Voice rough, I ask, "Is Zhuk in the day room, duchess?"

"I don't think so. There's glass all over the floor, so I'd hear someone coming in and I haven't. And I didn't see anyone out on the porch before he started shooting."

So the fucker gave himself an entrance from a distance—or was just trying to take her out while she was visible and crossing the room.

Cold sweat dripping down the back of my neck, I reach the end of the building and stop. The porch off the day room is just around the corner, but the bullets had to come from that direction, too. Stepping out into the open is asking to get my brains splattered against the wood siding.

"Where's Scarecrow?" Picasso asks her.

"Right here. He's been hit in the shoulder." Her voice quavers. "He says it's not bad but he's bleeding a lot. He gave me the radio because he can't hold it and his gun at the same time."

Good. Better that he's prepared to defend her if Zhuk makes it through.

"Hang in there, duchess," I tell her, then let the others know what I'm seeing. "I'm at the southeast corner. The back lawn is clear. He's got to be behind one of those trees by the creek."

It's the only cover available—and the only direction from which he could have shot out the windows in the day room.

"Zoomie?" the prez says.

"Almost there," she replies.

And once Zoomie gets up on the roof, there's no fucking way he's crossing that distance. She'll take him out if he tries.

If he doesn't try to cross, just waits for another shot at Olivia, it's still game over. In a contest between one fucker in a tree and the Hellfire Riders in their clubhouse, there's no question who'd come out on top—and still alive.

"Gunner's coming around to your position," Blowback says. "I'm taking the north side."

Thank fucking Christ. Because I just spent the afternoon at the courthouse, where a semiautomatic pistol might have raised more than a few questions—so I'm the only asshole out here who isn't armed. There's not even a rock within reach. Just some goddamn dirt.

"I'm at the hallway entrance to the day room and I've

got eyes on the kitchen," Grasshopper comes in. "Do I cross?"

Not when Zhuk likely has his assault rifle still trained on those blown-out windows, waiting for Olivia to make a run for safety. "Wait until Blowback and Gunner can give you cover— Hold up, I've got movement."

Not just movement. The fucker must have realized that the passing time was turning everything in our favor. In tan camouflage, a wiry figure breaks away from the tree line and crosses the back lawn at a sprint, assault rifle swinging to the side—

I hit the fucking ground. "Get your heads down!"

Zhuk starts shooting, sweeping the clubhouse from one end to the other, painting the entire face of the building with bullets. Windows in the upper floors shatter, glass raining as he makes another sweep. Providing his own cover as he comes.

Fuck. *Fuck.*

He eases up on the trigger as he hits the porch, as if pausing and looking through the broken windows to make sure there aren't any surprises waiting in the day room— and I'm right here, right fucking *here*, but my skull's no match for a round from an AK-47.

Glass crunches under his boots. Heading inside where he'll easily find Olivia huddling on the kitchen floor. I can almost see her, terrified and shaking, trying to stay quiet and hoping he won't find her and Scarecrow there. But he's been watching that damn room the entire time and knows exactly where she went.

And Grasshopper is right there. I can picture him, too—in the hallway just outside the day room, waiting for the fucker to walk into his line of sight. But if Zhuk makes it that far into the room, that close to the kitchen, then he's gotten far too close to Olivia.

My jaw clenches, every muscle tense. Because fuck *this*.

And because as soon as Zhuk's inside, he won't be looking behind him.

Another crunch of glass. Then another, but with a more brittle sound to it—not crunching against the wood of the porch but against the stone tile in the day room. He's inside.

Instantly I'm moving, gripping the porch railing and launching myself over. He hears my boots hit the boards and spins toward me but that's the fucking problem with carrying an assault rifle—it's hard to swing that shit around real fast.

A fist is faster.

Mine slams into the side of his neck and he reels back. Bullets rip into the plaster above the fireplace and I'm on him again before he can right the weapon, keeping on him because any distance between us means he can aim that shit and I'm dead. Instead I grab the blazing hot barrel and shove it upward, crowding in close and pounding my fist into his gut, smashing my boot into his knee.

The fucker goes down but he's not done. Still grappling with me over the rifle with one hand, his tattooed fingers scrabble through the shards of glass on the floor. Pain rips through my thigh, but I don't let up, using my weight against the rifle to bear down on his wrist, and I can't hear the crack of his bone over the thunderous bursts of gunfire but I can sure fucking feel it.

Abruptly the shooting stops but my ears are ringing and I'm seeing nothing but red. Ripping the weapon out of his loosened grip, I hammer the rifle's stock into his mouth. Blood and teeth splatter the tile floor and he goes down, all the way down, but it's not fucking enough, because I can still hear Olivia's scream when those windows went out. All that's in my head is her tears and her terror. All I can see is her face.

And when I'm done there's nothing left of Zhuk's.

Chest heaving, I straighten. Splinters from the ceiling beams and sheetrock dust are floating down around my head and shoulders. The end of the rifle's dripping with blood. There's a fucking mess on the floor but I give no shits.

Movement next to me draws my gaze. Blowback. My ears are so blown from the deafening noise of the gunfire that when I say, "Don't let her see this," I can't even hear my own voice.

He nods and says something—not to me, I realize, but to Grasshopper, who's at the entrance to the day room, staring at what's left of Zhuk's head and looking as if he's about to puke his lunch.

He'd better not. Olivia works too damn hard preparing our meals to waste a single bite on this piece of shit.

And I need to see for myself that she's all right.

I turn and my first step sends rockets of pain shooting down my leg. Fuck me. A four-inch shard of glass is sticking out of my thigh, my jeans soaked in blood. Gritting my teeth, I pull it out but that sure as hell doesn't feel much better. I can move again, though, so I continue on, hobbling toward the kitchen.

Gunner's in there, and at first he's the only one I see. That and all the shattered wine glasses, the bowl of fruit tipped over, apples and pears nothing but pulp on the counter and floor. The front of the island's been shredded by bullets, and I can barely fucking breathe, seeing how close he got to her.

The SA's crouching next to Scarecrow, who's sitting with his back against the dishwasher door. The amused expression on Gunner's pretty face tells me that the brother's wound isn't too worrying; instead he looks as if he's cracking a joke, maybe telling the kid it isn't much worse than a flesh wound.

I still can't hear a damn thing and my hand's on fucking fire where I grabbed the rifle barrel and my leg's a goddamn mess, but it's all nothing when I see her.

She's on the floor and holding a bloodied towel to Scarecrow's shoulder, tears streaking her face. Then she looks up and there's her smile, her big blinding smile.

Though it disappears a second later as horror takes

its place.

I suppose I've got Zhuk's blood splattered all over me. "It's a lot better than it looks," I tell her, then everything's better when she throws herself into my arms and buries her face in my neck, her tears burning my skin. I can't hear her sobbing but I can feel it—and feel her relief there, too, as my arms close around her.

A deep breath against her hair fills me up with her scent, and I look over into the day room, where Grasshopper's bringing in a sheet to cover Zhuk until we get Olivia through without seeing what I did to the fucker. She doesn't need that visual in her head. All that matters is that he's no longer a threat.

Job over. I meet Blowback's eyes and say, "Before you cover that up, maybe you want to take a picture of that trash and send it to Tataurov, let him know this is finished?"

He nods, but as he pulls out his phone and snaps the shot, I'm already rethinking that.

"Actually, why don't we hold off on sending that picture until tomorrow." And do a little date-changing of our own in the photo's metadata. "Because we might as well get another twenty grand off him, now that we've got all these fucking windows to replace."

I can't hear the brothers' responses to that, but judging by the grins I'm seeing, they're not arguing. Neither is Olivia. Her laugh shakes her against me—then she abruptly pulls away, her eyes wide with alarm as she stares down at my leg. When she looks up at me, I recognize that sweet, stubborn set to her mouth.

Looks like I'm about to get patched up again.

ALL THIS TIME WAITING FOR this job to be over, so Olivia can finally tell me what's got her so scared, and now I can't hear a damn thing. But the telling can wait.

Right now I'm utterly content, sitting here on the edge of her bed while she carefully cleans Zhuk's blood from my face. My thigh's already wrapped in a bandage, and my blistered palm and fingers covered in burn ointment. Those ought to hurt worse than they do, but Bull had some damn good meds left over after he healed up from his wreck a few months ago, when some crazy rich bastard rammed his rig into Bull's motorcycle, and so I'm all but floating.

And damn, she's pretty. Just so fucking beautiful.

I realize I've said it aloud when a blush pinkens her cheeks. And that's even prettier.

Her mouth curves, and I know she says something but I can't hear what—likely teasing me, though, because she's got that familiar glint in her eyes.

Same as the last time she was patching me up. Until I told her that I'd help her get away from the bastard who'd beat her, then it wasn't teasing in her gaze but her looking at me with so much hope and wonder that I wanted to be everything she needed.

Then she kissed me. And I hurt her. Pushed her away, throwing Keri Bishop's marriage into her face.

I wasn't wrong, being pissed—given what I believed then. But recalling it now and knowing how scared she was, how damn innocent her kiss felt, how all that wonder and hope was replaced with tears and shame…it just fucking rips me up.

Her hand cups my jaw now, her brows pleated together in concern. And I wasn't going to say this until those eyes were hazel, until I could say her name without frightening her, until she stopped pretending to be Keri.

But that's so fucking stupid. It doesn't matter what color her eyes are or whether I'm calling her Olivia or anything else. She's still the same woman. My feelings won't change.

And I almost lost her today.

"I love you, duchess," I tell her, and I can't hear my voice but I can feel the rawness of my throat as it comes out.

I made her cry again. Tears glitter in those blue eyes but this time wonder and hope are shining through, along with an emotion that appears pretty damn similar to what I just said.

Maybe she says it, too. I can't tell, because her lips are on mine and her kiss is just as sweet and urgent as the first time. And I don't need to hear her helpless moans as I hungrily feast from her pussy, not when the wetness of her cunt tells me how much she wants me. I don't need to hear her beg for more as I fill her with the thickness of my cock, not when the emotion shining from her passion-glazed eyes tells me over and over again that she's mine. And that she'll *always* be feeling me inside her.

438

SIXTEEN

OLIVIA

A LIGHT BREEZE FLUTTERS THE CURTAINS IN THE SUITE'S bedroom as I toss the final pile of clothes onto the bed. Yesterday we cleaned up the shattered glass, but since there's no rain in sight, the Riders haven't bothered with plastic sheeting to cover the empty panes before the windows are replaced. The morning's already warm, and I suppose by afternoon it'll be blazing hot, but I don't think I'll be here to see that. Instead I'll be seeing Erin, giving my stepfather a million dollars, and finally gaining custody of my sister.

And thinking of it, I can't stop smiling.

I hear the suite door open—and my heart, already so light and happy, fills almost to bursting. If life is all ups and downs, then this moment must be the highest I've known. Erin's almost within reach. And Duke loves me.

A high. But not easy.

Because Duke's not smiling. When I look over my shoulder to see him standing at the bedroom doorway, a brooding darkness has filled his expression.

"What the hell do you think you're doing, duchess?"

His voice is low and dangerous—and an even volume again. The first night and day following Zhuk's attack, his every word had been overloud, like someone talking while wearing headphones. When he woke up this morning, though, he said that his hearing was almost back to normal—if still a bit muffled, as if his ears were stuffed with cotton.

So no permanent damage, hopefully. But only time will tell.

And I pray that I'll have that time. That when this is all over, he'll still love me enough to keep me.

"Packing my things," I tell him, though the two open suitcases on the bed make that obvious. "Blowback said Ivan would be arriving today."

"So?" Duke returns bluntly. "You aren't leaving with him."

"Yes, I am. I have to."

"Why?" When I don't answer, his jaw clenches in frustration. "So Zhuk's dead and the job's done, but you're still not going to tell me a damn thing?"

"Because my part's not done yet." And I don't like keeping any of this from him but I don't have a choice. I hug my arms to my chest, my heart no longer light. Instead it's a rock lodged in my throat, painful and hot. "I have to see this job through."

It'll be over when Keri and I switch back again—which will probably happen the same way it did before, with me walking into a hotel as one person and leaving as another.

This time, I'll be leaving as Olivia. Forever.

I just want that forever to be with Duke.

"Why are so fucking loyal to that bastard?" It rips from him on a snarl. "Tataurov set you up as goddam bait!"

"I know." And I wish I could throw everything back in Ivan's face. "But he'll give me something I need."

"Money?"

"Yes…and no." If it was just money, I wouldn't be feeling this sick hurt in my gut right now. I wouldn't fight so hard to keep this all secret from Duke, and I'd risk losing the money rather than risk losing him. But I can't risk Erin. "It's more important than that."

Anger and frustration flattens his tone. "But you're not going to tell me what it is and let me help you? Why are you so afraid?"

"Because I don't want to lose *this*," I tell him and

my voice wavers under the strain. "Because everything has been so good here between you and me. And I'm so afraid that now, at the last minute, things will go wrong. Like they did before. So I just want to finish this job and come back and tell you everything." My throat constricts, squeezing the last into almost nothing. "Even the parts you might…not like."

His expression softens. "There's nothing about you I won't like. There's nothing about you I won't love."

My vision wavers with tears. "I hope so. And I *will* tell you everything when I come back. I just need you to trust me until then."

"Shit." On a heavy sigh, he shakes his head. "It's not about trust, duchess. It's about knowing that you've got something so important to do—so important that you're absolutely fucking terrified by the thought of not following through—and I've got no way to help you. Add to that, some motherfucker took a belt to you before you came here. And I've got a feeling you're heading back there. So it's not that I don't trust *you*. I don't trust Tataurov or any other fucker you might be dealing with."

That's why he's so frustrated? Not by my silence, but by not being able to help me?

I never thought I could love Duke more than I already do. But I can.

Moving closer, I tell him, "You *can* help me, by letting me see this through. Because if this job goes right, I'll never have to worry about that other thing again."

His eyes narrow. "You mean never worry about the fucker who beat you? You don't need to take care of that. I can."

And his voice says that he'd love to. I can't stop my quick grin. "Like you took care of Zhuk? I know you can. But like I said before…" My smile fades again and I can't stop my sigh. If he did anything to James, I don't know how I could make a clean escape. Because my stepfather's pride would never survive another man beating him, and million dollars or not, he'd never let me take Erin away. "It's not just about me. And I need to do this the right way or I might lose everything."

Jaw clenched, he regards me for a long, silent minute, as if debating. "All right, duchess. But if you don't come back within…how long will this take?"

"A few days?"

"Not good enough. If you're not here by Sunday, then I'm coming for you. That's two days—and still too long."

On a relieved, shuddering breath, I nod. "All right."

With strong fingers he catches my chin, gaze searching mine. "It'll probably be me and Jessie when you get back. She's got all her stuff packed and ready to move in."

"Good." I can't stop my laugh. All this time, I think he's been worried about my reaction to having a little girl around—when in truth, everything he does for Jessie just makes me more certain of *him*. "I'll be bringing a few things from home, too."

"Well, then—there's no point in you packing up all

this shit today, is there? Just what you need for a few days. Leave the rest and I'll have it all hauled over to my place."

All at once my heart is so light and happy again—and so full. Lifting my hands to his face, rising up on my toes, I whisper, "I don't know how I got so lucky that you ended up in my life."

Gruffly he replies, "It's the one good thing Tataurov's ever done."

True. And I can't tell him everything yet, but I can tell him this. "I love you," I say huskily.

Lightning flares through the storm of his eyes. Then his mouth claims mine, and when he lifts me against his broad chest, I don't think this *up* will ever have a *down*.

Except for the wonderful descent into bed…or the interruption that comes before we make it there. Because from the sitting room, I hear the notes from the piano that tell me Blowback's waiting in there again.

With a groan, Duke lifts his head and calls out, "This better be good, brother!"

"I got the police report you asked for."

Something lethal flares in his sea green eyes—then he looks down at me, drops a kiss to my lips. "I've got to go look at this."

A police report? "Is everything okay?"

"Better than. Someone's finally going to get what's coming to him." A hard, satisfied smile curves his mouth, then he calls out to Blowback, "Take it to the clubhouse. I'll meet you over there in five minutes."

"Will do."

Duke's hot gaze meets mine. His rough hands slip under my skirt and drag my panties down to my knees. "We've got three minutes before I have to head over there, duchess. You think I can make you come that fast just by sucking on your clit?"

Suddenly breathless, I shake my head.

And I'm *so* wrong.

For my final appearance as Keri Bishop, I take extra time on my hair and makeup—because, if I'm truthful, I've been letting those slip in the past week. I've been wearing eye makeup, but haven't bothered to do all of the fussy contouring that took up so much time those first days. And I've been putting up my hair in a braid or a bun instead of wearing Keri's trademark, just-rolled-out-of-bed golden waves—but I've also been cooking, and no one wants long blond hairs in their jambalaya.

Today, though, I do it all. I don't want to give Ivan any reason to think I haven't played my role perfectly. Carefully I pick out a short white dress that shows off my tanned skin, and slide my feet into strappy gold heels. From top to bottom, I'm all golden hair, golden tan, golden shoes—more like a goddess than a movie star.

But I can't wait to be Olivia again.

I'm sitting on the sofa and buckling the thin strap around my ankle when the suite door bangs open. My heart jumping, I glance up.

His gaze like an ice storm, Duke heads straight for me—though not as fast as he did before, the night he came after my phone. His gait is stiff, his thigh still healing from the shard of glass Zhuk stabbed him with.

Warily, I straighten and watch him come. Something's wrong. Something's *so* wrong.

"Duke?" I ask hesitantly.

Through clenched teeth, he snarls, "Do you want to explain this?"

A manila envelope is crumpled in his fist. With a snap of his wrist, he sends it flying toward me, where it lands on the cushion next to my hip.

"What is it?" With unsteady fingers, I pick up the envelope. The clasp is already open, and even before I slide the thin, stapled sheaf of papers out, he's telling me what it is.

"A police report." Ripping his hands through his hair, he stares at me as if I'm not a goddess, not even Olivia, but something small and slimy and disgusting. "Did you fucking *abduct* a little girl?"

Oh no no no. My gaze catches the logo at the top of the page. Winnfield City Police. I can barely speak through the sudden pain in my throat.

"How did you get this?"

"Does it matter? Did you do it? And no more fucking lies," he grinds out before I can answer. "It says right there that you kidnapped the mayor's daughter. Stole money from his house and took his kid. What were you hoping for—a ransom? Or maybe she was just going to end up in a goddamn basement."

"No. I would never have hurt her." Blinded by tears, I shake my head, desperately trying to think past the pain in my chest. "I was trying to get her away from him. And that money from his house was *mine*."

"So you did it," is his hoarse reply and his face is stunned, as if he didn't truly expect a confirmation. "You're not even going to deny it. You kidnapped a seven-year old girl—a girl almost the same age as Jessie, who's going to be living in my *home*. How the fuck could I ever trust you with her?"

Oh god. Desperately I reach for his hand. "Just let me explain—"

As if he can't bear my touch, he abruptly backs away, expression thunderous. "There's no fucking explanation that justifies it. *None.* And I thought I'd figured out who you were, thought you were so damn sweet and good, but I was way off. I can't believe I was so fucking wrong." A harsh laugh breaks from him. "You're a better actress than I thought."

My throat's a hot solid lump, my every breath ripping from my lungs like a hacksaw. "Please listen—"

"To more of your fake bullshit?" His gaze shutters and he backs up another step. "Maybe you better pack up after all, duchess."

Feeling as if my heart's been ripped from my chest, I stare after his retreating back. "Duke," I try to call his name, to bring him back, but through my raw throat it's nothing but a desperate wheeze, and I don't know if he can't hear me…or if he ignores my plea.

Then he's gone.

And I'm left shaking, feeling as if my world has just fallen apart. I knew he would find out eventually, because when I returned, I intended to tell him. But Erin would have been with me then, and I could explain everything. I'd intended to prepare him and to choose the most careful approach, so that he wouldn't look at me the way he just did.

I still knew I might lose him. I didn't know how much it would hurt.

I didn't know that taking a breath would feel like dying. I didn't know that to simply finish buckling my shoes would take all of my strength. But I have to keep moving. Because this has never been just about me.

And Erin's counting on me to save her.

So I buckle my shoes. And fix my makeup. And pretend that a part of my heart is still intact, even though it's been shattered as thoroughly as if Zhuk had filled it with bullets.

Carelessly I start packing again, filling each suitcase with everything I'm going to sell, until a sharp rap against the suite's open door pulls me away.

Grasshopper's at the entrance, looking at me expectantly. "Hey, duchess. Sounds like your husband's coming."

"Sounds like?"

"Yeah." He tilts his head, and suddenly I'm aware of a faint, familiar drone coming from outside—a helicopter. "That's not Zoomie. And I figure there's no one else who would fly in."

I can't think of anyone else, either. So it's time to go.

My breath shuddering, I sweep my gaze around the suite. I won't be expected to carry out my own luggage, and it doesn't matter if I forgot anything. None of it was really mine to begin with.

Except my heart. But it doesn't matter if I leave the shattered pieces of it here.

I won't use it again for a long, long time.

SEVENTEEN

DUKE

How many fucking times have I imagined the moment that pervert grabbed Holly, pulling her out of her seat? Or maybe he didn't grab her. Maybe he tricked her, saying that I'd sent him into the theater because I needed her to help Sandy in the bathroom. Maybe she didn't even realize that she was in danger until he started hurting her.

I've gone over it in my head a million goddamn times—and I still don't know what really happened when he took her.

I just know where she ended up. I just know she must have been terrified and hurting. Until she wasn't hurting or feeling anything anymore.

Now the only thing in my head is imagining this other little girl, and how Olivia got to her. The police report was scarce on details so my brain's just filling them in. It said she stole cash from the mayor's home—so when she's inside the house, maybe she sees a girl about Jessie's age and figures there's more money to get. Maybe she tricks the girl, because who wouldn't believe someone with a face and a smile as sweet as Olivia's? Or maybe she just drags her out of the house, kicking and screaming.

My head won't stop picturing it all—and my chest aches so much I can't fucking breathe. Because I can't believe Olivia would take a girl from the safety of her home, terrorize her like that. Not the woman I fell in love with.

But she's clearly not the woman I believed she was.

What the hell could make her do it? Olivia told me that she'd done something wrong once. Something wrong for the right reasons. Was she that desperate for money?

Probably the same reason she took this goddamn job.

A job that's finally fucking over. With my hearing jacked up, I'm the last brother to pick up on the noise of the helicopter coming in—but I'm the first who goes out to meet it. Because Tataurov's sure as hell not taking her with him.

There's still some bastard out there who beat her. She

might have faked everything else but those bruises weren't put there with makeup. And she told me this job would resolve all that shit but I don't know if I can believe a word of it now. So I'll get her home myself, then kill the fucker who beat her, so that she won't ever be hurt again.

And then I'll leave her there. Far away from me and Jessie.

The agony of that loss joins the stabbing pain in my thigh and the blistered burn still raging in my hand. Tataurov's chopper sets down at the edge of the asphalt parking lot, blowing dust and dried grass around like a cyclone, and the brothers eye their bikes uneasily as if judging whether the wind's strong enough to blow them over off their kickstands.

But I don't give a shit about my ride. My focus is on the man jumping down from the aircraft, the slick fucker coming toward me with his hand outstretched and wearing a broad smile.

Over the noise of the rotor blades, Tataurov yells, "That was a hell of a job you and your brothers did—"

My fist smashes that grin off his face. His head snaps back. Shouts clamor from behind him—then from behind me, as his security guards draw their weapons and the brothers suddenly don't give a goddamn fuck about their bikes.

Mouth bleeding, Tataurov holds up his hand to his guards, waving them away. The bastards stand down, holstering their weapons.

Bad fucking mistake. I take a step toward him, but before I can swing, soft hands catch my forearm and haul back. She's so fucking tiny, Olivia's got about as much chance of moving me as jumping to the moon, but clinging to me like she is, me hitting him again would jolt her forward and risk hurting her.

Her blond hair whipping around her face, Olivia gapes up at me with wide eyes. "Duke! What are you doing?"

"Only what he fucking deserves, using you as bait." With a twist of my arm I break her grip—then turn it around, snatching her wrist. Pulling her with me, I get up in his face. "You told an innocent girl she'd be safe and then put a target on her back!"

His eyes narrow. "An innocent girl? Don't you mean my *wife*?"

Olivia goes pale, her dismay clear though she pastes on a smile and tries to cover it up. But she's a fucking terrible actress.

"Yes, your wife!" she says in a rush. "Of course that's what he means."

Tataurov's gaze is on me. "Is that right? You think I used her as bait? What else do you think you know?"

I feel her suddenly and desperately pulling at me, as if trying to drag me away before I can answer. But I don't go anywhere, just stare down at the fucker. Because she's not leaving with him. Whatever she needs, whatever he was going to give to her—money, something else, *anything—*

I'll be giving it. "I know sure as hell that she's not your wife."

She'll never be anyone's but *mine.*

Abruptly she stops pulling. Stops pulling, and when I glance at her, the tightness in my chest becomes a crushing vise. Because she's staring up at me, her eyes wounded and disbelieving and welling with tears, appearing for all the world that I just betrayed her instead of betraying my own goddamn heart.

Because she's mine. And I don't care what she's done. I'll keep her away from Jessie but I'm not letting her go.

I'm *never* fucking letting her go.

In a cold voice that I better not ever hear a man use with my woman again, Tataurov tells her, "I believe that means our deal is forfeit, Ms. Burke."

Her lips part, and though I can't hear the anguished sound she makes, I see it in the utter desolation that crumples her expression. "But I never told him!" Wildly she tries to yank her wrist out of my grip, all at once fighting me, her voice rising. "I didn't say anything. *Please.*"

"Good-bye, Ms. Burke. Duke." He nods to me, then fingers the bleeding split in his lip, his mouth twitching with amusement. "Your club will receive its final payment shortly. And perhaps I'll secure the Hellfire Riders' services again. You were as effective as I heard you would be."

Just fuck right off, I begin to tell him, but as he turns away Olivia's despairing cry closes up my throat.

"Please! I didn't tell him!" She tries to follow the fucker, racing forward only to be brought up short by my hold on her wrist, but she's still trying to go, her heels digging in, her entire body straining toward him. "Please!"

My woman's *begging* another man. With my heart a pulped mess in my chest, I drag her back. "You don't need anything from him."

She whirls on me, tears spilling, her face stricken. "Do you know what you've done?" she cries brokenly, and when the sound of the helicopter rotors increase in speed she hauls back desperately. "Let me go!"

"Don't, duchess." I hold tighter as her arm slips. Already her wrist is red where she's fighting to get away from me. "You're hurting yourself, yanking your arm like this."

"What do you care? You're done with me!"

Voice raw, I tell her, "I'm not done."

But I don't even know if she hears me. Her gaze is fixed on the helicopter, where Tataurov is stepping between the landing struts, preparing to board. A sob breaks from her and she desperately pulls again. "*You're* the one hurting me!"

Fuck me. I am.

Quickly I adjust my grip but she slips right out of it, stumbling forward—and even as I reach for her again, she throws a single, devastated glance back at me.

Then races after him, hair blowing wildly as she ducks low beneath the helicopter blades.

"Olivia!" Raggedly I shout her name.

She doesn't turn. Heart pounding, I start after her, the wound in my thigh on fire and slowing every step. She clambers into the belly of the helicopter and gestures desperately to Tataurov.

Asking him to close the door.

Tataurov looks at me coming and nods to a guard.

The door slams closed. A second later, the helicopter's rising.

"Olivia!"

But her face doesn't even appear at the window. Fingers fisted in my hair, I stare after the helicopter, willing her back.

It just keeps going.

And going.

Do you know what you've done?

I've lost her. I've fucking lost her.

And I'm not seeing her taking some girl anymore, not imagining all the ways she could have done it. Instead all I'm seeing now is her face, her desolation and fear as she whirled on me. As she frantically tried to get away.

No one looks like that just because they need money.

"Jesus." Grasshopper comes up beside me, his gaze on the aircraft quickly disappearing from sight. "I didn't even get a chance to say good-bye. I turned around and she was gone."

Gone. But I didn't turn my back this time.

Instead she fought to get away from me.

And I can't say a damn thing in reply. I'm pretty

fucking sure it wouldn't be words that came out. Maybe blood, because everything inside me is shredded.

"Damn. I'm going to miss her." On a heavy sigh, Grasshopper shakes his head and turns back toward the clubhouse. "But I suppose I'll drown the pain of it in all the wet pussy we'll be bringing in again. You coming?"

To drown the pain.

I'm going to try.

But I can't fucking drink. The brothers are celebrating the end of a half-million-dollar job, and I've got a whisky in front of me that I can't even swallow because my throat feels as if there's a boot clogging it up.

Behind me, there's plenty of pussy for the having. The brothers didn't waste any damn time there, and the sounds of sucking and fucking are filling the clubhouse. But I can't imagine joining in. I can't imagine touching anyone but Olivia ever again.

Do you know what you've done?

The same thing I've always done. Because everything I am, every decision I've ever made, I can trace back to an empty seat in a theater. And everything I said to Olivia, every damn word I spoke after reading that police report, I can trace back there, too.

It's the reason she got into that helicopter.

It's the reason she's gone.

And I think from now on, it won't just be that seat in the theater that I'll picture when I'm tracing back to the moment that defines who I am, the moment that determines every decision I make. Instead I'll see her fighting to get away from me. I'll see her devastated tears, the despair and betrayal in her eyes. I'll hear her asking me—

Do you know what you've done?

I know what I've done. I've hurt her. I should have been protecting her, helping her—but I hurt her.

And there's a better way to drown the pain than this.

Grabbing the whisky bottle, I make my way past the girls writhing naked together on the pool table and putting on a show for the brothers. Every step on the stairs tears at the wound in my leg, but I welcome the pain, because saving Olivia from Zhuk was the one damn thing I did for her that was worth doing.

Now that the lockdown's over, the access door to the lodge is unsecured again. I make my way through, heading for the suite at the opposite end.

I almost turn around when I realize Molly's in there cleaning. Erasing any sign that Olivia had ever been here.

But I can't make myself head back the other way. Not when there's still something of her that remains. It'll all be gone soon enough.

Gone as quickly as she was.

Though there's more of her left than I realized. A mountain of luggage stands in the foyer. Her sparkly purse sits on the table. Her phone lies next to it.

Abandoned in her desperate rush to leave.

My chest aching, I touch the home button and her

screen lights up—and I don't know what the hell I'm seeing. I haven't looked at her phone before. When it was in my possession the device was powered off, and she never used it much. Just checked her e-mail every afternoon.

But there's a selfie on the first screen—Olivia, her hazel eyes laughing and bright—with her cheek pressed up against a girl's, and both looking into the camera. A young girl, but not as young as Jessie, with a shy smile and curly brown hair.

The screen goes dark.

"And here I was thinking you'd be over at the clubhouse awhile, but I see you brought your personal party in a bottle." Molly appears from the bedroom, carrying her cleaning caddy. With a lift of her chin, she gestures to the luggage. "She left all this?"

I force an answer through the jagged pain in my throat. "They took off before loading it."

A troubled frown pulls at her mouth. "A girl like her could probably make good use of all those expensive things. Sell it on eBay, maybe. I suppose we could ship it to her."

Staring at her, I echo, "'A girl like her?' You knew?"

"Wasn't hard to figure out. That girl is no more a big city actress than I am," she says dryly, and the dour look she sends in my direction slowly draws into an expression of concern. "Are you all right, Duke?"

All right? My gaze lands on the manila envelope lying at the center of the coffee table. The police report—which she tried so desperately to explain to me. But after weeks of waiting for her to tell me something, *anything* about who she was…I didn't even listen.

Instead I pushed her away. Left her alone, while she was hurting and afraid.

Blindly I look around the rest of the empty suite, and she's there in every room. Sitting next to me on the piano bench. Tending to my wounds in my quarters. And through the open door of the bedroom stands the bed where she gave herself to me so joyously, so fiercely. Her first.

Her only.

And she loved me.

"I fucked everything up," I say hoarsely.

Pursing her lips, Molly gives me a considering look. "So would you say that things went wrong?"

A short, harsh laugh is my reply to that.

But it's an answer that seems to satisfy her. "Then I've got something for you," she says, moving to the desk in the corner of the sitting room. "She gave this to me, said only to give it to you in the event things went wrong. I suppose she meant if she was killed by that Russian fellow. I brought it back today, because I figured she didn't need me to hold on to it anymore, but she left before I could return it to her. Since things *have* gone wrong, though, I don't think I'm going against her wishes by giving you this."

A sealed envelope. On the front, "Duke" is written in a pretty, feminine script.

"So…I suspect it's not a 'Dear John' letter," Molly says, then glances around the suite. "I'll just leave the rest of this cleaning until tomorrow. You have any problem with that?"

Already ripping open the envelope, I shake my head.

"All right. See you then."

I don't answer. As the door closes behind her, I pull out a folded letter—and another sealed envelope that Olivia tucked inside, addressed simply to "Erin."

Erin. Not Aaron. A girl's name.

Sagging back against the foyer wall, I begin reading everything she says that she would have told me, if she hadn't been bound by her agreement with Tataurov.

About her stepfather and how powerless she was against him.

About trying to escape with Erin, and how afterward no one would believe her word against his, no matter how many bruises she showed them.

About the the million dollars to pay off her stepfather, and the custody agreement.

About her fear that she would lose Erin forever if she didn't use a legal route this time. Then—

I wish I could have told you all of this in person, but if Molly has given this to you, then it means the worst must have happened.

And if I'm gone, I have two things to ask of you.

The first is that you don't blame yourself. I saw firsthand everything you and the others did to keep me safe. I know there isn't anything you wouldn't have done to protect me.

I also know that I'm not living in some Keri Bishop movie. Real life has taught me all too well that sometimes the bad guys win. Sometimes there's no happily ever after. Sometimes the prince beats his bride and sometimes the girl isn't saved in the end. It's just the shitty reality of life.

But I believe YOU are one of the good guys, Duke. The best man I've ever known. The strongest. You told me you would lay down your life for mine, and I believe you would. But I pray you haven't—and I pray that you'll continue being that man, the one I trust, the one I fell in love with.

Because I have something more to ask.

If I'm gone, then I don't care about right and wrong and legal anymore—I only care that Erin is safe. So please, go and get her and bring her home. I know it's a lot to ask. But I trust that she would be safe with you, with Jessie, and that she would be so much better off with a man like you to look up to. I think that she'll come to love you…and I think that you'll love her, too.

So I've included another letter in here for her. On the back of that envelope is her full name and address, so you'll know how to find her. She won't know you, but she'll trust what I've written.

And I haven't said this yet, either—but I love you, Duke. And I'm sorry, so sorry, that I couldn't be there with you both. I don't know where I'm going now. But I suppose it doesn't even matter, because I've already been in heaven. Surely there's nothing beyond the pearly gates that could compare to these

past few days with you.
With all of my heart, forever—
Olivia Burke

Don't blame yourself.

Already I'm doing what she asked me not to, reading every word again, feeling as if a gaping hole has opened up in my chest.

Do you know what you've done?

I failed her. Utterly failed her. That's what I've done.

But I'll *never* fail her again. And she's wrong about one thing: she *is* going to get her happily ever after. Because that *is* a fucking reality.

It's a reality I'll make for her.

Carefully I fold the letter, determination filling the ragged hole in my heart. Because the question echoing in my head is changing. It's not whether I know what I've done.

But what am I going to do now?

I'm going to find her. I'm going to bring her back home.

That empty theater seat and Olivia's desperate tears are *not* going to be the moments that determine the remainder of my life.

Instead every decision I make, everything I am—I'll be tracing back to the moment I see her again.

EIGHTEEN

OLIVIA

"Hurry, Livvie!" Erin urges from her post by the window in James's study.

I freeze with my hand still in the safe. "Is he back?"

"No. But hurry!"

A breathless laugh escapes me. What does she think I'm doing, dawdling?

Still my heart doesn't stop pounding and my fingers don't stop shaking as I quickly leaf through the documents inside. I find what I need at the same moment a pair of headlights swings past the window and Erin squeaks, "He's here!"

"Go, go," I tell her, hastily closing the safe and spinning the combination lock to the same number on the dial that was showing before I opened it. I don't know if James leaves little traps like that, but I'm not taking the chance. "I'll be right there."

She flees to the kitchen. I race upstairs to the guest bedroom, where the two backpacks we've stashed in the closet are waiting. I stuff the envelope containing our birth certificates into the first pack even as I hear the garage's overhead door opening.

Shoving the bags back under the lowest shelf, I sprint for the stairs.

When my stepfather enters the kitchen through the garage door, I'm still a little flushed, but my hectic color can be explained by the hot oven I've opened to check the browning of the pie crust.

Not burnt while Erin and I were rushing around, gathering everything we need to leave. Not burnt, and thank heaven for it. Lord knows the devil's hit me for less reason.

Even if James McCullen doesn't look like a devil. Tall and lean, with dark silvering hair and piercing blue eyes, he's a handsome man—which is probably part of the reason he has so much sway in this town. But I can see how the past day has taken a toll on him.

Which means it'll probably take a toll on me.

He eyes Erin, sitting at the table with a pre-algebra textbook open and her head bent over her spiral notebook.

"You doing your homework?"

"Yes, sir," she says obediently.

Sir. Never "Daddy." She only calls him "sir"—or when he's not around, "he."

James has never asked her to call him sir. But he doesn't seem to care that she doesn't call him Daddy, either.

His attention shifts to me next, and I feel the muscles in my neck and shoulders drawing up tight, as if to shield myself against that gaze. "When's that supper going to be ready?"

"Ten minutes," I tell him. Seven o'clock. Right on the dot.

Five hours until we're gone.

"You best be certain it's not late," he says, then crosses the kitchen—heading for his study.

As soon as he's left the room, all the tension melts from my spine. My hands begin shaking again, and I walk quietly over to Erin, slipping my arms around her shoulders. "Not long now," I whisper, because James never closes the door to his study and I can't risk him hearing a word. "Just pretend everything is normal."

She's not any better at pretending than I am. But instead of tension and fear, it's bright excitement that's gleaming from her eyes.

"Now go set the table in the dining room," I tell her.

She scampers off, and the moment she's out of sight,

it's everything I can do to keep from crumpling to the floor. It's been all I can do just to stay upright from the moment I boarded the helicopter two days ago. From the moment I lost Duke.

From the moment I lost everything.

Except I still have Erin. And she's all that matters now.

My throat burns with unshed tears as I finish up in the kitchen. I could have moved out of James's big house years ago, rented my own place, but that would have meant leaving Erin. So I've stayed. And even after I tried to take Erin away from him, he's never threatened to kick me out. I just have to follow his rules.

No going out at night. No drinking or smoking. Have a dinner ready after church. Make sure Erin has a lunch to take to school. Supper on the table at seven.

Those are his spoken rules. But of course there are the thousands of unspoken ones—all of which can change with his mood.

But I've never seen his mood quite like this. Yesterday, when a hired town car picked me up from the Shreveport airport and dropped me off at home—with no million dollars and no custody agreement—I was utterly terrified.

I still am, even though he didn't beat me yesterday. Maybe I'm terrified *because* he didn't beat me. Instead his expression drew into grim lines and he retreated to his study, where he polished off a bottle of bourbon. And I lay awake all night, waiting for the explosion to come.

I'm still waiting. I waited through breakfast and getting Erin ready for church, while the long night sat haggard on his face. Waited through Sunday dinner, when he asked about the jaunt I took this morning to Barb's Diner—where he thinks I was asking for my job back—and as I struggled through the anxiety of deciding whether to tell him that she hired me again or tell him that she didn't, because I wasn't certain which was more likely to set him off. But he accepted my reply that she wouldn't take me back without comment, and the waiting continued. We waited all through the afternoon, as he drank more. Waited as he drove away to Tess O'Dell's place, because that pretty widow always has some delicate issue that only the mayor can solve, when we frantically packed our things and prayed he'd take longer to solve the widow's problems than he usually does. But he didn't spend more time with her than usual, and doesn't appear as if *he* got much out of that problem-solving session, either.

Instead he seems to me like a grenade with its pin already pulled, and I'm just waiting for the inevitable explosion. Except it's been building up so long, I fear it might be worse than any explosion that came before.

So Erin and I plan to leave before it comes. Running was the very last option I wanted to take, because it means always looking over my shoulder, always being afraid.

But I had no idea Tataurov's offer was coming, so I've also had five years to plan. I've had five years of working at Barb's and squirreling money away in her safe, because I knew if I kept cash at home—or in a bank account where James's friends would be more than happy to check on the balance for him—he would take it from me.

In those five years, he's never been much worried about me running off. He refuses to teach me to drive and I don't have any close friends who would take me anywhere. No one at the bus station will sell me a ticket, especially if I'm with Erin. And he assumed the pay stubs I brought home reported all that I was making.

Barb has been there for me, though, putting away half my earnings and keeping it safe. And at midnight, she'll be waiting down the street to take Erin and me to Shreveport. From there we'll fly out on the first plane heading to the southwest states—somewhere near the border, where hopefully I can use the cash I saved up to buy new birth certificates. Then we'll just huddle down in a small town like this one. A waitress can find work anywhere.

And if a part of me dreams that we'll end up in a small town in Oregon, and one day a big biker with stormy green eyes and a good man's heart crosses my path again...

Well, it's just a dream. And they aren't worth much.

But the world sure does feel empty and hopeless without them.

Just as empty and hopeless as I feel without *him*. So I'll keep dreaming. No harm done.

And it's all I have left of him. Just a dream.

Supper's quiet, but that's not unusual. James presides over the head of the table, his back to the formal painted portrait of his grandfather, who glowers down at us from his permanent seat above the fireplace. After the heavy Sunday dinner, supper's only a light meal and doesn't take too long—yet it seems to stretch out forever, with every bite forced through the lump in my throat.

At seven-thirty, he pushes his chair back. "You girls clear this away and wash up now. No putting it off," he says, same as always—and, same as always, he heads for his study again. Not far. Just one door off the dining room.

Erin immediately gathers the water glasses. I begin stacking the plates, trying not to clink the dishes together too loudly.

Another of his unspoken rules.

Across the table, Erin grins at me, her eyes sparkling before she turns and skips away toward the kitchen. To her, I suppose this is a wonderful secret, a daring escape to be followed by a thrilling adventure. She doesn't understand yet how difficult it might become for us, always hiding, living paycheck to paycheck.

But I'm determined to give her the best life I possibly can. Even if it's a struggle, it has to be better than this— and if I write to Molly, maybe I can get back the shoes and clothes and jewelry, and ease the financial stress.

And then I'd at least have something to show for doing that damn job. Something more than a broken heart.

A heart that stops at the sound of crashing glass.

I spin away from the table. "Erin!"

She's sprawled on the floor in front of the swinging

door between the kitchen and dining room. Shattered glass is spilled across the boards, the edge of the rug soaked in water.

Frantically she tries scraping the glass into a pile with her bare hands. "I tripped, I tripped—"

Hauling her up by her waist, I swing her away from the glass, give her a push toward the kitchen. "It's okay, honey. Go go go."

Eyes shimmering with tears, she looks up at me, her chin jutted out bravely, her lips wobbling. "Let me take it this time."

Throat tight, I shake my head. "You are *never* going to take it. Go."

Trembling, I crouch beside the rug and begin picking up the glass.

James never hurries. Sometimes that's the worst of it. He'll take his time making his way out of his study. He'll take his time removing his belt. He'll take his time explaining exactly what I've done to deserve what's coming.

This time I hear him emerge from his study and stand at the entrance to the dining room, feeling that piercing gaze on my stiff back.

I flinch when he calls out, "Erin, there's still dishes on that table!"

Hardly a second passes before she hurries through the kitchen door, heading for the stack of plates I abandoned when she fell. "We're clearing them away, sir!"

"*You* seem to be." He comes closer, his black shoes

gleaming against the dining room rug until he's standing right beside my crouching form. "Olivia here is doing something else. What happened here?"

I look up and pain bursts across my face, whipping my head around, sending me sprawling to the floor.

Oh my god. Oh my god.

Blinded by tears of shock and pain, I cover my burning cheek, crying as I try to scoot away. He's never hit me like that before. Never in the face. Never where it'll show.

"Stop it!" Erin screams.

Strong fingers twist in my hair, agony shearing across my scalp as he drags me up to my knees and stares down at me with cold, hate-filled eyes. "You made a mess, Olivia."

And I realize the explosion is coming, but it'll be worse than I feared. Because he's got nothing to lose. I've got no job to go back to, and no one will miss me—except Erin. And maybe he won't kill me but if he no longer cares whether the bruises show, then I'm not leaving this house for a long, long time. He'll have no reason to hold back.

Desperately I search the floor, trying to find a piece of glass, *anything* to defend myself with. In horror, I see the clenching of his fist as he draws it back—

But the heavy *thwack* that follows isn't a blow. Instead James stiffens and staggers to the side, releasing my hair, holding the side of his shoulder.

Wielding the fireplace poker, Erin advances on him with bared teeth. "Leave her alone!"

Lips drawing back in a terrifying smile, he takes a

step toward her.

No no no. I scramble to my feet, get to her first, grabbing the poker and spinning to face him, holding it ready like a baseball bat. "Don't you touch her," I snarl. "Don't you even take another step or I will splatter your brains across the table, *so help me God!*"

Instantly the rage leaves his face but I'm not fooled. I know it's still there.

Placatingly, he holds up his hands. "All right, Olivia. Let's think about what you're doing."

I know what I'm doing. To Erin, I say, "Run up and get our bags."

He watches her sprint for the stairs and there's the rage, flickering in his eyes again. Just waiting for me to let down my guard.

"And what then?" he asks in that reasonable voice. "You leave this house and I'll come right after you."

The poker trembles in my hands. Because I know he will. That's why we intended to leave when he was asleep. We need a head start.

"So put the poker down, Olivia," he continues. "And we'll talk this out in a sensible way."

I'm not going to engage in any conversation with him, because that will be the beginning of the end. Instead I just grit out, "Stay *right* there," when I hear Erin coming down the stairs again.

"We need to tie him up," she says matter-of-factly as she enters the dining room, wearing one backpack and holding the other against her chest. "Or we won't get far."

She's right. We need to immobilize him.

But the only way to do that would be to get close to him—and if he got his hands on one of us while we were tying him, it would be all over. He'd use one of us as a shield against the other, and we wouldn't dare swing the poker again.

I see him realize it at the same time. Triumph fills his smile, the rage not so hidden now that he doesn't need to pretend.

"So what will it be, Olivia? You don't have any options here."

I do. But not one that I want Erin to see.

Throat raw, I tell her, "Go out to the front porch and wait for me, honey."

She looks at me uncertainly. "Why?"

"So she can bash my brains across the table," James tells her. "But only if I don't get that poker away from her. Then she'll regret not handling this in a more rational manner."

Voice breaking, my entire body shaking, I tell her again, "Go, honey."

"Better hurry." James's eyes narrow. "We've got company."

We do. I can hear the engine, and headlights are sweeping across the wall of the dining room. Someone's pulling into the driveway.

Cruel, victorious amusement fills his voice. "Looks

like it might be Emerson's new truck."

The police chief. Breath sobbing from my chest, I give a tight shake of my head, trying to deny the terrible reality crashing down on me.

It can't end like this. It can't. If Emerson catches me threatening James with a poker, I'll never see Erin again. James wouldn't forgive the embarrassment—and he'd let his friend lock me away.

"Livvie…" Face stricken with terror, Erin tugs on my shirt. "Let's just run as fast as we can."

But we won't get far enough. If I drop this poker, though, the only thing that will happen is a beating later, after Emerson leaves.

A bad beating. But then we can try again.

The sound of the doorbell is like a death knell.

"It's unlocked, old boy!" James calls out loudly enough to be heard from the front porch. "You can just walk right in."

And see me. I'll be the *first* thing he sees. The foyer is right next to the dining room and a big archway offers a view of everything inside.

The front door opens. Then closes.

"We're in here, Emerson!" James calls. "Just finishing up supper, but we've got plenty of apple pie left over if you want to join us."

I can't lose Erin. I'll bear anything.

Arms going limp, I drop the poker to the rug. James's mouth twists into an enraged snarl.

"Now you get upstairs and hide your face from—" Abruptly he stops, looking past me, his brows drawing together in confusion. "Who the hell are you?"

"It seems I'm the man you just invited in," is the reply—in a familiar voice, a voice like a glacier, all ice and gravel.

Unless I'm dreaming again.

Heart leaping into my throat, I look back. And it *is* him. Duke. He's not wearing his kutte, just a T-shirt and jeans, but he still appears huge and dangerous standing in the archway leading to the foyer—and he's looking at me with a storm in his eyes, his gaze tender as it meets mine.

Then hardening into a lethal, icy stare. Lips parting in realization, I touch my throbbing cheek.

A duffle bag drops from his grip to the floor, landing with a thump next to his left boot. His hard gaze slides down my length, pausing near my feet—on the poker—and a muscle works in his jaw. Next he grimly eyes Erin, who's wearing one backpack and clutching the other to her chest, and who's watching him with shivering uncertainty. When he looks past me, his deadly focus narrowed on James, I almost don't recognize the man standing there.

But I bet Zhuk would recognize the expression he's wearing.

James starts forward. "I'll welcome any man into my home, but I'm wondering what you want here, friend."

"I came to give you a million dollars in exchange for your signature," Duke says softly. "But I think I'll be holding on to the money, instead. Olivia—you and your sister grab your things and go wait for me in the rig out front. Get everything you need, because you're not coming back."

"We already have it." I take the extra backpack from Erin, sling it over my shoulder, and grip her hand. "Are you coming?"

His lethal gaze stays locked on my stepfather. "In a few minutes."

I don't look back at James. Erin's hand in mine, I lead her to the big pickup truck parked on the driveway apron.

"Who is he?" she whispers as I toss the backpacks into the pickup bed.

The best man I've ever known. "His name is Duke," I tell her. "He's the one who looked after me while I was gone."

"The one you said you liked?"

My chest squeezes tight. "Yeah. The one I liked."

"He's even bigger than you said he was." Erin settles into the center of the cab's bench seat and peers through the windshield. Old Man McCullen's glowering portrait can be seen through the narrow opening in the curtains. Not much else in the dining room is visible. "Do you think Duke is beating him up?"

I hope so. "I'm sure they're just talking."

Disappointment scrunches her face.

"And that was *so* brave what you did," I tell her, my voice thick. "When you made him stop."

"He deserved it." Even as her small hands roll into

fists, her lips tremble. "But I was so scared."

Throat burning with tears, I hug her against me, tucking her head under my chin. "I know. Me, too." I draw a deep, shuddering breath. "But we don't have to be scared anymore."

Even if Duke's not here to take me home. Even if he never wants me around Jessie. Whatever happens, the one thing I do know is that if I'm in trouble, he'll help me. Somehow, by some miracle, he'll help me.

He comes through the front door a few minutes later, carrying a sheaf of papers in one hand and the duffel bag in the other. Slinging the bag into the truck bed, he opens the driver's door and looks in, his gaze searching my face before looking to Erin. "How you doing, little lady?"

"Okay," she whispers nervously.

"Is it all right if I sit next to you?"

Wordlessly, she nods.

He slides in, tossing the papers onto the dash in front of me. My gaze goes to his bloodied knuckles, then to his face. Those stormy green eyes are watching me, and he tilts his head as if to indicate that I should look at that document.

Fingers shaking, I reach for it.

He sits back and starts the engine, saying easily, "I apologize for the cramped quarters here. I wasn't sure how much you'd want to take, so I rented a truck that we could use to haul it all away in. But I suppose those backpacks will fit on a plane. You ever been on a plane before, Erin?"

She shakes her head.

It's the custody agreement. I can't stop the small sob that breaks from me, though I try to cover it with my hand, raising tear-filled eyes to meet his.

"That's not what you think," he tells me gruffly. "But we'll talk about it a bit later, all right?"

Nodding, I glance down at Erin, who's suddenly looking worried again. Because I'm crying.

It only takes a smile—a smile bursting with all the joy and relief I'm feeling—to vanish that fear from her eyes. Duke whistles softly through his teeth as he begins backing out of the drive.

"Your sister sure is pretty, Erin," he tells her.

"Yeah," she says and snuggles her head against my shoulder, then adds a little enviously, "And her teeth are *so* white."

A *BIT LATER* IS IN Shreveport, near the airport, in a hotel. Erin's sleeping soundly in one of the double beds when a gentle tap sounds at the door connecting our room to Duke's.

Heart thundering, dressed only in the T-shirt and panties I plan to wear to bed, I quietly undo the locks on our side and hear the click of the latch on the other. The door opens, and he's standing there in his jeans, his chest bare and his broad shoulders filling the doorway.

Softly Duke asks, "Is she sleeping?"

I nod.

Instantly his big hand clasps the back of my neck and he pulls me through into his room, straight into his arms. His mouth captures mine in a hungry, possessive kiss, and I'm gasping and breathless when he pushes me back against the wall and lifts his head, his eyes searching mine.

A smile tilts his firm lips. "So this is you," he says in a deep voice. "Olivia Burke."

"Yes," I reply, nervously biting my lip as he continues examining my face.

Eyes hot like lightning, he skims his knuckles down the curve of my jaw, then uses the pad of his thumb to tease my bottom lip from between my teeth. His gaze darkens when his gentle search takes him to my bruised cheek, and when he meets my eyes again, he goes utterly still, simply looking at them.

"Not blue," I whisper.

"And even more beautiful than in your picture," he says gruffly.

I blink. "What picture?"

"In that *People* magazine article." Bending his head, he gently presses his lips to my bruised cheek. "I've known who you are for a good long while, duchess."

Oh. "So that's how you found me?"

He lays another gentle kiss against the side of my throat, where my pulse must be throbbing as quickly as a rabbit's. "That, and an address on the back of the letter you wrote to Erin."

Heat fills my cheeks. "Molly gave you my letter?"

His voice roughens, as if suddenly struck by deep, painful emotion. "She did."

So he knows everything now. "And that's why you came?"

"No." His head lifts and he looks into my eyes again. "I told you that if you weren't back by Sunday, I'd come for you. It's Sunday. So here I am."

I don't know what to say. Because he'd said he would come for me *before* he found out about the police report. And he's kissed me, but now that the fear and relief of escaping James is settling down, the memory of everything that happened before I left on that helicopter is crashing over me again, leaving me trembling in a wake of uncertainty.

Searching for something to anchor to, my gaze lands on the duffel bag at the foot of his bed. "Is that really a million dollars?"

"It is." He's watching me carefully now. "I flew to Las Vegas yesterday, had a conversation with Tataurov…and Keri Bishop."

My gaze flies back to his. "What?"

He nods slowly, eyes still locked on mine. "I figured you did your job—and since I was the one who fucked up your deal with him, I ought to be the one who made it right. And he was damn well going to pay what he owed you."

I catch my breath. "Oh my god. What did you do to him?"

That makes him grin. "Turns out, I didn't need to do anything but talk. Keri didn't have a clue what he'd set up with you. But as soon as she found out, she made it real clear he'd better follow through." Grin fading, his voice deepens again, his gaze flicking to my cheek. "And that's what took me so damn long today—waiting for his lawyers to get me a copy of that agreement before I flew east."

Simply a mention of that document suddenly has me smiling again, but it fades when he adds, "Olivia, that custody agreement's not worth the fucking paper it's printed on."

I stare up at him in dismay, my throat closing—remembering his bloodied knuckles. "Because the signature was coerced?"

"Maybe that, too. But mostly because a man can't sign away custody of a child to someone else with one damn stroke of a pen. You saw what I went through with Jessie—and that was about as easy as it goes." Face grim, he shakes his head. "Truth is, your stepfather probably thinks what he signed is binding, because Tataurov's lawyers made that document look real good. But even if he doesn't think it's legal, I doubt he'd ever claim it was forced. Men like him, they get off on pushing around people who are weaker, but never want to admit someone was able to push them."

Fear gripping my throat, I stare up at him. Ivan gave me a worthless document? "I need it to be legal. So he can't take her."

"We're getting the next best thing. Tataurov has strings on a judge in Nevada and he's willing to pull them. It'll be the wrong state but it'll all look right on paper. So we'll be flying to Vegas tomorrow and we can get all that sorted out. You'll have non-parental custody, all the right documents will be filed with the courts, and it'll appear as if your stepfather's revoked his rights. So not exactly legal—but it'll be enough."

Will it be? My gaze searches his for reassurance. I find it, but whatever he sees in my eyes makes his fingers tighten, holding me still, as if afraid I'm about to dart away.

Firmly he says, "If you're worried your stepfather's going to come after you, you just put away that worry. With Erin right there, I didn't want to risk her seeing me do too much damage—"

"She about brained him with the poker," I say dryly.

"Did she?" His grin flashes again. "Well, I did something a lot worse to him with that poker. Then I made it real fucking clear that the only way he'll continue breathing is if he lets you go and never comes after you." He pauses, his gaze intense on mine. "But I stopped before I wanted to, so you could leave without the cops looking at you. If I kill him the same day you take off, it'll raise a lot of questions. And it's one thing if they come after me, but they'd be coming after you. As it is now, I figure you'll never see him again—but you just say the word, and I'll take care of him permanently."

So it *does* sound as if we're free. I draw a long, shuddering breath. "I think better not to kill him." Because I don't want to risk Duke's freedom, either. "And thank you."

Softly he groans, his eyes closing as if in pain. "Sweet Christ, Olivia. *You* sure as hell shouldn't be thanking *me*."

Yes, I should. "You didn't have to come."

"Yeah, I did." Duke says it softly but there's nothing insubstantial about his reply—as if beneath those quiet words is a promise as solid as he is. A promise that he'll *always* come for me. Gently his thumb slides across my quivering lips. "But it looked as if you weren't waiting to be saved. You were just going to get out of there yourself."

And came so close to failing. My throat thick, I tell him, "I'd been hiding money away for years, so that we could run when we needed to. Until Ivan made his offer, I thought it would be the only way to escape."

"Now you have a million dollars, and soon you'll have custody." This is quietly spoken, too, but with a rough edge, and although his eyes are gently caressing my face, his body is rigid—as if preparing for a blow. "You can do anything, go anywhere. Put yourself through school, or buy a house on a beach somewhere. Anything you want."

But not *everything* I want. None of those options he just gave included *him*.

My heart splitting open, I nod and avert my face, so he can't read the pain there, can't see the new tears glittering in my eyes.

Tenderly, his fingers grasp my chin and bring my gaze back to his. "Or you can come home with me."

I still don't dare hope. "To the clubhouse?"

"To *my* house. After we leave Vegas with those papers, we can stop by Joyce's and pick up Jessie, and then we'll all go home and figure out our new life together." His stormy gaze searches mine. "Or is that too much to ask?"

"What exactly *are* you asking?" I whisper through trembling lips, too afraid to trust that he's saying what I pray he's saying.

"I'm asking whether you'll have me."

"Are you sure you still want *me*?" I need to be sure. In anguish I tell him, "That police report wasn't a lie. I really tried to take her."

"Because you were afraid he'd start beating on her, too? You think I can't see the difference between that and what my sister went through?"

I don't know. "You were so angry. You said nothing could justify it."

Regret darkens his eyes. "Seeing that report hit me hard. All I could think of was Holly—and I went off half-cocked, thinking you'd been playing me this whole time. Faking everything."

A tremulous little laugh shakes from me. "I'm not that good an actress."

"You sure aren't." Cupping my face in his hands, he says gruffly, "So you weren't faking when you said you loved me?"

"No," I breathe.

"Even though I fucked up?" His tormented gaze drops

to my bruised cheek. "I'm so damn sorry that I wasn't there to stop him, baby. I should never have let you go."

"It's okay," I say and when he starts to shake his head, I continue, "It was probably better this way—not sneaking out and running, but facing him. Standing up to him. Better for me *and* for Erin."

"And she took a poker to him." He grins again, as if that's still about the best thing he's ever heard. "She's a real firecracker, yeah?"

"Yeah." Biting my lip, I pause a moment before rushing into, "It's not too much? Two girls?"

"Not even a bit." Then his eyes gleam, and he glances toward the adjoining room. "Though we'll need to get used to locking our bedroom door…unless you think there's a chance she won't wake up?"

Giggling, I wrap my arms around his neck. "Do you really want to take that chance?"

Apparently not. Lifting me against his chest, he stops by the door to quietly flip the lock before heading to the bed. As soon as he lays me down I try to draw his mouth to mine, but he just pins my arms above my head, his lips hovering a whisper away from a kiss.

Voice deep, he says, "Tomorrow we'll be in Las Vegas. So how much of a chance do you want to take with me, Olivia Burke?"

My heart stops as I realize what he's asking. "Every chance," I say fervently. "But maybe…it's better to wait before we get married. Not because I want to wait. But because we're all being thrown together—you and me and Jessie and Erin—and it *will* take some time to figure it out, for us to really become a family. So maybe when we do it, we should do it for all of us. So the girls are part of the wedding. Part of becoming *us*."

"You're so damn smart. Problem is, the part of me that needs to claim you doesn't have a real big brain, and it wants to know you're mine." With a slow rock of his hips, he grinds his thick erection against me, sending fiery sparks of need shooting through my veins. And even as I'm gasping and pressing closer, he says, "How about this, then? I marry you and make you mine tomorrow. Because we've got this figured out, you and me. But we'll hold off on that big ceremony until the girls are ready for it."

"Okay," I agree breathlessly.

His head jerks back and he looks down at me in surprise. "I thought I'd have to persuade you. But that was easy."

"Well, I've got parts that aren't very smart, too."

"Do you, now?" Watching me, he slides his rough palm up the side of my ribs, up beneath my T-shirt. Anticipation shivers through me when he cups my breast. "Is this one of those parts?"

"Yes," I whisper, arching my back, my nipples aching for his touch.

But he's teasing me. Instead of caressing those hardened peaks, his fingers begin a slow journey down my stomach. Laughing, I squirm and try to make him go faster, but he's got me pinned, his left hand capturing my wrists and his heavily muscled thigh thrown over both of mine.

Then he abandons the quivering plane of my stomach and begins unfastening his jeans. "Now, this here—this is the stupid fucker I've got."

His long, beautiful cock. My laughter fades, replaced by urgent need as I watch him stroke his thick length.

"Duke," I whisper. "Please."

Voice rough, he strokes harder, then sweeps his broad thumb through a pearl of pre-cum beaded at the tip. "You need something, baby? You'll have to spell it out, because like I said—not smart."

Whimpering, I squeeze my thighs together to ease the hollow ache inside me. "I need you in me. Because I'm wet." So wet. "And so empty."

"Fuck." With a tortured groan, abruptly he's over me, yanking my panties down to my knees before urging my legs apart. "Look at me, Olivia."

I meet the storm-swept sea of his eyes and he surges forward, filling me completely. Pleasure washes through me, my pussy desperately gripping his cock, my body bowed on a wave of ecstasy. Slowly he rides me, my slick inner walls clinging to his heavy shaft through each long thrust, his fingers mercilessly teasing my clit. And he doesn't release my hands, doesn't release my gaze, even as I cry out helplessly against the onslaught, my breath coming in frantic bursts, the tension rolling higher and higher with each powerful stroke of his cock.

Then it breaks, and a deep groan rips from his chest as my pussy convulsively tightens around his thick length. His mouth finds mine in a hot, hungry kiss that doesn't end, devouring my lips as his big body stiffens and his cock pulses deep inside my clenching sheath.

His kiss slows and softens, but still doesn't end as he eases over onto his back, carrying me with him. With my hands free, I suddenly can't stop touching him, sliding my palms up the sculpted strength of his arms, across his heavy shoulders, and burying my fingers in the short thickness of his hair at his nape.

My lips feel warm and swollen when I finally lift my head, looking down into the storm of his eyes—my chest filled with so much emotion, I can hardly speak.

"I love it when you look at me," I tell him hoarsely. "You're the only man I've ever wanted to look my way, to pay attention. And you're one of the only people who has ever seen *me*. Olivia."

"I see you, Olivia Burke," he says gruffly. His throat works, then he reaches up to cup my face in his hands and gently draw me closer. "I see the woman I love."

"The woman who loves you," I tell him, then smile against his lips. "And I'm only Olivia *Burke* for one more day."

But his duchess…for always.

EPILOGUE

Almost one year later...

DUKE

When I ease my bike off the main road and turn up my driveway, riding past the mailbox decorated with a blanket of flowers, I spot about two dozen lawn ornaments parked in the farmhouse's front yard.

I don't even think I *know* that many people who drive cars.

But there's a good chance they aren't here for me, anyway. I've never seen anyone make friends as easy as

Olivia does—and I can't blame a single damn person for wanting to be near her.

Hell, it's probable that half the brothers riding in behind me are here to see *her* married. That a Hellfire Rider happens to be the one who'll stand up beside her just means there's a bonus attached, in the form of one hell of a party at the clubhouse the night before.

A party that I'm still feeling, because when the prez starts pouring you shots, you sure as fuck don't stop drinking.

And when the prez *keeps* pouring you shots…shit, that was probably some revenge for when we did the same to him, the night before he got hitched.

He's riding right behind me now, Thorne beside him, and just about every brother following. Everything for the wedding is set up in the big back yard, but there's decorations everywhere else, too. Flowers are twisted around the porch railing and streamers weave through the fence that lines the drive. More streamers are waving from the windows in the girls' bedrooms upstairs, making the house look like it's got long, fluttery eyelashes.

I lead the brothers down the drive and around the house, and come to a stop at the edge of the lawn. By the time they've all pulled in, there'll be a line of motorcycles stretching all the way to the old barn that Erin and Jessie keep begging me to fix up, so they can stable their horses at home instead of over at Molly's place.

But I'm holding off on that. At least until Christmas.

The back yard's already busy with people, and something smells real damn good. A few big white tents provide shade for the guests, and a few more tents cover the tables where Sara's setting up a battalion of silver chafing dishes. And Bull's my best man, but he abandons me quick when he spots her standing there, clapping me on my back as he passes by.

"Give me ten minutes, brother," he says.

I'll give him longer than that, considering the wedding doesn't start for another half hour—and all he has to do is stand there, so there's not much preparation involved. But he hasn't seen his wife since yesterday, so I'm sure as hell not going to give him shit about it. Not when I'm wishing that this half hour was already gone, just so I can see my woman, too.

But, fuck. Since I can't see Olivia right now, no reason not to make it real difficult for Bull to get any quality time with his woman.

And I'm not the only one headed in that direction. As I reach the buffet table, Gunner's right beside me, frowning as he scans the lawn. "Do you see my wife?"

Cheeks flushed and eyes sparkling, and looking real tiny snuggled up against Bull's giant chest, Sara tells him, "I think she's upstairs with Olivia. She was under the tent with Jenny, but apparently there was a makeup emergency and she went to help."

Seems like every old lady and female guest is congregated over by Jenny, but the crowd parts like the Red Sea as the prez makes his way toward her. He bends to kiss his woman, then emerges from the circle of old ladies a moment later with a baby snuggled against his broad shoulder.

One month old and the boy hardly looks bigger than the prez's hand. He's got a hell of a lot of growing to do to catch up with his dad.

Drawn by the smell of the food—or by the booze sitting in the tubs of ice—some of the other brothers are starting their own congregation here at the serving table. But every single one of them stops and turns to look as an old truck rolls up and Zoomie gets out. A huge, ugly mutt jumps out after her—which I figure is why she's driving instead of riding in like usual—but it sure as fuck isn't the dog that's got the brothers' jaws hanging open.

It's her. Wearing a killer dress—and heels. I don't think I've ever seen her in anything but boots.

"Holy shit." Beside me, Grasshopper's staring like he's witnessing something holy. "Those legs go on for fucking *miles*."

"The better to kick a motherfucker's ass for miles," I tell him. Then Blowback comes around from the other side of the truck and suddenly every brother's got somewhere else to look.

There's only one person I want to look at, but she's not here. Still, now I've got an excuse to go searching.

I meet Gunner's eyes, tilt my head. "I'll take you in to find Anna, yeah?"

I lead him through the screen door on the back porch, into the kitchen where every counter is taken up with more food that'll be heading outside. Jesus. I hope these fuckers are hungry.

From the living room, I hear giggling and someone poking at the piano. Then the girls are heading toward us in a clattering rush, wearing flouncy dresses and cowboy boots, their smiles about as bright as Olivia's often are.

"I'm pretty sure I saw Molly coming down the lane with a pair of white horses," I tell them.

Jessie rolls her eyes. "They're *gray*, Daddy. Not white."

"Yeah, Dad," Erin chimes in. "They're gray."

I stop all at once, so choked up I can't breathe.

Suddenly shy, Erin says, "We decided that today we'd stop calling you Duke."

"And Uncle John." Jessie's twisting her fingers nervously, her gaze searching my face. "Is it all right? Olivia said I could call her Mommy but then she started crying and ruined her mascara. But you aren't wearing any."

"I'm not calling her Mommy though, because it's weird. Even though she's been my mother my whole life, she's still my sister." Erin bites her lip. "But…is it okay?"

My voice raw, I ask, "Do I get to start saying you're my daughters, then?"

"Yes!" they answer together.

"All right. Bring it in." I crouch and they fling themselves against my chest, their arms circling my neck. And this feeling, goddamn. Still nothing like it.

Erin's the first to pull back—probably because she just realized who was standing behind me. Suddenly blushing, she says shyly, "Hi, Uncle Zach."

"Hi, Uncle Zach!" Jessie echoes, her gaze wide and adoring.

A thirteen-year-old girl with a crush is simultaneously one of the funniest and most terrifying things I've ever known.

A seven-year-old girl, it's just cute.

Gunner flashes his pretty, pretty smile at them. "I hear you two are going to be Olivia's mounted guard, riding down the aisle ahead of her."

Erin's blush deepens. "We're riding behind her."

"Because the horses might poop." Excitedly Jessie jumps up and down. "And we have lightsabers!"

"I can't wait to see it," he says. "You two will be the best guards a bride ever had."

While the stars of delight are still dancing in their eyes, I tell them, "Why don't you run out and meet Molly, then. Make sure your horses get settled before the ceremony starts."

He's grinning as they run off. "That is cute as hell."

"They kill me every fucking day," I tell him as we head for the stairs. "You'll see."

"Yeah, if the goddamn adoption ever goes through. Swear to god, we've had more inspections than I ever did in boot camp."

"The wait will be worth it."

"The wait has always been worth it." He's looking up the stairwell ahead of me, where Anna's appeared on the second-floor landing. "There you are, sweetheart. Stone just called. He's running late."

"Of course he is." She rolls her eyes and begins descending the stairs. "Maybe he'd be on time more often if he could keep his hands off his wife."

Gunner frowns. "What kind of sick bastard would choose punctuality over getting his hands on his own wife?"

The man's got a point.

"John! What are you doing?" Joyce is right behind Anna, shooing me back down the stairs. "It's bad luck to see the bride on your wedding day."

"It's a good thing our wedding day was almost a year ago, then," I tell her and keep on going.

I saw her that day, too, and not a stroke of bad luck has come my way for it. Instead it's been the best damn year of my life.

For Olivia, too—because she was incredible before, but away from her stepfather, away from that worry and fear, she just kept blooming. The first thing she did on coming home was buy a car, and had me teach her to drive it. She's taken up riding with the girls, and when she's not helping Molly at the clubhouse or working here, she spends a good portion of her time volunteering at the women's shelter in town.

And every night, she's in my arms, sweet and hot and giving me everything.

So, yeah. I don't think seeing the bride on her wedding day hurt a damn bit.

But hell if it doesn't make my cock ache. Because when I open the door to our bedroom, she's got one sexy heel propped up on the stool in front of the mirrored vanity. Her wedding dress is a simple, body-hugging white sheath that skims the floor—but right now, she's got the skirt hiked up over her sleek thigh as she adjusts her lacy garter.

Sweet Christ. *This* is why they don't want men seeing their brides before the wedding. Because one look, and the only thought in my head is getting her into the bed and fucking her for hours.

But I've only got thirty minutes.

I close the door behind me—then have to turn back when she says, "Don't forget to lock it."

The gold flecks in her eyes are sparking as I cross the room, her red lips soft and full and parted in anticipation. She straightens, but keeps her foot propped on the stool, her fingers skimming over golden skin on a path up the inside of her thigh.

Legs for fucking miles. And I'm on a course straight between them.

She gasps as I drop to my knees, my lips following the path of her fingers, tasting her silky skin, inhaling the sultry scent of her cunt.

And she's going to have to adjust her garter again.

With rough hands, I drag her white panties down,

taking that garter with them. Her fingers fist in my hair and she cries out when I get my mouth on her pussy, groaning at the first delicious taste of her. She's wet, so fucking wet, her juicy little clit so sweet against my tongue. And every lick just makes her hotter, wetter, until she's writhing against my face in a desperate need to come.

But it's my goddamn wedding day. So she'll be coming on my cock.

When I abandon her pussy, her frustrated moan lasts only a second before I'm turning her to face the vanity, bending her over in front of the mirror, and shoving her white skirt up over her perfect ass.

Then she's gasping in urgent need. "Duke! Please!"

"I've got what you want, baby." I watch her reflection as I fist my cock and glide the thick crown through her scalding wetness.

And there's nothing in the world like her face as I push deep. Sheer ecstasy overtakes her expression, her hazel eyes glazed with pleasure, lips parting on a shuddering cry. Convulsively her fingers clench on the edge of the vanity.

Her pussy clenches around my cock, her inner muscles gripping me so goddamn tight. Groaning, I get a good hold on her hips and begin fucking her, long and sweet and slow. She rocks back against me, until she's close, so close, her legs trembling so hard she's not supporting her weight anymore, but I've got her, I'll always have her. And my own knees almost give out when she comes, her pussy clamping around me like a vise, her head thrown back on a keening cry. Teeth clenched, I fuck fast and hard into all that luscious tight heat, then slam deep, filling her with my hot cum.

Not the first time. My chest heaving, I draw her up against my chest, my palm sliding down to cup the swell of her belly. "You both all right?"

She reaches back to cup my jaw, her red lips curving into a slow, dreamy smile. "We're perfect."

"Yeah, you are." Everything is. I kiss the side of her neck, her bare shoulder. "And to think last year, I thought the universe was lining me up for another kick in the teeth—making me fall in love with a married woman."

Her smile widens, so beautiful and bright. "You *are* in love with a married woman."

"Yeah, I am," I say gruffly. "But not just any married woman."

Only mine.

THE END

ABOUT KATI

Kati Wilde is a tight-lipped, loose-hipped woman of indeterminate age and low breeding. She writes romantic fiction to assuage her darker urge to write Transformers erotica. You can reach Kati at kati@katiwilde.com or any of the Club authors (Ella Goode, Ruby Dixon, and Kati Wilde) at 1theclub1@gmail.com.

www.katiwilde.com

Facebook: www.facebook.com/authorkatiwilde
Instagram: www.instagram.com/authorkatiwilde
Twitter: www.twitter.com/katiwilde

www.katiwilde.com/newsletter

CONTENT WARNINGS

All of the Hellfire Riders stories include swearing, violence, explicit sexual content including references to group sex, sex in public and voyeurism (some main characters only watch while others participate), references to alcohol and drug use, sex trafficking, illegal cage fighting, and murder (mostly only bad guys, but there are exceptions.) There are no cliffhangers and no cheating.

For Bull's book:

- the heroine is being stalked by an ex-boyfriend who has, in the past, gaslighted her and murdered her family

- a secondary character suffers the loss of a child during an armed robbery (this does not happen on page but before the book begins.)

For Duke's book:

- the hero's sister was abducted and murdered by a serial killer (backstory)

- the heroine is being physically abused by her stepfather, and one instance of it happens on-page

- a secondary character tries to sell a child (to another family member)